KISS KILL VANISH

ALSO BY JESSICA MARTINEZ

The Vow
The Space Between Us
Virtuosity

KISS
KILL
VANISH

JESSICA MARTINEZ

KATHERINE TEGEN BOOKS
An Imprint of HarperCollins Publishers

Katherine Tegen Books is an imprint of HarperCollins Publishers.

Library of Congress Cataloging-in-Publication Data
Martinez, Jessica, date.
    Kiss kill vanish / by Jessica Martinez. — First edition.
        pages   cm
    Summary: "A teenage girl flees her opulent life in Miami when
she witnesses her boyfriend commit a murder that was ordered by her
father"— Provided by publisher.
    ISBN 978-0-06-227449-6 (hardcover)
    [1. Organized crime—Fiction.]   I. Title.
PZ7.M36715Ki 2014   2013043192
[Fic]—dc23   CIP
                                                                    AC

Typography by Kate Engbring
14 15 16 17 18   LP/RRDH   10 9 8 7 6 5 4 3 2 1

First Edition

For Steve, Dave, Mike, and Josh, aka the boys

KISS KILL VANISH

ONE

"Jane, darling, you have to keep still."

Darling.

I keep still. My muscles are screaming to stretch, release, contract, do anything but press my bones and blood into this pose for one more agonizing second, but I keep perfectly still.

"If you weren't so beautiful, I wouldn't have to be such a perfectionist," Lucien mumbles.

My skin prickles. I stifle the cringe, but skin will be skin. "Maybe taking a picture would work better for this one," I suggest.

Only half of his face is visible from behind the easel, but it's enough to see his eyebrow *think* about raising itself. That single eyebrow holds enough disdain to be the most expressive barely moving eyebrow in the world. It's saying: *Ridiculous. A picture.*

What's ridiculous is that I was stupid enough to suggest it. I need to be necessary to his process. He has to find my presence as vital as breath and paint and canvas.

"I can't paint from a photograph when it's my living, breathing muse that inspires me," he says, voice slippery and melodic like it gets when he's about to wax poetic. Sometimes, like right now, there's a hint of faux-British in it—just enough to remind people he went to boarding school in London, not consistent enough to sound remotely genuine.

It's pretentious, but I prefer it to French, which he knows baffles me yet slides into anyway. He only does it every once in a while, to remind me how charmingly bilingual he is. Like everyone in Montreal doesn't speak both. Aside from me, of course.

"Painting from a photograph isn't an organic artistic experience," he rambles on. "Rembrandt, Renoir, Matisse, Picasso—none of the great portrait artists painted from photographs. Can you imagine da Vinci infusing all that life and passion into the *Mona Lisa* if he wasn't actually in the woman's presence?"

I stare hard into the wall behind him to keep my eyes from rolling. He deserves to be mocked; I wish I could do it. The old me would do it. But Lucien has no sense of humor, so no ability to laugh at himself, and in the most literal sense of the word, I can't *afford* to insult him. Instead, I say, "I'm no Mona Lisa."

And Lucien is no idiot. He presses his lips together, clearly reading my thoughts—*you're no da Vinci*—which is probably why he doesn't respond with another affected monologue. He resumes painting, eyebrow back where it should be.

Lucien is not a terrible artist. The last two or three portraits have at least felt like me, if not actually looked like me. Dark hair, dark eyes, and I recognize the heart-shaped face because he exaggerates it every time. But honestly. Da Vinci. And as for referring to his *muse* as if *she*'s not present to hear how weird this is—it's like he's pulling me into his pretensions, making me complicit in his annoyingness.

Still, I say nothing. Some days the layers of make-believe are wrapped around me so thick, so tight, it's hard to breathe.

Lucien tries to educate me because he thinks I'm a simple, ignorant girl living in a big city for the first time. If he knew that I grew up with a Klimt hanging in the dining room, a Dalí in my father's study, and a Degas over my bed, he'd lose the smug smile. If he knew that I'd wandered galleries and auctions in London, Hong Kong, Buenos Aires, Dubai, that I know my Manet from my Monet and my van Gogh from my Gauguin, he'd stop trying to teach me something.

If I told him who my father is, pouring his knowledge of the art world into my sweet little head would be the last thing on his mind.

I stare at the wall. I keep still. I don't think about Miami, or my father's cigar-sweet smell and crinkled hands, or Emilio's sad eyes. Instead I think about the ridiculousness of this pose, of the costume, of what I've become.

The pose, well, I've done worse as far as comfort goes. I'm sitting in the curve of a gleaming grand piano, on the hip, so to speak, leaning back on one palm, holding the other hand in front of me with a skinny, ebony cigarette holder between curled fingers. It's cheesy and seductive, and my wrist is sore from the leaning, but at least I'm not perched on a diving board like last time. It's the absurdity of it that hurts more than anything.

My costume is glitz and pizzazz, straight from the Roaring Twenties: black sequined flapper dress with a fringed hem and beaded spaghetti straps. It's the kind of thing I would've worn to a party in my former life. Not to turn heads in the way my sisters love turning heads in their slinky cocktail dresses with slits up to there, but to be different. To stick out.

I don't try to stick out anymore.

"Comfortable?" Lucien asks.

"Yes."

A lie. As much as I'd love to love the flapper dress, it feels like I'm wrapped in sandpaper. Since I put it on I've been fantasizing about ripping it off my body and scratching my skin till it bleeds. It doesn't help that the feather headband squeezes my temples and the plume flops over, tickling my cheek. But still, it's better than the 1950s bathing suit, and the Regency gown, which, humiliatingly enough, actually took his help getting into.

"Don't sigh like that. It changes the slope of your shoulder."

I un-sigh, but he frowns, so I half sigh. Half-un-sigh? He scowls. It's all so polar and intense, the way he responds to me. I'm either something to be fawned over or annoyed by; there is no in between.

Nobody from my old life would believe this of me, this subordination. Valentina Cruz was sub-nothing. She had no idea that spitfire and spunk and guts were a luxury. I miss being her.

"I'm serious," Lucien says. "Stop sighing." There's a glint to his voice, a flash of something metallic and unyielding, reminding me of what my costume and his flattery occasionally make me forget. Power. I hand it to him at the door of this lavish loft. But sometimes I start acting and he starts acting, and the whole charade makes me forget. I shouldn't forget. This is business.

Lucien pulls his brush across the canvas and glares at it.

When I really look at him, I have to admit it: Lucien isn't ugly. But he's one of those people whose personality is so pungent it soaks through his skin from the inside out. That first day outside the Metro station, maybe, I saw lemony hair, blue eyes, features all in good symmetry even if his face seemed a little thin. Now that I know him, though, those eyes are too deep-set and narrow, the tan is a suspicious orange, and his nostrils are freakishly small.

It's his costume that irks me most, though—not that he'd admit to wearing one. He's dressed as the quintessential artiste: windswept bedhead we both know he spent time and sculpting gel perfecting, scruff on his cheeks, rumpled clothes with the designer labels clipped off, and wire glasses that sit like two Os on his face when he actually remembers to put them on. Nonprescription, I'd bet. I'd wager a lot on it, actually, but gambling has always been my vice. I've bet on all sorts of things and people I shouldn't have.

The door swings open. I can't see it—I'm facing the opposite wall without permission to move—but I hear it, followed by the unmistakable clunk and clatter of a drunk man stumbling into a table, followed by the drunk man cursing out the table.

Lucien scowls but doesn't lift his eyes from his brush. "Marcel."

"Lucien." The voice is not as drunk sounding as I'd expected. It's swimming toward hungover, maybe floating on its back hoping the current will take it there. "Lucien's model."

I don't respond. I'm not getting paid to converse with repulsive siblings. I'm getting paid to keep still.

"We need to talk," Lucien says, his eyes still on his brush, still on his canvas, still full of sulk. He's such a child.

"Not now," mutters Marcel.

"Yes, now."

"But you're clearly busy with . . . with . . . with . . ."

Jane. I'm not saying it. I've been introduced to Marcel close to a dozen times, at least three of which he's been relatively sober for. But today, Lucien doesn't even say my name. No—what he thinks is my name. Either I'm not alive, or not to be shared this afternoon.

". . . with arts and crafts hour," Marcel finally says.

"I'm finished for today." He puts his brush down a little more decisively than usual. "Jane, go put your clothes on."

Put your clothes on. As if I'm perched on the piano naked. I'd allow myself a glare in his direction, but he's reaching for his wallet, coaxing green bills from a stack—no, a pillow—of fifties with his thumb, one at a time . . . *three, four, five, six*. Of course. The power. This is why I check mine at the door.

He holds out the cash, and I slide my hips off the piano, taking the wad from his hand without touching his skin. The slips of paper are soft as clouds between my fingers. Three hundred dollars. My impulse is to kiss them. I don't, and I don't ask to look at the painting either, since I know what the answer will be. This is only the second sitting for this portrait. It'll be another five or six before we move on, and I'm not sure I care what any of them look like anymore either. Money in hand, I make my way to the guest room.

When I emerge, I'm myself almost. My boots, my leggings, my sweater, my expression. The cherry lipstick refused to be rubbed off completely, so my lips are still a little stained, and the "glossy curls" Lucien annoyingly demanded have been finger-combed out, the ironed ripple effect gone.

I glance around for Lucien.

"He left."

Marcel. He's slumped against the doorway to the kitchen, cradling a tumbler of orange juice in his hand. I take him in. Black nail polish. Oily blond hair. Long, skinny fingers. Sly and leering.

"He said not to wait for him."

I shift my bag to my other shoulder, sensing the swing of my cash-stuffed wallet. "I thought he wanted to talk to you."

"I guess I'm not that riveting a conversationalist."

"You don't say."

He sips his orange juice, eyes still evaluating me. "You're not as pretty as the last one."

I pause, surprised only at how quickly we've descended into insults. I don't know him. Close to a dozen introductions to an inebriated guy don't give you much to go on, and yet, I've always sensed that Marcel and I share a gift for bluntness, bordering on rudeness. Plus, Lucien is gone. This idiot isn't my employer, and he's probably my age.

"And the last one," I say, "how long did she pose before Lucien got bored? Was it a month? Oh no, it was two weeks, wasn't it?"

He grins, but I'm not entirely sure why. "No surprise there."

I don't ask. The reminder—that I'm not the first obsession for Lucien's artistry to feed off of—is not upsetting like Marcel thinks it'll be. More a happy reassurance, really, that this creepy excuse for a job is temporary.

"Tell me," he says, "does he let you keep the feathers and sequins and garters and all that?"

"Let me? I don't want them. I don't wear costumes in real life." I let my eyes make an obvious sweep of his clothes. He's a cliché of a rock star with the leather pants, tight T-shirt, and lip ring. I'm not scared of him. I knew too many rich boys like him in my former life—gritty and slick, all pretending to hate Daddy while snorting coke paid for with Daddy's cash. "Are you sure he said for me to go? He usually schedules my next sitting before I leave."

"You know how artists are." Marcel laughs. It's not a kind

laugh. And his eyes aren't kind eyes. They're dark as a bruise, edged with eyeliner that's smudged under his left eye.

"No," I say. "How are artists?"

"Unpredictable. Flighty."

Lucien is neither. We both know it, and that's where the humor lies, but Lucien is flawed in too many other ways for me to stick up for him. So we share this moment, Marcel and I, knowing exactly what the other is thinking: Lucien is a joke.

"So why do you do it?" he asks.

"Sit for Lucien?"

"Yes."

"Are you that naive?"

"Naive," he repeats, rubbing the pad of a bone-white finger around the lip of the tumbler. "How old are you, fifteen? Sixteen? How do your parents feel about you posing for a twenty-one-year-old *artist* who makes you dress up in costumes so he can stare at you for hours?"

"I'm nineteen." I find if I deliver this lie with relentless eye contact, it isn't questioned, but Lucien is staring at his ink-black fingernail. Maybe he believes me. "And how old are you?"

"Eighteen."

"I don't live with my parents," I continue, ignoring how annoying it is that he's actually older than me, "and by naive I mean you obviously don't realize that some people have to survive without billion-dollar trust funds. Unbelievable, I know."

His eyes are flat, registering none of the shame he should be feeling, or even annoyance.

I did exaggerate. It's unlikely there's a billion dollars sitting in his trust fund. More likely it's just many millions for the second son of a soap tycoon. Ironic. Bar soap, body wash, liquid soap, hand sanitizer—I wonder if suggesting he use the LeBlanc family products from time to time would be taking our mutual rudeness too far.

"This is a business transaction," I continue. "Something I do to make rent. Are you familiar with the concept of rent?"

He narrows his eyes. "Are you?" That bruised gaze sees something it shouldn't, and the sudden spinning in my gut tells me he knows. His eyes say *liar* and he's right, because I'm not what I'm pretending to be. Not at all.

I take a steadying breath through my nose so he won't see that I'm rattled. Marcel is nothing but a drunk sack of dumb. The only truth he might guess is that I'm a runaway. I'm poor and desperate—the hallmarks of runaway-dom—but he can't possibly know that the precious three hundred dollars in my wallet would have been a single shoe in my old life. Lunch on South Beach with my sisters. A trim and blow-dry at Petra's.

And now, well, if Lucien hadn't seen me busking outside the Metro that day two months ago, if he hadn't stood and stared, leaning his shoulder into the wall, leaning his eyes into me for an hour before walking up and sliding a crisp hundred-dollar bill in my open mandolin case, I wouldn't have lasted another week. I was down to my last few dollars. I'd have had to . . . I don't know. Not go back to Miami.

Marcel's still staring like he knows exactly what kind of money I came from.

"Am *I* familiar with the concept of rent? Are you kidding me?" I snap.

"Don't get all riled up, sweetheart. I only meant you seem a little above it."

"You don't even know my name. You definitely don't know what I seem."

"Sure I do, Jane," he says, a smirk on his lips. No hesitation, no head scratching, no fumbling through June-Jenny-Joan first. "You seem bored. I guess a little angelic or sexy or whatever it is that gets Lucien's artistic juices flowing, but mostly just bored."

"Bored and getting paid for it," I spit back.

He stops and grins, showing his teeth—perfectly aligned and nicotine gray. "That's something to be proud of."

"I just pose. He doesn't—"

"Oh, you don't have to tell me what he does and doesn't do," he interrupts. "If you were sleeping with him, you'd be gone tomorrow. Lucien's a freak. His muses are only good as long as they keep their halos intact. That what's-her-name before you, she was gone two days after I walked into the kitchen to find her making an omelet wearing half of his pajamas."

"I'm going." I don't give him the satisfaction of seeing me shudder, or ask him to pass on a message to Lucien, or let his slimy eyes touch mine.

"She was gorgeous, though, whatever her name was," he

mutters before I slam the door shut behind me.

I'm waiting for the elevator, trembling with anger, when I hear Marcel's voice calling from the far end of the hall. "What do you play, anyway?"

I pass my bag to the other shoulder again, considering how deep today's humiliation really needs to go. I've never told Marcel I play anything. That means Lucien's sitting around talking about me, which makes my armpits sticky and the skin on my stomach itch. "Music," I say, and step into the elevator.

The skinny corridor separating us is too long to see his expression. The elevator doors close between us.

TWO

*E*ight minutes.

I shut my closet door behind me and sink to the floor. It's the small pockets of time that kill me. Eight minutes isn't long enough for a nap, but it's long enough to remember things that make me want to rip my eyes out, so I'm careful. I stay in the here and now.

Closet is a misnomer. It's the size of your average walk-in, but if you define a space by what you do in it, this is my bedroom. I sleep here. On this cot, under this synthetic blanket, I read and have nightmares and stare at the backs of my eyelids. I undress here, in the tiny space that I'm sitting in now, between the foot of the cot and the door. It's dim and drab, only big enough for the cot, a suitcase, a mandolin, and my body. But it's mine. I pay for it, and the money is clean.

Seven minutes.

The clock glows at me from the upturned crate beside my bed. I'm only on the floor because I'm too tired to move the suitcase off my bed. Maybe it's ridiculous—being here three months and still living out of a suitcase—but buying a dresser would be settling in. I don't want to be settling into this closet, this apartment with five roommates packed like pickles in a jar, in this run-down building in the most decrepit neighborhood in all of Montreal. I want to be passing through. Quickly.

I should be eating before I have to leave again, but Xiang is in the kitchen frying more garlic than has ever been fried at one time and in one place, and the unholy stench will permeate my skin and I will smell like garlic forever if I walk in there again. And I used to like garlic. Or garlic in Cuban food—black beans and *ropa vieja* and ceviche—where garlic belongs, swirled with cilantro and salt and lime. I don't know if this stench is worse or better than when Françoise and Nanette let those potatoes turn to mush in the cupboard last week. Worse, I think.

How Xiang's garlic escapades are deemed less offensive than the delicate *plunk*s of a mandolin, I don't know. And yet, I can't practice here. Too loud. The vote was five to one, and I voted. Reasons stated: apartment is too small, walls are too thin, we said no to Pierre's trombone, and Françoise and Nanette have occasional night shifts at the hospital, so they have to sleep during the day.

Six minutes.

I lean my body into the side of the bed and close my eyes to shield myself from the glare of the clock numbers. My blanket smells like Nanette's detergent. Which reminds me, I need to buy myself the same detergent and sneak a few scoops back into her box. I doubt she noticed any was gone, but still. She might be the closest thing I have to a friend here. As in, I think she would do CPR on me if I needed it, and not just to practice her nursing-school skills.

Real friends are another luxury I've left behind. Drea. Cameron. Kim. Tony. I miss them but not like they deserve to be missed, not as whole people, but as pieces, fragments sewn together into a patchwork of mindlessness and recklessness and fun. I miss Drea's fearless purple streaks. (When Lola told her they looked ridiculous, she laughed in Lola's face. *Nobody* laughs in Lola's face.) I miss Cameron's inexhaustible devotion to cutting class. And Kim's flask of mostly Dr Pepper. And Tony's horoscope obsession. The sadness of losing them all is easier to take like that, in one sewn-together clump of memories. Even still, it's lodged in my chest, and it hurts. To think of them as entire and separate people that I'll never see again, that would be unbearable. I can't.

They must hate me for disappearing. I wonder what they think happened.

Five minutes.

The real reason I'm not moving the suitcase: if I lie down, I will fall asleep, and if I fall asleep, I won't wake up, not even when the alarm on my cell rings in four and a half minutes to tell me that it's time to go.

Nanette's uncle locks up his café, Soupe au Chocolat, at

exactly midnight. If I miss him, I lose my only chance to practice, and if I don't practice, I lose the music Emilio taught me. It's our only link. I know it's irrational, but when I'm not playing I feel like the notes are fading from my memory and that the next time I get to play my fingers will stumble around the melodies but never actually find them. That can't happen. I'll never see Emilio again, but the music gives us a heartbeat.

It's his mandolin. I stole it, and I don't feel bad about it. When I cradle and pluck it like he showed me, the notes sound like raindrops, and I see his eyes. It's worth the exhaustion of staying up all night.

I should've come straight home after leaving Lucien's. At least I could've slept for a few hours then, but getting onto the Metro I could still feel them, the rich boys, like a film on my skin. They'd both been so unnerving in their own way—Lucien with his adoration and Marcel with his insults and innuendo. Creepiness to expunge, I got off at Station Place-des-Arts for the cleansing power of back-to-back Japanese samurai films at Cinéma du Parc. That did the trick, burned off the grime of both sets of slimy blue eyes on me.

Four minutes.

I didn't buy the clock. It and the cot were the only things in the room when I moved in. I hate them both. Every time the numbers on that clock change I'm a whole minute closer to outside.

I shiver again. Last month, a wet chill pushed its way up the Saint Lawrence River. It howled up the streets of Old Montreal, through the cracks of this decaying apartment tower, and into my bones. It lives there now, probably forever.

My stomach grumbles.

The palmeras! How did I forget? I root around in my purse until I find the white paper bakery bag miraculously uncrushed, the two coiled pastries still intact. They're perfect: golden and glossy with the sugar glaze. I bought them on the way to Lucien's as a reward for afterward, then forgot they were there. The first bite is almost too much. Butter and honey melt together into sunshine. The sign said PALMIERS, but I know better. They aren't French. The French can claim every other pastry in the world, but I grew up on these. When I close my eyes and chew, I could be in Little Havana, at Versailles Bakery with Papi and my sisters picking out freshly baked pastelitos.

The palmera is so sweet I want to cry.

Three minutes.

I didn't choose Montreal so much as it chose me. My pawned jewelry hadn't been enough for a last-minute ticket to Spain, and standing at the airport ticket counter trying to digest that information, I was too crushed and drained to form a new plan. I asked the lady how much tickets to France were, thinking I could make my way west by train, but they were even more.

"A ticket to Montreal is only half that," she said with one of those effervescent airline smiles. "You get the foreign experience without the overseas airfare."

Tear-soaked and swollen, I stared at her. Did I look like I

was trying to book an impromptu foreign vacation? On a one-way ticket?

"It's lovely this time of year," she added.

Montreal. I'd never been. I didn't know anything about it, but in my mind it suddenly appeared as a glittering ice castle, a fortress to hide myself in. Maybe it was even better this way. My father would be looking for me under every rock in Spain—in Madrid, where my mother's cousin lives, or in Barcelona, where I always said I wanted to go after graduation. A few months in Montreal might be smart. I'd get to Spain eventually.

Two minutes.

And I remembered what Emilio had told me.

It was one of those Key West nights on the yacht, but we weren't on the deck anymore. We were in his cabin, tangled in sheets and talking about places we wished we could go. Alone. Together.

"Someday I'll take you to Montreal," he murmured in my ear. "It's beautiful. You'll love it."

"When did you go to Montreal?"

"I've been lots of times," he said. "For your father. He hates it, so he sends me."

"I didn't know he had business in Montreal."

"He has business everywhere."

Montreal. Of all the random places.

I bought the ticket.

One minute.

I forgot to ask why Papi hated it. Now I know.

It's only November, and I can't remember the last time I was warm. If someone had a gun to my head and was forcing me to choose between braving the five-minute walk to Soupe au Chocolat and murdering a kitten, I'd have to think long and hard. I'd probably end up under the frozen café awning, but only because I want to play Emilio's mandolin more than anything else in the world right now, and I don't even know where to find a kitten. In Miami they're everywhere, but here, I think they've all been murdered by the cold already.

I pull myself to my feet and gather the things I need for the next four hours: mandolin, hat, scarf, coat, fingerless gloves, mittens to go over the gloves. And then I turn off the alarm before it can ring and force me to leave. I'd much rather it be my idea.

THREE

"You're late." Nanette's formidable uncle Jacques is standing under the awning with his arms crossed over his barrel chest. My eyes are drawn to the flaming orange sideburns glinting in the lamplight below the brim of his cap. He's bull-like, short and thick, all meat and muscles. Like my father.

I hate muscles.

But not Emilio's muscles, because Emilio is lean—not skinny, but taut and long and powerful, practically humming with energy.

I give Jacques a hopeful smile.

He shakes his head. "I already locked up."

"I'm only two minutes late. You'd leave me to freeze to death for being two minutes late?" I let my teeth chatter loudly enough for him to hear the rattle.

He huffs.

Raw, red knuckles appear at the cuff of his jacket, and he pulls the key from his pocket. "Only if you're stupid enough to freeze to death instead of going home." He pushes the heavy door open for me. "You smell like garlic."

I don't deny it.

Jacques's English is technically perfect, but it lacks the easy lilt of most Montreal natives who came out of the womb bilingual. It's nasal and gurgling. It swallows entire syllables. It makes me constantly question if he's slipped into his native French, and right now it's making me annoyed that I still smell like *grr-lique*.

As for Jacques's lack of subtlety, I don't mind. There's never a malicious undertone, and it feels good to have a conversation with someone who doesn't give me the creeps. His occasional rudeness is counterbalanced by the fact that he's my father's age (old men are allowed to be cranky, aren't they?), and he's doing me a favor, and he has a slight limp. According to Nanette, he grew up on a farm north of Quebec City, and the limp has something to do with a combine.

Jacques flips on the lights, and I place the mandolin case on the closest of the tables. There are too many of them for a space this small—massive pearly white circles crammed in like soap bubbles. Every other color in the café is a glossy variation of chocolate. The floors are bittersweet, the walls are milk, and the countertops are deepest dark.

"Garlic," he says again with a sniff. *"Terrible."*

I unwind my scarf. "All I can smell is chocolate. That's worse."

He gives me a nasty look, all scrunched and incensed. "You don't like chocolate? What's the matter with you? Everybody likes chocolate."

"Of course I like chocolate. But just smelling it is torture." Reflexively, I sniff. Molten chocolate with roasted coffee bean undertones. I'll be practically delirious from it in a few hours.

He motions for me to hand him my coat and my scarf. I do. He hangs them on the elaborate iron coatrack by the door with branches that curl like an unruly tree, then stands at the window, lifting the edge of the blind to peer out. "Don't open the door for anyone."

"I won't."

"And why did you walk here alone? That's not safe to do at night."

He said the same thing last time. And the time before. I fiddle with the zipper on the case and bite my tongue, because the parental concern doesn't feel bad. But I don't need someone to walk me here, and I don't need someone to walk me home. Montreal in the dead of night is ten times safer than Miami at noon.

"Do you have someone you can call to walk you home?" he asks.

"Sure."

He looks at me doubtfully. "Nanette said you have no friends."

"I'll be fine." So much for thinking Nanette is my friend.

"I'll go turn on the lights in the back for you," he says, and inches past me.

I rub my nose. It's still cold and rubbery feeling, like I'm touching someone else's face. "I have friends," I call after him.

"Maybe I heard her wrong. Maybe she said you're not friendly."

I watch him limp his way through tables and disappear into the back. A light goes on, followed by the scrapes and thuds of drawers and cupboards opening and closing. He reappears with a box under each arm. "Estelle will be here at four thirty to start the baking."

"Just like last time."

He puts one of his boxes beside the mandolin case. It's plain brown, the size of a small shoe box. "So I'll lock you in. If you leave, you won't be able to relock it, though."

"Right. Just like last time," I repeat.

"I guess I'll go then," he says. "No smoking. Or any sort of fire. Don't use the stove."

"I got it. Thanks."

He nods. "Good night."

He's one foot into the cold when I notice the brown box still sitting beside my case. "Are you forgetting this?"

"No, it's for you," he answers over his shoulder, the other box still tucked between his arm and his body. He closes the door behind him, and I listen to it lock from the outside, a metallic scrape followed by a clunk.

I run my hand over the box, warmed by the anticipation of a gift. It's been a while. Papi used to give me gifts, extravagant gifts, gifts that make me squirm with guilt when I think of them now. And sometimes Lucien gives me things—weird things like a book about pointillism, and old-fashioned opera binoculars, and a CD of cello music even though I told him I don't have a CD player—but none of these has felt like a real present. They've felt like wages.

The lid slips off easily, and I peer inside to see three perfect stacks of foil-wrapped bars. Chocolate. Quick inventory reveals two milk, four white, four dark, four hazelnut, two almond.

I'm shaking.

I slide onto the table, pull my legs up so I'm sitting cross-legged, and inhale half a bar of dark chocolate with my eyes closed, sucking on each precious square until I'm cocoa drunk and feeling too nostalgic to think about anything but what I shouldn't think about.

Last summer. Key West. That first night on the yacht, when the stars were like scattered diamond chips and Emilio showed me how to hold his mandolin.

Papi had gone to bed first. Then Lola. Then Ana. But I wasn't tired, because Emilio kept playing song after song and I couldn't stop watching his fingers tug and slide over the strings. Wistful. That's what he seemed, and I remember thinking it was so odd. How had I never noticed that possibility in him before? But I'd barely noticed him at all. Not because he wasn't good-looking—he was—but because he'd always seemed so stiff, just another of Papi's eager protégés with slicked hair and designer suits.

That night he was different, though, and it was more than

just his wind-mussed hair and T-shirt. Everything felt fated. Him. Me. It was supposed to be a family vacation, just Papi and us three girls and the yacht, but then some business crisis—an authenticity issue with an auction piece, a sculpture—meant Emilio had to drive documents down from Miami.

Authenticity issue. Ha.

But when you've known something forever, you don't see the evidence against it, not even when it's sprouting all around you, blooming and strangling like noxious weeds. Really. You don't. It's only after, looking back, that you see the choking innocents, and then you hate yourself.

Here's what I'd known forever: My father bought and sold priceless art. His clients were the wealthiest of the wealthy from all over the world. He worked miracles for them, procuring the rarest masterpieces for their eccentric collections, so there were always emergencies to be handled. Emilio was simply his latest lackey in a string of rotating men who handled them.

When Emilio showed up with whatever documents he was supposed to be bringing, the earnest assistant or minion or whatever you call a twenty-four-year-old slave, Papi insisted he stay for the weekend. It was a reward for his diligence, this invitation into our lives. And then everything changed.

It was the first of a whole summer of weekends, Emilio driving back and forth from Miami doing Papi's bidding, then, at Papi's insistence, staying in the guest cabin. Some nights he'd play his mandolin for everyone. And some nights just me. I'd pretend to go to bed, because I was only seventeen and Ana and

Lola were nineteen and twenty, which gave them first dibs on Emilio and on life in general.

But it was my door he'd knock on. *Valentina, come look at the stars. They're so much brighter down here than in Miami.* Not Lola and her relentless supply of push-up bras. Not Ana with her fawning. He came to me. I was the one he taught to play his mandolin, with his arms draped around me, still smelling just a little like cigar. *You have to pull the bowl of it against your body, no, like this, so your fingers are free to play.* Emilio with his light-brown eyes and loose brown hair and long brown limbs. *Here, feel my hand. See how relaxed it is? Yours is too tight. You'll strangle the music.* Emilio who, after Papi went to bed, actually smiled and melted into a real person. *Valentina, you have the most beautiful neck I have ever tasted. What? Why is that funny?*

It's been three months. Remembering shouldn't still sting so much.

I leave the box of chocolate, take the mandolin to a chair in the corner by the radiator, sit, and cradle the rounded back against my belly. Those simple Spanish folk songs aren't hard like they used to be. When I first arrived in Montreal and it was still warm enough to play outside, I spent hours by the Metro station, practicing over and over the few things he'd taught me. The wandering melodies. The tremolo. The finger patterns. If we'd had more time, he could have taught me more.

My fingers are stronger and more agile now, better able to control the tiny movements, and the patterns have sunk into my hands so the right notes sound at the right times. But still,

I don't sound like him. I play too deliberately, which makes the music plod when it's supposed to trickle and flow. I play with too much guilt.

But if I play with guilt, why doesn't he?

I discovered there were two Emilios. There was the serious one for my father, and the real Emilio who emerged slowly after everyone else went to sleep and we were two lone bodies on the deck, curled around the mandolin, night fog curling around us. It was the music that coaxed him out. After a few songs he would start to laugh at my jokes. He'd look out across the black waves all full of nostalgia and tell me the things you tell someone to make them yours: about when he was nine and his father left; about the soccer scholarship he gave up in Colombia to come work for Papi.

"Why would you do that?" I asked.

He only shrugged and said, "Money. My mother and sisters don't have much."

At the time, I thought sending his paychecks home to Colombia was gallant. But his gallantry is just as bloodstained as my luxury-filled childhood. We're both guilty.

Time vanishes like it has during the other nights I've spent at Soupe au Chocolat. I don't know how long I practice for—hours? days? years?—but there's sweetness in losing time. My fingers ache, and my eyes burn, and I'm so tired I hurt, but right now I can remember the Emilio I want to remember. The one who played melodies for me and the stars.

Not the Emilio with dead eyes.

* * *

"Encore? N'avez-vous pas un appartement?"

I'm startled. I'm awake. It's a woman's voice. I'm still curled around the mandolin, my fingers half gripping the strings. I taste bitter cocoa, and I don't know where I am, or what the voice is saying, or why my brain is stretching tentacles into the Spanish places and finding nothing.

"Mademoiselle, pourquoi dormez-vous ici encore?"

Estelle. French. Soupe au Chocolat. I pull myself out of my slump and twist around to see her kicking the snow off her boots. The clock says four thirty.

"Sorry. I guess I dozed off," I mumble as I stand, hoping my English convinces her to switch over. The room tilts until I blink it back to normal.

"You should go home and sleep in a bed," she says, bustling past me to the kitchen, her cheeks red and splotchy from the cold. "You have a bed, no?"

"I have a bed." I fit the mandolin back into the case, take my coat and scarf from the iron tree where Jacques hung them.

Estelle reappears. She's short like me, but with extra chins, and sausage arms beneath the sleeves she's trying to roll up. The sleeves are resisting.

"I'm going now," I say.

She ignores me and wrestles with the second sleeve without breaking her bulldog scowl to say good-bye.

Two steps out and the night wraps cold claws around my throat. I'm not nervous. I shouldn't be nervous. Still, I walk quickly, quicker than I should on the icy cobblestone, the mist of predawn tickling the back of my neck. This is Jacques's fault, this jumpiness. Old Montreal is not unsafe.

But it's not quite night and it's not quite morning, and the city feels like a sleeping beast that could wake at any moment and eat me.

I force myself to slow down just a little so I can check my phone. I missed a two thirty a.m. text from Lucien.

Tonight at 9. Saint Joseph's Oratory. Idea to run by you.

An idea. Great. As long as he pays me, Lucien can run all sorts of ideas by me. I consider texting back to say that if his idea involves posing as the Virgin Mary I'm not doing it, but it would only fall into the black hole where his sense of humor should be. Besides, there's a slight and horrific possibility that he's already thinking along those lines.

I shove the phone back into my pocket and quicken my pace. Old Montreal is all corners and crevices between uneven buildings, staircases, craggy stone alleys. My imagination takes over, and one crooked shadow falls into the next. Anything could be lurking.

But nobody is looking for me here. Emilio can't possibly remember talking about coming to Montreal together, and even if he did, he wouldn't try to find me. He knows he'd be safer if I disappeared forever. If I was dead.

I shouldn't, but I let myself remember that last night and his dead eyes, and that's enough to remind myself that I don't ever want to see him again. It should be that easy. But it's one thing to say it—*I don't ever want to see Emilio again*—and it's another thing to be sure that if I looked into one of those alleys and saw his long silhouette leaning against the stone, a glowing cigar between his lips, I could run away. I'm not sure.

That night. He knows I saw everything from his closet. He was the one who pushed me into it, his eyes wide with fear and his grip too tight. *Shhh! Your father will kill me if he finds you in my room.* He knows I stood trembling between suit coats, frantically buttoning up my blouse, still feeling his fingers around my arms where they had squeezed too hard. He knows I saw everything.

A bird squawks from a covered doorway, and I jump, nearly slipping into the gutter. My heart is racing too fast to keep walking so I run, back to my decrepit building, past the perpetually out-of-service elevator, up the filthy stairwell, through the communal space and kitchen, and into my closet. I heft my suitcase off the cot, chuck the mandolin and the chocolate on top of the suitcase, and collapse into bed.

Safe. Alone. The relief is sweeter than chocolate or palmeras or even memories of the beach. This is home, or at least until I get myself to Spain. This is a cold, disgusting hellhole, but it's mine. I pay for it with money that nobody was murdered for.

FOUR

"I'm not dressing up like a nun," I say, sitting down beside Lucien. We're in the last pew of the near-empty cathedral.

Lucien laughs like I'm kidding. The sound is offensively loud, bouncing off the stone columns and blooming over the entire cathedral, and an old woman turns and glares from up near the altar. He doesn't notice. "I wouldn't dream of making you."

Asking me. The correction goes unsaid, of course, but I'm starting to wonder if he can't hear my thoughts, the way his eyes narrow just a little.

"Hiding you under a habit would be such a waste," he says. "And I don't think they'll let me paint in here anyway." He stands and edges by me, motioning for me to follow him.

"Where are we going?"

"The cemetery."

I don't stand. I don't follow. "But that's outside."

"Correct."

"Outside and covered in snow."

"More or less."

"Less?" I ask. "Tell me how it's less covered in snow. I saw it coming in. It's entirely covered in snow."

He stops and squints. I can feel his eyes searching my face for his sweet, docile Jane, but his sweet, docile Jane is tired.

After spending most of the night at Soupe au Chocolat, I should've spent the day sleeping. Instead, I trolled thrift stores for a better pair of boots—a maddening and humiliating waste of time. Even used boots cost too much, so I'll continue stuffing my freezing toes into the scuffed, tight, ugly ones I have.

I swallow and look up at the stained-glass panels. The Virgin Mary stands stoically, surrounded by three adoring magi, the Christ child in her arms. I've been here once before, but it was during the day when sunlight pushes through the glass and bathes the cathedral in color. The scene is barely visible now with just the moon glowing behind it.

I turn back to Lucien. I need the money, but sitting for a portrait in the cemetery sounds like hell. No, worse. Hell would be hot.

"I'll double your sitting fee," he says.

Instantly, my heart is pumping twice as fast. Two hundred an hour, that's—that's ridiculous. In a month I could be in Spain with a cushion big enough to buy time, enough time to find a decent place to live and a decent job. And in the meantime, I could buy a pair of boots that fit, and dozens and dozens of palmeras.

He holds out his hand, palm up, just waiting for me to slide my fingers into it.

My stomach lurches, and the colors from the stained glass melt together.

I take it.

Lucien leads me outside, down the steps, under the black sky stamped with a full yellow moon. Once we hit snow, I drop his hand and follow him down the path to the graves, ice crunching like eggshells under my boots. Headstones rise from the snow like spikes and bolts, angry granite reminders that we're all going to die. Me. Emilio. My father.

All of us, like the man from the docks.

I wonder if he has a headstone somewhere, if the people who love him have realized that he's never coming back. It's only been three months. Whoever they are. Whoever he was.

"Hurry up," Lucien calls. He's already reached the top of the crest. I join him and see we're only at the first hill, that the graves and headstones and mausoleums stretch on and on and on. We're the only mourners.

"Aren't you curious?" Lucien asks.

I don't want to pose out here. Not as an angel. Not as a grieving widow. My bones are ringing with something worse than chill. I sniff, the cold already making my nose run. "Just tell me."

"I think you'd make a stunning grim reaper."

I nearly laugh, but his satisfied smirk stops me. "You're serious."

"Of course I'm serious. I'm thinking under that tree." He points to the left, the sleeve of his coat brushing my face. "The one beside that grayish mausoleum."

"But . . ." Rebellion. I feel it bubbling—volcanic rebellion, with cruel words like scalding lava flowing out of me and eating him alive. If only I could afford it. I exhale and watch the cloud of ice crystals escape from my mouth, rise up, and dissipate. Releasing the anger is easy, but I can still taste bitterness.

"But what?"

"But it's so stupid," I mutter.

"Excuse me?"

"They're all so stupid," I say again, louder, a glorious reck-lessness taking over. "Your paintings. The grim reaper, the flapper girl, the Southern belle, the Marilyn Monroe thing, that ridiculous Marie Antoinette getup—*all* of them. Your entire portrait collection is one tacky cliché after another."

He's perfectly still. His lips are parted, but not even a trickle of frost floats up from them. I close my eyes, wincing under the cold pressing in on me, wishing I could slice time and reconnect it to when this is all over. There will be carnage—a tantrum, insults, a firing (him), mouthing off (me). My stupid temper. Speaking my mind is a luxury I left in Miami.

The silence stretches and thickens between us, and even-tually I have to open my eyes. I'm met with the impossible. He's wounded. I'd thought Lucien was too arrogant for hurt feelings, but his face is stricken with them now. The bloated ego, the wealth, the artiste charade, all gone. Of course they were a cover for insecurity—I suppose I knew that but forgot? Our eyes meet, and his embarrassment infects me, burning my cheeks. It's painfully clear, but I can't look away. He wants to be special in a way money can't buy, wants to show Daddy he can do something remarkable and separate, be his own man.

"Lucien. I'm . . . I didn't mea—"

"I know what you meant," he says.

"But I don't actually—"

"Yes, you do." He breaks away from my eyes and stares out over the field of icy graves. I look too. Some of them shimmer, frost crystals and moonlight playing tricks with the dead. When he turns back to me the hurt is gone, like the moment never happened. And when he speaks, his voice is oily. "You're not exactly qualified to judge art, though, are you? I'm creating a series of parodies. All those clichés you find so ridiculous are intentional. I didn't explain it earlier, because honestly I didn't think you'd get it, but in order to mock stereotypes I have to reproduce them."

I open my mouth, but nothing comes out.

"Don't worry about it. Art is complex. I don't expect you to understand."

My pity is gone. Over. Like it never happened. My hand tingles, and the thought of slapping him flies through my mind. I close my mouth and swallow, then ball my hand into a fist before I do something stupid.

Lucien will never know that I've been to more galleries than he can name. He won't know that I've sat at auctions beside my father for hours and hours because I was the only daughter who cared, the only one who understood Papi's passion and who loved the art too.

Lucien will never know that I'm haunted by the art now.

"So we'll start tomorrow?" he asks.

It takes me a moment to remember that he's talking about the cemetery painting. Double the money. "We'll freeze."

"We'll take lots of breaks."

"I don't want to sit in the snow."

"You have to."

"I don't have to do anything."

He lifts his eyebrow. "What's the matter with you tonight? Are you sick?"

"No."

"Then stop being so difficult. You're in eleven portraits. You have to be in the last three."

The last three. I draw a slow breath of frozen air and feel it flow down to my toes, fill my fingers. Now who has the power? *Tactical error, Lucien. You need me.* "What about the one we're in the middle of? The piano one."

He shrugs. "It's not going where I want it to go. I need to let it breathe for a week or two."

"And what if I have something better to do?"

"You don't."

"How would you know?"

"Do you?"

I ignore the question. "You don't actually know me at all."

"Jane," he says, grinning. "Come on."

The irony of him not even knowing my real name hangs between us, unappreciated.

"I've spent dozens of hours examining you," he says. "You don't have an expression I haven't seen. I know every curve of your body. I know the exact difference between the color of the skin on the backs of your legs and the skin at your throat." He reaches out and pets my cheek with the back of his finger.

I swallow my shudder.

"I'm leaving Montreal," I say.

He pulls his hand back and drops it by his side. "Going where?"

"Spain."

"When?"

"Soon." He can't know that it's not possible yet, that I need more money, that I need more from him.

"Why Spain?"

"I have family there." There's truth to this lie.

"I'll triple your fee."

A crow caws, and a wave of dizziness rolls through me. Three hundred dollars an hour. It's too much to turn down.

"Not just for the grim reaper," I say, and hold my breath while the numbers multiply in my brain. Three more portraits, around six hours apiece, three hundred an hour, plus a few more hours for the flapper girl. That's . . . thousands. "I'm going to need that much for all the portraits still left to do."

He grins. He knows he has me. I'm greedy, and it makes me his. "Three hundred an hour for the grim reaper and the last three portraits."

"Deal," I say, and hold my hand out for him to shake. He takes it, pulls it to his mouth, presses wet lips against my frozen skin.

That seals it. My feet are weighted, cemented to the eggshell snow and ice while the sea of headstones reels around me. The impulse to get away is overwhelming, to get away from Lucien, go back into the cathedral, and find a confession box to pour my guilt into. I need absolution. Absolution for making deals with a devil. Absolution for being the daughter of somebody evil. Absolution for falling in love with a murderer.

Forgive me, Father, for I have sinned.

FIVE

Seven minutes.

I'm under my synthetic blanket, fully clothed, still shivering even though I've been back from the cemetery for over an hour.

I could show up at Soupe au Chocolat late. Jacques will wait, pretending to be just locking up whether I'm there right at midnight or twenty minutes after. He gave himself away with the box of chocolate; he doesn't hate me. He might even be nice.

Lola says niceness is a liability, which explains why she rarely attempts it. She's catty with friends and cruel to guys, who are revoltingly eager to lick up whatever garbage she tosses their way. She treats them like scum and they love her for it, until she's done with them, and then they love Ana, who thinks she's won because she ends up with the prize, until even the nice guys get tired of her neediness and slink away. Poor Ana.

Lola probably doesn't miss me—she's too self-consumed to

miss anybody—but Ana might.

I pull the blanket over my head, but that doesn't help. It's thick but weightless, so I can't breathe and I'm not any warmer. It was a dollar at the thrift shop where I bought everything I own. The only other blanket cost four dollars, and I needed that extra three bucks for the boots fund.

Six minutes.

Leaving Key West with nothing but a stolen mandolin and my passport was stupid. I see that now. But I had rage and terror to grapple with, and I'd never felt so much of both at the same time. I couldn't risk going back to the house in Miami first. Emilio or my father might already be there.

The four-hour drive from Key West to Miami airport felt like ten minutes. I guess I was shaking and crying so hard that time melted down into a puddle. I stopped once to get gas (the last time anything was charged to Valentina Cruz's Platinum Visa), and a second time to hock my diamond earrings and tennis bracelet. I only got two thousand for both, which still makes me cringe. I know for a fact they were worth five times that, at least, but I was desperate, a pawnshop's dream customer.

During the rest of that drive, still shaking and crying, gripping the steering wheel, I had the strangest, clearest thought: I wondered if my mother had been shaking and crying when she left too.

Five minutes.

Lola and Ana hate her. I should too, but she was never quite real enough to hate. They remember the holes she left, remember missing her. But she didn't leave a hole in me—I was only a baby. I grew up with nannies who cuddled and scolded and bandaged, while subtly planting the ideas that have always protected me: *What kind of woman does that? Who would abandon three daughters and a husband and all that money? She must have been sick, mentally unbalanced.*

But now that I've fled too, I wonder. When did she find out what art really was?

My phone buzzes. It's a text from Lucien.

Tomorrow at 2. I'll bring clothes. Don't wear makeup.

I shiver. It's purely reflexive, involuntary as gagging.

Four minutes.

The chocolate. I need it. But it's under the cot, and I don't want to get out of my synthetic-fiber cocoon until I have to. Only the junk bars are left: the hazelnut, which I'll eat even though hazelnuts taste like sweaty socks, because they're perfectly good calories and food is expensive; and the white chocolate, which I'll trade for real food the next time I smell something palatable being prepared by a roommate. Or I'll melt it down and use it as a moisturizer.

Maybe Jacques will give me more tonight.

Food costing so much—that goes on the embarrassing list of things I should have known. That and things getting dirty. Who knew that you have to clean constantly just to keep filth from swallowing you? Probably most people, which is why the list is embarrassing. But it's not my fault that the various nannies and housekeepers and paid mother-replacements did everything, and that none of them thought teaching us to cook, clean, or do laundry was part of their jobs. I guess it wasn't. And is it terrible that I never wanted to know?

Three minutes.

I'm getting what I deserve now, sharing a nasty little bathroom with five other people, living on generic-brand ramen noodles and pity chocolate. I learned to wash my clothes—my ratty secondhand clothes—at a Laundromat with no English instructions. I'm proud of that. It was humiliating, fumbling around with the knobs and the quarters and the detergent, but I figured it out with the help of a Korean woman who didn't speak English or French or Spanish but knew what she was doing and felt sorry for me.

Nobody felt sorry for Valentina Cruz. There was nothing to pity, except maybe ignorance. Up until three months ago, I was too busy spending dirty money on vintage couture to stop and wonder about the things that had always been. I grew up with Papi's business associates coming and going at all hours—young guys like Emilio, driving Porsches and wearing Gucci, happy to joke and flirt with Lola when Papi wasn't around, and older men with the same dangerous toys and fewer smiles. But the problem with growing up with a thing is that you never question it. It's normal.

Until nothing is normal.

Two minutes.

I should just leave now.

But it's too late. I'm already thinking about Emilio's closet.

From the crack, I saw Emilio let them in, my father and the man I recognized from the docks the day before. I remembered his sparse beard, his sloping shoulders and sagging belly. He'd talked to Papi and Emilio while Lola and Ana scoured the marina for guys.

From the closet he looked different than he had at the docks. His face was the color of cigar ash, and when he spoke I could hear the trembling. My father's face was full of things I'd never seen there before. Disgust. Cruelty.

They spoke in Spanish, their voices too muffled for me to decipher their words, even when I pressed my face right up against the crack. And then the talking stopped. My heart thundered louder, faster, fuller, because it knew something about that silence that my mind didn't. It had to have been my heart that told my eyes to look down.

But I couldn't.

Papi nodded to Emilio and crossed his arms over his chest. The man started whimpering, and I felt the *why?* swirl faster and faster inside of me. Why would Papi and this man come to the yacht at two a.m., and to Emilio's room, and why was my father staring at Emilio like that? *Look down, look down, look down.* My heart thundered it, but I couldn't.

Papi's eyes commanded something. *Prove yourself.* Yes, that. *One minute.*

I can't do this anymore. I'm not waiting for the alarm.

SIX

I'm late again, but Jacques waits. Of course he waits. He scowls, complains, drags a chair I haven't seen before—a soft, high-backed, brown leather dream—from the back office over to my radiator. And before he goes, he leaves another box of chocolate for me.

"Thank you," I say.

"You look terrible."

"Just tired."

"Maybe you should sleep."

"Maybe," I say.

He shrugs and pulls gloves over his hands, a hat over his head.

Again, I have to wait while he warns me against every possible danger, but it's worth it. The longer I play here alone, the more intimate the music becomes. It seems unreal to think that I used to play outside the Metro where anyone could hear. Where Lucien could see.

But Jacques does leave, and once my fingers are pulling at strings, I'm somewhere else. The music teases the real Emilio back to life. Like magic. And the other Emilio, the one with the floating arm and tight grip, the one with the dead eyes, doesn't even exist. I'm plucking from sweet memories only.

Like the night near the end of the summer that my father went into Key West for drinks with old friends and stayed overnight at their home, and Emilio and I had the deck to ourselves.

"What do you want to be when you grow up?" His voice tickled my ear, making it hard to concentrate on the words. Cocooned in his arms, in a blanket, wrapped in a breezeless night, we were smaller than small, nearly invisible. Just specks on a boat, two heartbeats. The ocean could roll and swallow us if it wanted to. Thick black mist hid the stars and the moon, clung to my skin, made his skin cling to mine. We were waiting for the rain.

"I'm not grown up to you?" I teased.

He kissed my shoulder. "You know what I mean."

"I want to do what my dad does."

Did I feel his arms stiffen, or is that a detail my memory added later? I wish I knew, but this memory is too well worn to be purely truth, so maybe I've slipped that in since. Maybe he was only silent, waiting for me to continue.

"I want to buy art," I said.

"You want to be like him."

I did, but admitting it seemed childish. "Art makes me happy."

"Of course," he said softly. Sadly, I think. Yes. That detail is definitely true.

I turned my head and spoke into his neck. "Art and you."

There. The words out, I suddenly felt the urge to move, to wiggle out, to fidget, but the weight of his arms and his silence kept me still as the seconds passed.

Finally, he spoke. "If your father had any idea about us—"

"Stop. You know he's not coming back till tomorrow. Why are you so serious tonight?"

When he wouldn't answer I tried to tickle him, but he caught my wrists and wouldn't laugh, so I nuzzled his neck until he caved and started kissing me. And then, of course, I forgot about whatever it was he wouldn't say. What he whispered between kisses was enough. *"You're mine."*

His. That hadn't occurred to me. Beneath my name and my clothes and my skin, I'd always belonged to just myself. Being his was better.

I tipped my head back onto his shoulder. The first drops of rain wet my cheeks. Neither of us said anything else.

SEVEN

Lucien's grim reaper has cleavage. Of course. Why wouldn't she.

I discover this disturbing fact while squeezing into the charcoal velvet dress in the back of his Range Rover, fogging up the windows with exasperated growls and strings of expletives. It's way too tight and has a scoop neck the size of China. Hopefully his grim reaper is supposed to be scowling.

I rub a circle in the window fog with my fist and peer out. Lucien is setting up the easel, shifting it an inch right, an inch left, an inch right again, looking back and forth between two crows on the naked tree branch above him. Naturally, he's wearing head-to-toe wool—coat, scarf, hat, and gloves. It is, after all, winter. Nobody with a brain would be exposing a China-sized stretch of skin to the elements.

I grit my teeth and turn to the next task: bleaching myself.

Staring up from my lap is a picture of the cadaver-faced model I'm supposed to copy. Her skin is geisha white. My Spanish mother and Colombian father didn't make pale anything, but today, apparently, I'm defying genetics by four or five shades because Lucien commands it. I check the cosmetics box he brought and find foundation shade 00, Palest Ivory. At least it's not Halloween face paint. I slather it on.

Next I paint thick black eyeliner across both lids and add smoky red shadow so it looks like an anemic poppy is blooming around each eye. Once the fake eyelashes are glued into place and my lips have disappeared beneath concealer, there's nothing left to do. I stare into the mirror to examine the whole.

Horrifying.

I pull the cloak over my shoulders, the hood over my head, and tie the gray satin ribbon at my neck. It's heavy. I feel weak under its weight, like hands are pushing down on me.

Snow crunches beneath my feet as I make my way toward Lucien. The crows fly away.

Lucien examines my body and face with fascination. "Perfect. Disturbing, but exactly how I envisioned."

I set my eyes over his shoulder, on the sharp edges of a mausoleum in the distance. I'd hate for my body to be laid in something so austere to freeze for eternity. I'd rather be cremated and have my ashes tossed into tropical waters. But then I remember the man from the docks and imagine the splash his corpse must have made after Emilio and Papi heaved it over, and my blood chills. Maybe not tropical waters.

"Cold already?" Lucien asks.

"What?"

"You're shivering."

"Oh." I make myself stop. "Where do you want me?"

He points to a spot beneath the tree, around six feet from the trunk. I find it and face forward. "Here?"

"A step backward."

I obey.

"A little to the left."

I obey.

"No, *my* left, and turn to face the tree."

I obey, I obey, I obey, shuffling one step at a time, until he takes a seat in his chair and says, "Good enough. Now look at me without turning your body."

I almost obey. I stare over my right shoulder, not at Lucien, but through the stained glass of the cathedral behind him and into memories of home. The massive window facing Biscayne Bay, framed by two stained-glass panels, stretching from floor to ceiling. As a little girl, I thought magic flowed through those slices of color and light. Why else would the room glow like that? How else could I feel rainbows wash through me?

"The scythe!" Lucien growls, chasing the colors from my thoughts. He drops his brush and jogs back to the car, pulling his knees up as he runs but still breaking through layers of crusted snow with each stomp. A surge of some emotion I don't even recognize rises up my throat. He's such an idiot. I think I pity him.

But then he jogs back with an actual scythe—metal pole and gleaming blade curled like a smile—and rests it on my shoulder. It's heavy and cold. I loathe him all over again. He repositions it on the same shoulder, then moves it to the other one, then the first again, frowning as he adjusts the neckline of my dress, pushing the cape behind my shoulders, taking my fingers and bending them around the freezing pole. His confidence should remind me of Emilio, the way his hands rearrange me like I'm his to rearrange, but Emilio's touch never made me cringe.

Eventually he goes back to his easel and sits. I stare at nothing while he paints. Gray sky. I don't want to think about stained glass anymore.

"What did you and Marcel talk about the other day?" he asks after a few minutes of silence.

It takes me a moment to remember. At first I just see Marcel's black fingernails and greasy blond hair, feel my skin prickle under his leering eyes. But then I do remember. We talked about Lucien. We talked about what happens when Lucien's models become more than just models. We talked about what I would and wouldn't do for money. "I don't remember."

Lucien snorts. "Well, he does."

"What's that supposed to mean?"

"It means he wanted to know what instrument you were playing when I saw you outside the Metro. And about a dozen other things."

"Like what?"

He squints at me, and I wonder if I asked too quickly—if

that's jealousy in his eye. "He thinks you're younger than you say you are. He thinks you're a runaway."

A crow caws from above. It's flown back, inched closer and closer without my noticing, close enough to see the blue shimmer on its oily wing. It jerks as it walks along the branch of the naked tree. "Why does he even care? Why am I any of his business?"

"You're not," Lucien says. "He was high, and when he's high he thinks he's God. My parents will be back from New York next week, his bender will end, and if I have anything to say about it, he'll be moving back in with them. He only stays with me when they're out of town."

"I'm guessing he won't be too heartbroken. No offense, but he doesn't seem to like you all that much."

Lucien snorts. "He likes living with my parents even less. My father is a domineering, self-righteous jerk, and Marcel is Marcel. They make each other miserable. Oh, and my mother can't stomach conflict, so she'll be miserable right alongside them."

Fascinating. Our fathers are filthy rich opposites. His is a vile mogul and mine is a genial murderer. I wonder whose is easier to love.

"Stop biting your lip," Lucien orders.

I stop biting my lip.

I don't know if I love my father anymore. That would have seemed impossible before last summer. Everybody loves my father. He's huge and warm and expressive, and he talks with his hands like his voice isn't already booming loudly enough to make his point. He's the king of grand gestures, and who doesn't love a surprise trip to Grand Cayman or a Tiffany's box on their pillow? It's not that I never noticed he made people nervous. I noticed. I thought it was because he's important.

But love him now? I don't know. I do know I hate him, and it doesn't seem like the two should be able to coexist.

I miss him. And Ana and Lola too, so much that I'm hollow. I feel like I left myself in Miami, dragged my shell up here to grieve. It's more chilling than wind or snow—the emptiness of being a costume.

"My parents are going to freak when they find out Marcel hasn't been going to school," Lucien says. "I'll be surprised if he graduates this year, although I'm sure my dad will be willing to make a sizable donation to grease that wheel."

School. I don't miss that. I should be a senior, but all of that seems so blurry and inconsequential now. Prom dates and pop quizzes and locker gossip.

"They should be used to it by now," he goes on, "but they always look at him like they can't figure out how things got so bad, how the golden boy got so unlucky. If they spent less time in Manhattan and London, and more time here, it wouldn't be such a huge surprise." He grinds his brush into the glob of gray paint on his palette. "Of course my father never has a hard time noticing *my* faults. His disapproval can span the globe to find me."

"Maybe he'll be preoccupied with Marcel now."

"So I should be thrilled Marcel's such a loser?"

I shrug. Lola's chronic spending and Ana's horrific grades had certainly made me free. I could skip school whenever Drea felt like dragging me to the beach, and I never even had a curfew to break. Papi never batted an eye, because I wasn't the one charging thousands on my card in a single afternoon of purse shopping, or repeating algebra and US history. Of course, favorite-child status wouldn't have been hard to procure anyway. My sisters care less about the Klimt in the living room than the latest edition of *People*, which makes them idiots in Papi's eyes.

Of course, Lucien doesn't know I have sisters. From the beginning I told him I'm an only child from Los Angeles, and thankfully he's too self-absorbed to ask questions.

"Marcel did have one good suggestion," Lucien says.

"What's that?"

"He said I should paint you playing the mandolin."

Too much. The intrusion is worse than his hands positioning my clothes and his endless orders and his demeaning compliments. The fact that I play the mandolin is the only real thing he knows about me, and I wish he didn't. It should be just mine and Emilio's. "I lent it to a friend."

Lucien stops painting and gives me a long, cold look. When he continues, it's without the chatter. My scattered thoughts are my own to rearrange. They go to Soupe au Chocolat, where everything is warm and I can suck on squares of chocolate and play the mandolin with nobody looking at me.

"Your expression isn't working." Lucien's voice cuts my thoughts. "Lose the tragic look."

"You want me grinning like a maniac?"

"No. But death isn't supposed to look forlorn."

I set my jaw and stare evenly across the horizon of tombstones. He's right. When I saw death it had three faces, and none of them was forlorn. I rotate through them, again and again until they blend and spin in a horrific kaleidoscope.

On the man from the dock, death was fear—fear so huge and hopeless the panic was infectious, seeping out of him and into me like a disease through that skinny little crack in the closet door.

And on Papi, death was cruel, but he wasn't the one dying. The cruelty was death's inverse, the other man's mirror. He looked so harsh. I should have closed my eyes so it didn't burn itself into my brain, but I didn't, and it did.

On Emilio, death was hidden—at first because he was facing the other way, but then, when he turned, he was composed. A perfect mask with dead eyes. His nothingness was worse than the other two faces combined.

I roll the scythe back and forth between my numb palms and try to replace the last memory with one from the yacht, one of Emilio's warm hands and soft lips telling me I'm more beautiful than music. I can't.

I do hate my father.

"For the love of all that is holy, will you please stop thinking about drowning puppies?"

I growl loudly enough for Lucien to hear. "But I'm the grim reaper! Isn't that what I do? Kill things?"

"The grim reaper *enjoys* killing things."

"Who says?"

"Me."

So God says Death enjoys his job.

And like a bolt of electricity, the question strikes and a shiver rolls down my spine: During those horrible seconds when I couldn't see Emilio's face—was he enjoying his job?

"Think *victorious scowl*," Lucien suggests.

"Victorious scowl," I mumble. As if there is such a thing.

I can't do this. I break the pose, turning my whole body to stare at Lucien. A pout is pulling his lips out and his eyebrows down. It's the face of a child who's always indulged, confused as to why he's not currently being indulged. I take a step backward.

"Are you going somewhere?"

Yes. To Spain to start over, where I can be Valentina again—wiser than the old one, but not just a shell. A person again.

If only freedom weren't so expensive.

I shake my head and turn my body back into the position he placed me in. I give him my best victorious scowl. He shuts up and paints.

Three hours and two thermoses of coffee later, we're both shivering and blue-lipped. Even with car breaks, my body is aching from the cold and my ears are stinging with exquisite pain. Lucien packs his easel and supplies into the back while I climb into the front. I have to pee, but I'd rather hold it than go into the cathedral and delay the hot shower I've been fantasizing about for the last three hours.

"You were brilliant," Lucien says as he joins me, flipping on the seat warmers and blasting the heat.

I close my eyes, bring my knees to my chest, and try to heal myself with warm thoughts: white-hot sand, roasting bare skin, burning rays. Lucien is full of it, as usual. I wasn't brilliant. I was a scowling shadow of myself. All I did was stand there.

We peel out of the parking lot, tires squealing. Lucien is a terrible driver, all screech and lurch, like a boy who's stolen his father's Porsche.

Emilio was an excellent driver.

"This painting is going to be exactly what the collection needs," he says. "The exhibition is going to be a shock to those hacks from art school. My teachers and my parents—they're all finally going to see what I've been trying to do. And Hugo is going to feel like a complete idiot."

"Who's Hugo?"

He cracks his knuckles, and I fight the urge to grab the wheel. "A guy I knew in art school. He's showing his collection this weekend, actually."

A rival. I'm not sure why this strikes me as funny—maybe the cold is affecting my brain—but I have to clamp my jaw shut to keep from laughing. Lucien has a nemesis, a real artist, one who didn't get his panties in a twist and quit art school, one who maybe isn't filthy rich but honestly struggling. Maybe this Hugo's bedhead is authentic and his glasses house prescription lenses.

"Are you going to see it?" I ask.

"I don't know."

Unexpectedly, I feel that twinge of pity in my stomach again. If he weren't so transparently needy, this wouldn't be happening.

"Come with me," he says.

"What?"

"Come to Hugo's art show with me."

"This weekend?"

"Yes."

A string of questions I can't ask rush up my throat. Go with him as what? His model? His friend? His date? Since that first day outside the Metro, I haven't spent a single unpaid second with Lucien. But I can't get paid for walking around a gallery and drinking champagne with his arm around my waist. I'm not an escort.

Anger builds as my skin starts to sting from the car's heat. I turn my vents away from me. I can't believe he's putting me in this place—having to choose between being his paid date and his something else, something voluntary.

Lucien's a freak. His muses are only good as long as they keep their halos intact.

I close my eyes and force Marcel out of my brain. If I refuse to go with Lucien, then what? He's humiliated and he fires me.

"Jane?"

"When is it?"

"Saturday night at Les Fontaines. Black tie." He sounds

confident, sure I'll say yes, sure that I've already said yes, which makes me think maybe I have. "It'll be fun."

I doubt it. It's not like I have a choice, though. It seems like a long time since anything I did with Lucien was voluntary. "What's Les Fontaines?"

"A gallery."

"Where is it?"

"It's one of those historical mansions up on the mountain. It used to be the home of a wealthy British diplomat around the turn of the twentieth century."

An art show. An actual gallery. I might even see something beautiful, which makes the line being crossed a little less terrible.

"Jane?"

"I'll go."

EIGHT

Hugo LaFleur's website is easy to find. The library computer groans, burdened with the searches of the un-interneted poor, but it gets me there while I try not to think about why the mouse is so sticky.

I click on the bio link, and Lucien's rival stares at me from a black-and-white candid. Dark, wavy hair that reaches his shoulders and a scraggly goatee make him look suspiciously like a pirate. I can't read his expression. It's ennui. Or confusion. Or indigestion.

I skim the short blurb for vitals: twenty-two years old, originally from Lyons, France, the recipient of some awards and a scholarship to McGill's art program. I move on to his work, navigating slowly from piece to piece. Jars with eyeballs painted onto the sides. Jars with lips painted onto the sides. Jars with ears painted onto the sides. Jars with nipples painted onto the sides. Jars with toes painted onto the sides.

I don't dislike modern art, but Hugo's jars seem contrived. He's trying too hard, saying too little. My father would smile—a sure sign he's untouched by whatever piece he's looking at—and move on. I have to assume that the ugliness of the jars is part of whatever point Hugo is trying to make, but that doesn't mean I want to look at them.

Or maybe Lucien's competitiveness has infected me, and I want to think Hugo LaFleur's work is pedestrian out of loyalty. I really hope not.

The thought of feeling loyalty toward Lucien is mildly painful, so I make myself defend Hugo's jars with everything I've got. Maybe they're more powerful in real life. Art isn't meant to be viewed on a computer screen—there's something wrong about dissecting someone's passion with a few clicks of a sticky mouse, isn't there?—and this particular screen looks like it could be older than me.

I log out and push away from the desk. The dread hasn't faded. There'll be no taking refuge in LaFleur's art.

Seven minutes.

I hate that clock. Some of the bars don't light up properly, so I'm always having to get my phone out to check. And it's just a clock, no radio, so I get to wake up to a long, high-pitched beep followed by three shorter, but just as high-pitched, beeps. *Beeeeep bee-bee-bee beeeeep bee-bee-bee beeeeep.* From a deep sleep, it isn't so much a sound as an assault.

I pull out my phone. The clock is right. It's 6:53, which means my hellish evening is about to officially begin.

I really hate that clock.

I hate a lot of things right now.

I hate Lucien.

I hate this dress. No, I don't. I only resent the dress, because the dress itself is beautiful, and the dress never did anything to me besides being the only thing Nanette had to lend. I *resent* it because it's lovely. I want it for a different place and time and set of eyes.

The fabric is petal soft and just barely pink. It's short but flowing, draped over one shoulder, then cinched below the bust. The asymmetrical hem looks like someone's taken scissors to a Grecian gown, making it fall to angles and points. I feel like a nymph, or a hand slipping into a suede glove.

Six minutes.

Nanette saved me. Not just with the dress, but with patent leather nude heels and a white wool coat and pearl earrings. She almost smiled too. I wouldn't have guessed she had it in her, since I've only ever seen her with a solemn I'll-intubate-you-if-I-need-to look, but maybe I don't know that much about her.

Asking was humiliating. She didn't get giddy and prying like I was worried she might, but her round brown eyes took in my lies with a sympathy I didn't deserve and left me with a guilt-knotted stomach. She thinks I'm going on a date, which technically . . . well . . . who knows. But she thinks I work at a café and that a customer asked me to the symphony. I'm not sure what I was thinking—could I have chosen a more movie-plot lie? Maybe an Italian prince, thrilled with his hypothetical latte, wanting to whisk me away for the weekend.

Luckily, Nanette has a believing heart. She's the type to assume others are truthful, and good, and who they say they are. I'm envious. I used to be that way too, before I learned that words are just aluminum foil—shiny and worthless, easily torn, crumpled, and chucked.

Five minutes.

Nanette was right when she told Jacques I have no friends. I don't, not anymore. And she isn't my friend, even though she lent me this outfit and found me a place to practice Emilio's mandolin. She did those things out of pity and guilt—pity for the girl with not a single dress and guilt for voting against me practicing in the apartment.

The mandolin isn't even loud. Jerks.

It's fine. Friends are an extravagance, just people who agree to lie to each other to make each other feel better.

I wish Emilio could see me in this dress.

Four minutes.

The wind is howling. My hair will be a mess by the time I get to the Metro, but I'm not all that worried about it. I was pretending to care about looking pretty, so I let Nanette put it up for me. Lucien offered to pick me up, but I gave him a firm no. Definitely not. After I said it, the look on his face dripped with pity—*how sad that you're ashamed of your poverty*—and I let the misunderstanding lie. I don't want him to know where he can find me. I go to him.

The wind's howl becomes a screech, conjuring memories of tropical storms. I've always hated storms. I used to hide in Lola's bed while the rasping torrents clawed at our house and eventually fall asleep beside her, exhausted from clenching and embarrassed for being afraid. But isn't it rational to fear something so vindictive? They scrape out whole cities and houses and lives, no regard for the helpless. No mercy.

My fear of storms—that was why Emilio and I were in his room that night and not on the deck where we should have been. The wind was making me nervous, and I couldn't relax with the whooshing of the ocean being blown skyward all around me.

Three minutes.

His room smelled like shaving cream. His skin tasted like water. His hands were warm. The wind's nagging was muted— I could hear the waves slapping against the side of the yacht, feel the boat rolling from side to side, but I didn't feel like we were going to be shaken off anymore. Swallowed, maybe.

But then the knock came, and his grip tightened like jaws sinking into my arms.

How many times do I have to relive this moment before it makes sense?

The sense is in his hands, I think, or in the way they changed. If I can just figure out which hands were the real Emilio's, I'll be able to hate him and mourn him. Or love him and mourn him. They went from plucking the mandolin strings to caressing my skin, then suddenly squeezing my arms tight enough to leave fingerprint bruises.

And finally, his hand was gripping something sleek and glinting that I understood, even while refusing to understand. A gun. Emilio's arm floated up in front of him, as if he had no control over his own body, as if his hand was being lifted by my father's eyes.

The whirlpool of *why* and *stop* and *no* accelerated, and I know I gasped, but the noise was swallowed by the reeling storm. I clamped my mouth shut. I dug my nails into my palms.

Two minutes.

Why am I reliving this again?

But he turned the weapon like it was the most natural thing to do, like he'd done it before. And with no hesitation or tremor, he exploded the world.

Too loud. Then no sound at all.

There was so much more color than I would have guessed. A brain. A whole lifetime of thoughts and memories and emotions blooming like a flower on the wall beyond him. One bullet, one head, one massive scarlet blossom.

Understanding came flash-like, illuminating everything. This. This juxtaposition of life and death, of vibrancy and shadow, of beauty in tragedy—this was the art my father dealt.

One minute.

And now. More art awaits.

NINE

"You clean up nicely."

I spin around to see a lanky figure slouched in the shadows. His features are mottled in the half dark, but a cigarette glows in his mouth and his cheeks pull concave as he sucks on it. Panic and hope squeeze my heart at the sight of his long, lean limbs. How did he find me?

"Did I scare you?"

Bitter relief. It's Marcel. The fist around my heart unclenches. "No." I steady myself against the icy railing, but it's too cold to grip with bare fingers.

"Stay and have a smoke with me."

"I don't smoke."

"Then watch me smoke. You've got the whole night to hang on Lucien's arm."

I'm about to say something rude, when I realize the potential of this situation. This isn't a date if Marcel clings to us all night. If I can get him to stick around and annoy Lucien, I may even survive with both my job and my dignity intact.

I take a few steps toward him. Once I'm in the shadow I can see him better, well enough to be reminded that he looks nothing like Emilio.

"You're not even going to comment on how well I clean up?" Marcel gestures to his tux. Armani, if I haven't lost my eye. His hair is slicked back and the eyeliner is gone, but I can see the glint of his lip ring. The malnourished pallor is the same.

"You look . . . cleaned up."

"Don't worry, I'm not."

"Aren't you freezing out here?"

"No," he says. "And I'd need a smoke break even if I didn't need a smoke break."

"What does that mean?"

"It's pretty stuffy in there. A lot of hot air. A lot of annoying people."

"And where's Lucien?" I ask again, losing his name in a shiver. With nothing but cheap stockings between my legs and winter, the six-minute walk from the Metro to Les Fontaines felt like an hour. I'm ready to be inside.

"Forget about Lucien," he says lazily. I wonder if he's drunk. "He's a liar. And as his brother, I feel like it's my duty to tell you he has the smallest—"

"Stop," I interrupt him with an outstretched hand.

"But you already knew that, didn't you." He grins. "See, if it was me, I wouldn't mind if you kissed and told."

"Shut up." I start up the stone steps, forcing myself to climb slowly. I'd love to run. But I don't. The stairs stretch on and on, and I can feel his eyes watching me take each one. I stop at the top, glance over my shoulder, and see him take one last, long pull on his cigarette. He's still staring. Head down, I make my way toward the ornate door.

I don't need to turn around again. I can hear the hollow tap of dress shoes on stone, twenty steps below and closing in.

The interior of Les Fontaines is distractingly artful, more castle than gallery. As I deliver Nanette's coat to the coat check, I take it all in: arches, candlelight, and vaulted ceilings. I've been swallowed by a fairy tale. If I wasn't so preoccupied with losing Marcel, I'd stop to run my fingers along the stone walls and feel the plush velvet curtain separating the lobby from whatever lies beyond.

A visit to the ladies' room confirms what I suspected: Nanette's updo has been ravaged by the wind. It's unsalvageable. Channeling my inner Lola, I pull the clips and bobby pins out, then do my best to finger-comb for a windblown curls effect.

I stare at myself in the mirror. Nanette painted my lips rose pink and dusted me with something shimmery, which makes me twinkle unnaturally in this light. I don't like it. It's like I'm staring at a painting of myself. I turn away.

From the ladies' room, I let the flow of traffic carry me to the main gallery, too entranced by the colors and scents of the lavish flower arrangements perched on pillars to notice what I should be noticing: I stick out.

Once I reach the entrance, though, I feel it. The women are dressed in obsidian and silver. A few sharp-colored accents cry out—a peacock feather sash, a poppy tucked into a smooth bun, a jade necklace, electric blue stilettos—but it's mostly black, and the harsh lines of ebony gowns against bare skin, the diamonds and sapphires choking tall necks, all pulse shrilly around me.

Nobody is wearing pink. Nobody is wearing simple pearl earrings. Nobody has their hair loose. I'd been so relieved Nanette had something to borrow, I didn't realize I'd be all wrong here. But it's winter—*real* winter, dark and cold and foreign. And I look like a little girl.

I spot Lucien by the bar, chatting with a bearded man and a tightly bunned Amazon in a charcoal gown. Lucien looks lost without his artist garb. The tuxedo is perfectly cut, his jaw is clean shaven, and I can see the comb lines in his hair from across the room. I'd have thought this would be his natural habitat, but he seems even less genuine than usual.

I let my eyes take in the paintings while I wait for Lucien to see me.

Naked women. They're everywhere. Twisted, lounged, splayed, and butterflied with oil paints on life-size canvases. I've spent too much time looking at art to be shy about nudes, but I'm inexplicably shocked. I was expecting more jars. Or something equally nonsensical, something I would be forced to spend the evening staring at, wondering what on earth Hugo LaFleur possibly meant by a bicycle covered in noses or kneecaps.

I feel the pressure of Lucien's hand against the small of my back before I see him.

"You're late," he says. "I was worried you got lost."

I turn, but he keeps his hand in place, so we stay too close, the arm of his tuxedo sliding over my arm. So this is how it's going to be. I glance around for Marcel, but I don't see him at the bar, which means he's probably off in a corner trying to get too friendly with a server, or on one of the balconies smoking something more calming than a cigarette. It's possible that my hopes for using him to distract Lucien were overly optimistic.

"You look like Aphrodite in that dress." He takes a sip from the champagne flute in his hand. I'd love one too. "I don't know why a goddess portrait never occurred to me," he says, touching the fabric draped over my hip. "Maybe after we're finished in the cemetery."

I take an oyster from a passing tray. It's cold and briny, and I let it slip down my throat before I can gag.

"So what do you think?" he asks with a nod to the nearest wall.

"I think your friend paints beautifully."

"He's not my friend." Lucien scowls, irked by the compliment as I'd hoped he'd be. "And nobody calls his paintings *beautiful*. You're not even looking at them."

So I look at them. Lucien's hand on my back, we push through the crowd to the nearest painting, then the next, and the next, and the next. We move at his pace, which is too fast and not fast enough; it's a blur, but I want it to end.

"See?" he says.

He's right. They aren't beautiful, and the artist didn't want them to be. They're angry, not just the models' faces but the emotion vibrating from each canvas. There's something garish and hateful about these women—not beloved. Certainly not beautiful.

"They make you uncomfortable," Lucien says.

"No." But I am uncomfortable. It's not the paintings, or not quite. It's that niggling feeling that I've been ignoring something big. All the incongruities I've been chalking up to Lucien's weirdness are being brought into focus by LaFleur's nudes. Everything seems sharper now. *This* is art—the bare human form in all its strength and vulnerability, musculature, rolls, bulges, and dips, every angle and shade on display. I've grown up knowing this.

But Lucien hasn't asked to paint me nude. Not once. I'd say no, but he doesn't know that. He thinks I'll do anything if he just increases the price.

The price is all wrong too, though. Three hundred dollars an hour is ten times the amount art school models are paid in Montreal. I checked. It was less disturbing when we started, when it was a hundred dollars, but I let the price surge, no, forced it to, without wondering why he'd pay so much. My excuses—he's rich, he thinks I'm interesting to paint, paying too much makes him feel powerful—smoothed over enough of the bumps for me to proceed, and I've been greedy enough to make believing worthwhile. But now, it's so obviously all wrong. Why doesn't this heightened focus point to something specific?

My stomach feels stirred, the back of my throat thickens, and my eyes burn.

"I can't imagine she's enjoying this," Marcel says, his voice so close to my ear I startle. He's behind us, between us, above us, all at the same time. I don't know whether it's relief or revulsion that pulses through me.

Lucien cringes and takes a step forward, pulling me with him. "I thought you left."

"Changed my mind," Marcel says, and inches behind us, not seeming to care that we don't turn around. His breath tickles my bare shoulder. There's no reason for him to be standing this close, but the annoyance on Lucien's face makes it bearable.

Marcel reaches over his brother's arm and holds out a champagne flute for me. "You must be thirsty. Lucien's stingy with the drinks. Wait." He stops, pulling the glass just out of my reach. "I can't remember—are you legal?"

I glare over my shoulder at him. Legal is eighteen here, but in practice, the Quebecois serve liquor to anyone with a pulse. "I've told you several times. I'm nineteen." I pull the champagne from his hand and take a sip. Clearly, Marcel doesn't care whether it's my buttons or Lucien's being pushed, just as long as he's pissing someone off.

"Oh, right," Marcel says. "*Nineteen*. So aren't you a little uncomfortable with all this?" He twirls his finger around at the paintings.

"Why would I be?"

"It's a bit provocative, don't you think?"

"Go away," Lucien interrupts. "You're the only thing making Jane uncomfortable."

"I don't know," he says. "I bet she finds having you speak for her far more annoying."

"Why are you even here?" Lucien asks.

Marcel snorts. "Because Hugo invited me."

I'm silent, listening but not listening, staring at a lounging woman frozen in paint with her hands over her breasts, wondering what she was thinking, wondering if she felt hated by Hugo, or if she pitied Hugo. Something in her expression reminds me a little of Ana. What an odd moment for homesickness to hit.

"I think the better question," Marcel continues, "is why did *you* come? Didn't you just tell Dad you were done with all this?"

"You don't know what you're talking about."

"Yeah, I do," Marcel says. "He said you'd be back in the office doing his bidding Monday morning."

Lucien's hand drops from my back as he spins around. "I don't do his bidding."

Marcel raises an eyebrow and smirks.

I see Lucien's hand curl into a fist at his side, and for one glorious moment, I think he's going to punch Marcel. I can't think of a better path for this evening to take. I'd rather be at the emergency room, or even jail, than spend another minute in this room.

But Lucien stops short of hitting him. He grabs Marcel's

lapel and drags him toward the entrance, muttering something I can't hear through bared teeth. Ah, brotherly love. I watch them leave. Their faces are turned away, but something in Marcel's scuffling swagger tells me he's smiling.

This is my chance. I'm alone, and if I conveniently lose myself in the thickening crowd, it could be a good hour before Lucien tracks me down. But that painting calls to me, and I have to look back at it. Yes. It does look a little like Ana.

It's more than homesickness this time. It's a flood of grief that sweeps over me, threatening to knock me over. I used to have a life and a family and friends and a home. I wonder what Ana's doing now. It takes everything to stay upright. I finish my champagne and slip into the crowd. I need to get as far away from that painting as I can.

Off the main gallery, I find a hallway with openings to smaller rooms. Pieces by artists I don't recognize fill the first, with only a few people milling around: a red-faced man chuckling into his cell phone; a couple huddled with their heads together, her satin-gloved hand tucked snugly under his arm. I wander around them and into the next room, my heels stinging from the forming blisters. I end up in front of a sculpture of hands—old hands, wrinkled and puckered like Papi's. The memory only feeds the sadness that's inflating in my chest, climbing up my throat. I leave without another glance.

The next room is smaller and blessedly empty. Glare shields the contents of a single glass case in the center of the room, so I step closer to see what's beneath. Music. Browning, tattered sheets of parchment, the notes minuscule and oddly square. Art or artifact? I lean over to examine the scores when I hear the *shush* of a door closing behind me, followed by an impossible sound. A whispered name.

"*Valentina.*"

My heart is in my throat as I twist around, because I already know. Emilio is rushing toward me with long strides, his hands up in surrender even as he's charging into me and gripping my arms with that terrifying clutch I've felt as many times as I've relived that memory, pushing me back and back and back and against the wall.

TEN

I can't breathe.

His face is one inch from mine. His breath is hot on my
checks. His skin is the same sun-golden brown I remember, his
cheekbones high and strong, his eyes so intense I would gasp if
I could open my mouth. I swear I smell the ocean.

"Shhhh!" he says, but I haven't made a sound. "We only have
a minute. You don't know me. Okay?"

I nod.

"Where are you staying?" he asks.

I feel my bones weakening under his grip.

"Where?"

I shake my head.

"You're scared of me," he whispers.

"I'm not." I shake my head again, but he knows I'm lying.
His grip on me loosens. He slides his hands down my arms and

wraps his fingers around mine.

"You have to let me explain. It's been killing me, knowing you—"

Laughter rings from beyond the door. Emilio drops my hands and turns away, pretending to examine the sheet music beneath the glass. *We don't know each other.* I'm shaking and my heart is thundering as I try to brace for whatever may come charging through the door. Lucien. Or my father.

The laughter passes. But Emilio's body doesn't relax, and he doesn't come any closer again. He looks at me hard.

I feel like I might fall.

"Where are you staying?" he repeats.

"An apartment in Old Montreal," I stammer. "How did you find me? Are you here alone?"

He shakes his head. I can see the urgency in his hands, the way his fingers tighten around the edges of the glass case. "I don't have time to explain now. Just, please, where are you staying?"

"283 Rue Saint-Paul." The words are out before I realize what I'm doing, how fast I've given in. But he came for me.

It's a mess, too twisted to untangle here and now. Who he really is, why he's really here—those are infinitely less important than the physical truth in front of me. He *is* here. I can see him and touch him, because he came for me.

I'd forgotten how his hair curls just enough to resist tucking behind his ears. I stare at his knuckles as they turn white from gripping the glass case. It looks like he could crush it. But he came for me.

Without warning, the door swings open and my heart lurches. In the doorway, with a fresh drink in his hand, stands Marcel. He grins sloppily at me. "So, I'm not the only one trying to hide from Lucien."

I can't speak. My mind is racing to keep worlds separate.

"He got a phone call mid-rant and sort of wandered off," Marcel explains, not noticing Emilio's figure hunched over the glass case. "Or maybe I was the one who wandered off. Hard to tell."

Emilio pulls himself up straight and turns, not once looking in my direction. "Marcel."

"Emilio."

I don't understand. I can't think. They don't know each other.

Marcel's grin has become something else without actually changing. Something strained. "I didn't know you were in town."

My stomach turns over, and I taste oyster. They do know each other.

"Just for the weekend."

"On business?"

"Of course."

Marcel looks from Emilio to me, then back to Emilio, frowning in confusion. He gestures to both of us, and the liquid in his glass sloshes over, but he doesn't seem to notice. "Wait, you two know each other?"

"We just met," Emilio says, perfectly casually.

Don't say my name. Forcing a brittle smile, I try to make eye contact with Emilio, but he won't look at me.

"Well, aren't you the social butterfly tonight," Marcel says to me with a raised eyebrow.

"Actually," I say, hoping he doesn't hear the quiver in my voice, "I was trying to get away from the crowd, and I thought the room was empty. Emilio was just telling me about these old music scores."

"Fascinating," Marcel says drily, glancing into the case. "So you're here to buy a LaFleur, I assume?" For reasons unknown, he tries to do air quotes around "LaFleur" and spills a little more of his drink.

Emilio shrugs. He looks so relaxed I'd believe he really was that calm if I couldn't see his knuckles still white from clenching. "Depends. My boss wants me to look at a few while he feels out buyers. You're a friend of LaFleur's, aren't you?"

Marcel grimaces, his distaste for Emilio becoming more and more obvious. "I think we both know I'm mostly here just to piss off Lucien."

"How do you two know each other?" I interrupt. Emilio gives me the quickest glance. A warning? Am I not supposed to speak?

"Through Lucien," Marcel mutters, which only ignites another line of questions in my head. Emilio and Lucien know each other too?

"He's here, I'm assuming," Emilio says.

"Of course," Marcel says, and turns to the frosted window.

"You know how he loves his *art*."

With Marcel's back to us, Emilio looks into my eyes. There's a message I'm supposed to understand. A question. I can't tell.

"I've yet to see any of Lucien's paintings," Emilio says, pulling his eyes away from me just as Marcel turns back around.

"You're not missing much. Jane's beauty notwithstanding, of course."

Emilio's confusion only lasts a second, but it's long enough for Marcel to notice.

"She didn't tell you?" he says with a chuckle.

"I just met him," I say through gritted teeth. "I had no clue he knew Lucien."

Emilio waits, looking expectantly from me to Marcel.

"Jane here is Lucien's muse," Marcel explains.

"You're his girlfriend," Emilio says, not a question, eyes betraying nothing.

Marcel laughs loudly, and the sound fills the small room. "That would make it less weird. She's just his subject. Or has your status changed tonight?" His lip curls with the suggestion.

Emilio's knuckles go even whiter.

"I'm his model." I force myself to look at Marcel while I speak. I don't trust my acting. I can't look at Emilio like I don't know him, like I don't care what he's thinking. "That's all."

"Except for this evening," Marcel says.

I narrow my eyes.

"That's why you're hiding from him, right?" Marcel says. "That's typical behavior for one of Lucien's dates, but a little odd if he's paying you to be here with him. Is he paying you?"

Blood burns my cheeks, humiliation and hatred pulsing because I don't know the answer to that question.

"I see you're still as charming as ever with the ladies," Emilio says, with a wry smile. "Last time I ran into you, you were hiding from some socialite with claws. In Amsterdam, I think."

Drunk enough to be easily distracted, Marcel gives a lazy *cheers* motion with the empty glass. "Ah, Ingrid. She was psychotic."

"And unprovoked, I'm sure," Emilio says.

I don't listen as Marcel reminisces about Ingrid the psychotic socialite. I'm wondering why Emilio was in Amsterdam, wondering why Marcel was in Amsterdam, wondering why they're both here, wondering why these two worlds have overlapped, not just once, but over and over.

"Well, I should go," Emilio says. "I've got an early flight tomorrow."

Panic seizes me, and I search for something to make him stay, something that won't make Marcel suspicious.

"Nice meeting you, Jane." He nods coolly in my direction, then to Marcel, and is one foot out the door before I manage to find words.

"You aren't going to stay to say hi to Lucien?" I ask, desperation making me talk too loud.

Emilio glances back, and I catch a flash of accusation in his eyes, there and gone before I'm even sure I've seen it. "You'll have to do it for me."

And there's that taste again. Oyster. I'm going to be sick.

"She can't. She's playing hard to get," Marcel says. Then to me, "You know it's only making him want you more, right?"

Emilio turns, walks out the door and away from me. I clench my teeth and watch him go.

He's gone. I'm alone again—alone with Marcel, a thousand unanswered questions, and a clawed-open heart.

"You look like hell," Marcel muses, like this fact is more interesting than unfortunate.

"I have a stomachache."

"Did I miss something?" He tips his head to the left. "Did Señor Suave say something to upset you before I walked in?"

"You're the one who upset me," I spit. Suddenly every emotion is funneled into my disgust for Marcel. "You made me sound like a paid escort."

He snorts. "I'm sorry, you're not?"

Without warning, my body is moving on its own. I see my two hands on Marcel's chest, feel the fine wool of tuxedo over wasted muscle before I understand what I'm doing. I'm shoving him. As hard as I can, I'm shoving him backward with all the gumption Jane lacks and all the strength Valentina has, and despite being nearly a foot shorter and fifty pounds lighter, I rock his center of balance and he careens into the wall. I don't wait to see him slide all the way down, but I do hear his glass shatter against the marble floor and a slurred string of curses before I slam the door shut behind me.

I find my way to the main gallery, ducking and weaving into the horde. I'm frantic. I scan, I spin, I scour, touching every face with my eyes. Emilio has to still be here. But Hugo has drawn a crowd, and they're crushing in around me, leaning and leering. Lucien's probably out here looking for me. I should be careful, but panic is making me stupid; I don't care if Lucien sees me freaking out or if I knock over a whole tray of hors d'oeuvres. I have to find Emilio.

Instead I find parts. Over my shoulder, I see his fluid gait, but then he turns and it's not him at all. Out of the corner of my eye, there it is, his hair curling softly up at his collar, but when I grab his arm, it's a startled stranger staring back. His laugh, his jaw, his hands, I find them all, but not together.

And his eyes aren't anywhere. He's gone.

The blister on my heel has burst and is bleeding, hopefully not all over Nanette's beautiful shoe. And I feel so flushed. My face must have a manic shine to it. I look around for a chair, but apparently the patrons of Les Fontaines aren't meant to sit, because there isn't a single one. Instead, I lean against a pillar, close my eyes, and feel the room sway with wine and money and angry nudes trapped in oil paint.

Emilio was here. He was here and he was beautiful. He said he never got to explain. *So explain.*

I'm hot and sweating. Maybe I'm not just in shock, maybe I have a fever, because for one bleary, pulsing moment I allow myself to doubt what I saw from the closet. Emilio didn't kill anyone. I was tricked, or it was terrible joke, or I was hallucinating, but whatever I thought I saw was not real.

Except of course it was real.

Cold fingers squeeze my upper arm, and my blood turns to ice.

"Where have you been?" Lucien demands. "I've been looking everywhere for you."

I stare up at him. He looks far away. "I don't feel well."

"You don't look well." He frowns and puts his palm to my forehead, sending a shiver through me.

"You're freezing," I say.

"I've been on the balcony."

"The balcony?"

"Upstairs. It overlooks the gardens and the fountains, which I think will be perfect for the next portrait. Or maybe we'll want to do one indoors first if we survive the cemetery."

I'm not listening to him. I'm staring over his shoulder into the crowd where Emilio used to be but is not anymore. Without warning, tears fill my eyes, and I'm filled with a shame worse than any costume or pose I've assumed for Lucien. "I'm not feeling well," I plead.

He sets his lips in a thin, straight line. "I'll take you home."

"I'll take the Metro."

"Don't be an idiot. I'll take you home."

I'm too weak to refuse.

While Lucien gets my coat, I do one more slow turn of the gallery. But not for Emilio. For the paintings. Swirling in my head, the miserable nudes collide with Emilio's impossible appearance and become something beyond coincidence. Something beyond fate.

* * *

Lucien drives me home in a car I've never seen before. It's sleek and small, tapered like a bullet, no backseat. He's mercifully quiet. My panic recedes as we get farther and farther from Les Fontaines, but I don't feel better. I feel empty. The lights streak by, and I realize that I've lived in Montreal for three months without seeing the streets like this. I've been tunneling beneath them, a Metro rat, or trudging through them staring at my feet. But with it all whirring by me so fast now, I feel light. This night has been heaven and hell, but now it's over and for a few minutes I lose myself in pure velocity.

Lucien finds my apartment, but I don't realize we're here until he stops at the curb. I don't even remember telling him the address. Maybe it's the car's soothing purr or the warm seat, but for the first time all night I'm not dying to get away from him.

"Go to bed," he says. "Call me when you've slept it off." He reaches out and strokes my cheek with the back of his finger.

I don't shiver. It's creepy, but affectionate too, and tonight Lucien is more pitiable than detestable. I don't have to look at him now to remember his face when Marcel humiliated him in front of me, which is why I don't pull away when he leans over to kiss my cheek. I don't breathe. His lips are cold and wet, pressed to my skin for a second too long.

He doesn't say good night. He pulls back and I get out, weak and dizzy on my heels, disoriented by the blast of icy air. He drives off while I'm still teetering toward the doorway, scrounging for my key in the dark. My fingers haven't yet found the right one when I see a bent figure, half a block up, leaning against the building. It's far enough to be hidden, close enough to be watching. He came.

As he walks toward me, my body tightens. Of course he came—did I think he wouldn't? It was all so fast and chaotic, though, I almost didn't want to hope. Or maybe I knew I shouldn't hope.

"Do you live alone?" Emilio asks when he's close enough for me to see the angry pink of his cold-pricked cheeks. He stops at an awkward distance, hands in his pockets.

"No. You look freezing. How long have you been out here?"

"A while. I thought you might have gone to his place."

"Of course not." My fingers are cold and shaking. I drop my key ring, then scramble to find it in the dark.

He's silent while he watches me, waiting for me to stand before speaking again. "But you don't live alone."

"I have roommates."

He sighs. Whether it's from exhaustion or frustration, I can't tell. "I can't come up then," he says.

I cross my arms over my chest for warmth. I don't know why he won't come closer. "Where are you staying?"

"The Ritz-Carlton, but I can't take you there."

"Is my father with you?" I hold my breath. The first snow-flakes of the evening slide between us. There's no flutter to them. Just sink.

He shakes his head. "I'm alone. Or I thought I was alone.

Now I don't know. Do you know anywhere private we can go to talk?"

I glance around, already knowing there isn't. It's midnight and everything is closed.

Or just closing.

"There's a place a few blocks from here," I say, slipping my keys back into my purse. I don't know what I'm saying. This won't work. I can just picture Jacques's face when I show up with a man instead of a mandolin. "We have to get there before the owner leaves, though."

"When is that?"

"Now."

We walk quickly. I try calling Jacques on the way, but there's no answer. He wasn't planning on me coming tonight, but I think he locks up at the same time every evening. I hope he does.

Emilio's long strides are hard to match, but I manage, bleeding blister and all. He's charged with that same current as earlier, and it's sucking me in. It's urgency laced with something more. Terror? And what was it he said? *You have to let me explain.* Yes, that. I'm racing through the dark and the cold, fueled by an impossible hope that Emilio only needs to explain, that whatever he says to me will alter reality; what I saw was not what I saw.

But Soupe au Chocolat is dark, boarded up, silent. Closed. I bang on the door anyway, but of course there's no answer. Emilio stands with his hands in his pockets, staring at the snow collecting on his shoes. It's coming down harder now—thick, wet clumps like thousands of falling stars. I knock harder, anger and desperation driving my fist into the door.

"Valentina," Emilio says finally.

I don't stop banging. "Maybe he's in the back room."

"Nobody's here."

"But he's always here at midnight."

"It's quarter past." He reaches out and grabs my forearm. "You're going to wake up the whole neighborhood."

I swallow and take a step back.

"Is it alarmed?" Emilio asks.

"What?"

He puts his hand flat on the door. "Do they have an alarm system?"

"No. Just a single lock."

"Amazing," he murmurs, fishing around in his pocket. "Not even a deadbolt. People are so trusting."

There's something wrong with me. I'm watching him take a tiny metal tool from a tiny silver case and wriggle it into the space between the door and the frame when I should be stopping him. I will never again be allowed inside this café if Jacques finds out, but all I can think about is that before tonight I never thought I'd see Emilio again, and now he's here, he came for me again, and he has beautiful hands. They're slender and strong. Musician's hands. He curses under his breath, slides the tool out of the door, flips it shut, and pulls a shorter hook out of the silver case. I'm mesmerized. Watching him manipulate the lock reminds me of having his hands cupped over mine, his nimble fingers pressing my inflexible ones into the mandolin strings.

The lock slides. There's an audible *clunk* and Emilio smiles— his first real smile of the night. But then he looks at me and he's serious again. "After you." He pushes it open.

I limp into the café and fumble for the light switch while I'm kicking off my bloody heels. It's blissfully warm. I hear him come in behind me and almost expect . . . what do I expect? For him to grab my waist and pull me against him? For him to kiss my neck and run his fingers down the notches of my spine?

I flip the light switch and turn around. Emilio blinks, taking in the glossy tables, the thirty variations on brown, the rich smell. "Chocolate," he mutters.

"It's torture." I take off Nanette's coat, then gesture for him to give me his. Once upon a time I would have helped him out of it.

He takes it off and hands it to me. "So you know the owner?"

"He lets me come here some nights."

I walk to my corner, but he doesn't follow. He stands rigid by the window and peers between slats in the blinds. "Why? What do you do here?"

I'm caught, blushing before I've even admitted it. I'm not a real musician like he is. He'll think I'm silly coming here and pretending I am, but no plausible excuse comes to my mind. "I practice."

"Practice what?"

I shrug. "Your mandolin."

"Nice to know where it went."

"I assumed you knew I took it."

"Well, you both disappeared at the same time. It was a safe bet."

I can't tell if he's actually mad. "Sorry."

"But not really," he says.

"No. Not really."

"I missed it."

I missed you. If only he'd said that. I push a chair to the radiator and sit.

We stare at each other from opposite sides of the café. This isn't what I thought it would be. This is strained. Awkward. I can't tell if we're mad at each other, or afraid of each other, or just afraid of the questions ballooning between us.

He pulls his bow tie loose and undoes the top two buttons on his shirt. "I hate this thing," he mutters.

He peeks out the blind again, but this time in the other direction.

"Who are you looking for?" I ask.

He drops the blind. "Why are you in Montreal?"

"Me? Why are *you* in Montreal?"

"Why won't you answer my question?"

"Answer mine first," I demand.

"Which one?"

I swallow. There are too many. Order should matter, one should trigger all the others, but in this moment I can't see a beginning or any sort of chronology to the confusion. There's just one question pulsing beneath all the others like a heart.

"How could you kill that man?"

His skin loses color with each step toward me. It's storm gray by the time he's close enough to grab me, but he doesn't grab me. He pulls a chair angrily off the table and throws it down beside mine.

The Emilio of my memories would never hurt me. He's gentle, and he whispers things that make me melt. He doesn't make me cower. I don't know who this man is or what he's capable of, but I'm cowering.

"How?" he repeats bitterly. His face is close to mine, his lips twisted as he spits the words at me. "Ask me who, what, even why—ask me anything else about that night."

"Why, then?" It comes out as a whisper, but I ask it. I have to know.

"Because I have to do what your father tells me to do."

"Have to?"

His glare hardens.

I don't look away.

"You don't know what you're talking about," he says. "Your father isn't what you think he is."

"You don't know what I think he is!" I say, feeling turned around. *I* don't know what I think Papi is anymore, but I hate his condescension. I feel raw and cut down. I feel like a child. "You know what I saw. You put me in that closet. You knew I was there and—"

"—and if I'd had any idea he was dragging Bruno in, I'd

never have put you there."

So the man had a name. Of course he had a name. Bruno. Somebody named him that, and the people who loved him called him that.

"You'd never have put me there," I repeat. "But you'd still have killed him."

He doesn't look at me. The anger from a moment ago has drained out of him. There's a vacuous acceptance on his face.

"You're a murderer," I say, unable to keep the disgust from my voice. "How do you live with yourself?"

He leans over, rests his forearms on his legs, stares at his hands. He doesn't meet my eye, and he doesn't deny it. Just stares.

I understand. The impossible explanation is not coming. No optical illusion. No hidden threat that made it self-defense.

"I had to," he says softly.

"You already said that."

"But you don't believe me."

"I . . ." I pause. "I don't see how someone could make you."

"You're saying you couldn't be forced to kill someone."

"Exactly."

"Even if there was a gun held to Ana's head."

My heart jumps at the mention of my sister. "What are you talking about?"

"Your father owns me. He's always owned me because I have a mother and sisters. You don't dabble in Victor Cruz's business. You're in for life because disloyalty is always punished, and the punishments can be carried out from thousands of miles away."

The sick feeling surges as my stomach plunges. "My father wouldn't—"

"He would. He does. All the time." The muscles under the smooth skin of his jaw tense as he clenches his teeth.

"You're wrong," I say, angry that my voice is shaking again. "You don't know that."

"I don't? What do you think your father really trades?" He gives me an incredulous glance, then goes back to staring at his hands.

"Art." The word comes out, and the absurdity of it clicks like a lens being snapped into place. Focus. Clarity.

"Art," he says quietly. "It's a good cover because there's so much money in it. And because he does trade art. It's his hobby." He looks up at me, and his face is full of pity. It's wretched. It's the look you give someone before you have to hurt them. It only lasts a moment, then his eyes harden again. "Listen carefully, Valentina. I'm telling you the truth. Victor Cruz controls a quarter of all cocaine production and exportation in Colombia. In the neighborhood I grew up in, in neighborhoods and cities all over Colombia, Victor Cruz is God. There are entire drug armies in Bogotá who make siblings and mothers and friends suffer when one of his employees is disloyal or disobedient. So when he tells me to kill some low-life dealer who's been stealing from him, I kill him."

I can't trust myself to speak. I close my eyes.

"I'd do it again."

Revulsion fills me, pushing out air and light. I can't look at him. "I don't believe you."

"I think you do."

"You're wrong."

"Valentina." The way he says my name is disappointment and derision at once. "You had to have had some idea."

"Stop."

"You knew."

"I didn't!"

"But you believe me now?"

Tears burn my eyes. He's making no sense, and yet he's making more sense than anything my imagination has concocted since I left Miami. How else can I explain what I saw? I'd considered an art smuggling scheme gone bad, or gambling debts unpaid, but for the most part I didn't let myself think about the why. Intentionally. And even if I'd allowed myself to dream up an explanation, I'd never have thought this.

Drug lord. Cartel boss. Cruz.

That's my name. Believing what Emilio is saying should be harder, but that's my name, the one I thought was respected because of Papi's influence in the art world, and the bitterness and pain in Emilio's voice when he says it are real. *Cruz.* He's not lying. It's something dark and evil and fearsome. It hurts.

My mind whirs with signs, inconsistencies, clues, a lifetime of things missed.

"Do you believe me?" Emilio repeats.

I nod, numbly. Do I have a choice? "But I haven't always known."

"I don't see how."

"I'm only seventeen."

He laughs bitterly. "You know how old I was when I started working for the Cruz cartel?"

I don't want to guess. I don't want to know.

"Eleven. But even then, I was always sure I wasn't going to get stuck in it. I'd slip through their fingers. I wasn't going to get pulled in for life just because everyone else was. My uncle and cousins. My friends. My father. They were all trapped, but I was going to be a soccer star." He shakes his head like his abandoned optimism embarrasses him. "I told you my father left when I was nine, but I didn't tell you it was in a coffin. My uncle screwed up one of Victor's big pickups, and one of his guys got killed. The next day a couple of thugs drove by and shot my father in our driveway while he was washing his car. Payback."

Tears of shock and disgust roll down my cheeks before I can wipe them away.

"I guess you're right, though," Emilio continues, ignoring my tears. "I had a choice. I still have a choice, and I choose to stay alive and protect my family. But there's something you should keep in mind while you're judging me for that." He waits. I know he's waiting for me to look him in the eye, but when I do, I wish I hadn't. His eyes are clear. Magnetic. They have me, and I can't look away. "I grew up in the slums. I've seen more blood spilled than you can imagine—my father's, friends', strangers' who were at the wrong side of my own gun—all because of your precious Papi. And while I was living that nightmare, you were in a mansion in Miami living on the proceeds."

Something ugly escapes, both sob and groan, before I can cover my mouth with my palm. *How can you live with yourself?* Did I really say that to him? I did. I press my hand harder against my lips to keep every sound and thought inside. He doesn't have to ask me that same question because I'm broken, and he knows it. Everything he's said makes sense, my entire life makes sense, and the shock and horror that's ringing through my body doesn't change that. I want to scream at him. I want to slap his face, but that would be pointless, because it would still be true.

I should have known. My entire life. A lie. How could I not have known?

I slump in the chair, spent, ashamed. My eyes are closed, and my hands are cupping my wet cheeks. I can't look at Emilio. I think I hate him. And myself.

When I feel his hands slipping under my legs and behind my back I'm startled, but only for a second. I turn my head into his chest as he lifts me onto his lap, and I cry against his heart as he whispers, "I'm sorry, I'm sorry, I'm sorry," over and over and over into my ear.

ELEVEN

We waste too much time.

There are things we should be talking about, things we could be doing, but at first the grief is so sweltering I can only melt into myself and let him hold me.

Emilio goes somewhere else too—to a lonely corner of his mind. There's an uneasy tension in his arms and his torso, and when I reach up and cup his jaw with my hand, I feel clenched muscle. He's bracing.

"How did you find me?" I ask, my hand still on his cheek, my thumb on his lips.

"I didn't."

"But you did."

"No. When I walked into the gallery tonight and saw Lucien's arm around you, I thought I was seeing things. Going crazy. Or that you were someone who looked enough like Valentina

Cruz to make me feel crazy. I was on the opposite side of the room and you were facing the other way, so I had to watch you for a while before I was sure. You're thinner now. But even from a distance, I recognized your mannerisms, the way you put your hand under your chin when you talk. Your walk."

"But—"

"I saw you go into that room and realized it was my only chance. It was just luck." My hand drops to his neck. I let my fingertips rest on the smooth skin over his clavicle. Luck. After everything he's told me tonight, luck sounds like a bad word, the curse that made my childhood perfect. Luck is a lie.

"How do you know Lucien?" he asks.

"Just randomly."

"Tell me how."

I picture the glittering mosaic by Sherbrooke station where I used to sit, remember the dull burn of an empty stomach. The hungry days seem like forever ago. During those first few weeks I spent nearly every afternoon sitting cross-legged below the mural, playing till my butt was numb and my back ached. "I was busking outside the Metro."

"What?"

"Playing mandolin."

"*My* mandolin, but why were you busking? Don't you have money?"

"I do now, but I was down to my last few dollars when Lucien found me. I can't get a real job here without a work visa, and I'd used all my pawned jewelry money on rent. Busking was how I got money for food." I stop and swallow. The memory is as clear as a cold sky. "Then one day he was there listening. He listened for a while, and then he put money in my case and asked me if I'd ever modeled. The timing was . . ." I trail off, refusing to say it. *Lucky. It was lucky.*

"Did you recognize him from anywhere?"

"No. What do you mean?"

"Do you think he'd been watching you for a while?"

Would I have noticed? I burrow my face into Emilio's chest and smell him. He's the same, but different somehow, too. I don't want to answer these questions. "I don't know. I guess he could've been lurking without me noticing. I tried not to look up. People walk away if you stare at them."

He thinks for a moment, then says, "I can't believe Victor Cruz's daughter has been begging on a street corner."

"It's not begging. And it doesn't matter, because I make enough working for Lucien now."

He grumbles something I can't make out.

"How do you know him?" I ask.

"Lucien keeps turning up at events I have to go to for the art side of Victor's business. Your father actually does buy and sell art, you know. He's sort of fanatical about it, which makes it an even better front."

I think of the galleries Papi's taken me to. The auctions. The museums. Hours and hours filling years and years spent soaking up what I thought was his legacy. The betrayal feels so sharp, so physical, I might be bleeding.

"I know Marcel a lot better, though," Emilio goes on.

"Why?"

"Because he parties with the big boys."

I don't ask who *the big boys* are. Marcel can party with the president for all I care.

A long pause hardens the air around us. The longer it lasts, the more impossible it becomes to force out words. I glance up, and he looks so distant and unbreakable with his thoughts that I barely recognize him. I put my head back down on his chest and feel his breaths instead.

"You're not the one who's been bought," Emilio finally mumbles.

"What are you talking about?"

My head rises and falls with him several times before he answers. "Lucien's working for someone. He's babysitting you."

"I don't understand. I thought—"

"He showed up right when you ran out of money, and now he's got you dependent on him, right? He's keeping you here in Montreal, away from Miami but not wandering around the world like you would be otherwise. He's keeping you safe. And let me guess, beyond that less-than-passionate kiss in the car, he's never actually tried anything with you."

I'm spinning, trying to keep up. Emilio saw the kiss, but that hardly seems like the important part. Nothing makes sense.

"Or has he?" Emilio asks.

"No."

"He's never wanted to paint you naked, then?"

No. He's right. It's one of the absurdities that became clear at Les Fontaines, and I've been cataloging them all, haven't I? Subconsciously I've had to, because snowflake after snowflake they've been floating down around me and piling up to something too real to ignore.

"No," Emilio answers his own question for me. "His boss wouldn't like that."

Anger burns in my gut. Lucien is a liar. I thought I despised him, but this new pain, even after the deeper betrayals of tonight, is sharp and real. Did I actually let myself pity him? I squeeze my eyes shut. I want to kill him.

"Victor," Emilio says calmly. "He works for Victor."

"No."

"Trust me. That's the explanation you want."

"What do you mean?"

Emilio thinks for a moment. "Lucien works for someone. Better your father than one of his enemies, or someone who thinks keeping tabs on you could be useful at some point. But it's been too long—they'd have already used you as a bargaining chip. Or killed you."

I cringe. "But why would my father hire Lucien to watch me? If he knew I was here, he'd come get me."

"I don't know," he admits. "Victor's been to Spain three times in three months looking for you. Or maybe just pretending to look for you. Maybe he wants you to come back on your own, and maybe he wants you kept safe until then." Emilio sounds doubtful. He brings his fingers to my hair and pulls them through. I can't remember the last time someone did this. After so much isolation, being touched feels sweetly painful. I hold my breath.

"Except he never knew why you left," Emilio says.

"You never told him I was in the closet that night?"

"Of course not. But he sent me here," Emilio says softly. "To an art show he knew you'd be at—if I'm right and he was paying Lucien to watch you."

"But he can't have known I was in Montreal this whole time," I repeat pointlessly, no argument, no reason. It's just unimaginable.

Emilio doesn't answer, twirls a piece of my hair around and around his finger, distracting me with the gentle tugging and his touch on my neck. I can't follow his hole-ridden logic when he's doing that.

"This is a test," he says evenly. "That's what it is."

"For who?"

"Me."

"What kind of a test? Why would he be testing you?"

"It's what he does. Loyalty has to be proven."

"But he knows you're loyal." I look up at him. "Right? That's why he made you shoot . . ." I don't want to say his name. Now that I know it, I don't ever want to hear it again.

Emilio is staring into the radiator, lost in his thoughts and a handful of my hair. "Do you think he knew about us?"

"No," I say, without thinking. But then I do think. I'd always assumed Papi would go ballistic if he knew about Emilio—he never liked the boys I hung out with, and they were at least my own age. And Emilio is twenty-four. If Papi had suspicions, I can't imagine him keeping quiet about them.

But there are all sorts of things about Papi that I could never have imagined. That night on the yacht changed everything. What do I know about who he really is and what he'd really do? Nothing, anymore. I know nothing.

"He must've known about us," Emilio says. "Let's say he did, but instead of confronting me, he saw it as an opportunity, something to hold on to for later. And when you disappeared, he tracked you down here and saw to it you'd be safe and decided it was a chance to test me. Let's say he sent me here, knowing I'd see you at Les Fontaines because he had Lucien take you."

"But why?"

"Because I'd have to decide whether to tell him I found you."

My heart punches against my ribs. "You aren't going to, though, right?"

Emilio doesn't answer.

I turn my face into the pleats of his shirt. "Don't," I say into his breastbone. "Please. I can't go back."

No answer. His smell—I know what the difference is now. No sea or salt, just spray starch and cigar.

"Come back with me," he says gently, his hand moving to my back. "You said it yourself—you're living in squalor. If you come with me, you could be in your own bed by tomorrow night."

"I can't."

His lips are next to my ear. "You don't want to be with me?"

I slide my fingers up his arms, feeling the muscle beneath. Being with him is all I want. If I could just get that picture out of my head—the blood flower, the crumpled gray heap, Emilio's perfectly straight arm, the same one I'm holding on to right now—I could have that. I could go with him. "You know I do. But I can't go back now that I know what he does, and what he makes you do, and what pays for . . . everything."

His arms loosen, dropping to his sides, and my back is cold without his hands holding the warmth in. I uncurl myself awkwardly and sit up straight, so I won't fall off his lap. "What happens if you don't tell him?"

He stares gloomily across the café toward the door.

"Maybe he'd think you just didn't see me. You didn't actually see Lucien, did you?"

"But Marcel knows. He'll tell Lucien."

Right. I rest a hand on his chest where my cheek was before. "What if you don't go back? What if we go somewhere else? Together?"

For a few seconds, I know he's going to say yes. His heart quickens beneath my palm. His hands find my waist. He's looking at my lips, and I see him remembering. He wants to tell me all the places he'll take me.

But he shakes his head.

"Why not?" I ask.

"My family. I've seen how he makes people pay. And where would we go?"

"Somewhere he couldn't find us. Your family too."

"Be realistic, Valentina. Even if they had that kind of money, there's nowhere that Victor couldn't find them. Or us."

"Of course there is."

"It doesn't exist," he insists. "He found you here."

He did. I don't know how, but he did. "Somewhere deeper or wilder. Siberia. The Congo. New Guinea."

"You don't want to live in the Congo or New Guinea," he says drily, "and I'm pretty sure neither of us wants to live in Siberia. It's not a fluke that he found you here, you know. He'd have found you if you'd gone somewhere else. He has people all over the world, people who can track us anywhere."

"Not *anywhere*."

He frowns at me. "You have to stop being so childish."

"Don't say that," I say, feeling the hurt rolling into anger, picking up speed. "If you don't want to be with me, own it and just say—"

I can't finish. Emilio is kissing me. His hands are holding my head like he thinks he can trap me in place and shut me up. I'm too startled to respond. But then his anger becomes something else and I feel it pouring into me, filling me. He's not shutting me up. He's telling me something. He's melding us together.

When he pulls away, I'm lost. For a few seconds I was Valentina, and now I'm nothing. He brings me close to him again, puts his cheek on mine, his lips beside my ear. "I want to be with you. Every time I imagine what my life would be like if it was really mine, you're in it. You are it."

I'm breathless. He wants me, but I'm not his. He's not mine. He's not even his own.

"Do you believe me?" he asks, still holding my cheek to his.

I nod. I'm not going to speak until my heart slows and my breath comes back. I hate this vulnerability, this feeling like I've been spun around and sliced open. He knows what he just did to me, and yet he can just pull away, leaving me shaken and winded with my heart still thundering. Maybe I shouldn't believe him.

"If I disappear," he says, "my family will pay. With blood."

I shudder, revolted. Emilio's right. I have been childish. I can't believe I actually wondered if I could love and hate Papi at same time, a man who would kill innocent people for revenge.

I can't go back and pretend I don't hate him.

"So I can't disappear," Emilio says. "You understand?"

"Yes. But I'm not going with you."

He frowns. I've surprised him. "You realize I can't lie to him, though. He'll know."

"So tell him. He already knows where I am, right?"

"Yes, but . . ." Emilio shakes his head. "He'll be suspicious if I don't bring you home."

"I don't see why. He can't expect you to drag me to Miami."

"But he can expect me to convince you, and *nothing* is more important than having your father think I'm his most loyal employee. He already doubts me. That's why he's doing this."

"Then don't tell him. He'll just assume we didn't run into

each other. Remember Lucien didn't see us together."

"How sure are you of that?" he asks.

"Pretty sure."

"Would you bet my life on it?"

I swallow. Would I?

"And Marcel saw us together," Emilio continues. "Don't you think he'll tell Lucien?"

I sigh and cup Emilio's face in my hands. *I can't go back because I saw your dead eyes.*

"I've been miserable since you left," he says.

I let go of his face and look down at my lap, at the fluted edge of Nanette's wrinkled dress. Above my right knee, a tiny hole in my stockings is just beginning to open up. Reflexively, before it even occurs to me that they're reparable, I stick my pinkie in it and pull, watching the web trickle up and down my thigh. It's something Valentina would do because she can, because panty hose are expendable. The guilt takes seconds to hit—these cost real money, money I had to earn myself.

"Come back with me," he presses, pulling my hand from the growing web of lace.

"Not now that I know what he is."

"Don't do it for him. Do it for me."

"I am doing it for you! I can't go back because of what he's done to you. He's made you a killer."

I glance up in time to see him wince. It's what he is, though, what he did. It's what he'll keep doing.

"I was born into this just like you were," he says evenly.

"Neither of us chose it. If I can forgive you for being a Cruz, you should be able to do the same." He stops for long enough to put my hand back on his chest and hold it there as if it belongs there. "It's the only way we can be together."

My fingers look spindly and weak between his, like they could be easily crushed. I don't know what to say. I don't trust myself. If he kisses me again, I might give in. "No," I say.

"Is it Lucien?" He doesn't hide the twinge of bitterness in his voice.

"What are you talking about?"

"He's getting paid to watch you, remember? He's getting paid to give you money, and kiss you good night and whatever else—"

"Stop it!" I yank my hand away. "I take enough of it from Marcel. I can't stand Lucien. I put up with him because it's better than begging on the street."

"I didn't mean—"

"You *did* mean it."

"Something about him irks me. And Marcel is dangerous—you should stay away from him."

"Trust me, I try. Marcel is just . . ." I stop, distracted by the tiniest fragment of a possibility. It's like something tickling the back of my neck, a thought but barely a thought. "I wonder if I could convince him not to tell."

"Lucien?"

"No. Marcel. I wonder if I could convince Marcel not to tell Lucien."

Emilio shakes his head. "Too risky."

"But what if it worked? You could go back and pretend you never saw me."

"We'd still be apart," Emilio says, and pulls me closer.

I have to look away to keep my thoughts straight. I have to not think about his grip on my waist. "But Papi wouldn't suspect anything, and we'd have time to figure out what to do."

"I'm not so sure Lucien didn't see us going into that room. Or coming out. He must've been watching if he was supposed to report back to Victor."

"But he was cold when he found me. I remember. I asked him why, and he said he'd been out on the balcony looking at the fountains. I need to talk to Marcel before he says anything to Lucien. Wait, do you think Marcel works for my father too?"

Emilio snorts. "No."

"Why is that funny?"

"Victor doesn't trust users." He takes both of my upper arms in his hands, turning me to face him, his fingers like cuffs. "We have to think through this rationally. What if Marcel's already told him?"

"He hasn't. They were fighting tonight. Lucien was going home, and Marcel is probably still out partying."

"So he'll tell him tomorrow then."

"That's what I'm saying—I'll convince him not to." My stomach twists at the thought of begging Marcel for anything. I picture his leer, his skinny hands. I push it out of my mind. "He'll listen to me."

"And why is that?"

"He just will. He owes me a favor," I lie.

Emilio leans back and sighs. I can see the defeat in his face. He's caving. "It's too risky," he mutters.

"But it's worth it. It'll buy you time."

"To do what?"

"To figure out a plan," I say. "What do you need to get your family somewhere safe?"

"That doesn't exist."

"If it exists."

He rubs the side of his neck, and I see again how tired he looks, how much older. "Money."

I can't help but smile. "Lucky for you I know some rich people in Miami you can rob blind."

He doesn't think it's funny. "Stealing from your father is suicide."

"Then steal from Lola. She's got so much stuff, she won't even notice."

Finally, it's there—the hint of a smile, a glimmer of hope in his eyes. "This is insane."

"No, it's genius."

"So I'll fly back in the morning like I'm supposed to," he says, "and you'll persuade Marcel not to tell Lucien that the two of you bumped into me. Lucien will tell your father the truth—that he took you to the gallery but he didn't see me, and then"—he stops, takes a deep breath—"and then I'll get some money together, and get my family out of Bogotá."

Hope balloons inside me. I'm afraid to breathe, afraid it'll puncture and collapse. "And once they're safe?"

"I'll come back for you."

I want to kiss him again, but he looks too lost in worry. Guilt thickens in the back of my throat, refusing to be swallowed. "Promise?"

His lips turn upward in the shape of a smile. If only it were real. "We'll go somewhere he can't find us."

"Siberia?"

He snorts. "Never. And not the Congo. I'll think of somewhere better while I'm trying not to think about all the ways this could blow up in my face."

"Don't worry about Marcel. I can handle him."

"You don't know Marcel as well as you think you know him."

"What does that mean?"

"Just be careful," Emilio says, glancing at the clock.

"I will."

"I have to leave soon."

"But it's only one thirty. Your flight isn't until morning, right?"

"I have to pack up, and take care of a few things."

I stand, instantly colder without the heat from his body. "What do I do if you don't come back?"

"I'll come back."

"When?"

"One week. I'll need a week." He stands too. He picks up

the tuxedo jacket from the chair it's draped over and slides back into it.

The smell of chocolate is suddenly too much. My stomach aches. A thousand terrible things could happen in seven days.

Emilio helps me hide the evidence: straighten the chairs, turn out the lights, relock the door from the outside with another tiny tool. And his time he holds me up as we walk over the fresh snow, back to my apartment, so I don't slip or put weight on my blisters. We memorize new cell phone numbers to reach each other at, but don't put them in our phones or even write them down.

"Don't ever call my other phone," he makes me promise. "Victor doesn't know I have this one. Emergency only."

"Emergency only."

I trust him.

Except I notice that he glances over his shoulder and into the alleys. I notice that his hand flies to his hip when a sound explodes from behind us, then drops when he sees it's just a dog barking. I notice that before he can kiss me good-bye he has to pull me under the steps where the shadow is thicker than mud.

But trust doesn't have to mean *not* noticing, does it? It could mean noticing and ignoring. I think.

I decide for certain while he's kissing me: of course I trust him. The pressure and rhythm of his lips beg me to. It's not angry like before, but it can't be gentle or easy, either. Urgency overrides both of those things.

"I have to go," he whispers, hot breath on my frozen cheek.

"But first I need something."

I wait. Whatever he wants.

"Run up and get my mandolin."

Except that. I pretend to think about it, listening for the impossible sound of snowflakes landing on snowflakes. All I hear is wind. "I don't think so."

"What?"

"You can have it back when I see you again."

He shakes his head. "Good to know you haven't lost your nerve, *Jane*."

"Don't call me that."

I let him kiss my forehead, while I close my eyes and fight the urge to clutch his jacket and not let go. He slips away before I can say *I love you*. He didn't say it either.

I'm alone in the shadow.

TWELVE

*S*even minutes.

I told Emilio I was sure. That was a lie, and now I'm paying for it with paralyzing indecision. I'm not sure of anything anymore—definitely not sure I can convince Marcel to keep my secrets. The earth is shifting beneath me. Shale. Quicksand. Sludge. Ice. I have to take my single step, but I'm sliding before I even plant my foot. I have to do it, though. I'm going to do it. I am.

I'll leave in seven minutes, at noon, before Marcel wakes up and recalls whatever fragments of last night aren't permanently lost to another booze-narcotic haze in his booze-narcotic haze of a life, and hopefully before he sees Lucien at all. The trick will be getting Marcel alone. I don't have his number, or even a place where I can find him without finding Lucien too. I have to just show up at the apartment and send Lucien out on some errand, to go get croissants or something. That should be all the time I need.

Picturing Lucien running out to a bakery just because I ask him to is mind-blowing enough. I've never ordered him to do anything for me before—he's the one who gives out the orders. I don't even know if he'll obey.

I suppose I could flirt with him if I have to. In theory.

Six minutes.

Marcel probably won't be up yet, but it's late enough that I should be able to force his eyes open. That might actually be fun.

I go over what I'm going to say, but that doesn't settle me down. I'm screwed. Marcel doesn't care about anyone—why would he agree to keep my secret? And yet, I can't think of a single way to spin it so it's in his best interest and not simply a favor to me. With any luck, he'll have partied too hard to remember anything about last night.

And there's something else I have to do today. It came to me last night during the hours I spent lying on the cot not sleeping. I need to ask Lucien for an advance. Six or seven sittings' worth—just one painting. I'll tell him I'm moving to a nicer apartment and need it for rent, and after last night and that painfully awkward kiss, he might say yes.

Of course, I won't be around to actually sit for the painting, but it's not like it's his money anyway. It's not even his father's. It's my father's.

Lucien must wonder who I am to Victor Cruz, but he doesn't

know. I'm sure of it. If he'd guessed I'm Victor's daughter, he'd treat me like a grenade. Soft hands. No sudden movements. He'd never talk down to me about art, and he wouldn't paint me over and over with such earnestness and be so blind to the pitiful results. He wouldn't have kissed me.

Five minutes.

Emilio's plane has already landed in Miami. I wonder if he's going to his apartment or straight to my house. No, not my house. My father's house. I close my eyes and picture Emilio there. I see massive bay windows, red-on-white decor, walnut floors, wall-to-wall art. I can picture him coming out of Papi's office with that earnest expression and a freshly lit cigar wedged between his fingers. Papi pats him on the back.

What brilliant actors—Emilio playing the son Papi never had, and Papi playing the father Emilio lost. The fact that I believed their charade must make me the biggest idiot in the world. Emilio hates Papi. And Papi . . . who knows what Papi feels about anyone. Or if he even does feel.

The fear hits me hard and swift, sits high in my chest, practically in my throat: I'm scared for Emilio. If Papi's as ruthless as Emilio says he is, I should be scared.

Four minutes.

There's always the possibility that Emilio has changed his mind. With a few thousand miles between us, his pulse is undoubtedly slower, his head clearer. The taste of my lips and the pressure of my hand over his heart are gone, and he has to at least be considering telling my father the truth again.

It makes sense that Emilio would think of his family. No doubt he'd earn an impressive reward, too. Papi doesn't skimp on gifts.

Or maybe Emilio's mind didn't need time and distance to change. Maybe he knew all along that he'd be telling Papi the truth. He said and did exactly what he needed to do to make me stay right here and wait patiently to be collected like a docile little lamb. Papi could be boarding a plane for Montreal right now.

But Papi can't force me to go home with him. Or maybe he can. I'm a minor in a foreign country, and he is my father. For all the things I didn't see about Papi, I've always seen his gift for intimidation. His temper. He gets what he wants.

I should run.

Three minutes.

But if Emilio was going to tell Papi, why wouldn't he have called him immediately, or started insisting I come home with him the minute he saw me last night? Instead, he pretended he didn't know me. He didn't out me to Marcel. He didn't try to force me to go back with him. He started risking his life for me the second he saw me.

So I'm gambling on his loyalty.

Gambling is an art. I've always loved watching Papi do it, and he used to let me bet on anything and everything: black-jack, roulette, poker, football, jai alai, bowling, cockfighting (just once, in Brazil, and never ever again), chess, boules. He didn't care when I took forever to pick my winner, or if I threw his money away on a lost cause.

I used to tell my sisters I was going to be a professional when I grew up, and they'd give me that indulgent half smirk you give to a child who says she's going to work in a toy store. They didn't understand that the games Papi played were more than just chance, that skill and intuition were the real wild cards.

Papi always said my problem was not knowing when to let go of a lost cause. But once I've picked, I've picked. I don't abandon my dark horse.

Two minutes.

Without that clock, I could convince myself time had stopped existing in the middle of the night. My mind is weaving in and out of yesterday and today. I'm not sure I slept at all. As soon as I curled up in bed, all the panic-pleasure-pain bled together, and even now, showered and dressed, I feel like my undreamt dreams are making me crazy.

Champagne, oyster, shock, betrayal, chocolate, kissing. It's an ingredient list for insanity.

I replay the moment when I first saw him last night. Long strides advancing, closing space, fast, his face full of hope and fear. I'm so tired, I could be delirious—the memory might be a dream. But if I'd imagined it, I wouldn't still be able to feel his hands in my hair or his breath on my neck.

Trusting Emilio is a gamble, but I can't walk away.

And now, to beg Marcel.

THIRTEEN

"*B*onjour, *ma chérie*." Lucien's doorman offers his cursory greeting with a quick glance in my direction.

"*Bonjour*," I mumble, and point to the elevator. I'd rather point and wait and nod and gesture than attempt more than a word in French. As Lucien doesn't mind telling me, my French "reeks of Spanish accent."

He picks up his phone. "*Un moment.*"

I watch the switch phone light pulse red. The light blinks and blinks until we both know Lucien is not going to pick up, but the doorman waits. He's wrinkled and tube-shaped, and at the moment, uncharacteristically nervous. He's let me up before when nobody was there to answer, but maybe there's another reason he won't let me up. Maybe he saw Marcel go up last night with friends—wasted friends, female friends, user friends. I have no idea, and I don't really care.

"It's okay," I say, holding up the key Lucien gave me. I've only had it for two weeks and haven't had to use it yet, but he pushed it on me after he got stuck in traffic and left me sitting in the hallway for an hour. He was annoyed that I left before he finally showed up.

The doorman sighs, mutters something I can't make out, and presses his magic button. The doors make the clicking sound of the lock releasing.

"Merci," I call over my shoulder. Next time, if there is a next time, I'll bring him one of my white chocolate bars.

The elevators here are nothing like the jerking death cages that service my building. They glide upward without a shudder or lurch, but I'm too busy reformulating my plan to enjoy it today. A woman up there might complicate things. If that's what it is, hopefully she'll be asleep. Hopefully she'll be dressed.

With each step down the long hall my legs become a little weaker and my purpose a little more nonsensical. I'm Alice and the hall is growing, or I'm shrinking, and I couldn't be any more lost if a grinning cat was my guide, so I focus on the details of my story, on the way I'm going to ask—not beg—Marcel to play along.

I'm here. I lock my knees and stare at the peephole. If I think anymore, I won't do it, so I don't think. I knock. I do it too hard, though, and when I pull my hand back, my knuckles are ringing.

No answer. He must still be asleep, or maybe he crashed somewhere else.

I pull out my key, slip it into the door, and turn. But the key doesn't catch—it isn't locked—and the door floats open. Lucien must not be here. He doesn't forget things like that. And considering that Marcel was slurring his speech by nine and stumbling around the gallery by ten, the open door makes sense. By the time he got back here he probably couldn't spell his name, let alone manipulate a key.

The main room is immaculate as usual. Except for a coat on the floor and a crumpled program from Les Fontaines on an end table, it looks as if the cleaning lady was just here polishing glass, setting square pillows in perfect lines, raking lines into the carpet. The blinds are pulled tight. A muted glow coats the room, the afternoon beyond seeping in through the cracks.

Marcel's bedroom door is open. Wide open. I don't even have to take a step to see in. The light is on and his bed is made up tightly, the cleaning lady's corners still razor sharp. I don't want to do it, but I feel myself taking a step toward his open door.

"Marcel?" I call, but my voice is too timid to carry. I try again, louder. "Marcel?"

Nothing.

I peer in, looking around for evidence of a woman—lipstick on a glass, a high heel, a bra, last night's perfume clinging to the air—but there's nothing. Not a hint of a romantic escapade. The room smells of the same sandalwood air freshener that's in all the rooms in the apartment, but of something else too. Something rotten. And strewn across the chair are the various pieces of a tux.

I shouldn't be here. Marcel has clearly come and gone; Lucien could show up any minute. But I'm being pulled, or not pulled but pushed by something repellent and invisible behind me. Dread has two hands on my back.

I reach down and pick up the tuxedo jacket, rub my thumb over the stitching. Not Armani. Was I wrong last night? No. This isn't the tux Marcel was wearing. I check the label. Gucci. I hold it to my nose and breathe in Lucien's cologne and the faintest breath of cigar.

Plop.

I don't turn to the sound. It's coming from the en suite bathroom, which, I sense without seeing, is open wide. For one moment, I let myself notice how satisfying the sound is, before it has meaning. It's round and crisp with its own tiny echo.

Plop.

Another drop. Except it's not the metallic *ping* of a leaky faucet where water meets metal, or the *splat* of a washcloth dripping on a marble countertop. It's water meets water.

I shouldn't be here.

Plop.

But the same dread that pushed me into Marcel's room turns my head now, drags me toward the perfect, echoing sound, pulls my eyes into the yellowed bathroom light where a painting has been brought to life. It's a grotesque version of Michelangelo's *The Creation of Adam.* Half of it, at least. Just Adam, no God.

Plop.

An arm, thin and purplish, juts out over the edge of the bathtub, manicured fingers dangling in the air, lifeless. His rippling torso is not the muscled perfection Michelangelo painted, but sallow skin stretched over rows of ribs, slumped sideways, marred with nipples like bruises.

Plop.

It's Lucien and it's not Lucien.

His eyes are glassy and frozen in their narrowness, staring into death. The signature smirk is now a slack-jawed gape. Dried vomit covers his chin and trails down his chest in a thin line like an old man's beard. The stench. It swallows up every other detail. The water level in the tub barely covers his thighs and crotch, which I now see are covered in vomit too.

Plop.

It's the faucet. The bathtub faucet is leaking, drops landing in the putrid water between his two spongy feet. Clumps of bile float between them, around his calves, and behind him, little islands in a sea of fetid water.

I shudder.

Around the sink, several empty pill bottles lie scattered like seashells.

Plop.

That sound is death's heartbeat, and it's making me insane. I have to stop it. I take two steps forward so I'm close enough to crouch beside the tub and twist the faucet, but in those two steps the sweet stench intensifies, clouding everything else.

Plop.

Gagging saves me. That first back-of-the-throat spasm hurls me out of my daze and into Lucien's suicide. I can't throw up in here. I can't leave anything of myself in here. My clenched fist opens, and Lucien's tuxedo pants fall to the marble tile with a *swish*. It's the sound a wave makes as it peels off the beach.

I have to get out of here.

Plop.

I stumble backward out of the bathroom, tripping on a men's dress shoe, giving Lucien's agonized body one last look before I turn and run.

I run to the door, down the hall, down eleven flights of stairs because I can't wait for the elevator, through the basement parking garage because I can't face the doorman, and into the outside world. The noon sun paralyzes me. It's cold. I'm hot. And the glare is so white and blinding, I have to stop at the sidewalk and wait for my eyes to adjust, heart thumping and body swaying from the dizzying speed of blood.

A plan. I need a plan. I'm gripping something foreign in my pocket, something that feels technical and deadly, like a grenade, but then I realize it's just my phone. I must be losing my mind.

Blasts of wind sting my cheeks as cars shoot past.

Maybe I don't need a plan. I can't go to the police—they'll figure out who I am, send me home to my father. And I have no way of getting ahold of Marcel. Besides, he'll come back here eventually and find Lucien, whether I track him down or not. I think of Lucien's glassy, unblinking eyes. Calling 911 isn't going to save him. Dead is dead.

Lucien is dead.

My knees will give out if I stand still, so I walk. I walk in the opposite direction of my apartment, still not feeling the cold, even as the wind picks up. I'm out of my body, but my mind is clear as glass as my feet carry me up the icy path on the north side of the Saint Lawrence River. Every detail is sharp, magnified to that dangerous point where distinction between important and unimportant is lost. Too much. I'm seeing too much, but I'm feeling nothing.

There are people—people walking their dogs, dogs walking their people, children making snowmen, couples strolling with fingers intertwined and fingers wrapped around steaming cups, people smoking cigarettes, cigarettes smoking people— but they're as random and plastic as movie extras.

Maybe nobody is real but me. This tableau of happy people doing happy things has an artificial sheen. They wouldn't be smiling if they knew how close death was, and what it looked like. Bloated, purple, twisted, vomit-covered.

Laughter and the mingled aromas of cappuccinos and warm croissants waft over from cafés, but I keep walking. I'm still smelling Lucien's stench. I'm still seeing his body slumped sideways like an accordion with his ribs fanned out, and how the whites of his eyes were cracked with crooked red lines.

The ugliness is its own tragedy, a surface tragedy separate from death. Appearance and effect meant so much to Lucien. There's nothing poignant or poetic about being found naked, caked in vomit. It's unlike him.

He must have picked it for its ambiguity. Drug overdose is a choose-your-own-adventure death: suicide to outsiders, accident to loved ones. But which of the two am I? Outsider or loved one? Neither.

I never would've guessed he was suicidal. But for all the hours we spent together, I barely knew him, and he certainly didn't know me. All those opaque pill bottles scattered on the counter—why didn't I think to look at their labels?

A bundled child and parent hurry past me, the little boy being pulled along by the mitten. He's laughing, she's scolding, and I'm overwhelmed by a sudden desire to be him. I want to be led by the hand and scolded. I want to trust the person leading.

I feel something. Finally. It's a low-pitched sadness, heavy and dull. Guilt. I should have known. Of course the king of self-love would be the king of self-loathing too. Seeing his rival's collection must have made him feel like a failure and a fraud, and fighting with Marcel about working for their father would've made it worse.

And when he kissed my cheek, I may have shuddered.

It's not just guilt, though. The more I think about him, the more this feeling starts to hurt like anger. He treated me like I was nothing, then let himself be damaged by me. What a self-centered bastard! Being friends was never part of our arrangement. I never consented to having the power to injure him.

Rage and regret push me upriver, my feet pounding the

ice-and-salt-crusted path, until I stop and look behind me. Shaking from the confusion, I see how far I've gone in a direction I never wanted to go. A mile. At least.

My fingers ache. They're still wrapped around my phone, and my memory supplies the number in Emilio's accented voice. *786-555-3548. Emergency only.* He was adamant, but if this isn't an emergency, I don't know what is. My shock is wearing thin, and fear begins to edge its way back in. What will my father do? Emilio shows up saying nothing about seeing me, and Lucien, his little informant, is suddenly dead. He might even think the two are related.

Which.

No.

No.

Not possible.

But Emilio said it.

I have to pack up, and take care of a few things.

FOURTEEN

Hours. They've passed. The shock has bled out of me, and now I feel empty and scraped raw. Gutless, guilty Valentina.

I'm curled on my cot like a fetus, still steaming from the shower, naked except for the stiff towel wrapped around me. With the draft and my sopping hair, I should be freezing, but my scrubbed skin is burning hot. Nothing is the same. Even the air I'm breathing has a strange, bitter flavor, and a web of new truths is forming in my mind: Everyone lies. Love is a tool. I am a tool. Love is a lie. Isn't that where I started? It doesn't even make sense.

None of it makes sense, but neither does the fact that Lucien is dead, and despite having no evidence to prove it, I know it was for me. A gift I wasn't supposed to know about.

At first I thought the clock was keeping me sane, but I've decided it's holding me captive. It's calmly swallowed hours, one apathetic minute at a time. I need to make a decision, many decisions really, and with every changing number the likelihood of me being the one to get to make those decisions shrinks. Taking a shower was supposed to break the spell, but I'm only weaker, and if I lie here naked and folded up for long enough, someone else will decide everything for me. My father. Or Emilio. But maybe that would be best.

I still haven't called Emilio.

Five. That's the number of times I've typed his number into my phone. It's also the number of times I've hung up before pressing call. Before I talk to him, I have to decide how much of what he said to me last night was a lie.

When that idea first slid into place—that Emilio killed Lucien—it felt like his lock-picking tool glided into my brain channels and clicked. Steadily. Definitively. Of course Emilio killed Lucien.

But then I remembered that my evidence is a whiff of cigar smoke on a lapel, which I'm not even sure I'm remembering correctly, and a motive that may be a lie. Maybe it was Papi who did it, or had it done. Maybe it was both of them. Or it could have been exactly what it looked like. Suicide.

Again, my mind cycles through what I know, what I've ignored, what a girl with a brain and an inkling of intuition should be able to see about the men she loves.

First, Emilio. Emilio is perfect. Emilio is slippery. He's always what I need him to be, except when he's what my father needs him to be, but otherwise he molds himself to my cravings effortlessly. But too effortlessly?

And Papi. Papi is a monster. That I used to love him is irrelevant, because even if Emilio is lying about other things, he isn't lying about who Victor Cruz really is. No. Nuggets of truth about Papi glitter from the murk and grime of my memories, things from my childhood, details that make sense like they've never made sense before. And I can't forget what I saw from the closet.

Lucien's death is the smoke dancing between the two of them. If only I could see whose cigar is lit. I close my eyes and remember the scent in my father's den, that taste on Emilio's lips, that smell fresh on Lucien's lapel.

Did Emilio kill him for us? He didn't have to, or at least not for reasons that I know of. Then again, I don't know anything anymore.

Or Papi could've had Lucien killed as a warning for Emilio. Maybe it was a punishment for something Lucien did, but I know even less about Papi's relationship with Lucien than Papi's relationship with Emilio.

Need food. I'm so dazed, the sensation confuses me. But I am starving. I'm instantly crazy with hunger, trembling as I rummage through my things for Jacques's chocolate. I can't remember the last time I ate.

The oyster? Yes, that was it.

I find the box of chocolate bars and pry it open, knowing already only one kind is left, knowing already that I'm going to do what I swore I would never do again, not after the White

Chocolate Mousse Incident of Christmas Eve 2010.

Desperate times.

I claw the paper off like a wild animal, do the same to the foil, then snap off a square, ignoring the slippery, waxy feel on my fingers, and put it in my mouth without looking at it. It doesn't melt. Not at first. It's smooth and sharp-cornered and as tasteless as plastic. I might be sucking on a toy or a small piece of electronic equipment. But eventually the surface separates into that familiar granular stickiness, so sweet and oily my tongue puckers and my gag reflex triggers and all the excess saliva pools, creating some sort of sugar-spit slurry. I've almost convinced myself to swallow when the unexpected happens and saves me.

My phone buzzes.

I spit the white chocolate mess into my wastebasket and stare at the black flip phone. It's set to vibrate, so when it rings for the second time it bounces along the surface of the crate toward the edge. It has to be Emilio. I have to pick it up. It rings a third time, and I grab it before it clatters to the floor. The number Emilio made me memorize, the one I've almost called five times now, is scrolling across the screen.

I can't.

I wait out the rings, trying not to picture him holding his phone, wondering why I'm not answering. Instead I picture Lucien. Dead, bloated Lucien. Before I talk to Emilio, I have decisions to make.

I bring my fingers to my temples and press hard, but it doesn't make my head ache any less. Emilio and Papi spin silk around my thoughts. Two spiders, one web, connected by common threads—art, drugs, money, ambition, power. And a common prey. Me.

But that's not quite right. I'm not prey, because my obliteration isn't anyone's objective; I'm not that important.

This feels more like a game of chess.

The image of Papi's chessboard appears in my mind, hand-carved characters in ebony and ivory, each individual piece its own work of art. He taught all three of us girls to play as soon as we were old enough to remember the names of the pieces, but by the time they were teenagers, neither of my sisters could be talked into a game. Lola refused because it was too boring, and Ana had become a perpetually sore loser.

Papi was the only one I could convince to play with me. He'd look like he was about to say no, then his face would soften and he'd say, *Fine. Pick your king, Valentina.* He was the perfect opponent—always losing, but only by a move or two—though now I see, he was winning all along.

I'm not under the illusion that I'm winning anymore. If this mess is a chess game, I'm not even playing. I'm the piece Papi and Emilio want to win with. I can be sacrificed by either, and the game still won.

Pick your king, Valentina.

He would say it like he didn't already know which color I would choose to play with, and I'd consider both slowly, like I didn't already know too. I picked black. Every time.

Pick your king, Valentina.

Like he doesn't already know who I'll choose.

I stare at my phone. Emilio is waiting.

The last time I called him a murderer he spun it around so he was the wounded one, a victim trapped in a drug king's world, and I'd been the monster daring to judge him for protecting his family.

A mess of possibilities tangle themselves together, but none of them make sense. I squeeze a handful of damp hair in my fist, and water dribbles down my forearm. It's time to pick my king.

FIFTEEN

The *Montreal Gazette* is not kind to Lucien.

I read about the suicide of the heir to the LeBlanc soap fortune in Monday's paper while sipping scalding black tea. A mangled pastry sits on a prim white plate, pushed to the far edge of the table.

Buying the pastry was stupid and rash, considering I'm back to being a jobless, destitute runaway, but it was practically sighing at me from behind the patisserie window, all flaky and delicate and wistful. It seemed like such a hopeful thing to do. Buy a pastry for breakfast. Drink tea from a real cup. Sit at a corner table in this café with its heavy golden light and quaint European ambiance, and close my eyes and—no. Not close my eyes. Keep my eyes open and not remember.

With all that hope I was going to finally call Emilio, but before I could make the call, Lucien's eyes found me. I felt them gazing up at me from the front of the abandoned newspaper at the next table as my teeth sank into that first bite.

The rest of the pastry is still waiting, twisted and smushed by my teeth and my grip before I pushed it away and snatched up the *Gazette*. Now I can't stop reading. And sipping. The tea is burning a path down my throat, but I'm too engrossed to stop swallowing.

Lucien LeBlanc died of a drug overdose. The reporter throws in a trivial "toxicology reports still pending" after the damning list of empty prescription bottles found in his room—sleeping pills, anxiety pills, depression pills, pain pills. It's made to sound like a typical medicine-cabinet-of-the-rich-and-famous cleanout.

The reporter doesn't give Lucien a profession. He doesn't get hobbies or passions or personality either. He's just a rich boy, a miserable man acting like a child. Of course, the deceased's younger brother's DUI and drug possession arrest from last year are mentioned, thrown in at the very end as a cherry on top. Marcel adds festive color to the tragedy, no doubt buys a few extra eye rolls from the paper's readership. *Rich people.*

The tea doesn't feel right in my stomach. It feels like sadness. It's a bad way to find out I'm emotionally attached to idiots I loathe. Loathed. The urge to go back to my apartment and wallow in misery and indecision for another twenty-four hours is strong, but I stifle it.

I force myself to finish the pastry, pretending I can taste it. I read over the list of drugs one more time, bottles and bottles of deadly things, fatal dosages and lethal combinations. I actively convince myself. This killed him. This. Not anything or anybody else.

I stare at the photo of Lucien. It's one of those staged-but-pretending-to-be-candid shots on the beach in rolled-up sleeves and khakis. His hair is perfect, but his smile is a little too wide, making his eyes all but disappear.

I take the cell phone out of my pocket and dial the numbers again. One last sip of tea and I'm completely singed from the inside out. Ready. I push the paper away, but Lucien still stares up at me, so I flip it over and press call.

It rings. Again. And again.

Between the third and fourth rings my eyes settle on the picture. The other picture. I was too lost in the words to see it before, plus it's smaller than Lucien's portrait. It's black-and-white, tucked beneath the memorial service information. In it, Lucien and Marcel stand together in front of a stone archway. They're younger. It must be from their British boarding school days, based on the jackets and ties. It's certainly more candid. Lucien looks like someone just called his name, not smiling but expectant, and Marcel is turned slightly toward his brother, arms crossed, grinning like he's waiting for a prank to play out. I've never seen him look at Lucien with anything but contempt. What happened to them?

"Valentina."

Emilio's whisper is like ice.

"Valentina, are you there?"

I squeeze the phone tighter, focusing my thoughts. *I called him.* "Yes."

"I've been worried sick. Didn't you see I tried to call?"

"Sorry." *I thought you might have murdered Lucien and wasn't sure I wanted to ever speak to you again, but now I've decided to pretend I'm not wondering if it's true.*

"I have news," he continues, talking louder now so I can hear the pitch of his voice, the faint Colombian lilt with blood and skin and muscle behind it. He must've found somewhere more private. "Something happened."

Something? Unbidden, Lucien's glassy, bloodshot eyes flash in my thoughts. "What happened?"

"Lucien killed himself."

I bite my lip and stay appropriately silent. People are silent when they're shocked. But for how long? I try counting breaths, but I lose track after three.

"Valentina? Are you still there?"

"Yeah. I'm just . . ."

"I know you were . . . friends, and I'm sorry. They're saying he did it the night of the LaFleur show. Pills. Are you okay?"

He sounds so sincere.

"Your father is the one who told me," he says, and I fight to listen to his words and not get lost in the melody of his voice. "He's acting cautious. I can tell he thinks something is up, but he's not going to admit that Lucien was on his payroll. At least not to me."

"What did you tell him about the show?"

"I told him about the paintings, said I talked to LaFleur. I didn't say anything about Lucien at first, but then he asked me, and I told him I didn't run into him."

"He believed you?"

"I think so. And I was telling the truth—I didn't actually run into him."

"Right. But Marcel?" I ask, and my eyes find the grainy black-and-white face on the newspaper in front of me. It doesn't look like he's wearing eyeliner. And his expression—it doesn't looks like he hates himself yet.

"What do you mean?"

"He saw us together," I say. "I haven't talked to him."

"I still don't think Marcel works for your father. I think we're in the clear."

I swallow. The clear means a fresh start. It means no past, no suspicions, no memories of closets and gunshots or naked, bloated bodies and empty pill bottles. The clear sounds like paradise. "So you're coming?"

"Not yet. This is going to take time."

"Getting the money," I say.

"That first and then getting my family out of Bogotá."

"Your family," I repeat, because it makes me feel better. Everything that he's done has been for them. I need to remember that the next time I picture Lucien's body or the gray slump of the man from the docks.

"I can't tell them until I have everything lined up, and then it all has to happen simultaneously. You'll need to be ready to leave, since we may not have a lot of notice."

"How are you getting the money?"

"Don't worry about it."

Irony burns away at my insides, hotter than the tea. Money was meaningless when I was swimming in it—expendable and constantly renewing itself—and it's everything now that I don't have it. It's freedom.

"I might need longer than a week," he adds. "Two weeks is probably more realistic."

"But should I just wait here?"

"For now."

I don't want to tell him how close that's cutting it. Lucien owed me for the last few sittings, but there's no way I'll see that money now, and rent is due in two days. My lips are still slick from the pastry splurge. No more wasting. No more treats.

"Once things are ready here, I'll come and get you," he says.

"Where will we go?"

"Somewhere beautiful." I hear a smile in his voice, and it's almost enough to make the fear and doubt float away.

"Like where?"

"How about Tahiti?"

"I'm over *le français*."

"Sweden?"

"I'm over the snow."

"New Zealand, then."

I know less about New Zealand than I know about nuclear physics. Sheep. Green hills. *Lord of the Rings*. That's it. "Maybe."

"I'm glad you called," he says, his voice low and gentle. "Talking to you reminds me of why I'm doing this. I miss you already."

"Then I'll call more often."

"Don't," he says abruptly. "It's not safe for me to carry this phone on me. This Lucien thing is making your father skittish. Text me, and I'll check it at night."

"What would he do if he found it?" I ask, wanting to know and not wanting to know.

"He's not going to. After today, I'm storing the phone somewhere else. I can't go ducking into the garage every time you decide to call me."

Decide to call me? I'm not sure if I'm imagining the irritation or not. "Are you really in the garage?"

"Crouched between the Porsche and the motorcycle."

"You're kidding."

"I'm picking a piece of gravel out of a tire tread as we speak."

It would be funny if the various outcomes I can imagine weren't so terrifying. "Who is he afraid of?"

"What?"

"You said Papi's skittish. Who is he afraid of?"

"He has enemies. Powerful people always have enemies."

I have to roll that idea around in my mind before it makes any sense. Enemies. The concept of being afraid *for* my father is so foreign. You don't worry that the lion is about to be attacked. "And he thinks you're working for his enemies."

"Not necessarily me. He's suspicious of everyone right now,

which means you have to be patient. Can you do that?"

I pick up a tiny flake of pastry with my index finger and put it on my tongue. Buttery snow. Outside the window it's snowing real flakes.

"Valentina?"

Can I do it? Do I have a choice? "What do I do if I don't hear from you?"

His voice is gentle again, intimate, like he's stroking my hair with the sound of it. "You will. If I was there and I could kiss you and say 'I promise,' you'd believe me. Right?"

I imagine it. If he was holding me, and if his lips were breathing those words in my ear, any words in my ear, he's right, I would believe him. "But what if something happens to you?"

"Nothing's going to happen to me. I'm being careful."

"You're hiding in the garage crouched beside my father's car."

"Checking the tire pressure. See? I think fast. Nothing's going to happen to me."

What if you change your mind? What if you tell him I'm here? What if you disappear without me?

"Nothing's going to happen to me," he repeats.

"Okay."

"And I won't disappear or change my mind," he says. "I don't want to be stuck in this anymore. I don't want anything but you."

I slump over, rest my forehead on the table. It's chilling. I don't remember letting him read my mind. I'm not sure I like it.

"Besides," he says, and I can hear the edge of a grin slipping into his voice. He's trying to charm me. "You have something I'd do anything for."

Kill for? I swallow the thought. It's gone. I match the flirting in his voice with my own. "And what would that be?"

"My mandolin."

I take the newspaper with me, but I don't go back to my little hole. Too depressing. I'm meeting Jacques at Soupe au Chocolat tonight, so sleeping now would be smart, but when I left this morning, Xiang was roasting something that looked like cabbage and smelled like rot.

Instead I sit on a bench in the Sherbrooke Metro station, the folded *Gazette* clenched between my body and my arm, the dusty mandolin case at my feet, and think about money. Gobs versus none. Then versus now. Valentina versus Jane. Now that Lucien's gone, my lifeline has been cut, and I'm officially destitute. There's survival money, which I could theoretically scrounge up busking for change in the cold, and then there's fly far, far away money, buy a cottage by a forgotten sea money, rescue Emilio's family money. That's the kind that Emilio's scrounging up.

I shouldn't let my mind wade so deep into the impossible, but I do: I think about going to Miami. Ten minutes in my house is all it would take. It's a useless exercise, but I give my imagination those ten minutes to run through the rooms and collect the right valuables, the untraceables. One or two of my father's watches or my sisters' necklaces would go a long way. Nothing is as valuable as the art, but I don't know how to find a buyer without getting caught.

I know where the safe with my mother's jewelry is. Rings, bracelets, and pendants, all too gaudy to be wearable but not old enough to be vintage—the stones would be worth something, and nobody would miss them right away.

I'm heartless. I must be, wanting to steal and sell the only pieces of her I have. But the woman owes me, and so what if I am heartless? Maybe heart is one of those luxuries you give up for the greater good. Freedom. Emilio.

The paper slips a little and I clamp my arm to my body, trapping it. If I'd never run away and I'd died unexpectedly, like Lucien but not like Lucien, an accident maybe, would a newspaper describe me any differently? I'd be a spoiled little rich girl.

I take the paper from beneath my arm and examine the photo facing out. Marcel's got a punch line stored up that he's about to deliver, something irreverent and teenage-boy hilarious, so probably not hilarious at all. I see it in his eyes. He's only a slightly different version of who I was last year. Sassy. Untouchable. Which makes me wonder: Would the old Marcel have been friends with the old Valentina? Maybe.

Marcel. The *now* Marcel. He would have access to money.

I refold the paper and clutch it harder between arm and body, suddenly conscious of my heart racing with the *click-click-click-click* of the trains speeding past.

SIXTEEN

" You."

Me. I can't think of a single response for Marcel. Not one for this moment. Not here on this lip of crusted snow with grave markers and dead flowers between us. Not with the last of the mourners still milling around like black ants on white cement. Different rules apply.

I take a step forward. His eyes are lighter than I'd remembered, his lashes blond. Maybe it's the lack of eyeliner, but he looks younger. His hair has been washed and cut and gelled perfectly into place. His skin looks polished to a shine, but drained of blood. He glows like a pearl.

Everyone around us is moving. His parents are wandering, robotically shaking hands and kissing cheeks, but Marcel seems pinned to this spot in the universe at the crest of the steps that lead from the cathedral to the graveyard.

"Nice hat," Marcel says, but the usual sardonic tone has been flattened. He might even mean it.

I tuck a stray strand of hair up into the black pillbox. A scoop of black netting separates my face from the world. It *is* a nice hat—thrift shop find of the year. Nanette's white coat covers the plunging neckline of grim reaper velvet, so as long as I stay buttoned up, I'm funeral appropriate. "I didn't want anyone to recognize me," I admit before realizing my mistake.

"Who would recognize you?"

Wouldn't I love to know. I glance around, wondering if my father has replaced Lucien's watchful eye on me with someone else's. "I thought your parents might. I'm the girl in Lucien's paintings."

"Trust me. His paintings are the last thing on their minds."

I missed the service intentionally, watching from a distance and wandering over once the crowd started to disperse. But now I'm close enough to see that Lucien's mother has the white-blond hair and porcelain features, his father the narrow eyes. I can see their expressions too. She looks vacant in the pharmaceutical way; he appears mortified but stoic.

"Shouldn't you be over there with them?" I ask.

"I should correct what I said about his paintings," he says, unnervingly straight-faced still. "*I* am the last thing on their minds."

As if on cue, both turn and start walking toward the cathedral. I wait for Marcel to move away from me, to follow them, but he doesn't.

"We came separately," he explains.

I set my face against the wind, trying not to show shock or pity or whatever it is I feel toward this scrubbed-clean tragedy. And who am I to judge? My father is a monster and my mother abandoned me.

"Did you just get here?" he asks. "I didn't see you at the service."

"I didn't want to intrude."

"So why come at all?"

The words are abrasive, but his sincerity disarms me. "Lucien was my friend." Does saying it make it any closer to true? I'm not sure. "Can't I just be here to pay my respects?"

He stares into my eyes, and I feel layers of false words and costumes being stripped away.

"Fine," I say. "I came here to see you."

He sets his jaw, not letting my eyes slip away. He's always been sallow, nearly yellow, but he's a different kind of pale today. Gray. Miserable. Not drunk. That look in his eyes now is disbelief, and I see why. Nobody came here to see Marcel.

The inappropriateness of what I came here to do slams into me, and my breath is gone. I can't ask him for money.

"Why?" he asks.

"I don't know. I thought . . ." I falter and start again. "Are you okay?" I hear myself ask.

He doesn't answer.

I'm an idiot.

"No," he says finally.

Silence. The cold is pulling and pushing us at the same time, making me dizzy. I feel like we could fall in any direction.

"Do you want to go somewhere?" he asks.

"Where?"

"I don't know."

"Okay."

I follow him to his car, something generically sporty and angry-looking, and get in. It doesn't feel like I have a choice, like this sudden sympathetic urge I'm experiencing is more of a compulsion than a decision. I sneak a sideways glance. He looks so wretched I almost want to squeeze his arm and tell him things will be okay.

"Movies?" he asks.

"Sure."

Marcel doesn't take me to the towering Cineplex Odeon. I'm relieved and worried at the same time—a testosterone-based, mindlessly violent action movie is what we need here. Something mind-numbing, please. Instead, we go to the Cinéma du Parc, where we stand and stare at the handwritten board.

"I've seen the Swedish ones," I say.

"And I've seen the Japanese one," he says. "That leaves French or Italian."

"Will the French one have subtitles?"

"Probably not. Who runs away to Montreal when they don't even speak French?"

"I'm not a runaway."

He shrugs. "Italian historical romance it is."

Marcel takes our coats to coat check, doing an average-to-poor job of not staring at my cleavage, and I silently curse Lucien for this dress. Then I remember he's dead.

There's no talk of money. Marcel buys our tickets, a cellophane bag of cinnamon walnuts, another of dark-chocolate-dipped apricots, and two black cherry sodas, while I wait and wonder. Where are his friends? Why isn't he with his parents? Why, when we've never had a single civil exchange, am I the one with him after his brother's funeral? Why is he not getting drunk or stoned out of his mind right now?

We survey the empty theater from the entrance.

"Where do you want to sit?" he asks.

I point to the last row. "If you don't mind sitting so far back."

"I don't care." I follow him to the middle of the row, where he sinks into a seat—old-fashioned, plush velvet.

He twists the metal top off a soda and hands it to me with the sweet fizz bubbling and dribbling over my hand.

I could've opened it, but it doesn't seem like the right moment to chide him for overstepping. We'll do chivalry versus feminism another day. Or not. "Thanks."

We sit in silence. I stare straight ahead, waiting for someone else to come in. Anyone else. Anyone at all. But apparently nobody in Montreal is interested in this particular low-budget Italian historical romance, because Marcel and I are still the only two takers when the lights dim and the velvet curtains part. As the screen flickers to life, I locate the exits and consider bailing before this gets any more awkward.

But the movie begins and I'm still sitting beside Marcel. My hand is slick from the glass bottle. My tongue tingles from the fizz. I guess I'm staying.

It's thirty excruciating minutes of bad acting and cheesy lines before Marcel makes his move. He stretches out his arm, slides his soda into the cup holder, and leans forward.

I hold my breath, gripping the chair arm between us.

He dips his head to his hands.

I shrink into my chair. I don't understand.

He starts to cry.

An Italian show tune breaks out, covering whatever sound he might be making, and all I have is what I can see: his long, slumped torso shuddering with the light from the screen illuminating his back.

I know what not to do. Instinctively, I know not to put my hand on his back. I don't rub his shoulder, or commit the unpardonable sin of trying to hug him. I sit. I watch him bounce as sobs shake his frame.

Ten, twenty, thirty minutes grind on. The musical Italian voices rain down, but I can't look up to read the subtitles. I can't look away from Marcel. The longer he cries, the more uncomfortable my own empathy makes me. I don't want to identify with Marcel, but if one of my sisters killed herself, the pain might kill me, and right now, watching him cry, it doesn't matter that he's a drug-addled douche bag, or that he and Lucien acted like they hated each other. Maybe I should hug him.

Finally, his shoulders go slack. Relief. Almost.

He doesn't sit back immediately, and I realize the worst of it: we have to suffer through the rest of the movie, say words to each other, maybe even make eye contact. The lights will go back on eventually. I wait for him to turn to me and in some way acknowledge what has just happened, but he doesn't. He leans back in his chair and watches the rest of the movie.

And so do I.

"This is a dump," he says, eyeing my building as he pulls up to the curb.

"Why, thank you." I struggle with my seat belt and its foreign prongs.

"Need some help with that?"

"No." I jab and yank for a few more seconds before the lock clicks open, releasing me.

I look at Marcel. Crying makes everyone ugly. Marcel's face is swollen, sweaty, and red, but he's not ugly, not quite. His eyes save him. They're raw and glittering, like polished ice. I could almost reach out and cup his face in my hands. I should tell him how sorry I am.

He hands me the untouched bags of walnuts and apricots. "Take these."

"Sure." No need to be shy about free food. "Thanks."

"We should do this again sometime."

I can't tell if he's joking. "Yeah."

It doesn't matter, though, because I'm leaving. Emilio is coming for me. And Marcel will get home and realize that he's just sobbed and sobbed beside a girl he finds ridiculous, his dead brother's dress-up doll, and the shame will eat him up.

I reach for the door handle.

"Wait," he says, thrusting his phone at me. "I need your number."

I hesitate, take it, and type in my number. If he calls, he's officially lost his mind. Not in a good way.

I'm back in my closet beneath my scratchy blanket when I realize I can't ever ask him for the money Lucien owed me for the cemetery sitting, let alone beg him for more. He'll remember this day and feel used, like his grief has been poached, though I'm not sure why I care. Losing my mind. Not in a good way.

SEVENTEEN

*S*even *minutes.*

I texted Emilio today. Three times. I shouldn't have done it, but it's been five days since I've heard his voice, and all the bad things that could've happened started multiplying and skittering around in my mind like crazed insects, and suddenly I was back in Emilio's closet staring through that crack, but this time it was my father holding the gun and Emilio cowering by the wall. I had to talk to him.

But now it's worse. It's much worse, because I texted him and he didn't respond, so I texted again, and still nothing, so I texted again, and now I'm lying here staring at the clock, waiting for time to inch forward so I can leave for Soupe au Chocolat. The sun only just set, but Jacques closes early on Sunday, so I can be there all night if I want.

Six minutes.

For sanity's sake, I remind myself of the things I know. Emilio said it was too dangerous to keep that phone on him, so it must be stashed away somewhere with all my unread texts piling up. He can probably only check it once a day. If that. And if he's working insane hours for my father, maybe he can't check it at all.

But reviewing the few things I know doesn't make me feel better about the things I don't know. Like, why give me a way to get ahold of him when I can't really get ahold of him at all? And why did he have that cell phone on him anyway? Who just walks around with a secret cell phone in case they're going to need one? The questions are like links in a chain—no answers, just another link and another link and another link, until the chain is too heavy and wrapped around me.

Five minutes.

Food-wise, these cinnamon walnuts are the best thing to happen to me in a long time. They're crunchy and sweet but not cloyingly so, and salty too. My bed has taken on a cinnamon scent and gritty feel, but I don't care.

I examine the contents of the bag. I've managed to ration them out for several days, but today is definitely the end. I eat the final walnut, then hold the bag up to my lips and pour the crumbled spice-roasted dregs into my mouth. More cinnamon in the bed. Whatever.

The food situation is approaching dire. I've identified several problems, the first being my lack of cooking skills. Rice is cheap, but I burn it. Every time. I'm good with peanut butter and jelly, but that's getting old. Pasta is easy enough, but I despise having to horn my way into that greasy kitchen and use the scratched, carcinogen-leaching pots and cabbage-shellacked utensils. Everything I make in there ends up smelling like fish sauce and leaving an oily film in my mouth.

Four minutes.

That leaves eating out. I've discovered the great tragedy of purchased food: expensive = delicious, cheap = revolting. I realize that it's my stupid rich-girl upbringing screwing me over, but I'd still rather buy one tray of high-grade sushi and starve for the rest of the week than eat fourteen 7-Eleven cheese dogs. It's supposed to be a little warmer tomorrow, so maybe I'll go sit in my old spot outside the Metro and make some pity change.

At least I have more chocolate bars beneath my bed. Jacques left me another box last time. I was so happy I almost cried.

I miss yesterday, when I still had the chocolate-dipped apricots. Those were harder to hoard, though—fewer of them to begin with. But apricots are a fruit. I may have even absorbed vitamins from them.

Three minutes.

Rent was due three days ago. Nanette's been nice about a lot of things, but I know this will not be one of them. She doesn't have the money to cover me. Nobody in this dump does; that's why we're all here. The question is how long crotchety Monsieur Cabot will take to remove me, and what I'm supposed to do if it's before Emilio comes.

Emilio. Maybe he's reading my texts right now. I pick up the phone, already knowing I haven't missed a call.

Nothing. Same as last time I checked, four minutes ago.

I wish I'd made him tell me exactly how he was going to get money. Then I'd have something solid to lean my anxiety against. What if Papi or one of my sisters caught him stealing something? I picture Papi's face, not the face I used to know, but the man I saw from the closet, and shudder. I don't know.

And if he hurt Emilio, what would I do then? I don't know that either.

My hand vibrates. Every nerve in my palm sizzles with the tremor, and I'm bringing the phone to my ear, sitting straight up, before that first ring can even end.

"Emilio," I gasp.

An inch of silence. That's all it takes for me to realize what I've done. Emilio is not the only person who has this number.

"No."

Panic courses through me, so hot and electric it's crippling, and now I can't speak at all. Marcel, Marcel, Marcel, Marcel. What does Marcel even know? I have to focus. He thinks I only just met Emilio at LaFleur's show. But now he thinks . . .

"Jane?"

"Marcel. Hi."

"Hi."

"Sorry, I didn't—I'm just—"

"Yeah," he says.

I take a deep breath and hold it. This is not the end of the world. I only said *Emilio*. So what? If he asks, I could say Emilio asked me for my number at the LaFleur show, and I didn't look at the caller display. Or I could say I have a cousin named Emilio. Lame, but he might buy it. I wish he'd say something.

"How are you?" he asks finally.

"Fine."

"You sound out of breath."

"Out of breath?" Lola's knowing voice comes to my head: *The best lies are the true ones.* She should know. She was a veteran class cutter, curfew breaker, sick faker—an all-around princess of lies. "The elevator is broken. I just climbed seven flights of stairs." At least the first half of that is true.

"Yeah?"

"Yeah."

"Interesting."

"Do you want to come try the elevator out yourself?"

"No."

"You saw my building. It shouldn't be hard to believe it's a little run-down on the inside."

"I never said I didn't believe you," he says.

"Fine, then."

He goes silent again, and I feel bad. That defensive freak-out was definitely uncalled for. "So, how are you?" I ask.

"Um . . ."

Wrong question. Now he's thinking that *I'm* thinking about the crying, which I'm not. Or I wasn't. Now I am.

"I'm fine," he says. "Actually, I'm hungry. Do you want to eat?"

I glance at the empty cellophane bag beside the cot. Of course I want to eat. I want to eat something expensive and delicious with take-home potential. If it wasn't Marcel I'd have already said yes, but it is Marcel, and I have no clue why we would go somewhere together again, or why he even called. I've already given up on asking him for the money Lucien owes me. Watching him sob his way through that movie made me realize I'm not quite heartless enough to make him feel used right now.

That doesn't mean I want to be around him, though. Grieving Marcel is still Marcel, just with the attitude and sliminess somewhat repressed. He needs to find a better shoulder to cry on, one belonging to someone who doesn't have to be heartless. And I really need to play Emilio's mandolin tonight.

"I know this good Japanese restaurant," he says. "Do you eat sushi?"

Damn him. "Yes."

"I'll pick you up in an hour."

EIGHTEEN

I wait out front in the dark. The entryway is temptingly warm, but I don't want Marcel seeing the greasy walls, or the crooked plastic plant with only four leaves, or even the permanently wrenched-open elevator. I spend the time staring at Marcel's number in my phone, promising myself to never mistake that number for Emilio's again. I should program him in, but I can't bring myself to put Marcel's name into my phone when I'm not even allowed to put Emilio's name in it.

Marcel pulls up, and I get in but not quick enough. I catch him giving the building a lingering, skeptical look. Or maybe the skeptical look is aimed at me.

"Hey," he says.

"Hey."

He pulls smoothly back into traffic, and the memory of Lucien's jerkiness behind the wheel bubbles up unbidden.

Accelerator-brake-accelerator-brake. Of all the stupid things to be sentimental about, spastic driving shouldn't be one of them. I push it away.

I run my palms along the leather, taking in all the things I somehow missed last time. The car is warm and soft, not masculine like the outside, and smooth as skin. And it's silent. I stare at the console. Surely this thing has a top-of-the-line sound system. I want him to turn on music, but I don't want to ask, and I'm not going to just reach over and do it myself. Maybe he doesn't even listen to music—but who doesn't listen to music?

I glance at him. His lip ring is gone. I'm still a little unnerved by the short hair and clear eyes, so I stare out the window while I work on something to say. I've got nothing. The silence is a big fat reminder of the obvious: we don't know anything about each other. This is weird.

"We might have a bit of a wait," he says finally. "This place is always busy."

"Okay."

"We can wander around, though. There are some cool buildings in the area."

"Sure." So Marcel is a respecter of *cool buildings*. That's something. Maybe he likes architecture.

The silence forces its way back between us.

"So, how was school this week?" I ask.

"I didn't go. 'Bereavement' is a powerful word." He changes gears, and the engine hums. "Nobody thought I'd be there anyway. I've had some truancy issues this year."

"Truancy issues."

"Meaning I don't go when I don't feel like it. What about you?"

"What about me?"

"Why aren't you in school?"

I picture where I should be: Trinity Prep, nestled in the palms of Coconut Grove between the boutiques and the ocean. I can see the terra-cotta roofs roasting under the sun, the sprawling Spanish colonials connected by hibiscus-lined walkways. I should be sitting on the north side of the quad with Drea and Kim, tanning the six inches of thigh between pleated skirt and knee-highs. I should be making fun of Tony and Cameron. Flirting with Diego.

Another twinge of nostalgia pulses through me. I miss those girls and the endless flow of gossip. I miss those guys in their navy blazers and cocky smiles. I had nothing deep with any of them, but I had fun. Fun is something.

I rest my hands on the thighs of my leggings—my cheaper-than-jeans go-to. Who'd have thought I'd ever miss that plaid skirt?

"Let me guess—you have truancy issues of your own," he says, pulling me back.

I bristle. "I'm nineteen. Why would I still be in high school?"

"I never said high school. Interesting that you immediately thought of high school, though. I assumed secondary education exists in whatever place you said you're from. Was it Colorado?"

"California."

"Right. California."

I shift uncomfortably in my seat. He's either trying to goad me into saying too much, or he really believes me and wants to know more. I don't like either.

"So Californians don't go to university," he says. "That makes sense. It's all Hollywood or Compton."

"Funny. I just wanted to live in Montreal."

"Why?"

A whole jumble of weak lies comes to my mind, but they're all equally unbelievable. I can't pick. "Seemed like an interesting place," I offer.

"Yeah, but . . . okay. Whatever."

The best lies are the true ones. The wisdom of Lola to the rescue again, and twice in one day, too. "And I wanted some space from my family."

He says nothing, and my insensitivity rings loudly in my ears. Did I really say that to someone who just lost his only brother? I slide my hand under my leg to keep from slapping my forehead and making things even more uncomfortable.

"So you aren't going to college," he says.

"I'm going. Just not right now."

He doesn't believe me, but I don't know if I believe me. College has always been a given, but the givens have been torn away. My lens is focused on now—running away from my family, basic survival, finding a way to be with Emilio. There's nothing else. College is another sacrificed luxury.

"I'm thinking of going back," he says, and it takes me a

second to understand what he's talking about.

"What, to school?"

"Yeah. Maybe. I only stopped going to annoy people. I used to sort of like school."

"Quitting school to annoy people—that's a little extreme."

"Well, I didn't exactly quit. I just stopped going."

"Right."

"And they really deserved to be annoyed."

"Your parents, I'm assuming."

"And Lucien." He says the name so casually, for a moment Lucien isn't dead. He's in a room somewhere, staring at a canvas and nibbling on the end of his paintbrush with that pretentious smirk on his face.

The illusion dissipates. "Did it work?" I ask.

He runs a hand through his hair, like he still can't believe it's short. "I think so. With Lucien, at least."

"Wait, I thought you both went to boarding school in England."

"I was only there for two years. I didn't want to be there without Lucien, so I left when he graduated."

I wait. He must hear the gap he's left—he wanted to be with Lucien; he wanted to annoy Lucien—but he doesn't fill it for me.

"So," I say, "have you seen much of your friends since . . . all of this?"

"No." His eyes are cold and fixed on the road ahead. "But they weren't exactly my friends. Just people I was using to piss off Lucien."

I must look appalled, because Marcel snorts and says, "Don't feel too bad for them. They didn't mind being used."

"Are you sure about that?"

He shrugs. "Whatever. Friends are overrated. You're in Montreal alone, I'm assuming."

"I'm here alone." I picture them again, the girls in shortened plaid and lip gloss, the boys with sand in their hair and bleached teeth. "I guess I miss my friends. I miss hanging out, not having to worry about anything."

"And you're worried now."

I don't answer him.

Marcel's face is less puffy today, less pale, to the point of looking like blood might flow through his veins, as opposed to vodka. Maybe it's just his profile, but the features are more pointed too.

"What are you so worried about?" he asks, catching me staring.

I look away, out the window to where the storefronts and signs and faces have become Chinese. I have to do a better job at steering this conversation. His questions are too focused, and it's getting harder to believe he doesn't know what he's aiming at. "Getting a job."

"How can that be hard? Walk into a Club Monaco or Anthropologie. You have retail sexpot written all over you."

I glare at him. "What's that supposed to mean?"

"Chill out. It's a compliment."

"That's how you compliment people?"

"I meant you look like you'd wear their clothes well, okay? If you think you're too good for retail, sorry. I misunderstood."

"I'm not too good for retail. I don't have a visa to work here."

"Oh."

There's nothing to say now. Our tenuous dynamic can't support him being a jerk and me being defensive. We settle back into silence.

I stare out the window and watch the signs turn from what I thought was Chinese to what I think is Vietnamese to what I think is Korean to what I just can't tell. Then we're back to the familiar mix of skyscrapers and fairy tale. I've nearly grown used to it, the way this city meshes Camelot and Metropolis. It's a fabric of old-world punctured by modern structures. I won't miss Montreal—when Emilio comes for me, I'll leave without looking back, without tears— but eventually I might be able to work up some sort of nostalgia for it.

Except then I'd have to remember the terror I've felt here. Maybe I'll leave nostalgia be.

The drive goes on and on, and by the time Marcel parks, I'm certain that the finest sushi in the world isn't worth another hour of this torture.

"It's right there," he says, pointing to a sign up ahead. KRU. The font is stretched and angled like a blade, the color of steel.

He roots around for something in the backseat while I get out of the car and walk ahead, pulled by my stomach and the promise of ambient noise.

"Wait up," he calls.

I have to force myself to slow down. Being civil shouldn't be so hard. Marcel opens the door for me and leans close as I pass through. "It's traditional Japanese," he says softly, like he needs to demonstrate how loud I should talk.

I whisper back, "In that case I'll order California rolls and a Diet Coke."

If he smiles, I don't catch it.

Inside, Kru is sparse and light. Lotus blossoms float in cups on tables, and crisply shaven bonsai accent ledges. I breathe. The air is delicate. It's ginger and soy and sake braided together, a fishtail of scents. Kimono-wrapped women glide from table to table, the fish on their trays glistening like bars of ruby and pearl.

"Omakase?" Marcel asks. He's watching me, so I don't let on that I know exactly what *omakase* is, that I've sat and watched expert sushi chefs make delicacy after delicacy of their own choosing plenty of times.

But then his face softens, and it's not so much patronizing as *nice*. I get it. He doesn't want me to be embarrassed about my own ignorance. That's worse, enough to make me abandon the dumb routine.

"How many courses?" I ask.

"Depends how hungry you are."

"Ten."

"You mean on a scale of one to ten?"

"No, I mean ten-course *omakase* sounds perfect," I say.

The hostess welcomes us in French, and after a brief

exchange with Marcel, seats us at the sushi bar. Side by side again. The movie theater, the car, now Kru—with any luck at all we'll never have to make eye contact.

The sushi chef nods at both of us, then speaks to Marcel in French too. He looks like a surgeon with his tight cap, solemn eyes, and gleaming cleaver. I watch his hands while he talks. Palm down, the left presses flat on the inky scales of a headless fish, and the right grips the knife. He slices the flesh in one fluid motion, as if it were butter and not meat. He does it again and again, discarding the skin and carving the meat into perfect blocks. It's violent and beautiful. I'm holding my breath. Why am I holding my breath?

"Are you okay?" Marcel asks.

"What? Oh. I'm fine." I fix my face into something less half-starved, more sane, and try to think of small talk. "So, it's not too busy. We didn't even have to wait."

"No."

Now the chef is slicing something red with white threads running through the fiber. It looks good. It looks expensive. I look around me for a menu, but of course there are none. We're eating *omakase*, so there's no need, except it'd be nice to see a price or two.

Of course, he's paying.

A mild jolt, just a hiccup of panic jerks me. No, he's paying. He knows I'm broke, and he paid for everything at the movies the other night. Plus, he asked me. Under different circum-stances I'd worry he was thinking this was a date, but it's clear neither of us is feeling that. Definitely not that.

We watch the chef slice eel and octopus, delicate operations of dismemberment and amputation. For some reason it makes me think of poetry. It's the way his fingers dance nimbly around the meat.

"You think this is weird," Marcel says.

"Eel butchering?" I ask.

"No. Being here with me."

"Oh." I lift my chopsticks from their holder. They're obsidian black and smooth. "No."

"It's fine. It is weird."

I click them together a few times. "Okay, it's weird."

The chef hands us our first plates, tiny strips of barbecued eel wrapped around shaved cucumber, and we stare at our food. The silence is less brittle now. He said it. I admitted it. There isn't much else to do besides eat the eel, because I need the food and he needs the company of someone who doesn't matter or care.

I take a bite and it melts in my mouth. Sinful, sinful meat. I can't remember the last time I tasted something so rich.

"My mom is demanding I start seeing her shrink."

I take another bite to save me from commenting.

"She thinks I'm not grieving."

I picture his hunched figure beside me in the theater, flickering with the movie on his back, shuddering beneath the barrage of sound. "And you don't think you need to go."

He shrugs. "I guess there's a certain way you're supposed to act in front of certain people at a certain time when your brother kills himself."

"As in cry at the funeral."

"As in that."

"Which you didn't do."

"I don't like an audience."

I'm not sure what this means. I'm not an audience?

"I could feel them all watching me," he says. "Would you have sobbed for the crowd?"

I picture my sisters. The idea of either of them dying is so sickening I can't keep imagining it. "I don't know."

"Do you have siblings?"

"Yes," I say before I remember that I'm not Valentina. Jane isn't supposed to have siblings, but I guess she does now. "Two sisters."

He stares at the curled, sticky flesh between his chopsticks. "So, maybe I seem crazy."

"Lots of people don't cry at funerals."

"Not that. I mean calling you, trying to hang out with you like we're friends."

I chew and swallow, but the sticky rice doesn't go down, just clings to my throat in a glob. I don't have to answer because we're both distracted as our plates are removed and the next course delivered: rectangles of seared white tuna, a breath of avocado draped over each like a wilting leaf.

"Maybe I don't know you," he says, "but I saw the way you

looked at Lucien when he was staring at his canvas. I know you hated him."

"I didn't hate—"

"*Stop.* It's okay. I hated him too."

Everything I could say is a lie. I didn't exactly hate him, but I couldn't stand him either.

We stare at our plates, white clouds covered in green velvet. I shouldn't have an appetite anymore, but I do, and the food is too beautiful to waste.

He takes the first bite. I follow. It's rich and fills my whole mouth with creaminess, practically a dessert.

"He wasn't always such an egomaniac," Marcel says, laying his chopsticks on his plate. "Before he came back to Montreal, he was different."

I think of the second photo from the *Gazette*. Even in grainy black-and-white, the difference was there. They were friends back then. "How?"

"He was smarter."

"Art school made him stupid?"

Marcel laughs bitterly. "No. Art school wasn't the problem. When he came back, he was all set to prove himself to the world, show my dad he was his own man so he wouldn't have to work for him. Art school was just failed attempt number one. The artist act was annoying, but it wasn't fatal."

Fatal. I pretend I didn't hear it.

Marcel leans back as bowls of shiitake soup are placed in front of us, mushrooms bobbing among scallions in a murky broth. The steam fills me with earthiness and salt. I breathe it in, take one sip, then drink it spoonful after spoonful until I give up on the spoon and drink from the bowl. I think I've dribbled a little on my sweater and I don't care.

"Hungry?" Marcel asks.

I lick the salt from my lips and eye his half-finished bowl. "What? It's perfectly acceptable to drink soup from the bowl in Japan."

"So you've spent time in Japan."

"I really like the soup."

"I'm sure Shinji here is flattered," Marcel says, gesturing to the chef.

The chef smiles at me from across the wooden board, where he's snapping the claws off a snow crab. Stringy pink flesh hangs from his fingers.

"I've just never seen a girl eat so fast," Marcel says.

"I'm hungry."

"Most girls I know don't eat. Most girls I know would rather talk nonstop."

"I'm nothing like most girls you know. And it sounds like you need to start hanging out with girls who are less annoying."

"I'm trying."

We sit in our first comfortable silence ever. But it's not entirely quiet. Traditional Japanese music plays softly, and chimes tinkle every few minutes or so when the door opens, but mostly I don't hear them. I'm considering the magical healing powers of food. I'm warming up. I may still be freezing to death for want of people and love and home, but for the moment food does a decent job of filling me. I almost feel like myself.

Marcel stirs a chunk of wasabi into his soy sauce. "This one time I dared Lucien to eat an entire spoonful of wasabi," he says.

"Tell me he didn't."

"I have the video of it somewhere. He was actually on the floor crying, and then he whined about not being able to taste anything for weeks. During the boarding-school days, I could get him to do anything."

"What was boarding school like?" I ask.

He shrugs. "Good."

"That's descriptive."

He pulls his hair between his fingers, testing the length again. "You know when things seem normal, good, fine, whatever, but then something changes and you realize that life *was* perfect, but only because it's not anymore and never will be again?"

His words ring like the door chimes, not loud but brightly. He said it exactly.

"It was that," he says.

I nod. Life *before*—that was perfect.

"I know what you're thinking," Marcel says. "Poor little rich boy."

"Not what I was thinking."

The chef slides two wooden tablets filled with tuna tartare in front of us. It's the color and texture of the inside of my cheek, but it tastes like heaven and the ocean. I try it with each accompaniment—crème fraîche, rice cracker crumbs, wasabi, avocado—before I notice Marcel is watching me.

"So, this isn't your first rodeo," he says.

"What's that supposed to mean?"

"You're better than me with chopsticks."

I shrug. "So you're not dexterous."

"Trust me, I'm good with my hands."

"What's your point?"

"You didn't learn to eat Japanese food from the sushi counter at a grocery store."

"Maybe I was just following your lead."

"You haven't looked at me once."

I look at him now. His eyes are icy clear.

"Fine. I've been to Japan a few times."

"You're well-traveled," he says. "And you grew up with money."

I say nothing.

"It's obvious."

"Yeah? Was it my fancy apartment that gave me away?"

"It certainly wasn't your clothes."

"Shut up." I tug at the synthetic sweater that seems to be shrink-wrapping around my body under Kru's lights. I'm not sure whether to defend myself. I am committing fashion crimes. Many.

Marcel takes a sip of his green tea. "I've always been able to tell. You have this unguarded look that reeks of a spoiled upbringing."

"Excuse me?"

"You do. It screams 'I'm too good for this.' It came out every time Lucien turned his back."

"Did not."

"Did too."

"Did not."

"Did too."

I roll my eyes.

"So you have money," he says. "What's the big deal? It's not like—"

"I *don't* have money. Maybe I used to, but I don't anymore."

"Whatever. Oh, and by the way, your holier-than-thou thing about me and my trust fund was great. Thanks."

"You're welcome. And thanks for insulting my clothes just now."

"Anytime. Since we're getting it all out in the open, your apartment really is disgusting."

I can't defend it. "You haven't even seen the inside."

He nudges my arm with his elbow, the first time he's touched me—ever, I think—and the shock of it makes me want to pull away, not in revulsion, but fear. I don't want to feel anyone's touch but Emilio's.

"Is that an invitation? If so, I'll pass. I'd rather not risk being exposed to asbestos and lead paint. You should be worried about that."

"It wasn't an invitation. And I'm moving soon, so I don't have to worry about toxins for much longer."

"Where are you moving to?"

"I don't know."

"Then why are you moving *soon* if you don't have a place lined up?"

It's too late to backpedal. "I stopped paying rent."

Our next plate is served—neat stacks of shaved radish and mountain vegetables drizzled with sweet-hot ginger vinaigrette—but I can't remember which course it is. Fourth? Fifth? They're running together now, and I'm having the niggling ache you get when you start to worry that something wonderful is going to end. Like summer vacation on the yacht, or a few hours alone to play the mandolin. Or being with Emilio.

Plates of salmon sashimi are placed in front of us.

"So how does a world-traveling little rich girl not have enough money to pay rent on a dive?"

I cringe. "I take back what I said before. It's not that I don't like to talk. It's that I don't like to talk about things I'm trying not to think about."

Marcel lifts the salmon to his lips. He doesn't ask me anything. He is redeemed.

I stare at my plate, at the meat that's the color of an orange hibiscus blossom and marbled with thin threads of fat, like it's been tied up with fine white string. Now would be the time to ask for money. It would be easy. I could tell him Lucien owed me, or about how Lucien promised me all that work at an increased sitting fee.

"So admit it," he says. "You're running from the law."

I laugh. "What crime did I commit?"

He leans away from me and squints at my face. "Arson. I can see it in your eyes."

"If I was a fugitive, which I'm not, it wouldn't be for arson. I've been afraid of fire since I was eight and I burned myself playing with matches." I hold out my arm to show him the band of scarred skin on the inside of my elbow. "My sister's idea. She, however, escaped unscathed."

"Okay, so not arson. Statutory rape. Your boyfriend is seventeen and his parents are pressing charges."

I roll my eyes.

"Unless you're not actually a legal adult," he continues, "which would be a real shocker."

"*I'm ni—*"

"I know, I know. You're nineteen." He chews thoughtfully. "I've got it: accomplice to murder."

The closet. The gunshot in my ears. The blood flower blooming on the wall. Emilio's rigid arm and dead eyes. Cold fingers of that memory wrap around my pounding heart, but I keep my eyes on my plate, my hands in my lap so they don't shake. "Why accomplice?" I ask.

"That's as good as a confession," he says. "So who'd you kill?"

I need a jokey answer, something stupid and light so he'll leave me alone. "My seventeen-year-old boyfriend. The one whose parents wanted me in jail for statutory rape. I set the whole house on fire."

"I knew it," he says.

A fan of seared Kobe beef is placed before me, each rectangular piece with a purple-raw center. I take a bite. It's deliciously salty and metallic, but I can't enjoy it. I feel like I'm eating my own heart. I wish I knew if Emilio was okay.

"So how do you know Emilio?" Marcel asks, and for one sickening moment I know he knows. He's eating his bloody beef calmly, but he knows what I'm thinking, who I am, and who really killed his brother.

"I met him at Les Fontaines. You were there, remember?"

"But when I called this morning, you thought I was him."

"He asked for my number," I say casually. "Not many people have my number. I just didn't look at it before I picked up."

"You sure sounded . . . I don't know. Excited."

"What do you care?" I fire back. "And how is that any of your business?"

Marcel abandons his beef, stares at his tea like he wishes it were something else. "It's not. You just don't know who he is."

"Really? Then enlighten me," I say before my brain can catch up with my temper.

"He's involved in some bad business. Lucien was too."

I hold my breath. I do and I don't want to hear Marcel's take on the *bad business*.

"After Lucien dropped out of art school, he was sort of desperate to do something big to prove himself. My dad was insisting he come work for him, but Lucien wouldn't. I don't blame him. My dad's a jerk. But then Lucien started working for this guy down in Miami. I think he met Emilio first, and then Emilio introduced him to this Cruz guy."

Time stops. It's only for a second, but it's long enough for Marcel to take a breath and my stomach to squeeze everything I've just eaten and my pulse to pound so loudly in my ears that I'm wondering if I'm having a stroke or an aneurism or some kind of neuro-vascular explosion. Cruz guy. I have to ask, "What was he doing?"

"Smuggling art."

"What?" I twist my whole body to look at Marcel's face. Papi is dealing art, not smuggling it. And art is the cover. Drugs are the dirt and the blood.

"Don't look so shocked."

"But . . ." Papi wouldn't steal art. He lives for it, practically breathes it. Marcel doesn't know what he's talking about.

"There's a lot of money in it," Marcel explains, like the economics of art theft are the unbelievable part.

"I know, but since when did Lucien need money?"

"Never. But he needed respect, which is the other thing working for this guy offered. I don't think Lucien even knew who Cruz really was until he'd been at it for a while."

Who Cruz really was. Did the whole world know but me? "What do you mean?" I ask, needing to hear it again, but dreading it too.

"He's the head of some Colombian drug cartel. The art fetish is more than a cover, though. According to Lucien, he was pulling in almost as much from stolen masterpieces as cocaine."

I picture the paintings I grew up staring at: the Klimt, the O'Keeffe, the Warhol, the Rodin. He's wrong. My father loves art, taught us to love it, travels all over the world to buy the finest. He wouldn't be stealing it. "So Lucien . . ."

"Lucien was one of his scouts. At first it was all legitimate, but eventually he got sucked into the smuggling side too. He had the right contacts from art school, so he'd go around pretending to be looking to buy. Plus, he was rich enough for people to take him seriously."

"And Emilio." I hear myself say his name and know I should stop. "He does the same thing?"

"No. Cruz runs his businesses in layers—the legal art dealing, then smuggling, then drugs. Emilio's pretty deep, does it all. He manages things, takes care of people, threatens people. Probably more than threatens people." Marcel stares at his plate. It's empty except for the small puddle of blood. "And of course, he always brings coke with him to grease wheels and make friends."

"Do you work for him too?" I can't hide the tremor in my voice, but I have to ask. I have to know.

"No. But I partied with Emilio. At first I did it just to make Lucien mad. I told him he was an idiot, and that he was going to get sent to jail or this Cruz guy was going to start asking him to do way worse stuff, but he ignored me. He had things under control. Suddenly he was important, not just some art school dropout, or Daddy's little pawn. So I screwed around more, stopped going to school, hooked up with Emilio's party-favor girls. I thought I could be wild enough to scare Lucien."

My stomach hurts. I've eaten too quickly. I stare at the plate in front of me, half-eaten seared shark, shiny with brine and oil. I can't remember when the beef was taken away, or when this arrived, and I can't remember taking those bites.

Emilio can't be who Marcel thinks he is.

The door chimes ring, a reminder that people are still eating and talking and living all around me. It seems impossible, though why would the whole world stop just because my world has? How long have we been here?

"Maybe you and Emilio aren't any of my business," Marcel says.

"We aren't."

"I'm just telling you he's dangerous."

"I believe you."

Marcel finishes his shark. I keep staring at mine; it keeps staring at me. Leaving unfinished food is *omakase* taboo, but the richness is finally too much. One more bite could be fatal.

When the chef turns his back, I nudge Marcel with my elbow and point to my plate. "Please?"

"You owe me," he says, and reaches for it.

Ominous words. They slice through me. My shark is being carried away, but I dive in, my chopsticks proving stronger and faster than his as they snatch it midair. It's in my mouth before he even understands that it's gone. "Changed my mind," I say between chews.

Our last course is roasted peaches and pistachio ice cream.

It's good, I think, but my taste buds are spent. Our bellies and brains are already too full, and I don't even make eye contact as he pays the bill. My cheeks burn, but I don't know if it's gratitude or shame that does it, or if there's much of a difference at this point.

The drive home takes longer. We hit light after light, get caught behind a bus making regular and long stops, and finally sit sandwiched between cars waiting for an accident to be cleared up ahead.

Still no music.

"Did Lucien seem different to you that night?" Marcel asks abruptly.

"I don't know." I say it without thinking. I don't want to think about it ever again.

He swallows. "I don't remember most of it. I was wasted when I showed up, and after that . . . well . . . Maybe if I hadn't been, things would have been different."

The compassionate thing to say is *of course not* or *don't blame yourself*, but if Marcel wants to take some blame, maybe less of it will be pressing down on me.

"I think I was a jerk to you," he says.

"You were."

"And I think Lucien and I fought," he says.

"You did."

He cringes.

"But that wasn't it," I say, not just because it's the nice thing to say but because it's true. "He didn't kill himself because of anything that happened between you two."

"Maybe not. But if I hadn't been so busy getting high that night, or this entire year, I'd have known something was wrong."

I can't make him feel better about that. Trying seems dishonest—dishonest in a way I don't have to be, and I have to be a liar in so many other ways right now.

"You have a way of saying the right thing," he says.

"I didn't say anything."

"Exactly."

I swallow. I look at him. The misery is intense, and yet it's only his eyes that show it, clear and sharp as pain. I want to tell him about Lucien kissing me, to turn it into something that it wasn't—a lover's quarrel or a rejection or something that could inspire a suicide—but that feels like a betrayal to Lucien. I don't know why.

I let Lucien kiss me because something about those last few hours had felt final. That night was an ending point for us. Emilio had come. I was finished being Lucien's doll. I don't want to lie about it and turn it into something it wasn't.

Traffic unclogs itself. We inch past the accident, and I have to stare. It looks like a sculpture—crushed metal and broken glass artfully arranged on a sheet of ice. The ambulances have already left it behind. We do too.

Marcel pulls to the curb, and I look out, shamed by the decrepit apartment towering down. I reach for the door.

"Wait," he says. "Before you go, I have to tell you something."

I brace myself for the worst: a declaration of feelings, or maybe an angry tirade. I think I'd prefer the tirade.

"This isn't because Lucien was obsessed with you."

"What's not?"

"The reason I called you."

"Okay."

"It's just you knew him. At the end, I was too busy hating him, and I don't know why, but being around you makes me feel better. Less guilty."

He runs his fingers through the cropped hair again, and this time I see they're long and white and trembling. Of course. I see it now, what I haven't seen all day because I've been too hungry and worried and self-obsessed. He's detoxing.

"Can I call you again?" he asks.

I nod.

"Good." He doesn't smile. I have a feeling Marcel's smile is gone forever.

My stomach is meat-heavy and the stairs are endless. I trudge upward. I'm three steps shy of the fifth floor when my phone rings. Trembling, scrambling, my fingers grope their way through everything in my purse, but can't find it. Panicked, I tip the purse upside down and shake violently, watching the contents clatter and flutter halfway back to the fourth floor. There. I see it. I lunge and grab it. I'm so close to hearing his voice, I can't think straight enough to realize it's stopped ringing.

But it's stopped ringing. It only rang once. A text. It was just a text. I pick up the phone and see it was from Emilio.

I need longer. More info when I have it. Miss you. Be careful.

I have to be quick. I sink to the cold concrete and text back, tears blurring my eyes as my thumbs fly over the keys.

How much longer? Why? Miss you too, but don't tell me to be careful. I'm not the one in danger.

I send it and wait. I suck the tears back up. I stare at the screen. I will the phone to ring, but it doesn't. I reread my response and realize I forgot to say *I love you*, but he didn't say it either, no, he didn't say it *first*. I type in *P.S. I love you*, then delete it. I don't need him thinking I'm juvenile and needy.

After ten minutes of nothing, I abandon hope. I get up, pick up my mess, and trudge back up to hell.

NINETEEN

"**A**re you going to the café tonight?"

Nanette's voice jerks me to life. I was sprawled across my cot nearly comatose; now I'm perched on its edge, heart racing. She probably knocked. I'm not sure why this feels like an attack.

Nanette raises her eyebrows and says, "Hm?"

That French Canadian *hm* is so endearing and aggravating at the same time. It's both *Are you?* and *Don't you think you should?* in less than a word.

But am I? I did plan to meet Jacques tonight. The last time I even intended to practice was the night I ended up going for sushi with Marcel, which was five days ago. And I want to play Emilio's mandolin—no, I *want* to want to—but right now, just thinking about the instrument makes me feel abandoned.

I can only feel abandoned for so long before it becomes anger, and I don't want to be angry at Emilio. It seems safer not to go to Soupe au Chocolat at all, to sit here in this shrinking closet like I have been for the last several days until it's so small I don't have room to roll over or even breathe.

"I don't think so," I say, picking up my phone to check for messages. Nothing.

Nanette's perfect little eyebrows furrow, but she doesn't frown. I'm worrying her.

"I don't feel well," I say.

"Are you okay?" she asks gently. She pulls on one of her pigtails. Her thick hay-colored hair is too short for a single ponytail, so she wears it in two tufts poking out below each ear. She looks like a baby deer. "You look a little pale."

"I think I'm getting the flu. You probably don't want to come too close."

She nods and backs away, saying, "Come get me if you need anything."

"Thanks." I don't know why she's so nice to me.

I close the door and sink back down into the cot. I don't look at the clock. I don't want to know when I would need to leave if I was going, because I'm not going.

I've given up on trying to do anything but sit here and worry. Emilio owes me a call, or at the very least, a text. I've spent every second of the last five days imagining the possible meanings behind his last text. He said he'd let me know when he knew more, so he must not know more yet. Unless something is very wrong.

Maybe it's time to call one of my sisters. Lola. No, not Lola.

Ana. No, neither. I love them both, but Lola is a little mean and Ana is a little incompetent, and all it would take is one nasty or stupid moment from either and Emilio could end up dead. There has to be a better way of finding out if he's okay.

This time I hear Nanette's knock on the door. Three short, hard taps. "Jane?"

"Yes."

She pokes her little deer head in again. "I forgot to tell you. Yesterday when you were sleeping, Monsieur Cabot called about the rent."

Rent. Rent. Rent. It's over a week late. But I don't have the money, so it doesn't even matter because I'm screwed.

"He said to tell you he'll forgive the late fee this one time only."

"What?"

Nanette tilts her head to the left and studies my face. "He said he got your payment for the next two months. No late fee."

My payment. Oh, no.

"Thanks," I mumble.

I wait until the door is closed and Nanette's footsteps retreat before I grab my phone. I'm so angry I almost forget to check messages. But then I do, and there are none, and the self-loathing for checking again when I just checked less than two minutes ago makes me even angrier. Blood pounds at my temples as I search for Marcel's number, pulses in my throat as I press call. He had no right.

But then Pierre sneezes—he sneezes from three rooms away

and it sounds like he's sitting beside me on this bed, reminding me that these walls are as sound resistant as wet tissue.

Fine. I slide my feet into my boots, grab my coat, and set off to meet Jacques. I grab the mandolin as an afterthought.

"You again," Jacques says as I come to a stop in front of him. "I thought maybe you weren't coming anymore."

I'm panting. It takes a moment before I can wheeze out words. "I've been really busy." My lungs are achy and tight from sprinting in the cold. I was sure I'd missed him, but when I rounded the final corner, there he was, lumbering up the street and away from the café.

He frowns. He's big and craggy, like barnacles could grow on him and he wouldn't feel it. His bulk reminds me of my father, and so does the way he's examining my face like he's forming opinions in stone. "You don't look good."

"I've been sick," I say, not entirely dishonestly. I've been sick of waiting, sick of loving someone more than he loves me back, sick of running away, sick of being rescued. That's a lot of sick. "So am I allowed in?"

He takes his time unlocking the door. "Nanette says you need a job."

"I need money."

"You need a job," he repeats.

I stifle my frustration. I don't want to explain. I want him to leave so I can call Marcel and yell at him for trying to buy me.

"I can give you a job," he says, jabbing a thumb in the

direction of the kitchen. "Not a lot of hours, but a few."

"I can't work here. No visa."

That should do it, but instead Jacques mutters, "Stupid English," as he flips on the lights, followed by something I don't quite catch, possibly in French.

"Sorry?"

"They can't tell me who I can hire in my own café," he says.

Canadian politics are about as interesting as competitive knitting, but I nod like I understand his pain and oppression, the possibility of money suddenly warming me. I hadn't taken Jacques for a rule-breaker. "What would you need me to do? I don't exactly have restaurant experience. Or baking experience." Or any experience, but I decide not to mention that the only jobs I've ever had were portrait modeling and busking.

He motions for me to follow him into the back. "Just some light cleaning."

Four hours later my hands are raw from scalding water and bleach. I started with the cheap gloves Jacques pulled from under a sink, but after three hours of scrubbing never-been-cleaned blinds, the latex ripped. Was I supposed to dilute the bleach more? I don't even know. And I certainly didn't know latex could tear like that—prophylactic companies everywhere should be notified.

I mentally multiply minimum wage by four as I peel off the holey latex. The number. I shudder. I should be grateful—I am, sort of—but I didn't know the work would be so unpleasant and the compensation so small.

When I was running here and my rage was still white-hot, the plan was to call Marcel and cut him down, but now my shoulder burns and I can't bend my fingers and my energy is gone. I'm still mad. He paid my rent without asking me or telling me, like he could expect something in return. Like Lucien, but not like Lucien.

Except if I had to earn that rent cleaning Soupe au Chocolat, it'd take me a full month, at least.

Too tired to drag myself over to a chair, I sit on the just-mopped floor and pull my knees to my chest. I was never supposed to be here in Montreal this long. It was my accidental destination, just a stopover, a waiting cell for money and then for Emilio and more money.

Now I'm stuck.

I take out my phone. It's four a.m.—too late and too early to call Marcel—so I text him instead.

Thanks.

I can't think of anything else to add. Yelling at him for his generosity is no longer an option. As demeaning as the gesture felt, my initial rage can't be rekindled, since I'm either too tired or too enlightened by hard labor.

With my last half hour, I try to play the mandolin, but my hands are so burned from the bleach and weak I can barely get through one song. It doesn't matter. It's getting harder to remember what it felt like on the yacht. All the benefit of all that doubt I've been giving to Emilio is fading. It doesn't feel like he belongs to me anymore, if he ever did. He belongs to my father.

On the table beside the mandolin case, my phone buzzes. I don't jump. I reach for it slowly, expecting Emilio and filling with dread from my toes up.

It's from Marcel: **You're welcome.**

I wait for more, cringing in anticipation, but it doesn't come. No flirting, no suggestion to watch the sunrise together, or any other thinly veiled booty call invite.

I text back: **Why are you awake?**

His response is fast: **I'm a vampire. Why are you awake?**

Me: **Just because.**

Him: **Ask me what I'm wearing.**

Me: **No.**

Him: **Ask me.**

Me: **Absolutely not.**

Him: **Do you swim?**

Swim. The sound of the word makes me weightless, sends my brain into a free float, and for a second my body feels the pulse of the ocean. I'm swaying against the pull and push. My arms want to slice through waves. I want to fly.

Me: **I don't have a suit.**

Him: **No worries.**

I sigh. The booty call was not even thinly veiled.

Me: **I don't skinny-dip with strangers.**

Him: **Ouch. I'm a stranger? Borrow a suit.**

Me: **Where are you?**

Him: **My place.**

It takes me a moment to realize that he doesn't mean Lucien's apartment, but his parents' house. Of course. Lucien said that Marcel would be going back home once his parents returned, and why would Marcel ever go back to that apartment now?

Me: **You have a pool?**

Him: **Yeah. I'll pick you up in an hour.**

When Estelle arrives minutes later, I'm ready to go. She mutters at me in French as I slip my phone into my pocket, grab the mandolin, and leave.

"Why all smelling like bleach?" she barks after me, but I pretend I don't understand.

I don't analyze what I'm doing as I hurry home, or as I'm rifling through Nanette's drawers looking for a swimsuit, or as I'm standing at the curb waiting for Marcel. Scrutinizing why I'm looking forward to this is unnecessary. It's been too long since I've swum.

TWENTY

In a thousand ways Marcel's house is cold. Every detail is acute, every space is stark, but the absolute coldest thing about it is the light. It's so white it's blue. The pool house—connected to the main house by a thin corridor—is the bluest of all.

It's nothing like my home in Miami. The decor there is white as well, but sunlight streams in and paints everything warm and yellowy except where the stained-glass windows bleed rainbows.

"This pool is hard-core," I say, sliding into the freezing water. Nanette had two suits to choose from: a crocheted purple bikini and a navy one-piece with a plunging back. I went navy for coverage.

Marcel is floating on his back, staring at the roof, his swim trunks ballooning around him. "What did you say?" he asks, pulling his head up. There is no shallow end, no place to stand, so he treads in place. His chest and shoulders glow like marble.

"This pool." I stroke cautiously, gliding across four lanes to the other side. "It's huge."

My legs feel strange, the muscles both wobbly and stiff at the same time. I don't think I've ever swum in water this cold. He's watching me, so I don't let on how my body is shrieking in shock and pain.

"Twenty-five meters," he says. "My dad used to swim competitively."

"Really?"

"He almost made the Olympics one year."

"Impressive."

"He's been pissed off ever since," Marcel says. "That's what my mom says, at least. I have a hard time imagining him not pissed off before, but whatever."

"You swim a lot then?"

"Used to. He tried to coach us, but he stopped fighting that battle when he realized we were both average."

"I swam in high school," I say, amazed at how easy it is to tell him something that is true. There's no danger in that. Just one true thing.

"Yeah?"

"Yeah."

"You can swim here anytime you want," he says. "Nobody uses it. I don't know why they even bother heating it."

"Wait, this is heated?"

"It's not an ice rink, is it?"

I survey the entire pool. It's a thin rectangle, carved into lanes by sharp black lines. There's no slide. There's no diving board. I can't even imagine a crowd in here, and I'm sure nobody has dunked anyone or done a cannonball. The sterility is eerie, but there's some comfort in knowing girls probably aren't routinely felt up in here. Bodily fluids are not exchanged. Thanks to Lola's world-famous parties, the same can't be said of the Cruz family pool.

"So you must come out here and do laps all the time," I say.

"No. Not until this last week." He swims to the opposite side and rubs his hand over his face. He's not what he looks like in clothes, not emaciated at all.

I look away.

"I've been out here every day since the funeral," he says.

I stare at the huge digital clock on the wall and search for something to say as the seconds and tenths of seconds and hundredths of seconds whir by. "And your parents?"

"What about them?"

"I don't know. How are they taking everything?"

"My dad is in New York on business, and my mom has spent the last week sleeping. So they're taking things exactly how I'd expect them to take things."

Picturing Marcel alone in this echoing, blue-lit palace makes me shudder. "Swimming must be a good release, then," I say.

"I'm out of shape, but yeah. It's something to focus on."

I dip the back of my head into the water and let the cold envelop me. Floating feels nice, even if I am bracing against a shiver. I get it. He's alone, and he's trying to stay clean, and I'm strangely proud of him. "Are you sure your mom doesn't mind that I'm here right now?"

"She won't be coming out of her room," he says. "And she wouldn't care even if she were lucid enough to care."

Above me, a grid of black beams holds up the ceiling and frames the skylight. It's still pitch black and starless out there. The cold isn't biting anymore, and I'm starting to think I could float here forever when Marcel's hand touches my arm.

I flinch and jerk upright.

"Holy startle reflex," he says.

"You snuck up on me."

"You were going to hit your head." He points to the concrete ledge I was drifting toward.

We're nose to nose now. Water drips down his face, and his skin shines satiny under the cold lights. He's like a Renaissance sculpture I swear I've seen before, but I can't quite remember the name or the artist or the museum.

He's looking at me uneasily, undoubtedly wondering why I'm examining his face like we've just met.

"What?" he asks.

"Nothing. Want to race?"

He smiles. "For real?"

I barely know what I just said. I was only trying to cut the awkward. "Let's race," I try again, more convincingly this time. Maybe I do want to race. Maybe I want to beat somebody at something.

"How about I only use my arms," he suggests.

"A little cocky, don't you think?"

"It's called chivalry."

I swim away from him, positioning myself at the head of the second lane. He swims to lane three. Facing the pool, he spreads both arms out behind him on the ledge, stretching his shoulders and chest. The way his arms are bent makes him look like a bird of prey. Soaring. Ready to kill.

"Chivalry is boring," I say. "Besides, you said you were out of shape."

"I am. Goggles?"

"Please."

He turns and pulls himself out of the pool. I hoist myself onto the edge and watch him walk to an equipment cupboard and pull out two pairs.

I'm going to lose. I'm a pretty good swimmer for my size, but unless his form is terrible, this race is already over. The laws of mathematics and aerodynamics say so—the muscles in his back and the length of his limbs are undeniably superior.

He comes back and sits beside me, handing me the silver pair. His are black.

"What stroke?" he asks.

"Whatever you want."

"What's your event?"

"Five hundred freestyle."

"Ugh, really?"

"What?" I say. "You don't have the stamina for it?"

He fits his goggles onto his head. "You did *not* just question my stamina. Screw chivalry. I'm using my legs."

"No cheating. And no letting me win."

"Deal. We need a wager."

I fit the silver goggles onto my head and test their suction. Perfect. "Sure."

"The loser has to perform CPR on the winner."

"Nope."

"The loser has to swim an extra lap naked."

"You're going the wrong direction here. I change my mind. No wager."

"Don't pretend you've never swum naked."

"So, ten laps, freestyle, right?"

"What do you think I was wearing when you texted me earlier?"

"Stop talking." I stand up and put my hands on my hips.

He stands too.

"Are you ready to be humiliated by a girl?"

He smiles.

I step up onto the starting block, place my left foot out front, and bend down so my chest touches my thigh.

He joins me.

I grip the edge of the block, and when I glance in his direction, all I see is the slope of his shoulder covering his face.

"Ready?" he asks.

"Who counts?"

"Me."

"No, me."

"Then why'd you ask me if you already knew you were going to do it?" he grumbles.

"Okay, we do it together."

"Five . . . four . . . ," he starts.

I join him on three. By two my muscles are burning with excitement, dying to uncoil. I've never been so psyched to get pummeled. I just need to try so hard it hurts.

"One."

We spring. His body is beside mine in the air, but when we slice through the water, he's already beyond me. Underwater I'm a missile, but when I surface for that first breath, he's even farther ahead. For a while I keep up, or not quite keep up, but hold a respectable gap between us. But by the fourth lap his half-pool lead becomes three quarters, and every muscle in my body is exhausted. I'm getting sloppy—my arms are chopping through the water with more violence, but I don't see him again until he laps me. And then laps me again.

When Marcel pulls his body from the pool, I still have three lengths to go, but I don't stop or slow down. He's watching. The least I can do is lose with style. My whole body screams for oxygen, but I force myself to sprint the final stretch. But only a few strokes from the wall, I suck a mouthful of water into my lungs. It feels like fire burning me from the inside out, and I collapse sputtering against the end of the pool, too disoriented by the exhaustion to even pull myself up.

Hands grip my arms.

They squeeze too tight, and my mind falls back into

memory. *Why is someone always grabbing and pulling and push-ing me?* These hands pull me out of the water and onto the ledge, but they don't let go of me right away, so I use my last ounce of energy to twist away from them. *"Get away from me!"* I yell, and wrench myself free.

Marcel lets me squirm away.

I sit on the ledge, sputtering until I've stopped coughing up pool water. When I finally open my eyes he's sitting on the bench, staring at the clock. Hundredths of seconds, then tenths of seconds, then whole seconds disappear as we both stare at it.

It feels like one of us should apologize. But not him.

"What's the matter with you?" he finally asks. He sounds more curious than angry, so I don't come back with an insult.

"Lots of things."

"I was just trying to help you."

"I'm sorry."

"Are you okay?"

"Yeah. I got a little water in my lungs, that's all. I'm fine. I'm sorry," I say again. "I was just startled and a little oxygen deprived." I stand up and everything spins, but I don't sit back down. "Good race," I mumble.

"Good race? A couple of seconds ago you were screaming at me for trying to help you."

"I didn't want your help."

He stares at me and I shrink. "What happened to you?" he asks.

"Lots of things."

My chest still hurts. If I could just catch my breath and calm down, I'd deflect his questions, but I can't. Weak, out of shape, tired—I don't know what I was expecting when I dove in. My diet of chocolate and water can't be doing much for me, either.

"You look pale," he says. "You should sit."

I don't argue, but I don't go sit by him on the bench either. I sit back down by the pool and let my legs dangle. I try leaning back on my palms, but my arms are too shaky to support my weight, so I slump forward instead.

My legs have changed color. It's the light. I look up to the skylight and see that the sky beyond has turned from black to purple. There's a hint of orange at one edge.

Marcel sees it too. "Morning."

"Morning."

We stare at the new sky for a few seconds before I say, "Thanks for not letting me win."

"You're welcome. I think the loser is supposed to give the winner CPR, but if you're not up for it, I'd be willing to reverse that."

"I'll pass."

"Are you sure? I'm really good at it."

The purple is being bled out of the skylight frame, and the orange is surging. "This would be a nice way to watch the sunrise if it wasn't so cold," I say.

He gets up and grabs two towels from the equipment closet. "At the risk of getting myself shoved again, here you go," he says, tosses one to me, and sits down beside me.

"Thanks." I wrap it around myself.

He lies back to see the sky better, and I do the same. We watch the battle of orange and purple. Orange wins, and then a splotch of pink appears, threatening to spill over the whole skylight.

"Sort of gory," I say. "For a sky, I mean."

"I guess."

We watch a little longer before I decide to say it after all. "I wish you hadn't paid my rent."

He pauses. "Okay."

"I mean thank you, but I wish you hadn't. I can't pay you back."

"I wasn't expecting you to."

"I know," I say, "but it put me in a weird spot."

"There's no weird spot. It's forgotten. If you want to feel weird about it, fine, but I'm not going to."

"I don't *want* to feel weird about it. I—"

"Don't worry," he interrupts. "I won't do it again."

I take a giant breath, feeling better and worse.

The pink is fading. It's not being forced out by anything else, but a warm yellow behind it is waiting for it to dissipate entirely.

"Can I ask you something?" he says.

"Yeah."

"I need you to answer honestly. I don't want the answer you think you should give."

I shiver beneath my towel. What's one more promise I can't

keep, one more lie? "Okay."

"Did he ever talk about me?"

I hesitate. Telling him yes would be the nice thing to do. But the truth? "Not a lot, but sometimes."

"Did he hate me?"

"He didn't kill himself because he hated you."

"That's not what I asked."

I sigh. "Why would you think he hated you?"

"You won't answer. That means he hated me."

"No. Brothers fight. They piss each other off. I don't think he hated you."

I count several of Marcel's measured breaths before he speaks again. "Then why did he do it in my bathroom? Why didn't he do it in his bathtub?"

I turn my head. He's only inches away, still staring up at the sky, and from this angle his cheeks are sunken. His features look even sharper, his lips bluish.

He saves me from answering. "So I would be the one to find him."

The snapshots of memory—Lucien's bloated body crusted in filth, the stench of vomit, the pain-twisted features, the *plop* of the water—pile up and fan out like photographs tossed onto a table before me, a montage of horror. "Did you?"

He turns his face to mine. His eyes are bloodshot from the chlorine. "Yes."

I should have realized. I should have thought about it longer and seen that someone had to find him after I left, and that someone would, of course, be Marcel. Pity and guilt sit on my chest. My head is too heavy to lift, and I have to blink back tears, but even blinking is too much effort.

Heartless. It's cruel not to tell him that I don't even think Lucien killed himself, but I have to be heartless.

Except maybe I can be a little less heartless.

I roll onto my side, pull my arm out of my towel, and rest the back of my hand on his cheek. It's soft and cold. I pretend I don't notice him shudder, but it makes me wonder how long it's been since anybody touched him.

Beyond that shudder, he doesn't respond, so I don't have to pull away. He just lies there, glowing under the yellow satin sky. I wipe the drop of water from his jaw with the backs of my fingers, and he doesn't flinch or reach for me.

His not reaching for me—it makes abandoning heartlessness okay. It's only temporary. I prop myself on my other elbow, lean in and press my lips to his cheek. It isn't stubbly like Emilio's, but smooth and smells like chlorine. The kiss is long enough to feel his jaw clench beneath my mouth, but he doesn't pull away.

Without a word, I stand. He watches me wring the water from my hair and rewrap my towel, then sits up.

"I'm going to change," I say.

"Me too."

I'm standing naked in the first of two changing rooms in the pool house, shivering as I pull underwear and bra over goose-pimpled skin. I was slow in the shower, but it was so gloriously hot and the steam was so saturating, I couldn't make myself get out until I felt sure I could never be cold again.

Except now I'm cold again. The hook on my bra is bent and requires steadier hands than I have at the moment, so I'm fumbling in frustration when I hear the sound. It's soft, but I'm sure. It's my phone. I abandon the clasp so I can dig through my clothes before my brain registers that something is wrong. The ring was too soft. It takes me a moment to make sense of it all, to remember that my phone isn't in this bag. It's next to my purse. And my purse is where I left it: on the bench by the pool.

I fumble faster, give up on the bent hook, pull on my sweater, and slip into my pants, but not before I drop them on the wet tile and half soak them. I wiggle into the wet pants and it doesn't matter, it doesn't matter, it doesn't matter, because Marcel is in the other changing room getting dressed, and if he isn't still there, if he's out by the pool, he wouldn't answer my phone. He wouldn't.

I skip socks and boots and run out to the pool deck. Marcel is sitting on the bench, already dressed, my purse beside him.

"Hey," I say, but I'm so flustered and breathless, the word barely comes out.

He doesn't answer. He's staring at the black rectangle in his hand. My phone.

"Did my phone ring?" I stammer.

He ignores the question, turning the phone over and over in his hand. When he finally does look up, the rawness from before is gone. Vulnerability is a memory. "Who the hell are you?"

TWENTY-ONE

Fight or flight. I remember learning it in biology. It goes like this: I sense danger and my adrenal glands secrete adrenaline, which increases heart rate, dilates pupils, and tightens muscles, all preparing my body to attack or run. But I have to choose which one.

Attack or run, attack or run, attack or run. I have to choose.

I've already run. I've been running for months, and I'm not any further from danger. It's liquid, filling my thoughts and my dreams, following me into my apartment, through the streets of Montreal, and into Soupe au Chocolat, bleeding into the cracks of my mind. It chases me everywhere, and I feel it in everyone. In Lucien. In Emilio. In Marcel.

Flight failed.

"What are you doing with my phone?" I demand shakily.

"It rang."

I walk toward him with long strides, my hand outstretched. "Give it to me."

"You didn't answer my question. Who are you?"

"I didn't say you could touch my phone," I say through gritted teeth, and reach for it, but he stands quickly, holding it out of my reach.

He snorts, and a wild, cruel look takes over his face. "And what would you do if I dropped it in the pool?"

I jump for it, but he's too tall and I hit my jaw on his collarbone when we collide. I feel his left arm wrap around me, pinning me to his chest, and when I arch my head up, he's staring down at me. Chlorine has turned his eyes red and puffy, but the rest of his face is all hard lines. Bone and veins and muscle. His arm tightens around my back, and panic explodes inside of me. He's too strong. I can't think.

"I'll give you your phone back. Just stop lying, and tell me who you are."

I try to wriggle free, and he flings the phone. My heart plummets—now Emilio can't reach me—before I see it was a trick. His hand made the motion, but he didn't let go. A mean smile stretches across his face. "Would that break your little heart, *Valentina*?"

I make another pointless lunge, but the end of his swimmer's arm is miles away.

Frustrated, I go limp. If I could, I'd slump all the way to the floor, but Marcel's grip is still forcing me upright.

"Don't worry," he says into my ear. "I told Emilio how well I was taking care of you. Wait—should I not have told him about the kiss?" He laughs. It's mocking and angry, and I can feel my blood getting hotter and hotter. I wriggle, but his grip only gets tighter, and he's still laughing.

"Let go of me," I growl.

"Calm down." He lets go, lifting both hands like he's under arrest. "You're the one who attacked me. And I didn't say anything on the phone—just listened to lover boy say, 'Valentina? Valentina? Valentina?'"

His fake Spanish accent makes me want to claw his face, but I don't want to get close enough for him to grab me again.

"So you're one of Emilio's girls," he says, and the regression is complete. He's the old Marcel, the real Marcel. I should never have forgotten he existed. "He usually only hooks up with slutty blondes. What's with the alias? Do you work for Cruz too?"

"None of your business."

Those words trigger something. The teasing is over. His voice gets tighter and lower, and the anger turns to full fury. "It was Lucien's business, though, wasn't it? And now that he's dead, it's my business to know why you were lying to him, and why one of Cruz's thugs is calling you. *Who are you?*" He extends his free arm over the pool and dangles the phone between a thumb and a finger.

"Valentina Cruz."

His arm drops to his side, my phone still hanging loosely from it. His face reveals nothing, not understanding or anger or even shock, but the muscles in his chest go concave like the air has been sucked from his lungs.

I step toward him. Flight has failed. It's time to fight. One more step and we're chest to chest, the phone close enough to pluck from his slack fingers, but first I yank my right knee straight up as hard as I can. I don't stop when I feel my leg collide with the unsuspecting softness above the seam of his jeans. I let the momentum drive my knee upward until I'm certain it can't get any higher, and whatever used to be between me and his pelvis has been catapulted up into his throat.

He crumples without a sound. As his knees hit the tile, he drops the phone, and it helicopters across the wet floor behind him, careening parallel to the edge of the pool.

I dart forward and grab it, leaving Marcel bent at every angle and wheezing with his forehead pressed to the tile. I check, just to make sure he was telling the truth. No texts. One call from Emilio, lasting eleven seconds. Long enough to say my name several times and hang up.

Emilio must be freaking out.

Behind me, Marcel makes a strangled sound, and the anger surges again. I spin around to see him lying on his side, one hand over his face, the other between his legs.

"Don't *ever* do that to me again," I spit.

He vomits.

I have to wait. I have to wait a while.

Incapacitating my ride home was not part of the plan. Admittedly, there was no plan, but having done it, I can't say I wouldn't do it again. I would.

"This isn't an apology," I say as I kneel beside him and clean up the vomit with the rag and cleaner I found under the sink in the changing room.

"Noted," he moans.

I finish with that and bring him two towels. "Lift your head," I order. He obeys and I slide one under him. He's shivering— I hope from the cold and not some life-threatening response to testicle crunching that I don't know about—so I spread the other across his body. "Here." I hand him my makeshift ice pack: three large handfuls of snow packed tight and wrapped in a trash-can liner. I think it's pretty inventive, but he doesn't comment. His personality seems to have retreated completely.

I'm not scared of Marcel, not anymore. He's not crying, but that glassy stare screams grief more than pain. It's the movie theater all over again.

I wait. I don't know how long it will take his reproductive organs to decide life is worth living again, but I'm stuck here until they do. We're at least twenty miles north of the city, and I can't even take his car, since I don't know how to drive a stick. I sit on the floor with my back pushed against the wall. After a few minutes my butt bones ache, but he's still on the cold, wet tile, so I stick it out on the floor beside him. He's already declined several offers for help to a chair.

And while I wait, I worry. I need to call Emilio and tell him I'm all right, but then I'll have to explain what happened. He's going to freak out when he finds out Marcel knows who I am.

Unless I don't tell him. If Marcel was telling the truth about answering the phone and saying nothing, I could tell Emilio the phone was in my purse or my pocket and I accidentally answered—but without hearing it or knowing it? I can't decide whether he'd believe me, or whether it matters if he knows that Marcel knows my real name. And would he care that I've been spending time with Marcel? That we're friends?

Of course he would.

Marcel pulls the ice pack out of his pants, crushes the ice between his palms, and shoves it back down his pants.

Friends is the wrong word.

My head hurts. I need to tell Emilio the right thing, but Emilio's mind has become foreign terrain. I can remember his touch, the smell of his skin, his laugh, but I can't predict his reaction to this. I can't really predict his reaction to anything. That makes me nervous.

Maybe I never knew Emilio that well in the first place. I was so quick to forgive him when he explained why he did what he did, but now Marcel's words burn like the glowing end of a cigar. One of Emilio's girls. Slutty blondes.

Nobody would be holding a gun to Emilio's head, forcing him to be a womanizer.

"You're his daughter," Marcel's voice interrupts my crisis.

I curl my fingers into fists. "Yes."

"Were you working with Lucien?"

"Not exactly."

"What does that mean?" He lifts his head, and his face

confirms it: his injuries are only half physical. He looks broken.

"I ran away from home three and a half months ago. I had no idea Lucien was working for my father until the night he died. Emilio was the one who figured out that he was being paid to keep an eye on me."

"I don't get it. He was babysitting you without you knowing it?"

I flinch. "Pretty much."

He grunts. "Is this the part where you tell me you're not nineteen?"

"Is this the part where I knee you again?"

He drops his head into the towel and shudders.

"I'm not sorry," I say. "About that, I mean."

"You already made that clear."

"Good."

He's silent for only a moment, but it's long enough for me to realize where the questions are about to turn. "So you didn't just meet Emilio the other night."

And the last wall crumbles. The pressure of lies, of being a liar, is finally enough. "No."

"Emilio's your what—your boyfriend?"

"Yes."

"But . . . you ran away and he didn't come with you."

"I didn't tell anyone that I was leaving."

"So you left him."

"I left everybody. Everything."

"Why?"

I don't answer. There are limits.

But Marcel smells blood. "Why?"

"I'm not going back," I say.

"Is that why Emilio was here, to make you go back?"

"No."

"He's one of your dad's enforcers, though."

"My father doesn't use that kind of enforcer on his children," I mutter through clenched teeth, though I'm not sure what he has done with me is any less disgusting. I'm part of a loyalty test. A *test*. For someone else. I push it from my thoughts. "Emilio didn't know I was in Montreal. My father did, which is why he was paying Lucien to watch me. We think my father sent Emilio to Montreal to see if he'd report back that he'd found me."

"That makes no sense," Marcel says. "Why wouldn't he?"

"He wouldn't rat if he was more loyal to me than to my father. He wouldn't rat if he wanted to run away with me instead."

Marcel picks up his head again and stares me down. "Valentina Cruz, you're insane. If you knew who Emilio really was, you wouldn't be throwing away your life for him."

"You don't know what you're talking about. I'm not throwing away my life for Emilio. My life had to be thrown away because of who I am. And when I left, I thought I'd never see Emilio again." I stop to catch my breath and feel that sick ache in the very bottom of my stomach from having said too much. What has Marcel ever done to be worthy of my secrets?

"Fine," he says. "Then why are you still here? Why isn't he with you?"

"You can't just leave Victor Cruz without a plan," I say. "He's taking care of the people who would be . . ." I'm so ashamed I can't finish.

"Punished," Marcel says for me. He's pulled himself into a sitting position facing me, legs bent and arms resting on knees. He shakes his head. "You win."

"What?"

"Your family is worse than mine."

I ignore him. It's true and insulting, but we seem to have come to a tentative peace. He may be almost capable of driving me home. "How are you feeling?"

"Like an idiot. I thought you were a fugitive from the law. I thought Lucien was in love with you. And I thought you were putting up with me out of guilt over Lucien's suicide. So I was zero for three."

One for three, I silently correct him. Marcel didn't guess where my guilt over Lucien comes from, but it's real. It's tethering me to Marcel when I should be staying as far away from him as possible.

"But maybe Lucien *was* in love with you," Marcel adds.

"He wasn't," I say with more conviction than I feel. "I was an assignment."

I shut my eyes and think of my last few seconds with Lucien, the pressure of his lips on my cheek. And what about all those paintings? At some point, the project became real to him. At some point, I became more than an assignment. I'm sure of it, and the realization makes me unspeakably sad. "I'm sorry."

"For kneeing me? I thought you weren't sorry."

"I'm sorry about Lucien."

My understatement echoes off the walls until the silence swallows it. "I'm sorry I . . . grabbed you," he says. "That was not . . . I don't know. Lately, sometimes I feel crazy." He runs both hands through his hair but leaves his head in his hands like it's too heavy for his neck to pick up. "Not a good excuse, but . . . yeah."

"Okay."

It's not that his words don't feel true. They do. I believe that he's sorry and I'm not scared of him, but I also know we won't recover from this. This fragile grief buddy thing we have won't survive the night we just had. He won't call me again. If he does, I won't go out with him. Weird, once broken, can't be fixed.

"You want me to take you home?" he asks.

"Yeah."

Seven minutes.

The café is calling, but I'm not going to clean. Not tonight. I've earned a break from the depressing reality of minimum wage, so I'm going to play the mandolin for the entire night instead. I've been curled up in my closet since Marcel dropped me off fourteen hours ago, minus a few trips to the bathroom and one to the kitchen to steal two handfuls of oyster crackers from Nanette's cupboard. That water stain on the ceiling is starting to look a lot like the Virgin Mary, or maybe Texas. I don't know what that means.

If only I'd been able to hear his voice, I wouldn't still be lying here in my cot like a mental patient. I'd have hope. I'm too tired for hope, though. Spending all last night scrubbing blinds and swimming made for fogginess all day and a deep fatigue now, but I can't seem to sink into sleep. I'm floating on the surface. The bleach and chlorine didn't help, either. My eyes and hands burn, but I'm too busy replaying every unreal moment with Marcel to go borrow some lotion.

I can't believe I missed Emilio's call.

I can't believe I told Marcel everything.

Six minutes.

The phone and I are on a break. I refuse to look at it, but I can feel it emitting its magnetic gamma rays or whatever from the floor beside the crate.

The second Marcel pulled away from the curb, I called Emilio. I had to. I was scared, and I knew his voice would make everything right again.

It went to voice mail. I didn't leave a message.

What doesn't make sense is that he hasn't tried to call me again. He hasn't even sent a text. If there was something so important that he was actually calling me after all these days, why wouldn't he at least text?

Thinking about it makes me even crazier: I hate the phone, but I have to check the phone, and then I have to throw the phone at the door, because the phone deserves it. The noise isn't nearly as satisfying as I'd hoped. It's more of a bang-thud than a clatter, and then Pierre barks something in French from across the hall that I have to assume is a string of swear words. I'm not sure which ones.

Five minutes.

I can force myself into Emilio's brain and almost make sense of things. It's the unworking of a math problem, though, looking at the facts and deducing his thoughts.

He called. He expected me to pick up. Instead he got silence, maybe the whir of the heater or some other ambient pool noise, and possibly some suspicious breathing, thank you very much, Marcel.

Emilio hasn't called back because he thinks something has happened to me. Papi would never hurt me—he knows that—but maybe he thinks one of Papi's enemies has gotten to me, or he could think Papi sent someone to collect me and take me home. If that were the case, that someone could have my phone and be ready and waiting to report back if Emilio calls.

I like that answer. It means Emilio hasn't given up on running away with me, or decided the risk is too high. He just has no safe way of getting ahold of me. He could be on his way here now, but it seems like too much to hope for. I shouldn't let myself even imagine it.

Four minutes.

I want to kill Marcel. I really do, but then I remember the times when he's seemed so different, so genuine. It makes me wonder if, under different circumstances, we couldn't actually be friends. Then I remember how he grabbed me and threatened me and terrified me, and how I crushed his testicles with my knee. So maybe not.

But I can recognize that he's a real person and not just a vile caricature without wanting to be his friend.

Still, if he hadn't answered my phone, I wouldn't be in this position with Emilio. If I ever see him again, I'm going to kill him.

Three minutes.

I pull my knees to my chest and stare deep into the water stain. If it's the Virgin Mary, she has chosen the wrong ceiling to appear on. This is not a sacred place. I am not devout or even good. But I'm not sure if I ever had a chance, if there are even redeeming choices to make now. I can be less bad, but that gets hazy. Abandoning my family seemed less bad than staying and pretending I didn't know the human cost of my wealth. Although, if I'm causing Emilio to put his family in danger, that seems unconscionably selfish. If anything happens to them, I don't see how I could forgive myself, or how he could ever forgive me.

But Emilio's no saint, either. Thinking through his crimes makes me cringe, and once I'm cringing I can't stop, my fists and shoulders and stomach clench on and on. Everything can be explained, though. So why am I still cringing?

Two minutes.

One of Emilio's girls. What does that even mean? Obviously I know what it means, but I need the salient stats—heights, weights, relative attractiveness, degree of sluttiness—for every single one of them. I already know their hair color, thank you again, Marcel.

Marcel. He knows. I have to make him tell me exactly what he's seen before I can force myself to believe it was all part of the game Emilio had to play. Surely, that's a girlfriend's prerogative: sordid details for me to stew over.

I do want to believe. Emilio's always made me feel like I was the only girl in the world, but how hard would it have been to fool me? All he had to do was ignore my sisters and I was his. The thought of him running his hands over someone else's skin makes my fingers curl into fists and my stomach drop. How am I still cringing? It's supposed to be a wave. There's supposed to be a limit on how long you can be stuck mid-recoil.

One minute.

Time to go. I pick up the phone and drop it into my purse, because even if I wish I was strong enough to be on a break, I'm not. He could call again.

I pick up the mandolin case and glance around the room, struck by its bareness. I've kept it this way on purpose, a reminder to myself I'm not going to be here long enough for comfort or art or anything close to beauty. Apparently I should've reminded myself harder. I'm still here. It's still naked. Worst of all, I'm used to it.

I go.

I practice too long. I practice until the music is just music, and that nauseates me. I put the instrument in its case and stare at the heater.

Of course it's just music. My body is a plucked string, still shaking. I've been lied to by everyone, and even, strangely enough, by the mandolin. The rambling folk tunes convinced me they could recreate Emilio, but they can't. They can only use him up. I've been spending the magic little by little without realizing there was a finite amount.

I pull the lid from Jacques's kindest gift ever—a box of truffles—and put one in my mouth whole. I can't even taste it.

I tip my head back, close my eyes, and try to imagine what Emilio is doing right now. I can't. Here I thought the memories were triggered by melodies in a self-renewing loop, but this whole time they've been seeping out, drop by drop, note by note.

TWENTY-TWO

"So do you want to come with us?" Nanette asks.

"Hmm?" I'm not listening. Whatever she's been saying has not been as interesting as watching my mug of soup twirl around through the microwave door. The can said heirloom tomato bisque, but it looks like your standard tomato soup to me.

"To the Jello Bar?"

I pull myself away from the microwave. Nanette's eyebrows are raised hopefully (her version of a smile), and she's wearing a sequined tank and tight jeans. I barely recognize her out of her scrubs. She should be annoyed with me for pretending to listen to her for the last minute or two, but Nanette's emotions don't seem to exist in extremes.

"There's live music tonight," she adds.

"Oh. Thanks. I have some stuff I have to do."

"Okay."

"Have fun, though," I add as an afterthought.

She nods and leaves.

I'm a jerk. And I really need to buy her a bag of pretzels to replace that one I borrowed.

The microwave groans on. I stare out the tiny window over the kitchen table, where more snow is muffling the world beyond. Montreal's silence is denser now that Emilio has come and gone, piling up like that windowsill snow, filling minutes and hours that have become weeks, until there's nothing but white silence. Every day I don't hear from Emilio my view shrinks, my prison wall thickens.

It was better before. I'd left a murderer in Miami, and the heartbreak was deep, necessary, and final. But then he showed up and told me things, and made me . . . what, forgive? More like hope, and hope sucks. Hope has made the heartbreak deeper, unnecessary, and unending.

The microwave beeps. I take my mug to my closet, sit cross-legged on the cot, and take a sip. It's tepid. That microwave sucks. Not going back to heat it on the stove may be the best evidence of the depth of my pathetic state, but realizing this doesn't make me any more likely to fix it. So it's not hot. So what.

The mandolin is beneath me. Sometimes I can ignore it, but today I feel it pulsing under the bed like the telltale heart, and I'm half tempted to chuck it out into the hall so I can drink my lukewarm heirloom tomato bisque and stare at the wall in peace. I don't bring it to Soupe au Chocolat anymore. I just clean. The job isn't fun, but it's a job, and it's better now that Nanette has clued me in on the correct ratio of bleach to water. Turns out it's more like one to fifty—another valuable life lesson I managed to dodge. I didn't tell Nanette that I mixed it half and half that first time, since she already must think I'm the biggest idiot. The upside: I've made enough money to buy a skirt.

I wonder if Lola and Ana know about diluting bleach. I'd be surprised.

It's been over a week since I saw Marcel, over a week since Emilio tried to call, but it seems more like a month. I've done enough worrying to fill a year. The worrying hasn't helped me decide what to do, though. I could go back to Miami. My father would welcome me with open arms, and I'd go back to school like I never left, purposely ignoring the things I need to ignore in order to sleep at night.

Emilio's in Miami. I could be with him. Who am I to have principles, anyway?

But my brain can't just leave it at that—the decision isn't the end point. I have to imagine what it would be like, knowing the things I know and living in my father's house, surrounded by beautiful artwork but suffocating under the ugliness of his crimes, knowing that Emilio is off doing whatever it is my father makes him do.

All of those things I wish I could forget—maybe forgetting them would be much worse.

So I'm still here, pretending to wait for someone who isn't coming back.

I pick up the mug and take another sip. Room temperature now. I put it down and lay my head on my pillow, and at some point I fall asleep.

It's hard to say whether it's the phone that wakes me, or the rush of hope that sweeps through me after it rings. Hope. Didn't I talk myself out of that?

I grab the phone and see Marcel's number. I shouldn't be surprised—it had to be one or the other—but I was sure we'd outgrown each other, or out-used each other.

"Marcel," I say.

"Hey."

"Hi."

"Sorry, did I wake you up?" he asks.

I glance at the clock. 3:17. "I don't know. I was sort of in between. Don't you ever sleep?"

"Not lately. I wasn't sure you'd still be in Montreal. You are still here, aren't you?"

"Yeah." I don't explain that Emilio hasn't called or shown up or tried any other way to contact me. I don't want to hear anything more he has to say about Emilio.

"Good," he says. "Do you want to come swim again?"

"What?"

"Come swim."

"I heard you. I just . . ."

"What?"

"I thought maybe we'd both . . ." I pause and wait for the right words to come. "I assumed that knowing who I was would

222

be enough for you."

"I'm over it. Don't you want to swim?"

I'm startled. "I still don't have a bathing suit."

"You still don't have to wear one."

"I guess I could steal my roommate's again."

"Whatever. I'll be there in a half hour."

I get dressed, braid my hair, and go hunting for Nanette's navy suit again. It's not hard to rationalize more borrowing. If she were here, I'd ask her, and I'm sure she'd say yes, so I stuff it in my purse and go down to the street to wait. As for swimming with Marcel, it's not hard to rationalize that either. I've barely spoken to a soul or left the apartment in a week.

Snow falls around me, melting on my hair and shoulders. I don't mind. I'm excited to swim. I'm excited to go somewhere. I'm excited to talk to someone. That's all.

Like last time, we bypass the main house, driving directly to the pool house.

"Are your parents around?" I ask.

"No."

I refuse to dig. He'll elaborate if he wants to elaborate, which he clearly doesn't. A girl can wonder, though.

I change and meet him at the head of the pool, where he's waiting with extra goggles.

"Let's warm up for a few laps," I suggest.

"Fine by me."

I hesitate at the edge, remembering how cold the water was.

He doesn't, though. He dives in headfirst, so I watch him for the first lap. His stroke isn't better than mine, but his limbs are so much longer and he looks tireless. He'll beat me every time.

I follow him in, slipping in like a sliver. It doesn't take long to lose myself. I do breaststroke for the first couple of laps, then freestyle for another two. I know I've found my rhythm when I'm thinking about absolutely nothing except how the water feels sliding over me. When my fingers touch the wall and I look up, Marcel is sitting at the head of his lane watching me, goggles pushed up on his forehead.

"So where did you learn to swim?" he asks.

"The ocean."

"What, the dolphins taught you?"

"No. I had a human teacher, but you asked where. Are you not warming up?"

"I already did. You've got a more natural stroke than I do."

"I know. I watched your first lap."

He smirks. "So you're going to beat me today, then."

"Probably not. Let's do it." I climb out and join him.

The first part of the race is similar to last time. I hold a respectable half lap between us for a while, then the distance begins to grow and my limbs turn to jelly. But this time he pulls ahead even more in the second half and ends up finishing much faster than last time. I hit the wall and collapse against the pebbled ledge.

"I feel like I've been hustled," I say between gasps. "Again." I'm too exhausted to pull myself out of the pool, so I rest my forehead on my arms and wheeze like an asthmatic.

"If I was hustling you, I'd have insisted we bet on it." His voice is above me, but I can't lift my head. All I see are his calves. They're muscular and fuzzy with wet blond hair.

"Do you need a hand?" he asks.

"No."

Marcel doesn't move, though, and after a few seconds his hand appears in front of my face. I take it and let him pull me up so I'm sitting on the ledge.

"You're welcome." He stands beside me, hands on his hips, staring at the pool. "You have no stamina."

"And your stroke is pretty weak."

"Yeah, but you have so little stamina, it doesn't matter."

"Let me guess," I say. "You got the sportsmanship award back in your swim team days."

He snorts.

The swimming pool at Trinity Prep bubbles up from my memory in vibrant color: the electric-blue tile, the yellow lane dividers, the cherry swimsuits. Last year's caps for our final tournament were gold. I wonder what color they are this year. "So what's the deal?" I ask. "Have you been swimming every day since last time I was here?"

"And lifting."

"Are you training for something?"

"No." He pauses. "It's something to do."

I open my mouth and close it. I want to tell him I'm impressed, not so much with the working out, but with the changes. It's obvious he's staying clean. Since Lucien's death, Marcel has morphed into something altogether different. He's lost that greasy, haggard look, and today, even more than the last time I saw him, he seems alive.

I have the feeling nobody else is going to congratulate him. "Good for you."

He grunts, and a swollen silence follows. Fair enough. I didn't need help getting out of the pool. He doesn't need someone to care.

"Hungry?" he asks.

"You have no idea."

"Get that," Marcel says, pointing to the fifth item on the menu.

Tourtière. I don't say it aloud and embarrass myself. "Why? Is it ground sheep eyeballs or something?"

"Interesting guess."

I squeeze my braids, dripping water on the hardwood floor of the charcuterie. Braids made sense for swimming, but now I'm feeling four years old. Not being able to order on my own doesn't help.

I eye the deli case of cured meats and sausages at the front of the line. All those slabs and cylinders of marbled fat and clotted blood look too freshly dead. At least for breakfast. "Maybe I'll just get a croissant."

"*Tourtière* is pork pie. You'll like it."

I'm about to tell him he has no idea what I like, when I realize he might. And I'm ravenous from nearly swimming myself to death again. "What are you getting?"

"Ground sheep eyeballs."

"Maybe that's why you're getting faster and I'm staying the same," I say. "Mutton protein."

"You do realize you're only slower because you're a girl, right?"

"That sounds like an insult."

"That sounds like science."

I take a step forward as the line moves up. "Okay, what are you really getting?"

"Charcuterie."

I nod.

"It's a plate of cured meats," he says. "Sausage, pâté, foie gras, whatever else they decide to throw on there."

"I knew that."

"No, you didn't. Have you thought about learning some French?"

"I *did* know that, and learning French would be a waste of my time." I'm too hungry to care how ignorant I sound. "I'm not going to be here long enough to make it worth the hassle."

"So you have definite exit plans then," he says.

I hesitate. "No."

"Good."

The other customers buzz around us in line. Some wander to fill the tables up front after they make their purchases, but most leave the charcuterie with their food wrapped in brown bags and string. We're even farther north of the city now, a twenty-minute drive from Marcel's house, but not really in Montreal anymore. It seems we've moved back in time too. This could be rural France a hundred years ago if it weren't for the cash register up front and the cell phone under the cheek of the woman behind us. I close my eyes and lose myself in the noise and smells. Salami. Foreign chatter. Salted pork. Yeast.

I don't want to think about what it means that I'm confiding in Marcel, or about whether disclosing my uncertainty about when I'm leaving is disloyal. It feels disloyal.

"I could teach you a few basics," Marcel pesters on. "Small talk, swearing. You know, the necessities."

"Everyone in Montreal speaks English. Besides, I don't trust you not to switch around the small talk and the swearing."

"That's fair. I wouldn't trust me either. Speaking another language might be useful, though."

"I speak Spanish."

"Well maybe you should order your food in Spanish then and see how that goes."

The line moves forward again. It's our turn. Marcel puts the menu on the stack and smiles at the pretty, gap-toothed girl behind the counter. He opens his mouth, but before he can say a thing, I blurt, "*Tourtière, s'il vous plaît.*"

She stares at me. Blinks.

I don't look at Marcel. He's undoubtedly smirking at my pronunciation, so instead I keep my eyes straight ahead and pretend he's never been so impressed.

I'm almost ready to congratulate myself when the girl opens

her mouth and emits a perfectly strung chain of sounds. There are no separate words, just one giant unrecognizable mass of language. Based on inflection and how she's staring at me, I'm pretty sure it was a question.

In the corner of my eye, Marcel folds his arms. I can feel him grinning without actually looking at his face. This situation might not be beyond repair. *"Pardon?"* I ask the girl.

She says it again slower, but it's just as meaningless, and when it's over, she's still staring at me, waiting for a response. I decide to gamble and say, *"Oui."*

She stares at me a second longer, then turns to Marcel and says, *"Parlez-vous français?"*

Marcel shrugs at her and turns to me. "The people behind us are getting a little antsy. I think I'll go find a place to sit."

I roll my eyes. "Seriously?"

"What?"

"A little help."

"What was that? I didn't quite hear you."

I breathe through my nose and turn back to the girl, who is now saying something else, something just as incomprehensible as the last thing she said.

"You need help?" he asks me. "Did you ask her if she speaks Spanish?"

I turn around. With a long line of potential translators to choose from, I start with the man directly behind the woman on her phone. He's old and sour-looking, and when I say *"Anglais?"* he puckers and puts up his hands like I'm aiming a weapon at him.

"Anybody?" I call.

"We're not in Montreal anymore, babe," Marcel mutters.

"*Espagnol?*" I try.

Marcel laughs. "Okay, this isn't going anywhere. She wants to know if you'd like anything else."

"*That's all?*"

I don't realize that I'm shouting at him until I feel the eyes of the entire charcuterie on me.

He shrugs.

"Tell her no thanks, jackass. Just the *tourtière* is fine." I leave the line to find a table.

"Wait," he calls from behind me. "You want me to call her a jackass? Really?"

I don't turn around.

There's only one open table. It's right by the window, so I sling my bag over the back of the chair and sit, staring out into the depressed fairy tale. It should be beautiful, frozen branches and suspended icicles, but the sludge from the cars and deep gray of the sky paint a film of dreariness over the whole. A pang of loneliness rings through me. It makes me hate Emilio for being gone, and Marcel for being nice and mean in the same breath, and myself for being so difficult.

Marcel joins me without a word, sliding the steaming *tourtière* in front of me. He starts to eat, but I can only stare at my food. My food I didn't even pay for.

"What?" he says finally. "You can't seriously be mad at me."

"I'm not mad at you."

"You are. You're insulted every time I help you, but then when I won't help, I'm in trouble. Or am I in trouble for stepping in and helping?"

"You can't be in trouble. I'm not your mother or your girlfriend."

"Yeah, well, I've never had that kind of mother or that kind of girlfriend."

I'm a jerk. Remembering the hunger that was threatening to kill me just minutes ago, I pick up my fork and take a big bite. It's salty. It makes my tongue curl with its perfect saltiness, and it's so warm and filling I almost tear up. More. I need more.

I'm halfway through before the guilt creeps up my throat. I put my fork down. "Sorry."

He doesn't look up.

"For being a jerk," I add.

He keeps eating only a tiny bit slower, though, and I sense his surprise. Maybe I've embarrassed him.

"Would you accept low blood sugar as an excuse?" I ask.

He lifts an eyebrow and mumbles, "Sure." It feels sincere. A single word, it shouldn't seem like a real pardon, but it does. That makes me feel bad too, though. Is he so quick to forgive because people are always asking his forgiveness, or because nobody ever does?

We eat in a warm sort of silence. He offers me a piece of cheese and prosciutto, and I lend him my knife after he drops his, but the rest is conversationless.

"That was really good," I say as we make our way back to the car.

"Worth the drive, right?"

I nod, but I meant all of it, not just the food. Dread is starting to creep along my skin at the thought of being delivered back to my apartment. "Swimming wasn't bad either," I add.

"Yeah." He pulls out of the parking lot and onto the small highway that leads back to the city. "Could've been worse. I could've had my balls crushed again."

"Why would you even bring that up?"

"Right. Sorry. Must be some post-traumatic stress disorder thing."

"I'm still not going to apologize for it."

"I still didn't think you were going to."

"Good," I say. Out my window rows of trees lift their skeletal arms upward like they're praying for spring. It's a pose of desperation, the way their skinny black limbs grasp at nothing and everything.

"Maples," Marcel says.

"They're kind of ghostly."

"I guess."

I can't pull my eyes away from their stripped frames. To think that by the time they're covered again I'll be thousands of miles away should make me happy. I shouldn't have doubt pouring into me like sand, filling every inch. Doubt feels just as fatal as hope.

"So, swimming," he says. "You want go again tomorrow?"

I turn from the maples, but I can still feel them scraping away at the sky. "Sure."

I'm not dreaming. I can't be, because I'm not asleep. I'm lying in bed trying to sleep, which makes this remembering or imagining, even though it doesn't feel like either. It feels like my subconscious is forcing me to watch a movie of its own creation. If I was inside a dream, I wouldn't be aware of the saltiness still on my lips or feel the weight of the half-digested pig in my stomach. I'm definitely awake.

Only I'm not here, I'm in Key West. It's a ripe orange dusk, and my fingers are laced with Emilio's as we wander in and out of shops. It's all clutter—kitschy souvenirs and eclectic charms—but it's beguiling clutter. I want to look, but Emilio is leading me away from it, farther from the shops toward the thick smell of roasting meats and fried plantains. I let him.

My sisters are on the yacht, resting after too much sun and wine, and my father too, all lost in their own worlds. So Emilio and I concocted separate excuses to go into town, not that anybody was listening, and now we're pretending this is allowed. We're pretending that he isn't my father's employee and that I'm older than seventeen. We're pretending he can pull me to him suddenly and kiss me on the sidewalk without looking around anxiously before and after.

No, I'm not asleep. This isn't a dream, or my imagination. I remember.

I remember my green cotton sundress, limp from the

humidity, and I remember that Emilio tastes like tequila. His cheek scratches my skin when he leans down to kiss my collarbone. Right there on the street, he does it like he's allowed to, his fingers sliding under the thin green strap. The terror of it is still delicious enough to make me shiver, even now.

He lifts his head, smiling, like he only just realized where we are. He kisses my lips again, but only for a second before someone bumps into us and we break apart. I glance around us. Tourists are everywhere, tipsy and sunburned, getting louder every second.

He turns me around and we walk, this time with me in front, his hand gripping my waist. I'm sticky from the mugginess of swarming bodies. The crowd thickens around us as people spill from the shops and restaurants and tiki bars into the streets, but we aren't part of it. We're two cool stones in a hot river of leering, sweaty faces and groping hands. They leave their wetness on my skin, and this is when I start to feel that familiar helplessness of a nightmare.

Is this part still a memory? I don't think so. I can't remember. Why would I be imagining it, though?

Emilio pushes me on, farther into the crowd, but I don't want to go this way anymore. I'm drowning in music from too many restaurants that's no longer music but a tide of pulsing noise. The colors around me have turned lurid. I don't trust these faces and bodies, but Emilio's hand is like an anchor. I can't float away.

Until the anchor lifts.

I spin around and he's gone, swallowed up by the crowd. *No.* Panic fills me, tastes like salt, smells like meat sweating over a fire. I was wrong. I'm the one who's been swallowed up by the crowd, and Emilio has delivered me to them.

The phone rings. I sit up in the dark, weak and wounded from my dream, and the imaginary betrayal. It rings again, and this time it hits me. It's him.

I hadn't realized—not until this moment—that I'd stopped believing he was going to call.

Fingers shaking, I pick up the phone. "Emilio."

He sighs. "It's you."

"It's me."

Neither of us can speak. I'm in shock; he's too relieved. At least I think he's relieved. A sigh can mean other things too.

"Where were you when I called?" he asks. The heaviness of his voice startles me. It's so severe, it barely sounds like him. "Someone picked up your phone, and I thought . . . I thought a lot of things."

"I'm sorry. I didn't know until after."

"After what? What happened?"

"Nothing." I close my eyes. I sound like a cagey teenager trying to wiggle out of trouble.

"*Something* happened. Who had your phone? I could hear someone breathing into the receiver, and I've been sick ever since, imagining the absolute worst scenar—"

"It was only Marcel," I blurt.

There's no sigh this time. No gasp, no cursing, no laughter.

His voice is lower and expressionless. "Why did Marcel have your phone?"

"We were hanging out. But why didn't you call again? Or text?"

"Since when do you *hang out* with Marcel? I couldn't call because I thought someone had your phone. And why did Marcel have it?"

"He didn't," I say. "He just picked it up when I was changing."

"What?"

"Nothing. He . . ." I trail off, muddled and sweating. I put my hand to my cheek. I'm flushed even though my room is cold. This conversation isn't how I imagined it would be. He's supposed to be supplying the excuses and the apologies. I'm supposed to be forgiving him.

"What are you doing, Valentina? Why are you spending time with the brother of your father's dead informant?" he asks. "I shouldn't have to explain how dangerous that is—we don't even know for sure that he's not working for your father!"

"Marcel isn't working for my father."

"You sound awfully certain. Is that what he's been trying to convince you of while you've been *hanging out*?"

"You were the one who was positive he wasn't!"

"But that doesn't mean I would take the unnecessary risk. If you're wrong, and if Marcel finds anything out . . ."

I'm uncomfortably close to tears. I know what he wants me to say, but I wait for him to finish his own sentence.

". . . he'd tell Victor."

"But he *doesn't* work for my father," I repeat.

"If Victor finds out what we're planning, he'll have me killed. You know that."

"Stop!" I feel sick. He's right. What have I been doing? Why would I jeopardize Emilio's safety like this? I open my eyes and stare at a strip of paint peeling off the door. If he knew everything I'd told Marcel, he'd . . . I don't know. Yell at me. Hang up. Leave Miami. Disappear without me.

Maybe all those things.

"I know it's hard for you to hear," he says. "I know he's your father and you don't want to believe it, but that's exactly what he'd do. He'd kill me."

That interrupted dream comes flooding back to me. How could I even imagine Emilio betraying me when I'm the one putting him in danger?

"Valentina." His voice is gentle now, pulling at me like fingers.

"What?"

"I thought I'd lost you."

"You can't lose me."

"I thought someone had taken you."

"Nobody even knows I'm here."

"Your father knows you're there. Probably a handful of his employees too."

"But Papi wouldn't hurt me."

"Valentina," he says again, but this time it's too cloying, like he's talking to an idiot, or worse, a child. "Your father has enemies. You have to be careful—"

"*Stop*. I'm fine."

We listen to each other breathe, and I imagine he forgives me for telling Marcel everything. I don't have to actually tell him that I've done it. I'm sorry. He loves me. I love him. That should be good enough.

"So you're hanging out with Marcel," he says.

"It's nothing. He's been going through a rough time. After Lucien . . . he just needed a friend."

He grunts. "Last time I checked, Marcel had plenty of friends."

"Well apparently they weren't the kind of friends to stick around after his brother killed himself."

"And you are."

He waits for me to explain, but I don't want to. I don't feel like justifying whatever Marcel and I are.

"I guess I didn't realize you knew each other that well," he says.

"We didn't, but I was sort of there for everything. He needed someone."

"You already said that. And I know Marcel. He's very good at making women feel needed."

Ha. What would he say if he knew Marcel had said the same thing about him? "He needed a *friend*. Why are you acting like this?"

"Like what?" he asks.

"Jealous. Like I did something wrong."

"I'm not jealous of Marcel. And it was nice of you to offer a shoulder to cry on, but you've got to stop seeing him. He may not work for your father, but he knows who Victor Cruz is."

I lie back down in my bed, the sweat-drenched T-shirt chilling my spine. I've never lied to him before. "But he doesn't know who I am."

"Are you sure?"

"We aren't doing this again," I say.

"He's not the kind of guy you want to be around."

"Why?"

"Just trust me."

Trust me. Trust me. Trust me. I need to trust someone. It should be Emilio. It is Emilio. "I don't want to talk about Marcel anymore."

"Me neither," he says.

"I miss you. I was so scared something had happened to you, or you'd changed your mind about leaving."

"I haven't. I won't." His voice is gentler now that the jealous glint is gone. It feels like warm sun on my skin. "I love you."

I rest my hand on my stomach. Butterflies. Wings flap and the rest has to disappear. "I love you, too. Why didn't you call again?"

"I told you. I thought someone had your phone, maybe had you too. I couldn't risk calling and linking the two of us even more than we already are."

The butterflies are still swarming and swooping beneath my hand, almost distracting me from the fact that he's not making sense. The holes in his story are too big, though. If he really thought something bad had happened to me, he'd have figured out a way to track me down. "So why are you risking it now?"

"I couldn't take it anymore. I had to hear your voice and make sure you were okay."

"Oh." I stare at the water stain, which is looking less like the Virgin Mary and more like a stingray with a twisted left fin. Calling me is too dangerous, but missing me is too painful. He must've called me in a moment of weakness.

"You sound disappointed," he says.

"I'm not, but I want you to tell me you're coming, that it's time to leave."

He sighs. I imagine him rubbing his temples, running a hand through his hair. "I need you to be patient," he says.

"I am being patient. But I think I should come back." I've said it before I think the words through, but instantly I know I'm right.

"What are you talking about? You can't come back. Not now."

"Why not? I could tell Papi running away was a mistake, then leave again with you when you're ready to go."

"No," he says. "He'll suspect something."

"But don't you think it's more likely he'll suspect something if I stay here?" My heart is beating faster now, the ideas trickling down from my brain to my fingers and toes like currents of energy. "He knows I'm here, and he knows Lucien is dead so my money is running out. If he even suspects you saw me when you were here, you'd be safer if I came home."

"You were the one who said you couldn't go back and pretend."

"I couldn't do it forever," I say, "but I could for a little while."

"He already knows about us, remember? That's why he sent me up there to see if I'd rat you out. You can't just come back and pretend like before."

"Why not?"

"He'll know something's up."

"Then I could say I came back because I missed you."

"No."

"Emilio, please," I say, hating the begging in my voice. "Just think about it for a minute."

"*No.*"

"Why?"

"Because this isn't just about us!"

Shame burns my eyes. He's right. I'm selfish. But he's not being rational, either. If he thought it through, he'd see his family would be safer with me back in Miami too. "What aren't you telling me?"

He doesn't answer. He should say he's telling me everything there is to tell. I might even believe him.

"What's the real reason you don't want me to come back?" I try again.

"It's not safe here." His voice is missing something. Shine. Rhythm. Feeling.

I can't help it. I picture his eyes like they were from the slit in the closet, lifeless and cruel. "Why not?"

"Your father has enemies—"

"Enough with the enemies! I lived in that house for seventeen years, not knowing about any of it. You're telling me I've spent my whole life in danger?"

"No."

"Then why are things suddenly not safe?"

"They just are."

I catch my breath, not sure if I want to understand. "I don't believe you."

"Fine. But don't come back."

"My sisters are in that house. If something dangerous was about to happen, my father would do something about that."

"If he knew."

I pull myself into a sitting position, gripping the phone tightly. "What does that mean?"

"I'll make sure nothing happens to your sisters."

"What are you talking about?"

"Nothing. Everything will be fine. I'll be there soon, maybe next week even, but you can't come here, Valentina. You can't."

"Tell me," I beg, knowing he won't. He won't. I don't get to know. I don't get to make the plans or the decisions. I don't get to choose. I have to hide and wait for my rescue. My jaw aches, and I realize I'm grinding my teeth.

"Let's talk about where we'll go," he says softly.

"No."

"Come on. You wanted to go to New Zealand, didn't you?"

"That was your suggestion."

"Then where do you want to go?" he asks.

"I don't care."

"Valentina."

"What? Don't pretend what I want even matters."

He sighs. "Of course you matter."

"*I* do, but what I want doesn't? How is that possible?" I'm pouting like a child, but I don't care. I'm tired of waiting, of being alone.

"Sorry." He doesn't sound sorry. He sounds determined, and I'm not so sure he knows what he's supposed to be sorry for anyway. This conversation should have gone differently. "I'll call you soon," he says, "when it's time to leave."

I don't say anything.

"Valentina. You know I love you."

Do I? I swallow and try to remember his touch. When he was here and I could feel him, then yes, I knew it. "I love you, too."

I wait for him to hang up first. After he does, I realize I didn't tell him to be careful. Now it's too late.

TWENTY-THREE

"**W**hat are you doing here?" Jacques asks.

I follow his skeptical eye from my mandolin case to my skirt to my lip gloss and blown-out hair.

"It's busy," I say, ignoring his question. I've never seen Soupe au Chocolat peopled before, but now I understand what it's supposed to be like. Lively. Pulsing. I've only known its empty skeleton, but the people are the blood. They crowd around the bubble-like tables, break up the layers of brown, fill the air with color and warmth and smells other than chocolate. "Is it always this busy?"

Jacques shrugs. "Typical afternoon crowd."

"Oh."

"So you're here to eat?"

"What? No. I thought I'd stop by and ask about maybe picking up some extra work." I clutch the mandolin case with both hands so he can't see my fingers trembling. It's taken me three days to work up the guts to do this. I'm not backing out now.

"You can't clean while we're open," he says, avoiding eye contact. "And I already have too many servers."

"Actually, I was wondering if I could play my mandolin. You know. For tips." Desperation climbs up my throat and colors my cheeks. Blushing is harder to hide than shaky hands.

Jacques stares at the mandolin case, scratches his arm, glances uneasily around at the crowd.

"I'm not bad," I say. I hope that's true. I'm not terrible, but I'm not exactly great, either. "I made pretty good money busking outside the Metro before it got cold."

Another worried look at his tables.

"And I really need the money."

He sighs and points. "Back corner. And not too loud."

"It's a quiet instrument," I say over my shoulder as I follow the direction of his finger. Hope fizzes up inside of me as I get the mandolin out of the case. I'm doing this. It may take a while, maybe even a few weeks, but if Jacques doesn't mind and his customers aren't too stingy and I don't waste a cent of it, I'll eventually have enough money for a plane ticket home.

I play without looking up. I watch my fingers, pretending the people away. Still, I can feel their judging eyes and hear the occasional clink of coins in my glass tip jar—even the rare rustle of a bill being stuffed in.

When I run out of music and do look up, the people are different. The earlier diners have been replaced by another round of customers, so I cycle through my repertoire again. And again. I don't know how many times I do it, because I get lost in the melodies, happy for the first time in I don't know how long. I'm going home. I'm not waiting to be rescued, and when Emilio sees me, he'll be relieved I didn't listen to him because we'll be together and we can sort through this mess if we're together.

Jacques's barrel torso enters my peripheral vision, and I break off awkwardly midphrase.

"Time to pack up," he says.

I stop, eye the half-full tip jar.

"Wednesday night is poetry reading."

"Night?" I glance out the shop window and realize what I somehow missed. The light has changed, afternoon melting into dusk. "Poetry?"

Jacques shrugs. "Not my thing, but the customers like it."

"Can I come again tomorrow?" I ask as I lay the mandolin back in its case.

He looks thoughtfully at the tip jar. "I guess."

"Thank you."

He doesn't say *you're welcome*, but he hands me a coffee to go and a brown paper bag with a croissant in it.

"Thank you."

I don't count my money in the café. If he'd wanted me to stay and take up a precious table, he wouldn't have given me the food to go, so I stuff the jar in my purse and sip my coffee as I walk back to the apartment. The wind is biting, but I'm warm with hope and caffeine. That croissant is going to taste like heaven. Anticipation floats me all the way home.

Safe in my closet, I kick off my shoes, sit on my bed, and take the tiniest bites possible. It might be lighter and richer than anything I've ever tasted. Once I've swallowed the last mouthful and licked the pastry flakes from my fingers, I pull the jar out of my purse. I dump its contents on the bed. Coins. Bills. More coins than bills. I separate them, lick the butter on my lips and count. Then I count again. And again. Eighteen dollars and ten cents. I played for four hours and made eighteen dollars and ten cents. That's less than five dollars an hour. That's nothing.

The hope trickles out of me penny by penny. Eighteen dollars. A plane ticket to Miami will cost at least five hundred. That's . . . The math hurts. That's too much. I'm not going home. At that rate, I'm not making enough for food.

I lie down, empty. The hope and caffeine have been used up. I've still got butter on my lips, but the rest of the croissant seems to have settled into a ball of grease and gluten right below my ribs. I could wait for Emilio. Or I could steal from Nanette, or maybe even from Jacques, and then send them the money once I got back to Miami. Or I could call my father. I can't decide which option makes me want to throw up the most.

I pull my phone out of my bag before I can think too hard about what I'm doing and dial.

"Jane." It's just a syllable, but I can tell Marcel is smiling. "Or am I supposed to call you Valentina?"

"You'd better stick with Jane."

"Why Jane, by the way?"

"You don't like it?"

"I didn't say that. I'm just curious."

"Because it's nondescript," I say.

"As in plain Jane."

"I didn't want to be noticed."

"And how'd that work for you?"

"Not so well."

He laughs. "Should I come get you?"

"What?"

"To swim. That's why you're calling, right?"

"Oh. Yeah."

The pool is cleansing. I feel strong, carving a path through the water with my hands, propelling my body forward with each kick. Marcel beats me by a larger margin than last time, but it doesn't matter. Or it matters less. I spend the entire swim going through what to say, how to ask so it doesn't sound like begging. By the end, though, I'm too tired and too ready to have it over with to say any of the things I planned.

I pull myself up out of the water, panting. Marcel is sitting with his legs dangling in the pool, no longer breathing heavy at all. If he ever was.

"You okay?" he asks.

I nod and blurt out, "Can I borrow some money?"

"Of course."

I'm not sure what I expected. A smirk at the very least.

"I need kind of a lot, though."

He shrugs.

"No," I say, "like six hundred dollars."

"Okay."

"Seriously? That's all?"

He hands me a towel, and I realize I'm shivering. "Did you think I'd say no?"

"Um, no? I don't know. I thought you'd want to know why." I don't add that I thought he might make me beg.

"Do you want to tell me why?"

I shouldn't. I thought I'd have to, but if he's willing to give me the money no questions asked, there's no reason to. Unless he's my friend. Unless I care that he might miss me when I disappear. "A plane ticket to Miami."

"I thought you were waiting for Emilio."

"I was. But something is wrong."

"What do you mean?"

"I don't know, but I need to go back."

"Oh. So why don't you call your father?"

"I don't want him to know. I'm not going *home* home."

Marcel snorts. "Sorry. It's just . . . seriously?"

"What's so funny?"

"Your father is Victor Cruz. He'll definitely know if you're in Miami."

"How?" I ask. I wring the water from my braids, watching the water trickle over my thighs. "Lucien isn't reporting back anymore."

"I wouldn't be surprised if he had someone else watching

you. And he probably has someone at customs on his payroll. I'm guessing the minute your passport gets scanned, he gets a phone call."

"Oh." Of course. That must be how he found me here.

"And once you get to Miami, don't you think people will recognize you? Where are you going to stay?"

My teeth are chattering now. The towel is drenched. "I hadn't thought about it."

He doesn't need to say anything else. I realize now how naive the plan was, if I can even call it a plan. It was a fantasy: fly to Miami, break into my house, take enough untraceable jewelry for Emilio and me to live off, and convince Emilio to come with me. I might as well have had us riding off on a unicorn at the end.

"Never mind," I say. My throat thickens, and tears blur my vision. Marcel's staring at me. I need to go change before I lose control completely.

I start to stand, but he puts his hand on my leg. "Wait."

I sit back down, blink the tears away, and try not to look at his hand or feel anything at all. He's staring through the water into the artificial blue of the pool floor, his mind elsewhere. He could be gripping a sandwich for all he knows.

"The Burlington crossing can be a pain," he mutters. "Alburgh is pretty quiet, though. At night, especially. I've only had my car searched once."

"What are you talking about? Why did you have your car searched?"

"Everybody has their car searched at some point. It's a statistical probability when you're crossing the border regularly."

"Oh." I can't ignore it any longer. I look down at his hand.

He pulls it away. "You wouldn't be any harder to hide than a suitcase full of guns."

"You've smuggled guns across the border?"

"Of course not. But people do, and they get away with it."

"What are you suggesting?" I ask.

"I'm suggesting we road trip."

We draw up plans in Marcel's room.

It's the first time I've been into the main house, but Marcel doesn't give me a tour. He barely turns on enough lights for us to make it through the first floor and up the two flights of stairs. I don't need it illuminated to get the drift, though. It's cavernous and immaculate, with anemic watercolor landscapes covering the walls. It's my home in Miami drained of blood. No wonder Lucien was so desperate to escape. No wonder Marcel is still trying.

"Is this really going to work?" I ask, staring at the bookshelves that line two walls of his room. Not what I was expecting of a high school dropout. Aside from the books, there isn't much personality in the room, but I get the sense that any gratuitous personality is wiped clean by the daily maid.

"Maybe." He's hunched over his laptop, pulling up maps of the various routes from Montreal to Miami. "Maybe not. You still want to try?"

"Yeah. Yeah, I do."

TWENTY-FOUR

Six minutes.

I'm leaving. It's hard to believe, but if that clock is still actually functioning, Marcel should be here soon.

Parting with my junk hurt. Surprisingly, it was more painful than pawning my tennis bracelet and earrings to get here, which doesn't make any sense. At least a dozen times over the past couple of months I've pictured myself gleefully chucking the synthetic blanket into the Dumpster out back, hurling the scuffed shoes and threadbare sweaters into the icy Saint Lawrence River, but I couldn't do it today. I thought I hated them, but at least they were mine.

Instead, after Marcel dropped me off, I gathered the few items I'm taking with me—a change of clothes, a few pairs of underwear, basic toiletries—and put them into a grocery bag. The rest I reluctantly lugged to the Salvation Army donation box.

I realized too late that I should've kept the blanket, that I was still hours from midnight and Marcel's warm car. I've spent the entire evening freezing on the cot without it. It's been bearable only because it's the last time. By this time tomorrow I'll be somewhere warmer—not Miami yet, but somewhere warmer.

Five minutes.

My grocery bag of clothes, the mandolin, and me. That's all that's left. I'm huddled on the cot, staring at the clock on the floor because I used the crate to lug everything else to the Salvation Army.

I'm lucky Nanette isn't home. She's the only one who occasionally pokes her head in here, and if she did today, my leaving would be obvious. Marcel and I both agreed not to tell anyone. He insisted nobody would miss him, or at least not for a week, which seems both unbelievable and totally possible. Almost as unbelievable and totally possible: he's driving me to Miami. 1,639 miles. Twenty-nine hours. That's not a reasonable favor to do for someone, not even a friend, but I couldn't make myself try to talk him out of it. He said that he needed a break from winter anyway, and that he's always loved South Beach. He said he had friends there to stay with. So I guess I'm letting him.

Four minutes.

But Nanette. I owe her something. I owe her lots of little things, actually—detergent, peanut butter, ChapStick, crackers, not to mention wear and tear on her bathing suit, and heels that I've bled into. A thank-you. I owe her a thank-you. When this is all over, I'll send her something, anonymously if I have to.

Of course, Emilio's going to be pissed off at first. I can fantasize all I want about how happy he'll be to find me on his doorstep, but I can't forget what he said. *Don't come back. Promise me you won't come back.* And the way he said it—those words sank like stones.

He was scared when he said that, though. Terse out of fear. After the shock wears off, after he understands that I'm not in danger because nobody knows I'm in Miami, he'll come around. I'll make him. I'll show up at his apartment in Brickell, and he'll be mad, but he'll let me in, and he'll have missed me. We'll walk down through Bayside Marketplace to the docks, dip our toes in warm water, and be in this together. I'll melt his anger. I'll make him forget.

Three minutes.

If I can.

Marcel said midnight is the best time to leave because it puts us at the border by two, and by that time border patrol agents don't care about anything except going back to sleep.

Guilt creeps up my spine, one notch at a time. I'm using Marcel. But if he knows it—and he does—is it really so bad? He wants to take me to Miami. He was the one who suggested it, so it's not like I put the idea in his head.

I still don't want Marcel to see this apartment. Not the lobby, not the busted elevator, definitely not the musty common room or this fetid closet. How is it possible I'm still so vain? I don't know, but it's bad enough that he's seen the outside of this derelict embarrassment. I'll wait outside.

I pick up the plastic grocery bag and the mandolin case and give the closet one final glance. The water stain on the ceiling looks like it's grown again, the edges pushing outward, getting ready to swallow everything. The room is empty, except for the cot and the clock.

I unplug the clock, but I don't take it with me. It's not mine. And besides, I'm done waiting.

TWENTY-FIVE

Marcel is late.

Icy fog wraps around me, and I shiver. The grocery bag and mandolin weight me to the sidewalk like anchors while I take turns entertaining the best- and worst-case scenarios. The best: he's just late. The worst: he's changed his mind. In a moment of typical old-Marcel flakiness, he offered to do this, then realized that a few days of ogling uninhibited South Beachers isn't worth the risk of getting arrested for human trafficking.

No. That's not the worst-case scenario. The worst-case scenario is he's lying to me and has been for as long as we've been friends, which I guess is what we are now. He's working for my father, or for one of my father's enemies.

I'm crazy. Paranoid. Since that night in Emilio's closet, there's an endless thread of doubt winding its way through my thoughts, and it's tangled in everything now, twisting every interaction. Anybody could be a liar, a murderer, an enforcer, an informant.

I pull out my phone to check the time. It's 12:33. No wonder I'm so cold—I've been out here for a half hour. I watch my frozen thumbs press the buttons to dial Marcel's number, but before I can finish, Lucien's Range Rover careens around the corner. Even though I can see Marcel's distinctly squarer jaw, a fleeting panic washes over me at the thought of Lucien behind that wheel, followed by an irrational tide of betrayal. I shouldn't be mad at a dead man, even if he did lie to me. As quickly as the anger surged, it ebbs, and I'm left with cold, cold guilt.

Marcel stops in front of me, leans over, and pushes the door open without getting out of the car. "You getting in?" he asks.

Did I hesitate? I must have. I pick up my things, throw the bag and then the mandolin over the seat, and climb into the familiar leather chair. Thankfully, the smell of coffee covers any lingering scent of Lucien's cologne. "You're late. I thought you'd changed your mind."

"I never change my mind," he says, and holds out a coffee for me. "It'd mean I was wrong in the first place."

I roll my eyes and take the cup. "And you're never wrong in the first place?"

"No. I just never admit it."

Marcel peels away from the building and I don't look back, but I feel a distinct pull as it recedes, as if I'm still connected to it by a string. The sadness surprises me. It's complicated, leaving a prison and a haven.

I sip slowly, drinking in my final views of Montreal. I'll never come back. It's beautiful tonight, dark and glittering like a giant, deadly snake, but once I'm gone the memories will be enough to keep me away. Forever, I think.

"Why are you driving Lucien's car?" I ask.

"Mine's more likely to get searched."

I nod. That makes sense. The Range Rover is luxurious in a less-likely-to-be-breaking-the-law way than Marcel's European sports car. This'll draw less attention. "So where am I going to hide?"

"I put some blankets in the back. You can lie on the floor between the second and third rows and spread them out on top of you."

"And if they search the car?"

"Then we're screwed."

"Right." I don't know if he means legally, or as far as my father is concerned. He should be most worried about Victor Cruz. "And how far away is the border?"

"An hour and a half. You can sleep if you want."

"Okay."

I recline the seat, but I don't sleep. I don't even close my eyes. I stare at the roof, and of all the unlikely things to think about, I picture Lola and Ana. Missing them still surprises me, but I feel this ache of nostalgia right now and every other time I've thought of them since leaving Miami. Four months feels like four years. Of course, the memories have become increasingly rosy—unrealistically so. I do remember that they're mostly vain and self-absorbed, but I remember the sweet things too, like when all three of us would cram into Lola's bed during storms and sleep there the whole night, even after the storm had ended, even when we were too old to be afraid of thunder.

For all her faults, Lola has this confidence that feels like it extends to me, like she thinks I can do anything and just her thinking it somehow makes it true. And Ana is the softest shoulder to cry on, probably because she does a lot of crying herself. She's the one who helped me rinse off the blood and bandage my leg when I was ten and tried to shave it completely dry. She didn't even make fun of me.

Not having a mother to miss—that sounds so tragic, but Lola and Ana are the reason it's okay. They're the reason I'm okay.

It'll be hard, being in Miami and not seeing them, but I can't. No. Even if I thought breaking their bubble of innocence was a good idea, I can't trust either to keep real secrets. Lola not telling anyone about my dented fender one week after I got my new car doesn't mean she's capable of anything on this scale.

"Not tired?" Marcel asks.

"I guess not."

Marcel turns the wheel, and when the car leans left, my stomach leans right. We're leaving the city. Everything darkens as well-lit civilization fades, the road becomes a little bumpier, and eventually farm smells seep into the vehicle. I smell pig first. Then cow, I'm guessing, though I'm no farm girl. It might be sheep or horse or who knows what. Skunk hits my nose the strongest, so pungent my stomach lurches and I want to gag. I lift up my head. "How much of the drive is farmland?" I ask.

"I don't know. I've only driven as far as Burlington. You want a percentage or something?"

"Never mind. The smell is getting to me, but I think I'm just nervous."

"Don't be nervous about the border," he says.

"Too late. Are you sure you want to do this?"

He shrugs. "What else am I going to be doing?"

I don't answer, because I'm almost certain it's rhetorical, but I can think of a dozen better things for him to be doing than getting arrested or putting his life in danger getting tangled up in this mess. I put my head back down and go back to staring at the roof. In all the nervous seconds I've spent thinking about Miami since Marcel offered to take me home, I can't believe I didn't once think of what the drive would be like. I don't have a book to read. I don't even have a magazine, just the smell of farm animal excrement and the sound of my own thoughts. Maybe I could fall asleep.

"You should probably climb back there," Marcel says, jarring me out of my drowsiness. "We're about five minutes from the border."

My face must register the rush of panic I feel, because he adds, "Don't be nervous."

"I'm not." It's a pointless lie, since I already admitted to it, and he must see my hands shaking as I pull myself over the seat, then over that row into the next. What am I doing? "Wait, what's our story if we get caught?"

"We don't have one. If we get busted, it's over—we're going to jail until your father comes to rescue you and kill me. Don't go all the way to the back in case they want to look in the trunk. Yeah, between the second and third row."

I sit down in the back row and try to see his face in the rear-view mirror, but it's too dark. "Why aren't you nervous?"

"I don't have much to lose."

I slide onto the floor, pulling the folded blanket off the seat and over me. It's soft and dense and perfectly heavy—the kind of heaviness that folds warmth in without suffocating you. I'm surprised by how extravagant the weight of a real blanket feels. I'd forgotten.

I pull the blanket over my head and inhale to check for breathability. It's good. It smells sweet and lightly floral, like fabric softener, and I have a sudden impulse to either cry or throw my arms around Marcel and thank him. It's irrational. Everything else he's giving me is so much bigger: the risk, the time, the money. But he could have grabbed any old blanket.

Marcel is lying. If he really felt like he had nothing to lose, he wouldn't be here with me. He'd still be partying, using, hurting himself until he'd really lost everything.

I feel the frequency of the car's hum changing. We aren't stopping, but we are slowing down.

"Showtime," he says. "I'm not going to talk anymore. I don't want them seeing my lips move."

"Okay." I squeeze my eyes shut. My cheeks are burning, but

I can't tell if I'm hot or just flustered. *Calm down, calm down, calm down.* I repeat the words as the car slows even further, but when we hit a speed bump still going too fast, I drop my calm resolve and let out a yelp as the car bounces and my head knocks against the floor. Pain pulses across the back of my skull. If we make it through this, he's getting yelled at for that.

The car stops. I think my heart does too. Marcel clears his throat, and the smooth electric purr of the window opening sends a shiver through me.

"Good evening," a voice outside the car says. It's not friendly, but it's not unfriendly either. Male. Older. "Traveling late tonight."

"Yes, sir." Marcel's tone is almost unrecognizable. He sounds respectful—polite, but nothing to hide.

"Where are you heading?"

"Burlington."

"For how long?"

"A week."

"Citizenship?"

"Dual."

"American passport, please."

Neither of them speaks for at least ten seconds, and I picture the guard inspecting it, scanning it into his computer, doing whatever it is that they do to track entry. My own passport is resting on my stomach, collecting sweat between the faux-leather cover and my skin. I lift up my shirt to feel it, held in place by a makeshift money belt I fashioned out of my ripped stockings. I assumed Marcel knew what he was talking about when he suggested that Papi had an informant in customs, but now's the first time I'm really thinking about what that means. I can't travel into the United States without my father finding out. Maybe forever. Is getting me a fake passport something Emilio has already thought of? I pull my shirt back down and refuse to think about it.

"There you go," the voice says. "What are you planning on doing in Burlington?"

"Visiting my grandma."

"Your grandma? She expecting you in the middle of the night, son?"

"Yes, sir. I told her I'd come right after my shift ended. She's ill and doesn't sleep well anyway. Cancer."

I cringe. Too much. The sick grandma is overplayed, a rookie lie. I'd have thought Marcel would come out with something more subtle.

"I'm sorry to hear that," the man says, his voice noticeably softer. "I hope you have a nice visit. Any fruits or vegetables in the car?"

"No, sir."

"Firearms?"

"No, sir."

"Go ahead and pop the trunk for me."

"Pardon me?"

"I said pop the trunk, son."

My bones are liquid. Marcel said this wouldn't happen. A

clunk sounds to my left as the trunk pops, and I instinctively force the air out of my lungs, willing my body flat. I don't think I'm visible from the trunk, but I'm not sure. I should've checked to see how much space there is under the seat, but Marcel said they wouldn't search the car.

Cold air pushes its way through the blanket, and I have to force myself to breathe it in. My lungs hurt. Rustling. I hear it close by, just a little to the left of my face, but I can't turn to see what it is or how close it is. Then sliding, like a box or a duffel bag being pushed. Silence. An agonizing moment. Still nothing.

Slam.

The shock jolts every nerve. He closed it. He isn't still digging around inches from my face, but I can't stop clenching every muscle in my body. What if he opens the side door to check the rows? Should I roll under the seat now?

"Have a safe trip, son." The voice is up front again.

"Thank you, sir," Marcel answers.

"And watch out for deer. They're all over the roads at night."

"Yes, sir."

The car rolls forward. The window hums as it closes, and I'm suddenly aware of the ache on the back of my head spreading out like a claw. The speed bump. Everything's clenched, and my lungs burn. I'm not sure when I stopped breathing. I pull the blanket off my face and gasp. It's a euphoric combination, all that oxygen and relief swirling through my body.

"How's it going back there?" Marcel calls.

I take another gulp of air and yell, "You said they wouldn't search the car!"

"I said they *probably* wouldn't search the car. And he didn't really search it. He just poked around in the back."

"And your *grandmother*?" This time the yell turns into a laugh, one of those uncontrollable laughs that's dangerously close to tears.

"Yeah, works in every situation."

"It shouldn't." I sit up and sigh, wiping my eyes. It's dark. I feel drunk. It's so much darker than Montreal or Miami, no lights, no moon, no stars. I'm in a black hole, somewhere between my two lives.

"You coming back up, or are you going to lie on the floor for the rest of the trip?"

I climb back over the seats, still shaking. "Thanks for the concussion. That speed bump nearly knocked me out."

"Sorry. That thing came out of nowhere. Are you okay?"

I touch the back of my head. A goose egg is forming. "Yeah."

"Sorry," he says again.

"You can make it up to me by finding a bathroom to stop at."

He snorts. "I'm sure there are several million lovely trees out there for you to pee on."

"I'm a girl. I can't pee *on* a tree."

"Fine, next to a tree. We're not going to find anything open between here and Burlington."

"And how far away is that?" I ask, staring out at the black

forest on either side. It's probably teeming with wildlife. Bears. Cougars. I don't even know what else.

"An hour."

"I'll hold it," I grumble.

"Tell me if you change your mind—preferably before you pee in my car."

"If I had more than a single change of clothes, I'd consider it as payback for the speed bump."

"You know you're going to be stuck in this car for the next few days, right?"

"Yeah."

"And you'd pee in it just for revenge."

"Maybe," I say.

"I respect that."

"Thanks. Revenge sometimes requires a little personal sacrifice. My sister Lola once took out her boyfriend's mailbox with her BMW. On purpose. She was without her car for two weeks while the body damage was repaired."

He pauses long enough for me to regret bringing up Lola. "So that wasn't a lie, then. You do have sisters."

"No, it wasn't a lie. It's not like I lied about everything." But when I think about it, I can't remember what I did tell him the truth about.

"Older or younger?"

"Older. Nineteen and twenty-one."

"Hmm. So are we still pretending that you're nineteen, or

are we admitting that it's unlikely that you're the same age as your older sister?"

"Shut up."

"So you're what—seventeen?"

"Move on."

"I knew it," he says.

"I said move on."

"Okay. What are your sisters like?"

"Um . . . beautiful and narcissistic."

"Do I get to meet them?" he asks.

"Absolutely not."

"But beautiful and narcissistic is my favorite combination," he says. "Beautiful narcissistic girls love me."

"Both good reasons for you not to meet them."

"Oh, I get it," he says. "You want me all for yourself."

I rub my eyes, suddenly too tired to be dealing with this version of Marcel. "Why do you always have to do that? I hate that."

"I was kidding, Valentina. Chill out."

I stare hard at the patch of lit road directly in front of us. The car swallows it up so fast, we can't be seeing more than a second or two ahead. I don't like it when he calls me Valentina. It sounds wrong coming from his mouth, but I don't want to be called Jane anymore either. "Sorry. I'm just worried."

"The risky part's over."

Is it? Maybe for him. We made it through the border, but I

still have to convince Emilio not to be angry with me for coming. And I have to break into my own house and steal my own things without getting caught, plus I have to spend days in the city where everyone that I know lives without a soul finding out that I'm there. And even then the risky part isn't over. I have to come and go without anyone else getting killed.

We're quiet for a while, then he asks, "Why don't you play your guitar thing?"

"My guitar thing?"

"Ukulele. No, banjo."

"Try again."

"Okay, I can't remember what it's called," he admits, "but you should play whatever's in that case back there. You might feel better."

"I'm not going to feel better until you find me a semi-clean twenty-four-hour gas station."

"That's not going to happen, princess."

"We've got to pass something."

But he's right. We roll through a handful of sleepy towns, and everything is closed. Rural Vermont, apparently, has a bedtime.

"Pull over," I mutter when things move from critical to dire.

Marcel slows and veers onto the shoulder. Gravel and snow crunch beneath the tires, and the patch of road we illuminate now is the mottled gray of sludge and ice.

"I don't suppose you have toilet paper."

He laughs.

"Tissues?"

He rummages around in his jacket pocket and retrieves a couple of receipts. "Enjoy," he says, holding them out for me to take.

Awesome. I grab them and step out of the car, careful not to slip on the ice.

"Watch out for wolves, princess," he says.

"Don't call me that." I give the door a hefty slam. Wolves. Great. I hadn't even thought of wolves. I make my way to the back of the car and survey the inky black forest. I'd have to be crazy to wander out into that. And ultimately, would I rather have my body ripped apart by wild animals or pee uncomfortably close to the car?

I run back up to the driver's side of the car and motion for Marcel to roll down the window. "Don't turn around," I say.

"What do you take me for? No offense, but watching you pee is not real high on my list of things I'm dying to do."

He keeps talking, but I'm already running to the back of the car. Crouched with one hand on the bumper, both eyes on the forest, I go.

"Better?" he asks as I climb back in afterward.

"You have no idea."

I'm buckling my seat belt when a car flies by.

"Too bad that didn't happen thirty seconds ago," he says.

I shudder. I hadn't even thought about being visible to passing cars.

"So I was looking at the map," he says, pulling back onto

the highway, "and it turns out we're closer to Burlington than I thought we were."

"How close?"

He grins. "About five minutes."

Before I can stop myself, I'm punching his shoulder as hard as I can. I've thrown three good ones before I consider the possibility that he actually did misread the map, but I don't want to stop punching. Besides, he deserves it for the speed bump. I throw two more before he grabs my fist midair.

"Okay, that's starting to hurt. And I'm trying to drive here."

I take a few exaggerated deep breaths. "*Now* I feel better."

"Great."

I stare at his hand wrapped around my fist. "I'm done punching you. Let go."

"I don't know if I can. This isn't the first time you've been unpredictably violent."

"When you annoy me, I hurt you," I say. "Seems very predictable to me."

"I don't think that defense is going to hold up in a court of law when you're being tried for assault and battery. Maybe we could find some anger management course to enroll you in once we get to Miami."

He loosens his grip, but he doesn't let go. I yank my hand free. He puts his back on the steering wheel, and we both stare straight ahead. *Once we get to Miami.* When we get to Miami, Marcel is going to drop me off at Emilio's apartment, and we won't ever see each other again. He knows that. I know that.

"Or maybe I'll just mention it to Emilio," he adds. "He has the most to benefit from you getting psychiatric help for that temper."

"I don't lose my temper when I'm with Emilio."

"I bet."

"I don't. He doesn't intentionally piss me off."

Marcel smirks.

"What's that look supposed to mean?"

"There was no look."

"Seriously, what?"

"Nothing. It just doesn't sound like very much fun, being with someone who doesn't rile you up. That's all."

"We have fun."

"Okay."

"And since when are you a relationship expert?" I say.

"Since never. Go to sleep. I might need you to drive later."

I recline the seat and roll away from him to face the window. It's easier to be sad when nobody can see your face. This bruise inside my chest shouldn't be there—I should be relieved we got past the border. I should be thinking about how many hours I am from having Emilio's arms around me. I close my eyes, but I can't get comfortable. "I need the blanket," I mumble, and crawl over the seats to find it.

"There's a pillow in the back if you want it. And would you mind bringing the cooler up here?"

I find the pillow and a small cooler beside his duffel bag. It's surprisingly heavy. "What's in here?"

"Soda. You can help yourself."

"Maybe later." I bring it up to him.

"Are you okay?" he asks.

"Yeah. Just tired." I gesture to the backseat. "I think I'm gonna sleep back there."

He doesn't argue.

I stretch out on the third row, and even with a seat belt digging into my hip, I'm more comfortable by myself. Marcel's sympathy feels more dangerous than his teasing, probably because it reminds me that I *am* using him. I'm not going to think about it. He offered to do this.

The hope that I might dream of Emilio pulls me under, but I'm too tired to dream about anything.

TWENTY-SIX

Light. I can feel it before my eyes are open. It's not the stabbing morning light that cuts through the crack in your blinds and burns a hole in your head, but a gradual lifting of darkness. It's warm and yellow before you even notice it's there.

I don't open my eyes. That would force me to acknowledge a list of ugly realities: where I am, what I'm doing, what a huge mistake it is, etc. But now I've thought too much, and it's all flooding in. I'm going back to Miami. Marcel is taking me there. Emilio doesn't want me there. My father can't know I'm there.

And that's just the surface. The next layer is relearning what still makes me sick, even though I should be used to it by now. My father. Who he is. Emilio. What he does.

I force my eyes open and sit up. It still smells like animals.

"Hey," Marcel says. "I thought you might be dead."

I blink and wipe the sleep from my eyes. "How long did I sleep?"

"I don't know. It's ten."

"In the morning?"

Marcel lifts his eyes from the road, glancing at me in the rearview mirror. "I don't know how to answer that."

"Right. I mean, obviously morning. I can't believe I slept for that long, though."

"I was sure you'd wake up when I stopped for gas," he says.

"We stopped? Did you get some food?" I make my way back up to the front, but my seat is now covered in candy wrappers.

"Yeah, but I ate it all trying to stay awake. I think we're about a half hour from Lancaster. We can stop there."

I stuff the wrappers into a plastic bag, toss it on the floor, and sit down. "You look exhausted."

"This is what five energy drinks in one night looks like."

"Why didn't you just pull over and sleep?"

"I thought you wanted to get there as soon as possible."

"I do, but I don't want you to kill yourself."

Kill yourself. I cringe, but Marcel pretends he didn't hear it. "Can you drive after we stop for food?"

"Sure." I buckle my seat belt and pull my hair up into a ponytail. My teeth feel gritty, and I probably look like I've been sleeping on my face for the last eight hours, but that hopeless ache is gone. We could be in Miami by tomorrow.

"I'm glad you're up," he says. "I was starting to go crazy. I even listened to some self-help audiobook I found in the glove box. I'm pretty sure my mom put it there for Lucien. She's a big fan of motivation in a can."

"Yeah, how was it?"

"I'm now ready to embrace my authentic self and nurture my dreams."

"Beautiful."

Snow stretches to the horizon in every direction except for the narrow gray ribbon of road carved into it. The sky is bluer than Marcel's pool. Wherever Emilio and I end up going, I want the sky to be blue like that.

"Question," Marcel says, interrupting my thoughts. "Emilio doesn't know you're coming."

"That's not a question."

"Thanks, I'm getting there. Why don't you call him and tell him? I mean, he'll be happy to see you, right? What's with the secrecy?"

The good thing about a sky that blue is that it pulls your eyes up from dreariness. It makes you forget the less beautiful parts of whatever is below.

"Valentina?"

"He told me not to come."

"What?"

I clear my throat. "He told me not to come. He said it isn't safe."

"Then why are—"

"Because I can help him, and I'm tired of waiting to be rescued like some damsel in distress. And I think there's something going on that he's not telling me."

He gives me a sideways glance.

"What?"

"Nothing. That wouldn't surprise me."

"Don't lecture me. You only know the bad things about him, but he has to pretend to be that person. You don't know who he really is."

"But you do."

I ignore the skepticism in his voice. "Yes."

Marcel doesn't say anything else.

We stop at an IHOP for breakfast, and I use the facilities to brush my teeth and change my clothes. After we've stuffed ourselves with banana waffles (me) and chocolate chip pancakes (him), we swing by a gas station to top off the tank.

"Are you sure you don't mind driving?" Marcel asks as I adjust my seat and mirrors. He's already reclined the passenger seat, folded the pillow beneath his head, and cocooned himself in the blanket.

"Of course. I just stay on I-81?"

"Yeah," he mumbles. "Preferably going south."

"Right."

His eyes are shut by the time I've pulled out of the gas station, and he's snoring lightly after two minutes.

Driving isn't bad, at least not for the first few hours. Bald, snow-patched hills roll by, and it's easy to get lost in the monotony, let my best memories take over. Like that windy day in Rome last fall when my sisters went boot shopping and Papi took me with him to galleries. He critiqued and browsed and bought, asking me, *And what do you think of this one?* over and over as we wandered past paintings. I'd been tagging along all my life, but for some reason I was suddenly old enough for my opinion to mean something.

In between stops, we had lunch at a restaurant with a patio. Canary-colored tablecloths flapped in the wind like wings, anchored by vases of scarlet geraniums. Papi ordered me lobster mushroom ravioli that tasted earthy and salty. We dipped chunks of bread in a swirl of tangy balsamic and oil, and chewed, and talked about the paintings we still had to see.

He talked like he loved the art. I thought he did.

Strange. At some point his truths became his lies, but I can't see the line separating them. And do his admirable qualities cancel out any of his sins? I don't think so. Even if a person can be divided up like that—into truths and deceptions, good deeds and bad ones—and they cancel each other out like pluses and minuses in a gigantic life equation, he'd still never make it to zero. I don't even know a fraction of what he's done, but I know enough to see his love for art can't redeem him. His love for me can't do that either.

This is the problem. I let my thoughts take the good memories and turn them bad. All of them.

Marcel grunts and rolls over so he's facing me. Sleep makes his face serene.

Hating him seems like a long time ago. I don't feel pity anymore either. Something about him has changed, and he's not so pitiable now. Thinking about his life makes me sad, but that's different.

I turn on the radio. Keeping it soft so it won't wake Marcel, I cycle through the stations. But even when I land on a familiar song, the lyrics slide off me and the music is annoying, so I turn it off and start listening to the first CD of *Finding Your Authentic Self.* Within five minutes my authentic self is severely annoyed by the patronizing voice and message, but I can't bring myself to turn it off. It's hypnotic. I hate it, but it's strangely soothing too. And there's something appealing about the idea that I could listen to this woman tell me all the keys to happiness and then I'd have it.

When the first CD ends, the second begins automatically, and I don't stop it. What else have I got to do?

Five discs later my brain is mush and the only thing my authentic self is telling me is that I have to use the bathroom.

Marcel lifts his head as the car slows on the exit ramp. "You didn't kill us," he says, and yawns. "Good job."

"You were worried?"

"Nah. You don't seem like the bad-driver type."

"As if you can tell."

"With girls? Yeah, I can."

"This oughta be good." I turn into a kitschy Greek restaurant, complete with columns and chipped statues lining the path from the nearly full parking lot.

"The bad drivers are spazzes. The good drivers are sexy."

I roll my eyes. "That's one of the stupidest things I've ever heard. Is Greek okay?"

"Yeah. And you should be flattered."

"I'm too disturbed to be flattered."

He gets out of the car. "You know it's true."

I get out of the car too. My legs feel weak, and I'm suddenly starving. "And there are only two types of girls?"

"Fundamentally, yeah."

"My authentic self is appalled by the misogynistic crap that's coming out of your mouth."

"Oh no," he groans. "You listened to it?"

I follow him up the walkway. "My IQ dropped at least ten points from beginning to end."

He holds the door open for me. "I warned you."

Inside is packed.

"Game weekend," our server tells us with an eye roll, as if we're locals ourselves and just as annoyed with the pesky alumni clogging up the tables. "It'll be a tomb again by Monday."

"I hope this is good," Marcel whispers to me as she wipes down our table.

"This many West Virginians can't be wrong," I whisper back.

"Good or bad, we'll be sweating garlic for a week. I'm sure Emilio will be thrilled to have you back in his arms."

I have no comeback.

Cutlery clanking relentlessly against plates and dozens of conversations should cover the echo of what he just said. But the words are still there, still loud, still bouncing back and forth between us. Marcel's face is impassive as he ducks into the booth. I don't sit. I rest my fingertips on the wet table, which, even after the wipe down, feels like it's coated in the grease of a thousand spilled meals.

He looks up. "You staying?"

"I need to use the bathroom," I mumble, and leave him to peruse the sticky menu.

I use the toilet, then stare at my haggard reflection. My authentic self looks like hell. I pull out the small bit of makeup I have in my purse and try to fix things, but the effort looks too obvious. I certainly don't want Marcel thinking I'm trying to look good for him. I wipe it off and go back to the table.

The menu is long, and the descriptions of most of the entrées are similar. I look around at the food on the other tables. It all looks the same too.

Eventually, the waitress comes back and takes our order: moussaka for Marcel, artichoke pie for me. "It'll be awhile," she explains as she scribbles on her pad of paper. "The kitchen is backed up, and Debbie's son has the pukes, so we're short staffed out here."

"No problem," Marcel says, handing her our menus. Once she's gone, he adds, "I hope Debbie's son didn't get the pukes from eating here."

"So how far are we from Miami?"

"About halfway, so thirteen hours."

"Uuggggh." I put my forehead on the table and immediately regret it. Sticky. I actually hear my skin peeling off the surface when I lift it again. "Seriously?"

"Yeah. I think we should take a break and spend the night here."

"I don't think they'll let us sleep in this booth."

"I meant in a hotel with showers and real beds. How much of a hurry are you in to get there? It's not like he's expecting you."

He's right. There's no deadline, no set event I'm trying to make, so why do I feel this unsettling urgency? "I guess we could stay here tonight. If we leave early tomorrow, we could be there by evening, right?"

Marcel shrugs. "Sure. We could leave at seven and be there at nine or ten p.m. with a few stops."

When we're done with our meal, we find a Holiday Inn close to the highway, and Marcel checks us in while I tidy the car. I watch him saunter back, a little-boy grin on his face, and I'm struck again by the transformation. A few weeks ago he was sobbing in a movie theater, and a few weeks before that he was shooting up and checking out.

"I've got good news and bad news," he says.

"Good news first."

"They have a pool."

"Great, I don't have a swimsuit."

"What?" he exclaims, getting back in the car. "Who goes to Florida without a swimsuit? And what did you do with the swimsuit you've been wearing at my pool?"

"It was my roommate's, and I have plenty of swimsuits

waiting for me in Miami. Why are you getting in the car?"

"So we can park on the other side. It's closer to our room."

"*Our* room?"

"That's the bad news. They've only got one left."

I roll my eyes. "Are you kidding me? This is like a bad sitcom. I get the bed."

"Let's wrestle for it."

"I don't think so."

"But it's a king," he argues, pulling into a parking spot on the other side. "Are you seriously going to make me sleep on the floor after an entire night of driving?"

"Whatever," I grumble. "Just stay on your side."

He pulls two key cards out of his pocket. "Kidding. Your room." He holds one out to me. "And my room." He waves the other one.

I grab the card.

"I can't believe you were willing to share a bed with me. There are a bunch of other hotels in town you could have insisted we check out."

"All right, shut up." I get out of the car, grab my mandolin and bag of clothes, and head toward the nearest entrance.

"We can still snuggle if you really want," he calls after me. "I'm just next door."

The room is small but appears clean, and the bed feels gloriously soft after the car seat and my cot back in Montreal. I toss the mandolin and my bag on the chair, strip off my grimy clothes, and step into the shower. It's freezing at first. Then scalding. I can't seem to find an in-between, so I stick with scalding and let it burn the dirt and sweat and garlic stench off me.

By this time tomorrow I'll be with Emilio.

I step out of the shower scrubbed new, and wrap myself in the terry-cloth robe. It's a little stiff, but I can almost imagine I'm at a spa and not a Holiday Inn. I wander out into the tiny room and stretch out on the full-size bed, then marvel at how beautiful it feels to be able to lie like this, none of my limbs touching each other. My cot was barely big enough to roll over in.

The remote beckons from the bedside table, so I pick it up and turn on the TV. Finger-combing the tangles out of my hair with one hand, I flip through channels, trying to find something interesting. Anything interesting. I flip past shows I haven't seen in months, shows I used to care about, stopping for a minute or two at the most. They seem so inconsequential. Stupid, even.

I take the mandolin out of the case and pluck at the strings, while watching a paunchy celebrity chef make Italian meatballs. Italy. That's a thought. Those islands—Sardinia, Sicily, and the other one I can never remember—are supposed to be beautiful, but I wonder if they're remote enough. I wonder if Emilio has ever been there.

The knock at the door startles me, even though it could only be one person. "Yeah?" I yell without getting up.

"Come swimming with me," Marcel calls.

I grumble, turn the TV off, and drag myself off the bed and

to the door. Marcel is on the other side, already in his swimming trunks.

"I already told you I don't have a suit," I say.

"There's a Walmart right around the corner. Should we go get you one?"

"I just showered. And I don't feel like swimming."

"Of course you feel like swimming. Can I come in?"

"Fine." I take a step back. He's right. A swim would be perfect right now, but I need to be alone for a few hours. I need to be able to worry about Emilio without Marcel reading my face.

"Nice outfit," he says, flopping down on the bed.

"There's one in your room too, I'm sure."

"Yeah, well, I'd go change into it, but I don't think lover boy Emilio would want me lounging around your room in a bathrobe."

I ignore him.

"Although, you're both keeping plenty of secrets from each other already—what's one more to add to the pile? Let me guess, he's the jealous type."

I close my eyes and rub my temples.

"That means yes. Ironic considering he's the one who—"

"Marcel."

"What?"

"Enough."

"Fine. So you think he'd be all right with us hanging out in our matching bathrobes? You know, I may not be the greatest boyfriend, but I'm very good at taking care of other people's girlfriends. Gifted, really."

"Marcel," I repeat louder.

"Valentina."

"Back. Off."

Silence settles around us, heavy and uneasy, full with a new understanding. Friendly teasing is over. Friendly everything is over.

I close my eyes, because I can't look at him while I say what needs to be said. "I'm in love with Emilio, and you need to . . ." *Stop flirting with me. Stop looking at me like that.* "After tomorrow I'm not going to, you know   we're not going to see each other."

He laughs. But it doesn't sound like the Marcel I've become used to. "Oh, don't worry about me, princess."

I open my eyes.

He's not lying on my bed anymore. He's sitting up, arms crossed, face set and unreadable. "I'll be fine. And you're welcome for the lift."

"No, it's—" I stammer. "It's not that I don't appreciate everything you're doing for me. I do. But I feel like you're doing it for the wrong reason, and that—"

He cuts me off with another laugh, even louder, even harsher. "And that I'll be left heartbroken? No offense, but Emilio's sloppy seconds aren't exactly my thing." He stands. "I'm going swimming."

He's gone before I can think of anything to say. The door slams with a finality that vibrates in my bones. The end.

I don't move. I stare at the faded brown curtains and convince myself that this sloshy sick feeling in my stomach will go away. It's there because hurting a friend sucks, and Marcel has been my friend.

I move to the bed, curling into a miserable ball of damp terry cloth and overstuffed pillows and regret. I turn the TV back on in hopes that something banal will swallow me up, but it's all flat images telling flat stories that I don't care about. I turn it off and watch the phantom images fade from the screen where the picture used to be.

This has to be fixed. I can fix this.

I get up, rifle through my bag to find the shorts and tank top I brought to sleep in. Not exactly swim attire, but it's unlikely the Holiday Inn police are going to yank me for it, so I throw them on and grab my room key on the way out.

According to the sign inside the elevator, the pool is on the second floor. The elevator spits me out in front of the changing rooms, which I bypass, following the arrow and the humidity and the smell of chlorine to a glass door entrance at the end of the hall.

Luckily, I hear it first. Giggling. Female giggling.

I stop just shy of the doors and take a single step backward. I'm out of view behind the safety of a dusty plastic fern, but I crouch anyway to peer through the edges of the fogged-up glass. He's there. In the hot tub. And his arm is draped around the bony shoulders of a blonde in a gunmetal bikini. She's got huge, laughing, fuchsia lips spread wide enough to fit my fist through.

Grinning, he leans in and whispers something into her ear. She giggles again, louder even, tipping her head back. Mascara smudges are melting down her cheeks, and she's glistening like roasting meat.

Well then.

I take a few more steps backward before I turn and walk quickly back to the elevator. I punch the button again and again and again, willing the elevator to come quicker. Not that there's any chance he saw me, or that he's anywhere close to getting out, judging from the way he was looking at her when he leaned in to whisper.

I don't know why I'm surprised.

The elevator opens and I get in, but it isn't until the doors thud soundly shut in front of me that I realize my heart is racing. I'm more than surprised. I'm angry. No, not angry. Disappointed. But why would cleaning up his act include abandoning his man-slut tendencies? Emilio warned me about him.

I jab the four over and over, like that'll make the elevator move faster. How long has he even been down there—thirty minutes? And he's already just one giggle away from second base with a complete stranger in a hotel pool? Nice work, Marcel.

It wasn't the girl, though. It was the look on his face more than the giggling or anything else. That look. Eyes half-closed. Old Marcel.

And I was worried he was falling for me—I would laugh at myself, but I'm too drained. If old Marcel is back, a little dirty-blond hot tub action is probably the least depressing part of it, and I don't even want to think about what that means. Marcel isn't my responsibility anymore. Actually, he never was.

Once I'm back in my room, I brush my teeth and my hair without looking at myself, turn off the lights, and slide beneath the taut, scratchy sheets. It's only nine thirty, but I don't want to think. I want to be asleep already. But with my eyes closed, lying perfectly still, I see her in that gunmetal bikini, just skimpy triangles tethered with string. And her lips. The giggling. And his lips barely an inch from her collarbone.

These sheets are straitjacket tight. I yank them free on one side but still feel strapped to the bed. I pull out the other side too and throw my head back down into the pillow. It sinks too far. I'm suffocating, and all I can think about is that blond hair falling over Marcel's wet bicep. Her head tipped back, her throat pushed out. So much sweat. His chest too, slick with it.

Stop it, Valentina!

By tomorrow night I'll be wrapped in Emilio's loose, soft sheets and warm brown arms, and none of this will matter. It doesn't matter. It never mattered.

I repeat that over and over. And eventually, I fall asleep in a tangle of itchy sheets.

The giggling finds me in my dreams, melodic and seductive. It's me. I'm laughing. My lips are fuchsia and open, but then I close my mouth and the sound keeps coming. That's when I remember I'm sleeping, but the giggling isn't coming from inside my dream. It's coming from the other side of the wall.

I open my eyes. The clock says 2:37. And there it is again, muffled but unmistakably her.

Unbelievable.

I have to make it stop. In the dark, I fumble for the remote on the bedside table. It's not there. More giggling. Anger burns away my grogginess, and I'm instantly alert, twisting the knob on the bedside lamp and tossing the extra pillows around until I find the remote wedged between the headboard and the mattress. More giggling. I press power, flip to VH1, and plant my thumb on the volume button until it's blaring loudly enough to cover everything else I don't want to hear.

I don't fall back asleep.

TWENTY-SEVEN

Marcel knocks at exactly five to seven.

"What?" I call through the door without opening it.

"Are you ready to go?"

I am, but I definitely didn't think he would be. I peer through the peephole. He looks showered, dressed, refreshed. Disgusting.

I open the door a crack without removing the chain.

"Did you just wake up?" he asks, ignoring the chain and my glare.

"No."

"So let's go."

"Give me a sec."

I close the door, pick up my bag and mandolin, and give myself a glance in the mirror. I look haggard and cranky, like

I've spent half the night being screamed at by music videos. One more day.

The lobby smells like burned waffle and boiled eggs. Marcel checks out, while I scan the continental breakfast offerings. The muffins look okay, if oddly shiny, so I put one in my bag along with a banana and a carton of chocolate milk.

"Grab me something, will you?" Marcel calls from the front desk. "I'm going to go get the car."

I turn back to the breakfast spread, stewing over the fact that whatever anger he had for me last night is gone, and that all this food looks like it's been waxed and polished. Based on the way he stomped out of my room before he went swimming, I was sure there would be chilliness this morning, but the rest of his night seems to have erased all the earlier unpleasantness with me.

I take a fork, stab a doughnut—the half-mangled one with the least frosting—and scrape it onto a paper plate. I add two sulfur-reeking eggs, which immediately roll around picking up doughnut crumbs and frosting, and a box of grapefruit juice for him to wash it down with. I hope the combination makes him puke.

I wait outside, his plate in one hand, my things in the other. The air is crisp, but the cold doesn't pour into my lungs and burn like I've grown used to it doing. By tonight, I'll be walking around with bare legs, no goose bumps.

Marcel pulls up. I get in the back and hand his plate over the seat to him. "I'm going back to sleep."

"Um, okay."

I don't give him the satisfaction of hearing me acknowledge that I spent the second half of the night wide awake. He has to have heard the TV blaring from my room. He has to know why. Instead, I curl up with the blanket and let the hum and sway of the car lull me to sleep.

We do drive-through for lunch. Taco Bell. His choice, which is my own fault for refusing to offer my opinion when asked. It reeks up the car, but it's better than sitting across from each other and staring into our steaming burritos in silence. I eat in the backseat, not even caring that I have no excuse for still being back here, and he eats without once glancing at me in the rearview mirror.

"Do you need me to drive?" I ask after a particularly disgusting Texaco bathroom in Valdosta, Georgia. It's midafternoon. He has to be tired.

Marcel twists the gas cap on and starts toward the Texaco store. "Nah. You want a magazine or anything? A snack?"

I shrug. He's not mad at me—he's made that more than clear. He just doesn't care about the fact that I'm mad at him, and maybe I shouldn't even be mad at him. He is what he is. It's not his fault I got confused and thought he was any different. "A magazine."

"Which one?"

"I don't care."

I get in the backseat, change my mind, and climb up into the front seat, change it again and am in the process of climbing over into the back again when Marcel returns with *InStyle* and *People*.

"Thanks," I mumble, sliding back down beside him. Whatever.

I read both from cover to cover. It's something to do—read words, turn pages—but none of it means anything anymore. Beauty, fame, fortune, scandal. It seems funny that these worlds used to be interesting, that I would lie on the beach with my sisters, scouring glossy page after glossy page because this season's eye shadow trends mattered and celebrity cellulite battles were entertaining. And now it's nothing. It's sand. Stand up, brush it off. Or wait for it to be rendered pointless by the heaviness of real life, a single wave.

I put the magazines down.

Outside, everything is changing again. Yesterday was nothing but winter under a bruised sky, snow-cloaked farms melting into gray. I'd started to feel like we'd never escape the dying grass and naked trees again, but today the hills have been slowly lightening. It started while I slept this morning, the sun seeping into individual blades of grass one at a time, and now I see green. Actual green. Leaves, grass, trees, bushes.

Marcel leans forward and turns on the radio. The static is so loud after so many hours of silence that I jump. He rotates through the stations, never staying on one for longer than five seconds. It's incredibly unsatisfying, only listening to bits of songs, but he doesn't seem bothered.

"Are you going to pick something?" I ask.

"Maybe."

He cycles through the dial several more times, and out of nowhere, I wonder what he said to the blonde to make her laugh. What was he whispering in her ear when I saw them in the hot tub? And in his room? He turns off the radio, runs his hand through his hair, and yawns.

"Tired?" I ask.

"A little."

"You want me to drive?"

"I'm okay."

I reach around to the cooler, pull out another energy drink, and hand it to him.

"Thanks," he says. "Hopefully you can't overdose on these things."

Overdose. Overdose. Overdose. At least this time he was the one who stumbled into it.

He snorts, finally hearing what he said, then adds in a voice that barely even sounds like him, "I still can't believe it, you know? It's such a . . ."

A shock. A waste. A tragedy. All of them, really, but I don't know which one Marcel will pick.

"It's such a joke. A stupid way to kill yourself. It doesn't even work half the time."

"Oh."

"The Lucien I knew would've put a gun in his mouth. Less

pain, more drama. Then again, the Lucien I knew loved himself way too much to commit suicide."

I know he's right. I've always known it. "Maybe he didn't." I close my eyes, wishing the words could be sucked back in.

"It wasn't an accident. There's only one reason you take dozens of sleeping pills and painkillers and antidepressants, and it's not to get high. Still. I'd never in a million years have thought a fight with my dad, or a stupid art show, or a fight with me . . ."

His voice breaks, but he doesn't cry. I don't look at him. To our right, the sun is just about to touch the earth. The whole sky glows with all that orange energy, and I wish I could stare into it without hurting my eyes. I feel dangerous, like doing something dangerous, or saying something dangerous. "It wasn't you."

"I don't want a pep talk."

I owe him the truth. I owe it to Lucien too, but when I open my mouth the words aren't there, and I realize it's not simply what he deserves and what I owe. I can't do it. "It was me."

"What are you talking about?"

I'm blushing already, embarrassed by the lies I'm about to tell. "He kissed me. He told me he loved me, and I was so—" I stop and shake my head weakly. Maybe I can't tell him the truth, but I won't leave him thinking it was his fault for the rest of his life. "I was so mad and tired and drunk, and I said . . . I said the cruelest things. I felt trapped and used, which isn't an excuse, but I didn't mean for . . . I didn't know. I'm sorry." That choking, thickening-throat feeling surprises me, and the first tear slips out before I even realize it's there. It's strangely satisfying to be crying; it's the truth beneath my lies, because if Emilio killed Lucien, I am sorry. I'm so, so sorry. The guilt squeezing my heart is so tight, I feel like it might stop beating.

"Why didn't you tell me?" Marcel asks slowly, cautiously. I can't tell how angry he is. Not yet.

"I was afraid you'd blame me, but I don't care anymore, because you should blame me. It had nothing to do with you. You know that—you two argued all the time. He was upset because I broke his heart and told him he was a fake and a creep and I insulted his art. . . ."

I don't want to go on. That should be enough. I shouldn't have to dig up all the names I ever wanted to call Lucien. I wipe my cheeks with my palms.

When I finally get the courage to look at Marcel, his face is ice. He hates me. It's for the wrong reason, but it's a relief.

"I'm sorry," I say one last time, but I don't want him to forgive me. It's best if he hates me forever.

"I don't want to take you to him," Marcel says softly.

"What?"

"I can't take you to Emilio."

"So what, you're going to just dump me on the side of the road? I didn't know Lucien would—"

"I don't want to talk about Lucien anymore."

I pause, confused. "But you won't help me get to Emilio because I made Lucien kill himself."

"Nobody made Lucien do anything," he interrupts. "And I'm not a priest. I don't need your confession, especially a fake one you're only giving so I won't feel responsible."

I wipe my cheeks again, but the tears are already gone. My cheeks are hot.

"I don't want to take you to Emilio," he says again, this time more forcefully. He's angry, but not in the way he should be. "He's not someone you should be with."

"Don't," I say, finally understanding. "Not again. You don't know the real Emilio, and I'm tired of hearing what you think you know about him."

"I'm worried about you. You're being naive and stupid, and you don't know what you're doing."

"You don't get to worry about me!" I yell. "Worry about yourself. Worry about diseases you picked up from the skank in your room last night! Worry about your crazy parents and getting your screwed-up life back together, but don't worry about me!"

The sun is gone. It happened so fast, I missed both the moment it kissed the earth and the moment it slipped under.

Marcel doesn't speak again. We spend our last hour together in perfect silence, as the shimmer drains from the sky. The gold becomes purple, the purple becomes black, and the stars should be shining, but the lights of the cities—West Palm Beach, Fort Lauderdale, and finally Miami—steal the glory. Their glitter is all electric. I recognize the rainbow of neon lights on downtown's towers, gaudy and gorgeous and fake. Home. It's a hollow sort of relief.

I shouldn't have said it. I shouldn't have said any of it, but it's too late now, no time to repent or forgive. What's a little more guilt for me to live with in the long run?

I direct Marcel to the ritzy blocks of Brickell, nestled between downtown and the causeway to Key Biscayne. I didn't need to worry about finding Emilio's in the dark. It's all familiar, every corner and turn easily found in my memory.

"Here," I say, pointing to a cream building on our right. It isn't one of the tallest or newest, but it's one of the prettiest, with its rippled Spanish roof and curled iron railings edging the balconies and the walkways. Swollen hibiscus bushes with bloodred blooms line the courtyard.

Marcel turns into the parking lot, and an unforeseen panic slams into me. We're here. I'm not ready. I spent twenty-seven hours in the car anticipating this moment, but then Marcel distracted me and now I don't know what I'm doing.

Should I call Emilio and tell him I'm in the parking lot? Or should I just walk up to his door? I don't know why I'm nervous. It's Emilio.

Marcel puts the car in park. If he asks me if I want him to wait while I call Emilio, I'll say yes. Or if he asks me if I want him to wait while I go see if Emilio's home, I'll say yes to that too.

He doesn't ask either of those things, though. He doesn't say anything.

I reach behind the seat and find my bag and the mandolin. For the first time it seems wrong that this is all I have. There's nothing else in the world that's really mine, and the mandolin isn't really mine.

I open my door and the moist, floral air hits my nose. I'd forgotten the heaviness of night flowers. I can't smell them without thinking of Emilio, and suddenly the anxiety is gone. Childish. "Thank you," I say.

Marcel nods and stares out at the tangled vines, letting his gaze crawl up the building with them.

"No, really," I try again. "Thank you. And I'm sorry."

"Me too."

I'm not really sure which of his sins he's apologizing for, and he doesn't know half of what I'm sorry about, but the exchange is genuine. And as far as endings go, we could certainly do worse.

I slide out of the car and slam the door before he can ruin it by saying anything else. My legs feel thick and slow after so many hours of sitting, and I wobble a little as I enter the lamp-lit courtyard. I look up. Second floor, south corner. His light is on. Every part of me wants to run to the vine-wrapped spiral staircase, but Marcel is watching, so I walk. At least I think he's watching, but when I turn to give him a wave good-bye from the base of the staircase, he's already gone.

TWENTY-EIGHT

have no plan. It's hard to believe that now, standing on Emilio's doorstep, knuckles still sore from knocking for the second time, waiting for him to answer. But what was there to plan? He'll see me, I'll tell him I had to come, that we can do this better together, and he'll understand.

I look again to the windowpane. Blinds block my view of inside, but a yellow sliver of light spills onto the cement beside me. And is that sound his TV or his neighbor's? I rub my knuckles and lift my hand to knock again, but before I can, the door flies open. A wild-eyed Emilio stands in front of me. Suit pants, undershirt, wet hair, the smell of aftershave. I take in the details but no air. My mouth is dry. I force my lips open before I even decide what I'm about to say. "I had to come—"

His grip on my arm stops me, the force of his yank shocking me out of my fairy tale. I stumble forward, or he pulls me in, his fingers still squeezing my arm even after I'm inside and the door is closed.

"How long were you out there?" he demands.

I let out a whimper. "You're hurting me."

Instead of relaxing his grip, he pulls me closer. I'm inches from his face, breathing in his aftershave. "Did anyone see you?"

"I—I don't know. I was only out there for a few seconds. Maybe a minute at the most." I gulp for breath, for control, for understanding of this too-raw hostility. "Emilio. You're hurting me."

He loosens his grip and turns away from me to lock the door. "How did you get here?"

"Marcel."

He spins back around. "Are you trying to get me killed? You realize this means your father knows, right?"

"Marcel doesn't work for my father!"

"You don't know anything."

"He snuck me across the border in the back of his car and drove me all the way here."

He shakes his head, incredulous. "And you think he did that out of the goodness of his heart? Why would you trust Marcel?"

The answer. I can't find the words for it, and maybe the sight of Emilio half-dressed and the smell of his wet hair are twirling my thoughts around and rendering me senseless, or maybe there isn't a single, logical reason for me to give. I don't know why I trust Marcel, but I do. Or I did. "I thought you'd be happy to see me."

"Happy to see you?" He runs a hand through his wet hair and closes his eyes like he's in pain. "Valentina . . ." He doesn't finish. He turns away from me and walks into the bedroom, slamming the door behind him.

The room glows like a stage, the lights a little too bright, the shadows nonexistent. I take a few shaky steps forward. I'm not going to cry. I drop my bag and the mandolin beside the glass coffee table and slide onto the corner of his couch. My fingers curl into my palms. If I could, I'd curl my whole body up and disappear. Instead I slump back into the soft leather and look around me.

The apartment is small but clean—cleaner than I'd remembered. It feels impersonal, the sharp angles and black leather and glass tables, and not just in a bachelor pad way. It feels like an office, but even offices have cheap prints on the walls. I glance around. A clock. A mirror. A TV.

No art.

Why hadn't I noticed that the last time I was here? I know the answer—because *he* was with me. When Emilio is in the room, any room, there are things that I don't notice. Sometimes they're important.

I can hear him banging around in there, but I'm too tired and hungry to do anything but sit. All that time I spent waiting for him, freezing to death, living off Jacques's chocolate and Nanette's charity, all the nights I spent convincing myself he would be with me if he could, and now that I'm here he's too angry to be in the same room with me, to even talk to me. It doesn't seem like this could be happening.

When Emilio's door opens behind me, I fight the urge to jump up and turn to him. The sounds tell me what he's doing—picking things up, putting things down, opening a cupboard, pouring a drink. Finally he comes around to the chair across from me. He leans forward and puts a drink on the table for me, taking a sip from the one in his hand.

"I don't know what to say," he starts. He's not looking at me. And aside from dragging me in by my arm, he hasn't even touched me. The light-blue dress shirt he's put on makes his tan skin glow, and he's gelled back his hair. I don't like it when his curls are hidden.

"You're going out," I say.

"I have to meet some people for drinks. Business, of course. Then I'm going to your father's."

"What people?"

He clinks the ice cubes in his glass. "You shouldn't have come."

I stare at my own drink on the table—Coke, from the looks of it. I'm thirsty, but I don't pick it up. I could cry. I feel the tears waiting to pool and spill, but I don't let them get close enough to need to blink. Stupidly, I say it again. "I thought you'd be happy to see me."

"I'm sorry. I am, but it's just not safe for you to be here and now—"

"But nobody knows I'm here," I interrupt.

"You don't know that." He stares over my shoulder to the

window. The blinds block everything, but his mind is out in the courtyard shadows. "Why couldn't you just wait for me like we talked about? You have no idea what you're getting in the middle of."

"Then tell me!"

His face doesn't change, and I understand that he's never going to tell me. I might as well be talking to myself. He takes one more sip and glances at his watch. It's titanium, smooth, exquisite, expensive. I've never seen it before.

"You have to trust me," he says. "We can talk when I get back, but promise me you won't go anywhere."

I can't stop staring at his watch. "I have no car," I mutter. It's not as gaudy as the ones my father usually wears, but I can tell it's a ten-thousand-dollar piece. At least.

"And don't call anyone—not your sisters, not Marcel, not your father, not anybody."

"You think you have to tell me that?" I ask, breaking away from the polished glare on his wrist. He's looking at me. Finally, he's looking at me, and for a second I see it in his eyes—the fear that explains his anger—and I want to forgive him. "I'm here for you," I say. "I can help you get the money so we can get away from him forever. Or is that not still the plan?"

He stands, leaving his drink on the table. "I can't talk about this now."

I stand too. I don't know why. I feel too dejected to walk him to his own door, but my feet move me along behind him anyway. If it's not still the plan, what am I doing here?

He takes his suit jacket from the back of a chair and slides his arms into the sleeves. Without thinking I step toward him to help him, easing the jacket over his shoulders, pulling the lapels forward, adjusting his shirt collar. I let my fingers rest on the warm skin at his neck.

He doesn't respond, and I realize it was a mistake. Touching him. Coming back. Believing the things he told me in Montreal. All of it. There are so many mistakes, I can't see where they started, where I need to go back to.

I take my hand away, but he catches my wrist and brings it back to his neck, pulling me in with his other hand, and his lips find mine before I realize what's happening.

One hungry kiss. One million stars. We're back on the yacht, stealing time, and everything else is inconsequential. I'm spinning, or he's turning me around, pushing me against the door, but I'm still lucid enough to know that the pressure of his mouth and the pain of his words can't both be true. So I choose this. His hands in my hair, his lips whispering my name between kisses—this is the Emilio I believe. I had fears, I think. It's not that they weren't legitimate, but I just can't quite remember them when his mouth finds my neck and his hands drop to my hips.

But then he pulls away without warning. "I'm sorry," he says into my hair.

I can't think to speak. He's sorry. For kissing me? Or for everything else?

"After tomorrow, we'll be able to leave. And when this is all over and we're far away from here, promise me you'll still love me."

I nod, numbly.

"Say it."

"I'll always love you."

"I have to go. Wait up for me?"

I nod again.

He pulls me away from the door, and leaves without another word.

My daze doesn't lift. I drift from room to room, and eventually the walls stop spinning, my heart slows, and the tiny apartment becomes artless and impersonal again. He's gone. But he's coming back.

I wander through the bedroom, the office, the kitchen, then find my way back to his bedroom. It smells like him. His sheets probably feel like him. I peel off my cold-weather layers—boots, sweater, leggings—pounds lighter as I drop each on the floor. They're so ugly and worn and full of lonely memories. I'm never wearing them again.

I find a soft brushed-cotton T-shirt in Emilio's dresser, slip it on, and fall into his bed. He said to wait up, but he'll be gone for hours, and I've been up for so long I can't remember when this day began. Or can I? That laugh. The hotel. Marcel. I close my eyes and hear the wail of a siren, wiping away the memory. I'm never going to think about that again.

* * *

When I open my eyes, I'm lost. If I dreamed, I don't remember it, and the blissful haze of before is gone. My skin is prickled with a chill. Except it's warm. I fell asleep with the lights on, but it still takes a few moments to place that sleek, curving lamp, the clock with all the numbers 12:53 lit up properly, the faintest smell of hibiscus. All that before I remember.

I sit up. "Emilio?"

No answer. I swing my legs out of bed. Maybe the gnawing dread is just hunger. I make my way to the kitchen, but Emilio has the disappointing fridge of a man who eats out. A lot. A block of cheddar and a stale bagel seem like my best bet, so I take both, along with a knife from one of the drawers, and head for the living room couch. I don't turn on the TV. I sit slicing rectangles of crumbling cheese, listening to the muted chirp of a million tropical insects.

It's all wrong. No more hoping and ignoring. I have to think everything through and force the strangest of these details to make sense. For starters, Emilio is not trying to get the money together to rescue his family. I was willing to believe that lie for as long as he told it, but he didn't even say it tonight. I said it. He said I had to trust him.

So he's changed his mind? So he loves me, but not enough to put everyone else he loves in danger? But then why not just tell me? And why would he kiss me like that, beg me to trust him, act like we're still going to escape together? If he's come up with another way, why wouldn't he tell me?

The answer collides like a fist in my gut. Something clatters.

It's my knife hitting the floor, but I've already forgotten the sound because my heart is louder than a blade bouncing on tile, and I'm standing, running toward the door, stopping, turning around, grabbing my bag of clothes and shaking it out onto the couch. My phone. I pick it up, but my hands are shaking, and it takes me several tries to dial Emilio's number. It rings. It rings nine times, but I keep waiting, shaking, squeezing it to my ear, knowing he won't pick up. He probably doesn't even have that phone on him. It's probably somewhere in this apartment, turned off. Useless.

Like me.

Emilio is going to kill Papi.

TWENTY-NINE

The phone becomes heavier and heavier in my hand. I stare at the buttons. Too many choices. I could call my sisters, but that wouldn't do any good. They don't know anything. They don't even know who Papi really is, and even if I could explain it all to them and actually make them understand, what could they do about it? Obviously I can't call the police. And I know a thousand people in this city, but I can't trust a single one of them.

I have to call Papi.

I watch my thumb key in the number, but it hovers over the call button. I can't do it. I squeeze my eyes shut and see Emilio's face, and feel his hands, and hear his laugh. If I call Papi, Papi will kill Emilio.

I clear the number and put the phone down. There has to be another way. If I knew where Emilio went, I could go find him and convince him not to do it, but he could be anywhere. Or he could already be at my house. *My house.* Should I go home? I have to go home. But I have no car and no cash.

I replay the moment of him leaving, his lips in my hair, whispering, pleading with me to love him after tomorrow. *After tomorrow.* Does that mean I have time to figure out how to stop this, or is he going back to my house tonight to do it?

Is he there right now?

The panic surges again, and I'm all unfocused energy. It feels like I'm watching someone else, but I'm not. It's me rummaging wildly through Emilio's things, emptying out his desk drawer, scattering the contents of the bedside table across the bed. He must have cash somewhere. I don't need much—cab fare to the south end of Key Biscayne won't be more than twenty-five dollars—but all I can find is loose change. Two quarters in the couch. A handful of nickels and pennies under receipts by the phone. Another quarter in his desk.

The drawer in the kitchen yields nothing but typical junk drawer odds and ends, and I'm about to move on when I see the key ring. It's small and plain, just a thin metal hoop with a single key, stuck to the inside of a roll of packing tape. I only stop because it looks familiar. But whatever memory it's attached to doesn't surface as I peel off the layer of tape holding it against the cardboard. I only know I've seen it before. It's the right size for a bike lock or maybe a drawer.

Or a cash box. Like lightning, the key connects to a memory. Last year. Swim team car wash. I complained the event was completely pointless, so Coach put me in charge of the money as punishment. I was right. Nobody at my school needed to raise funds for anything, and the event turned into a public water fight/wet T-shirt contest.

I flip the key over, examining the blunt grooves. It's hardly high tech, but maybe that's the point. It's unexpected. And maybe somewhere, Emilio has an old-school cash box.

My search for anything resembling a cash box yields nothing. I've already ransacked the place looking for change, but this time I look for locked drawers. Even though the key looks too small to fit into a safe—or at least into any of my father's safes—I lift the mirrors and look behind furniture. Nothing.

I shouldn't be surprised. Emilio obviously thinks my father is watching him, probably believes he has someone search the apartment from time to time. If he's hiding anything, it won't be easy to find.

The adrenaline of panic is starting to wane. Despondency settles in. I have no money to get home and no plan to stop Emilio once I'm there—or at least not one that won't end with him getting killed. My only hope is that I have until tomorrow to change his mind. Again and again, I replay his words, but I know my memory is muddling up what I did hear with what I wish I heard. *By* tomorrow? *After* tomorrow?

I don't know.

I tape the key back where it was before and start putting things away. Weighted and sluggish, like I'm underwater, I gather handfuls of pens, rubber bands, paper clips, and drop them back into the drawers. My halfhearted attempt to organize them only lasts for a few minutes, because I can't remember how anything looked before. And what does it matter now?

I finish with his office and move to the bedroom. According to the clock, it's three thirty. If Emilio walks in now, I'll have to explain the mess, but dreaming up a story that makes sense of this wild rampage seems impossible.

I replace the contents of his bedside table, pausing at the unframed photograph I'd thrown on the ground without even looking at it. I examine it now. It's him beside an older woman who could only be his mother, and three teenage girls. His sisters. They remind me of my sisters, the way their arms are hooked around one another's waists. That's how Lola holds on to us when someone points a camera in our direction, like she can cement us together with her skinny arms and a flash.

Emilio's sisters are beautiful. I'm not sure why I never tried to imagine them before.

I slip the photo back into the drawer, but those hopeful smiles and hooked arms are burned into my mind forever. I wish I hadn't seen them. They weight one side of the equation, and choosing between Emilio and Papi is already wrenching enough. All those lives combined, though—are they more important than Papi's? And those girls are innocent. Papi is not.

I close the drawer, refusing to believe what I might have been considering for one second, and move on to the bathroom. I only glanced under the sink before, but that was when I was looking for change. Toilet paper, a leather toiletries bag, cleaning supplies. I reach for the toiletries bag, suddenly needing to smell his aftershave, like that will make my decision any easier. It's unexpectedly heavy. I place it on the countertop and unzip the black leather bag slowly. No aftershave. No cologne. Just a small silver box with a tiny slot for a key. Trembling, I hurry back to the kitchen, dig the packing tape out of the drawer, find the key, and take it back to the bathroom.

I know it'll fit, even before the key slides easily into the hole. I turn the key, lift the lid, and there lies a tidy stack of bills. Hundreds. The pile looks thin, but when I thumb through the crisp bills to count them, there are forty. Four thousand dollars. I smile. I was wrong—Emilio is squirreling away cash. It's taken so long because he has to be careful about it, and maybe the watch was a gift from my father that he has to keep wearing. That makes sense. I put the money back, relieved and giddy and nearly laughing out loud at myself. There's no reason I should believe Emilio would hurt Papi. He must know it would change everything between us if he did.

I pick the bills up and count them again. Still forty. I wonder if this is all. Maybe he's already taken care of his family and this is just for us. Or maybe he's stashing it in more than one place. It doesn't matter, though, because he said that after tomorrow we'll be set, so whatever he has planned must be yielding enough cash to take care of everything.

I put the stack of bills back again, noticing this time how shallow the tray is. The box isn't tall, but the tray only goes down about halfway to the bottom. I grasp the edges and pull up. It doesn't take much force. The tray pops and I pull it out.

Staring up at me from the bottom of the tray are two passports, and something else. A wallet?

I flip through the well-worn pages of the first passport, the Colombian one, stopping to inspect the photo page. It's a good picture. *Emilio Samuel Diaz.*

I pick up the second. American. The pages are stiffer, waxier, and it doesn't open naturally to the photo page. Same good picture. *Carlos Ernesto Garcia.* My eyes dart back and forth: photo to name, name to photo. That picture is better than good. It's perfect.

So Emilio has a fake American passport.

All the questions swarm at once. Did Papi get this for him? He must have. Or does Emilio use it when he doesn't want Papi to know where he is? That makes sense if Marcel was right about Papi having someone in customs on his payroll. Maybe Emilio got this passport just so we can disappear together, but if that's true, don't I need one too?

I reach for the final item, rubbing the black leather with my thumb. It looks like a wallet, but it's too heavy. I open it.

On one side is a badge, a gold crest, an eagle hovering on top, wings spread above the script: *Federal Bureau of Investigation.* I bring it closer to my face, unnecessarily because it's perfectly clear. FBI.

The opposite side shows a different picture of Emilio, this one unsmiling and with the other name below. *Carlos Ernesto Garcia.* I read it over and over this time, letting my tongue curl over the *r*'s without making a sound. I stare at the signature below it.

"I wish you hadn't found that."

I twist around to see Emilio's eyes burning through me. He's standing with both hands raised over his head, gripping the door frame. It's a pose of frustration but not submission.

"What is this?" I whisper.

He drops his hands but doesn't move toward me. "This makes everything much more difficult than it has to be."

"What is this?" I repeat, louder.

"You shouldn't have come back to Miami."

"*Tell me what this is!*" I shout, shaking it between us.

He reaches for the badge, but I rip my hand away, and he grabs a handful of the air between us. "Calm down."

"Why should I calm down? Explain this to me! What is this?"

He folds his arms, content to let me hold it. "My credentials."

"Your credentials."

"Yes."

"*Your* credentials."

He doesn't correct me.

"Carlos Ernesto Garcia." The syllables tumble out, nearly nonsense, so I say it again. "Carlos Ernesto Garcia. You are an FBI agent."

He nods.

I take a shaky breath. "Then who is Emilio?"

"Come sit down."

"I don't want to sit down!" I scream, and he closes his eyes like my tantrum is exhausting him.

"At the very least, stop yelling, then. I've got neighbors."

Without thinking, I hurl the badge at him, but it misses, slapping the wall and dropping to the tile floor. Neither of us reaches for it.

"I asked who Emilio is," I say. "Answer me."

"Emilio Diaz is an employee of Victor Cruz."

"But not a real person," I say.

He turns around and leaves the bathroom.

"But not a real person," I call after him. He doesn't answer, so I march past him, heading straight for the bedside table. I grab the picture. "And your mother? Your sisters? Not real people either?"

He sits on the edge of the bed, still not meeting my eyes. "You're angry. That's perfectly understandable. But now that you know who your father really is, it should make sense."

"I only know because of you, and apparently everything you've told me is a lie."

"Not everything." He finally looks at me and reaches out, slipping his hand around my waist.

I step back and his hand falls away. "Don't! You lied about everything!"

"I didn't lie about your father."

"I don't want to hear about my father anymore! Not from you!"

"You wish I hadn't told you? You'd rather not know?"

I don't answer. I don't know. No.

I put my hand up against the wall. I feel drained of blood, but I won't sit down. "You killed a man. I saw you kill a man."

"That man was going to die anyway. I wasn't going to blow my cover over something that inevitable. The United States government has spent over a decade trying to bring down the Cruz cartel."

"But you shot him!"

"Right," he says calmly. "That's something I'm authorized to do as an FBI agent working undercover as an enforcer in a drug organization."

"*Authorized* to do?"

"It's not something I enjoy," he says. "But it's not just Victor we're bringing down. It's the whole cartel."

The room is spinning.

"Sit down, Valentina," he begs, and his voice is gentle in that way that used to be so distracting.

I don't move. It's not that distracting anymore. "You're telling me the FBI kills innocent people."

"That man wasn't innocent. He'd spent his entire life distributing drugs, dragging children into the drug trade, selling coke to dealers who sold it on the streets. Trust me. He had plenty of blood on his hands."

Blood on his hands. Now I do need to sit, but not beside Emilio. Blood is on everyone's hands. My father's. Emilio's. Maybe mine too. "What about Lucien?"

"What about him?"

"You killed him too, didn't you?"

"Lucien killed himself."

I shake my head. "Stop lying to me! I know he didn't kill himself!"

"Does it matter?"

"What kind of question is that? You can't possibly be allowed to kill just anyone who gets in your way." I stop to swallow. I'm picturing Lucien's purple lips, the foam dribbling down his naked chest. I'm out of breath. "And he wasn't even in your way."

Emilio shakes his head. "He would've told your father that he saw us together—"

"No! I'm so sick of that lie. He didn't see us together."

"Not at the gallery. After."

After. My mind flies back to the last time I saw Lucien alive. I touch my lips, remembering that cold, sad kiss. "He drove off before I even saw you."

"I thought so too, but when we left the café, I noticed him on foot."

"He followed us to Soupe au Chocolat?"

"I think he was probably following you everywhere. He was more than a little obsessed."

My skin prickles, remembering the chill of Montreal and thinking of being watched and tracked like prey.

"Lucien is incidental," Emilio says.

"To you, maybe."

Emilio smirks. "Are you saying you cared about Lucien?"

"No, but his brother did. He had a life, you know. He wasn't just something *incidental* for you to crush."

"Stop blaming me. Lucien decided to throw away his life when he got caught up with Victor. Nobody made him do that."

I have no recourse. He's right, but his callousness is so disturbing I want to grab his face and shake him. "How did you do it?"

"Insulin," he says softly, but still without emotion. "He made it easy for me, already being half-drunk when I got there and having all those pill bottles around to empty out. Nobody looks for a tiny injection mark when it's clearly an overdose."

My stomach flips, and I sink to the floor, my hand trailing down the wall as I drop, drop, drop, until I'm in a heap. I see Lucien's bloated body, then Marcel's tearstained face, over and over, the two on a never-ending loop.

"There are things I wish I didn't have to do," he says.

I look up. "Like me."

He's staring at me. I pull my legs to my chest and his T-shirt over my knees. I hold his stare, daring him to say it, deny it, explain it. He doesn't.

"So I'm a work assignment," I spit. "I can't imagine the U.S. government pays you to screw minors."

"Come here," he says gently, reaching his hand out to me again.

I stare at it, at the lines on his palms where I used to slide my fingers, pretending I could read his fortune. "No. Just say it."

He drops his empty hand. "That I used you? Fine. Being with you gave me access to information I wouldn't have been able to get any other way. I'm sorry. It wasn't ideal."

I turn and look back into the bathroom so he can't see my face. My fingers curl into fists around the hem of the T-shirt, digging into the cotton. *It wasn't ideal.* Something feral and impulsive bubbles inside of me, and I picture myself lunging at him, clawing tracks down his beautiful face with my nails. I wonder if he'd think that *wasn't ideal* as well.

"That doesn't mean I don't have feelings for you," he says, but I'm afraid to keep listening. I can't stomach a declaration of love right now. He adds, "I didn't expect to fall in love with you."

"Don't," I say. I need him to stop talking so my heart can break in silence.

Emilio looks down, shamed but not really shamed. Not repentant. "I wasn't exaggerating when I said we've been trying to nail him for over a decade. At this point, my bosses aren't asking questions about things they don't want answers to. They know sometimes things get complicated. Entanglements are necessary."

It seems impossible that what he's saying is true, but what do I know about what FBI agents are allowed and not allowed to do? "How old are you really?" I ask.

"Twenty-four."

I snort. "You know, my sisters are legal and prettier than me too. I'm sure you could've had either of them."

"They aren't prettier than you."

I twist my grip on the hem of the T-shirt, hoping I dig holes into it.

"And they're idiots," he adds. "They don't go places with your father. He doesn't tell them things. You were the one with the most potential."

"Potential? I was clueless! I didn't even know what my father really did!" I laugh in spite of the tightness in my chest that's making it hard to breathe.

"I was wrong," he admits. "But by the time I figured that out, you were providing valuable access to everything happening in Key West, while Victor had me going back and forth between Miami and Bogotá. Once he found out about us, I didn't need a good excuse to be in Key West. He just assumed I was trying to wiggle my way down there to be with you."

"Wait, you *knew* that he knew about us?"

Emilio shrugs. It stings, another lie, another slap on my cheek. Making me fall in love with him, lying to me, breaking my heart—he answers to it all so easily with a shrug.

"You told him," I say.

"Not exactly, but it wasn't hard to give him just enough of a clue. It was a gamble. He could've flipped out. And it worried me that he never let on that he knew, but then it all made sense when he threw us together in Montreal, and I realized he was testing my loyalty."

Those words dig through me like claws. So this is betrayal. I thought I'd understood it when I found out who Papi really was, but this is so much bloodier and irreparable. My whole body feels like torn flesh.

I stare at the familiar angles of Emilio's face and remember looking up at him on the yacht's upper deck. I was blinded by moon glow on cheekbones, and folk music, and the smell of the sea. He was too beautiful to doubt, or I was too stupid to see.

Not anymore.

"So you never planned on running away with me. You were never coming back for me. The money to steal, the family to protect—those were all lies."

"They were necessary for my cover."

"*We* were a lie," I press on, leaning toward him. "Say it."

"I'm sorry."

"You're not sorry if you'd do it all over again."

He doesn't deny it. "There's something you need to see. Stay here." He stands and walks off, leaving me alone.

My eyes settle on his badge while I listen to him rustling around in his office. It's lying open on the floor between me and the bed, the gold eagle shiny and frozen. It's so patronizingly noble I want to grab it and hurl it at his head again when he walks back in. I don't get the chance, though. He comes back holding a laptop, sees me staring at the badge, and scoops it up.

"I hate you," I say. I don't know if I mean it, but it feels good to say.

"Fine. If you want to hate me, go ahead, but there are a few things you have to see first." He sits on the edge of the bed and opens the laptop. "Sit."

I don't want to sit beside him. Cooperation feels like submission, and I'd rather chew broken glass than let him think I respect his *authority*. Plus, from this distance it's easier to have him see just my rage. It's louder. It's surface. But if I sit beside him, he'll know I'm being hollowed out by this hurt, and that would only make it more unbearable.

"Valentina, you can't keep choosing to be ignorant. It's time to grow up. Sit."

I sit—beside him but not touching him—hating him, trying not to smell his aftershave.

He angles the laptop in my direction. "They're in reverse chronological order. That took place last week."

I barely hear him. I've muffled his voice, putting it behind the splashes of color on the screen. It's a photograph. There's a lot of blue. The sky is that hopeful shade of morning that appears after the fog has burned away. There's much less green, only a patch on either side of the shot, but it's a vibrant jungle green that brightens the whole picture—fat, shiny leaves under fuchsia blooms. They're potted plants on either side of what looks like a driveway. In the middle of the driveway is a daffodil-colored dress, not too bright or that cold butter-pale, but the perfect in-between.

And everywhere else, there's blood.

"That's Bogotá, in case you're wondering," Emilio says.

I wasn't wondering. I was examining the patterns on the death-smeared pavement. They're not at all like the blood flower. There was a dripping elegance to that, gravity styling the gore into something graceful. This isn't graceful. This looks like someone took a fat brush to her insides and wiped it clumsily around. Footprints here, long dashes there, and I can see from the stains on her upturned bare feet that she was walking in her own blood before she was dragging herself in her own blood before she collapsed in her own blood. The center of that perfect-yellow dress is scarlet and so is one side, though the top is miraculously spotless and her face is clean too. She is small-chested. Pretty. She's wearing white flower earrings and a gold cross around her neck. Her smooth black hair is tied in a white ribbon. She's young. Younger than me.

"Name's Yolanda Rojas. Fifteen years old. Her father, Javier Rojas, was caught stealing from Cruz—skimming profits from the dealers who worked under him—and Yolanda was payback. That's typical Cruz style. He didn't have Javier killed—just blinded. And he may or may not walk again, but as I said, it just happened last week, so he's still in the hospital."

I can't look away.

Emilio clicks to the next shot.

This one is dark, all shadows and mixed shades. It must've been taken at dusk, or maybe right before a storm. There are more people, but it's less personal—five rigid corpses lined up in a row like little dolls, hands tied, feet pointing skyward. Dolls. Broken dolls. They have no heads.

"Decapitation is a relatively new thing for Victor. It freaks people out, though, draws more media attention to the deaths. These five worked for another cartel, so this was most likely retaliation for something or other. That one took place three weeks ago, but he pulled a nearly identical stunt back in September."

I stand up.

"You've only seen two," Emilio says. "I've got nineteen in that file, and that's only a fraction of the murders we can pin to him."

I turn my body away from him so he can't see my face.

"Hard to look at, aren't they? It's easier to sit there and accuse me of being a monster." He grabs my arm—not hard, but his touch startles me—pulls me toward him, and turns me around before I can jerk away. "Decades of *this*. This is why the FBI doesn't care if I have to shoot a scumbag drug shipper. And this is why they'll turn a blind eye when I get involved with a *willing* young woman to get access to information. You're not the victim here. You're the daughter of one of the sickest, most dangerous men in the world, and you can't even stand to look at a couple of pictures of what he's done. Do you want to know exactly what Victor's sick goons did to Yolanda Rojas before they shot her?"

I might vomit. Emilio's face is close to mine, but I refuse to look at him. I stare at the wall, blurry through the tears that are pooling and betraying me. Why am I seeing Papi's face in my mind? There it is. Jovial, like he's just thought of something to say that will make me laugh. I can't scream that it's not true. I see now. Emilio's staring at me, waiting for a response, but I won't give him one.

"I can't believe you're here," he says, dropping my arm. "I can't believe you found my badge. And the timing. You're forcing my hand here."

"What are you talking about?"

He raises an eyebrow. "Don't tell me you've forgotten. This is the first weekend of December."

"The Vizcaya Gala," I mumble.

More castle than mansion, Vizcaya is where Papi chooses to gather his people—art dealers and buyers, celebrity artists, the wealthy of Miami who buy Warhols like they buy Ferraris, the segment of socialites who consider themselves erudite, and of course the pretenders who know nothing but spend enough to make up for it. They all flock to Papi's annual gala for the auctioning off of his latest acquisitions, to bleed money all over one another as publicly as possible.

"I have good memories of Vizcaya last year," Emilio says.

Finally, I look at him. No, I glare. He can't seriously be reminiscing about the first time we met.

It was Papi who introduced us. Emilio was Papi's newest minion, eager just like all the others, but different too. More intense. And he was so beautiful I couldn't not watch him work the crowd, laugh at Papi's jokes, charm the women with the biggest rocks on their fingers like he wasn't afraid of anyone. From the dew-drenched lawn I watched him go with Fernando down to the jetty to smoke. But then Fernando left. He was finally alone, so I took a deep breath and joined him, my heels in one hand, a drink in the other. I remember how the stone was cool and wet, and I could hear the Atlantic licking the pier beneath us. Cigar smoke coiled out of his lips. I asked him if he'd ever swum in the ocean at night. He smiled. He asked me if I knew what a mandolin was.

I hate him.

"What are you planning?" I ask.

"It's what Victor's planning that's more interesting. He's paranoid. Thinks everyone is a spy."

"It's not paranoia if it's true!"

Emilio cracks his knuckles, and I'm struck by his ability to tune out my emotion. Has he always been so good at that? I'm not sure.

"He has the yacht here in Miami to collect a shipment coming in on a cargo boat that's supposed to be carrying plantains. That should be happening in the morning," he says. "In a few hours, actually. And then of course the Vizcaya Gala is going on tomorrow night—like his little party will distract people from the fact that he has fifty-five million in coke sitting in Biscayne Bay."

Fifty-five million dollars. It's so improbable it's almost funny. But Emilio isn't smiling. "What are you planning?" I repeat.

"The drugs are being seized, and Victor's little party is being raided. And I can tell what you're thinking, so no, you're not running off to warn anybody about anything."

"You can't tell me what to do. You don't own me."

"And yet I can't let you wander out of here either."

"You're going to arrest me?" I sneer. "I haven't done anything illegal."

"If I do take you into custody, it'll be for your own protection."

"I bet."

"This investigation is too important. We've finally got everything we need to convict him of the worst of it."

I picture Papi in a prison cell. It's what he deserves and where he belongs, but it's too pitiful. He's still my father.

"But your being here . . ." Emilio's eyes travel over me. "That makes everything more complicated."

"I don't believe you," I say.

"Which part?"

"I don't believe you were allowed to use me."

He laughs, but his face is tight. "At the end of the day, it's not about what you believe."

"That's it, isn't it—why you didn't want me to come back to Miami? Nothing to do with my own safety or screwing up the investigation. I could get you in a lot of trouble."

"No."

"Afraid they'll take away that pretty badge?"

He closes the laptop, like that'll shut me down too.

"So now what?" I push on recklessly. "You can't just kill me like you killed Lucien."

He stands and walks out of the room, leaving me on the bed. My words continue to ricochet around the room while my thoughts argue with one another: If he made Lucien's death look like an overdose, why couldn't he do the same to me?

Except Emilio would never hurt me. But this man is not Emilio. There is no Emilio.

I look frantically around me for something . . . something I don't know what. Heavy or sharp. There's nothing.

I hear the drawer in his office opening and closing.

A sharp-cornered frame gleams from the bedside table. Tempting, but too small. I grab the lamp by the neck. It's heavy enough, but it's not like I can hide it behind my back.

Footsteps. He's coming.

I rip the cord from the wall, grab the lamp with both hands, and slip into the space between the open door and the wall. Trembling, I move my hands up the neck of the lamp to where I can grip it best, swing it behind my head, and wait. He isn't hurrying. The footsteps down the hall are deliberate, each one followed by the softest *clink*. What is that clink? His watch?

My arms tingle. My heart pounds. Sweat pours down my neck, and I pray it doesn't make me lose my grip on the lamp.

"Valentina?" His shirt passes by me on the other side of the hinge, inches from my nose. He stops where I can't see him on the other side of the door. My heart. He must hear it.

He takes another couple of steps forward, and I see all of him, or the back of him, with the source of the *clink* in plain view. Handcuffs. They dangle from his right hand. No time. I nudge the door with my hip so I have enough room to swing. But the hinge creaks. *Now.* He's turning. *Now. Now. Now.* Every muscle in my body contracts as I bring the lamp over my head and down, and his face turns just in time for me to see the shock in his eyes as the lamp explodes against his forehead. The sound of a million chimes shatters over us. He staggers backward, crunching over porcelain, a web of blood stretching over his face, skinny scarlet lines pouring down.

I run. Barefoot, I run over cold shards and hot blood, from the room and down the hall. I hear him cursing and stumbling behind me, but I don't turn to see how close he is or how badly he's hurt.

By the time I reach the front door I can't hear him chasing me anymore, but I don't stop. Not for shoes or pants or phone or breath. I glance over my shoulder, but I don't stop even when I hear him scream, "*Valentina!*" from the hallway where he's collapsed. It sounds like the scream of a tortured, desperate, lovesick animal. But he never loved me.

I fling the door open and run.

THIRTY

Hibiscus. Jasmine. Magnolia.

My body is numb. I feel nothing but the pounding in my chest as I tear down the steps and across the courtyard, but somehow I can smell the heady stench of floral rot. The air is sticky sweet and pulsing with it. Too much.

I don't stop to think which way to go once I reach the curb. My legs propel me in one direction and I fly, feeling nothing. Birds squawk and shriek in the low-hanging branches over my head, which means it's nearly morning, but it's still dark. They scream loudest right before the sun rises. That's when paradise sounds like hell.

Slap, slap, slap, slap. I can't feel my feet, but I hear them smack against the pavement. The sidewalk carves a tunnel through the foliage, shadowed from moonlight and street light and the beginnings of a sunrise. I can barely see, but that's safer. The dark can hide me. I know vaguely where I'm heading—away from Brickell and downtown—but destination is irrelevant as long as Emilio's not behind me. I check over my shoulder without slowing my pace and see nothing. Still, he could be driving around looking for me, or maybe he's called someone else to come get me. The FBI. The police. I don't know.

Once my adrenaline starts to wane, the obvious becomes painfully clear. I'm shoeless, pantless, and phoneless. I need help, and though practically everyone I've ever known lives in this city, there's nobody I can trust. Not now. Not ever again.

I pause at an intersection, and in the distance, I catch sight of a figure on the street. Running. Toward me. A surge of panic hits me and I nearly stumble backward, but then I see it's a runner. A woman. When she gets close enough I wave my arms, praying she doesn't look at me and run in the other direction.

"Excuse me," I call.

She slows to a walk, eyes wide as she fiddles with something in the side of her hydration belt. Mace. She holds up her clenched fist to show me the canister.

"Do you have a phone?" I ask shakily, taking a step toward her so she can see me better, both hands held out.

She swears.

"I just need to make one call."

"Are you okay?" She puts the Mace back in her belt and pulls out a cell phone. "Do you want me to call the police?"

"No. I just need to call my friend to come get me. Please."

She's staring at my feet, no, behind my feet. I follow her gaze and see the trail of dark splotches. Blood. My feet are suddenly throbbing. There isn't just one point of pain, but dozens, like the soles are on fire, and the flames are climbing up my calves.

Speechless, she hands me her phone, her eyes never leaving the trail behind me. I close my eyes, concentrating. His number. A jumble of digits appear in my mind, but are they in the right order? I need them to float magically into place. I've seen them enough times now, since I could never bring myself to program his name into my phone. All the times he called when I hoped it was Emilio. A fresh rush of anger pushes the numbers into place, and I've got it. I hope. I dial. He won't be awake, and if he is, he's probably in no condition to drive.

Marcel picks up, and I choke out his name.

"Valentina." His voice is groggy but clear.

I let out a sob. The relief is so strong I can't think what to say.

"Are you all right?"

"Yeah," I manage. "Can you come get me?"

It takes Marcel only ten minutes to find me. Jogger girl waits for the first few, but I eventually convince her that I'm fine, that I locked myself out and stepped on a broken beer bottle, that she should go. She can't possibly believe any of it, but she trots off anyway.

Once she's gone, I wish she wasn't. The sky has lightened to cobalt, and I'm more visible every second. I lean into the trunk of a palm tree and watch the corner where I told Marcel to come. More runners pass. Homeless people. Early commuters. Feral cats.

Finally the black Range Rover glides up onto the curb, and I begin limping toward him before he even stops, pain shooting up my legs with every step. His face is hard with rage, but I don't let myself think about it. Not yet. I look down. Almost there. I reach the door, pull it open, place my foot inside, and try to climb in, but lightning shoots up my calf when I put my entire body weight on the ball of my foot. I start to fall back, but Marcel grips my upper arms and hoists me up onto the seat.

"Thank you," I mumble, righting myself, tugging the T-shirt down.

He leans across me, closes my door, and pulls back onto the street. "What the hell did he do to you?"

"Nothing. Just drive."

He drives, anger rolling off him like smoke, his knuckles white from choking the steering wheel. I should have already thought through what I'm going to tell him, but my feet hurt, and the shock is wearing off, and I want to cry, so I say nothing. He says nothing. We make it through downtown, to the MacArthur Causeway, and halfway over the bridge to South Beach before either of us speaks.

"Okay, let's hear it," he says.

"I don't know where to start."

"Start with your feet."

"My feet?" I look down at them. Easy enough to explain. "I broke a lamp on his head, then I ran over it." From the top they look fine, except for the rust-colored stain between my toes where the blood has worked its way up and dried. But when I lift my right foot and see the sole for the first time, I almost gag. It looks like hamburger where the flesh has torn and ripped away. Only three jagged chunks of the porcelain lamp are visible—one in the heel, two in the ball—but there could be a dozen more that I can't see in that pulpy mess.

I don't check my left foot, but it feels about the same.

"You need to go to the ER," he says.

"*No.* Just take me to . . ." I almost say *wherever you're staying,* but I don't even know who he's staying with, or where we're going right now.

"I'll take you to my hotel," he says.

"I thought you were staying with friends."

"Well, I'm not."

I lean my head back and close my eyes, picturing Emilio staggering down the hall behind me, blood trickling down his forehead onto his perfectly pressed shirt. Except he's not Emilio.

"You cold?" Marcel asks.

"What?"

"You're shivering."

"Oh." But I'm not just shivering, I'm convulsing. My teeth are chattering, and I feel like my whole body is tightening around an earthquake.

He turns on the heat. "The blanket is still back there. You want me to pull over and get it for you?"

"I'm not cold."

I stare out my window. Palm trees fly by, too fast to count, skinny bars against the background of cruise liners and ocean. I thought I missed this view—the pristine white ships rising out of sapphire waves—but I don't feel nostalgia. I feel throbbing in my feet and my chest and my eyes.

We drive through the trickle of Miami Beach's earth lovers—dog walkers and joggers and Whole Foods patrons with their cloth bags and organic greens. It's all familiar, but I'm separate. Just a spectator. The luxury condos and hotels flip by like a movie.

Marcel pulls into the valet lane of the Setai. "Wait," he says to me, and hands the valet a bill from his wallet. He comes around the front of the car, opens my door, and slides an arm under my knees and behind my neck.

"I can walk," I say.

"Don't be an idiot." He lifts me out of the car.

The lobby is glossy and dimly lit, but not so dark that I shouldn't be embarrassed. The T-shirt may or may not be covering my butt, but I'm too spent for humiliation. I could insist on walking and I might look like I'm on my way to the pool, but I'm not convinced I wouldn't pass out if I put an ounce of weight on either foot, so I lay my head against Marcel's shoulder and give up.

Once we're in his room, Marcel takes me to the round marble tub and sits me on the ledge. He turns on the water. "Is this okay?"

"It's a lot nicer than the Holiday Inn."

"I mean, is the water too hot?"

My feet are still up on the ledge, but I take my right and dip a toe in. "No, it's good."

But when I try to put my whole foot in, the pain makes me gasp.

"Here. Put it under the running water." He reaches for my foot. I shake my head, but he takes it anyway and holds it under the faucet.

I grit my teeth until the burning recedes into numbness and I can't feel anything. Ribbons of blood twist from my foot, curl around the drain, and disappear. All that pain. Gone. Emilio. Gone.

Good.

Marcel takes my left foot and does the same. It hurts just as much, but this time the pain is the start of something new and constructive. Like anger. This is the last of Emilio hurting me. I'm finished being lied to by him and my father. And I'm finished being taken by surprise. Valentina the victim is gone, swirling-down-the-tub-drain gone.

Marcel lifts both feet out of the tub and wraps them in a towel, then leaves me in the bathroom. I hear him pick up the phone. "Can I get a first aid kit brought to the room, please? . . . . Tweezers and bandages . . . Yeah. . . . Oh, and Neosporin too. Thanks."

The phone clicks, and Marcel comes back to the bathroom. He sits across from me on the other side of the tub, and I take a good look at him for the first time. He looks tired, his hair all mussed and his eyes puffy.

"I woke you up," I say.

He raises an eyebrow. I don't know what that means.

"I'm sorry," I say.

"When do I get to go kill him?"

"You don't." I pull my right foot out of the towel and hold it up for him to see. "How bad is it?"

"Pretty bad. Now tell me what happened."

"Can you get me some pants first?"

"Deal." He goes off to find me something to wear, and I reposition my feet in the bloodstained towel. Not telling Marcel is the smartest thing. It's the safest thing, too. Smart and safe, though—it seems like I've abandoned both already.

"Shorts?" he asks from the doorway, holding up a pair of khaki cargos.

"Sure."

"Do you need help?"

I shake my head. He hands them to me. There's a knock at the door, and he goes off to answer it while I carefully ease them over my feet, then wiggle into them without actually standing up.

I have no reason to trust anyone ever again. But if I had to trust someone, it'd be Marcel. That seems so obvious now.

"I have tools," he says, holding up a first aid kit. "Where do you want to do this?"

"The bed?"

He carries me to the four-poster king-size. He sits at the foot of the bed, puts a pillow in his lap, and places my towel-wrapped feet on top of that. "So there's some rubbing alcohol in this first aid kit."

"Go ahead."

"It's going to hurt."

"I know."

"A lot."

"Just do it."

The pain is searing and white hot. Even with clenched teeth, I can't stop myself from gasping.

"Sorry," he says, then runs a swab over the other foot. Just as bad. I'm shivering with the pain, but then it fades and is over just as quickly.

Comparatively, what follows—the tweezers digging around in my raw, hanging flesh—barely hurts. Marcel holds each piece of porcelain up for me to see.

"Nice one," I say in response to the third sliver he pulls out of my right foot.

"Thanks."

"You should consider a career as a surgeon."

"Two problems with that," he says, and holds up another chunk of porcelain. "It might make my dad happy, and it'd require me to go back and finish high school. You said you'd tell me what happened if I got you something to wear."

"Did I?"

He rolls his eyes.

"First tell me about the blonde in your room," I say.

"What? Nobody's been in my room but you."

"Not this one," I say. "The Holiday Inn."

"How'd you know she was blond?"

I don't answer.

He keeps his eyes on my foot. "Does that bother you?"

"No."

"Yes, it does."

"No, it doesn't."

"Yes, it does. That's why I did it."

"You slept with some girl you didn't even know just to make me mad?"

"I didn't sleep with her. But yeah, I had her in my room just to make you mad."

"And I'm supposed to believe that?"

He pulls another sliver out, a tiny one, and holds it up before putting it beside the others on the spare towel. "I don't care if you believe me. It clearly did make you mad, though, which means I accomplished my goal."

"You jerk."

"You had it coming."

I wince.

"Sorry. I think this is the last one in this foot."

I lie back into the pillows and stare at the crown molding.

"Your turn," he says.

I tell him. I start at when he pulled away from Emilio's apartment, and after that the words tumble out on their own. Emilio lied to me. Used me. Never loved me. Saying it scrapes at the humiliation a little, but I feel better after hearing it aloud. I omit the part about Lucien, of course, but I'm used to this deception and the guilt that comes with it. "So you were right," I end with.

"I'm sorry," he says.

"Are you smiling?"

"No."

"You think this is funny?"

"Not at all. I'm just picturing you swinging a lamp into Emilio's head, and it's a nice image for me."

I allow myself a grin.

"How badly did you hurt him?"

"I don't know. There was a lot of blood, but he was still trying to run after me, so it's not like I killed him. I could hear him calling my name."

"I can't believe I delivered you to him," he mutters. "You realize if you hadn't cracked his head open, you'd be handcuffed to his refrigerator right now."

I shake my head. "Maybe he was going to arrest me."

"For what? You hadn't done anything. He just wanted you out of the way so you couldn't warn your father."

"And do you think I'd do that?"

"Warn your father?"

I nod.

"I don't know. Would you?"

I don't have an answer. It seems like something I should know instinctively, something I shouldn't have to weigh out to decide.

Marcel picks up my left foot and examines it. "This one isn't as bad, I don't think."

But the left isn't numb from picking yet, so it's excruciating all over again as he digs out the first sliver. My right is still throbbing, but it's a different kind of pain now that the shards are out. Pulsing but no pressure. "I don't want my father to go to jail for the rest of his life, even if he deserves it. Which he does. I should hate him now that I know who he is, but he's still my father. I—" I stop short of saying *I still love him.* I don't know. "But I don't want to save him, either."

"Doesn't seem like you'll have to."

"What do you mean?" I ask.

"Whether you warn your father or not, Emilio has to assume that's what you're doing. He's probably already called off whatever he had planned for tonight."

I sift through the fragments of my conversation with Emilio. It's all so muddled. I wish I'd been clearer headed. "I don't think so. Emilio wants to catch him with the drug shipment that comes in this morning."

"That was before you got away," Marcel says. "I bet you anything he's changing his plans now."

I laugh. It feels surprisingly good. "Maybe you're right."

"Of course I'm right."

"He's been doing everything to avoid having his cover blown, and now, because of me, he's totally screwed."

"He deserves it." Marcel wipes the tweezers on the towel, leaving a streak of blood behind them.

"He might just forget the shipment and move in on Papi faster, though."

Marcel is quiet for a moment. "What do you want to do, then? Whose side are you on?"

I look away, out the sheer curtains into the bay where yachts are bobbing like toy boats. They're both liars and killers. They both used me. "Neither."

"So do nothing. Go back to Montreal, or to Spain, or wherever you want to hide, and let whatever happens happen."

"But if I walk away and my father ends up—"

"It won't be your fault. Nobody forced your father to be who he is."

What he's saying is true. The picture of Yolanda Rojas still burns in my mind. I know what Papi deserves.

"You aren't even flinching," Marcel mumbles. "Doesn't this hurt?"

"Not anymore."

He holds up another sliver. "I think this is the last one. Pass me the Neosporin."

I hand it to him. "I don't want Emilio to win either."

"You want them both to lose."

"What if I convince Emilio I've turned on Papi and want to help?"

"Might be a little hard. You did just try to kill him."

I run a hand through my hair. The humidity has changed it already, made it wavy again. It feels like mine. "That can be explained—I overreacted, I thought he was going to hurt me."

"Why would he believe you?"

"Because he knows how repulsed I am by the things my father has done. He showed me pictures. . . ." I can't explain that part. I shake my head. "I could make him believe that I want Papi behind bars."

"And then . . ."

"And then sabotage whatever he has planned for tonight."

"Valentina, it's the FBI you're talking about messing with. And sabotage? Seriously? What do you even have in mind?"

"I don't know, but if I walk away, Vizcaya is going to be a bloodbath. Papi and his guys aren't going to go down without a fight, and obviously Emilio and whatever team he comes storming in with will all have weapons. Innocent people will be there. My sisters will be there. Emilio isn't thinking about anything but his own ego and about taking Papi down in the biggest way possible."

"Should I bother pointing out that you can't walk, or is that not a concern?"

I look down at my feet. Strips of white medical tape wrap around the tops, holding the gauze in place. The throbbing is fading. "I'll be okay. They hurt much less now that the shards are out."

Marcel stares at the floor. "You're crazy, and I'm not taking you back there. He could do anything to you. There's no way the FBI knew he was using you like he did."

"Which is why he'll *want* to believe that I've turned against Papi."

"But he's safer if you're out of the picture, and you already know he has no problem breaking rules."

"I have to call him."

"Listen to yourself! That's insane! Why don't we just take off?"

"I'm not running away again!" It comes out too loud. I don't want to be yelling at Marcel. "You have no idea what it's like to find out your entire life is a lie, and that the people you loved the most were using you."

"Right." He moves the pillow and my feet off his lap and stands up. "No idea."

I glance around the room, spotting the phone on the far bedside table. "I have to call him now. Before he does anything drastic."

"Before *he* does anything drastic?" Marcel waves a hand at my feet. "You're a mess, still bleeding all over the place, and you're going to go running back to him so you can blindly screw with a federal investigation?"

"I'm not letting him get away with using me!"

"So you'd risk your life for revenge."

My life. I don't even know what that is anymore. It's a reaction. It's a lie. It's being an object for other people to use. "Yes."

Marcel holds up his hands and walks toward the bathroom without looking at me. His fingers and knuckles are caked with my blood, and he's muttering something I can't hear.

Over the sound of the faucet I shout, "I'll tell him I want to be there to see him arrest Papi."

The water turns off. "And why would he let you do that?"

"Because he's afraid of me. Like you said."

Marcel reappears in the doorway, leaning against the frame like he's afraid to come back in.

"Help me," I say.

"And why would I do that?"

"Because you're my friend. Because you hate Emilio." I swallow, and close my eyes. He deserves to know. "Because Lucien didn't kill himself."

He freezes. His lips are parted slightly, his eyes are trained unblinkingly on the gauzy curtains and out into the bay of toy boats. The air between us is dead. He's stiller than a painting, all the blood and breath far from the surface. He's a statue held captive in a moment of agony.

I swing my legs off the side of the bed and stand. Painful, but not debilitating. I hobble toward him. Every muscle in his face is tight, like a cage around his mind. I put my hand up to his jaw. Nothing happens. His skin is warm, his jawbone rigid, and I realize I thought he would melt or respond in some way. He's not melting.

"I'm sorry," I say.

"You think, or you know?" he mumbles.

"I know. Before last night, I only suspected, but when I confronted Emilio, he didn't deny it."

"But . . . why?"

"He said it was because Lucien would tell my father we were together in Montreal, and that would ruin the investigation. He needed to stay in my father's inner circle."

Marcel swallows and says it first. "Maybe Lucien found out who Emilio really was."

"Maybe."

Marcel blinks, still lost in the bay.

I wait for his sadness, but when it doesn't come, when his eyes narrow, I know I've won.

I put my hand on his chest, half expecting him to flinch or push me away, but he doesn't. "You'll help me?" I ask.

"I'll help you."

THIRTY-ONE

I dial Emilio's number. My hand trembles as I bring the phone to my face. It's ringing. I've rehearsed every word with Marcel, but now all I can think of is the sound of Emilio screaming my name as I ran. Like a monster.

Marcel sits across the room on the couch, frowning at the room service menu, pretending he isn't listening. I twist my body around so I'm facing the head of the bed, dragging my aching feet with me and propping them on a new pillow.

"Hello?"

I close my eyes and make him wait.

"Hello?" He sounds angry.

"It's me."

"Valentina."

My name. *My* name. And like that, my nerve is back, because he has no right to say *my* name like that, like he owns me, like he thinks he only has to say the right words and I'll do whatever he wants me to do.

"Where are you?" he asks.

"At a hotel."

"You didn't go to your father's?" I love the disbelief in his voice. He must've spent the last two hours freaking out.

"Of course not."

"Have you spoken to him?"

"Of course not. Just because I hate you doesn't mean I'm running back to him."

Emilio is silent, appraising my answer, recalculating his plan. "You shouldn't have attacked me. We could've talked about this like reasonable human beings."

"I'm not very good at talking like a reasonable human being when I'm handcuffed and sedated and whatever else you were going to do to me."

"What are you talking about? You know I'd never hurt you."

"I don't know that," I say.

"My head's still bleeding, by the way."

"Good."

"Come back," he says, suddenly gentler. "We can talk about this."

Does he really think I'll forget who he is and what he did if he talks sweetly enough? I don't answer.

He must assume I'm considering the offer, because he keeps needling. "You didn't let me explain. Just because I'm under-cover doesn't mean that I don't love—"

"Shut up," I say flatly. "That's exactly what it means. Lucky for you, I have no intention of wrecking your perfect plans for tonight."

"You don't."

"I don't. Papi deserves to rot in hell, but I don't see why you're putting a bunch of innocent people in danger."

He snorts. "Innocent people? That party will be packed with people who feed off the cocaine industry, just like it was last year and the year before and the year before. Innocence is checked at the door."

"But my sisters will be there."

"That's not ideal," he admits. "But it's your father who's put them in danger. Not me."

"You know what I think? I think you're willing to gamble with all those lives because you have to come out looking like the hero. Am I right? You're picturing an award, a promotion, your face in the news—whatever it is they give to the agent who takes down the great and terrible Victor Cruz. I get it. It'll make your entire career. And the bigger, the more spectacular, the more of his goons you get, the more public the whole scene is, that all just makes you look better, right?"

Silence.

I push on. "And what do you care if Papi's guys kill a few people in the confusion? Nobody can blame you for that. You're a hero. Who knew heroism could be so complicated?"

"Enough," he says. "I put my life in danger every single day I spend with your precious Papi. You don't get to talk to me about heroism. You're on the wrong side of this, Valentina."

Is he right? I meet Marcel's empty stare and remember the grotesqueness of Lucien the last time I saw him. There is no right side of this. I take a deep breath. "I'm going to stay out of your hair tonight, but you have to promise me that whatever you have planned doesn't go down before midnight."

"This is an FBI, DEA, and ICE operation years in the making," he says. "Since when do you think you're calling the shots?"

"Since I decided there should be consequences for statutory rape. Unless you want to lose your job and go to jail alongside the Cruz cartel, you're going to promise me that a team of FBI agents doesn't storm Vizcaya before midnight."

He doesn't say anything. I wish I could see his face.

"Why midnight?" he says finally.

"That's when my sisters will be leaving."

"And how do you know that?" he asks.

"Don't worry about it. I'll get them out of there. And I don't care what happens to Papi after, but before midnight, no raid, no arrests, no SWAT team or whatever else you do. Deal?"

I hold my breath. He takes his time. I try to picture his face again, but I can't.

"You know," he says, "it's my word against yours. Nobody's going to believe a drug lord's teenage daughter over an FBI agent. You don't have as much leverage as you think you do."

"Leverage," I say coolly. "You're right. I would need proof to have real leverage. Something like a recorded phone conversation where you admit to it."

Silence.

"Still there?" I ask.

"You're not . . ." He trails off.

"Of course I am. But if you don't believe me, raid Vizcaya before midnight. The police and the press will all have copies before tomorrow morning, and I'm sure they'll be more than happy to let you listen to it."

He curses.

"Don't freak out," I say. "I'm not going to screw this up for you. I want to see Papi go down as much as anyone else."

"Really?" he says sullenly. "I never took you for the vengeful type. You were always such a daddy's girl."

I was. It's true, but I can't think about that right now. "I've seen too much," I say shortly. "Oh, and one more thing, Emilio. I want my mandolin back."

"It's not yours," he mutters.

"It is now."

Marcel and I devour breakfast in bed, silver room-service trays propped on pillows around us, their dome tops scattered upturned on the floor. I'm halfway through my second omelet before I stop for a breath.

"Glad I ordered three," Marcel says, handing me a napkin.

I wipe my chin. "I didn't even know I was hungry."

"Adrenaline. You're crashing."

"I guess. Are you going to eat that?" I ask, pointing to his bacon.

He hands it over. "So let's talk about tonight."

I nod, taking a bite. He's right, but I'm too jittery for details. "Did you hear me tell him to shut up? It was perfect. I told him to shut up, and he actually shut up."

"Good job. Now tonight."

"Tonight we go to Vizcaya." I pull a cream cheese Danish from one of the silver trays and sink my teeth into it.

"Maybe," he says.

I chew.

"What if you go to Vizcaya, and I go to your yacht and screw up the drop-off?" he asks.

I swallow the lump of Danish. "That sounds stupid and dangerous. We're going to call the police and tell them it's coming like we talked about."

"But then the police seize the drugs, and Emilio gets credit. I don't see how that's revenge."

"Emilio's going to be plenty pissed off when my father gets away, and my father is going to lose the millions and his ability to do business when the drugs are seized. Everybody loses."

Marcel pushes his plate away. "Not enough."

"What are you suggesting then?"

"Did I ever tell you how I got kicked out of boarding school?"

"No." I picture the black-and-white newspaper photo of Lucien and Marcel in their school uniforms. "You told me you chose to come home when Lucien graduated."

"Oh. Actually, I chose to get kicked out."

"Nice."

"I had no choice," he explains.

"Of course you didn't."

"I didn't want to stay there without him, and my parents wouldn't let me come back. So I set a few fires."

"Tell me you didn't hurt anyone."

"'Course not," he says. "I'm an expert at recreational, non-lethal arson."

I nod. I already know the answer, but I have to ask. "And that will help us how?"

"I'm going to set fire to Victor Cruz's yacht."

I turn and survey the ravaged trays. He's watching me, waiting for my reaction.

"If that's okay with you," he adds.

If it's okay with me? The yacht is my childhood, my sisters, vacations to the Virgin Islands with Papi—all the things I used to want to remember.

But it's already worse than ashes. I'll never again set foot on the yacht without thinking of the smell of Emilio's skin, his hands circling my wrists, his breath in my ear. Or the closet and the blood flower.

I repeat Marcel's words in my head. *If that's okay with you.*

"It is," I say.

"Are you sure?"

"Burn it down."

My wardrobe issues don't occur to me until after breakfast settles and Emilio announces he's going out to buy pyro supplies and something black to wear. I look down at my own outfit. Emilio's T-shirt, Marcel's cargo shorts, no shoes. It's all I have.

"Hold on," I say, swinging my feet off the pillow. "I need to come with you."

"You need to stay off your feet if you plan on walking tonight. How do they feel, by the way?"

"Good."

He picks up my feet and puts them back on the pillow. "Liar."

"But I have to buy a dress and some shoes and some makeup."

"So make a list."

"What?"

He takes the hotel stationery and a pen from desk and hands them to me. "I can handle the dress and shoes. Just write down your sizes, and what makeup you want me to pick up."

"You aren't serious."

"You think I can't pick out a dress?"

"That's exactly what I think."

"How about this: If you don't like it, I'll take you to pick one out yourself."

"You know we won't have time," I mutter, and scribble on the edge of the pad to make the pen start.

"It won't matter. You'll love it."

I write a short list of cosmetic staples and my sizes and hand it to him. "Not slutty."

"We'll see."

"I'm serious. And I need a wig. I don't even know where

you'd find one, so good luck."

"A wig?" He folds the paper and puts it in his back pocket. "Is that really necessary? I thought you were going to be hiding in a room or closet somewhere."

"I am, but I have to get into the party in the first place."

He gives me a hard look.

"Don't worry. I'll leave as soon as you call to tell me your part's done. Which reminds me, I'll need a phone."

He takes the paper out of his pocket. "Adding it to the list."

I work through the timing in my head one more time to make sure it checks out. Papi should get a call from his people telling him the yacht's on fire the same time as I hear from Marcel. He should take off without ever seeing me or knowing that I'd saved him. That would be best. But if he's still there and it's getting close to midnight, I'll have to tell him who Emilio really is.

"What about your sisters?" Marcel asks.

"I'll find them and make them leave with me."

"How?"

"I'm still working on that. So, the dress. I need you to find me something amazing. Can you do that?"

Marcel puts his hand on the doorknob but doesn't twist it. "It's him. You want to look good for him."

He's staring at the potted orchid on the table beside the door, a white blossom with petals like pearls.

"Yeah," I say.

He twists the knob, turning away from me.

"Marcel, stop," I call, and he does, letting the door catch on his shoulder. "I hate Emilio more than I've ever hated anyone in my entire life. I mean it. Buy me a dress that makes him want to kill himself."

He smiles. "Done."

THIRTY-TWO

Rain.

I wake up to the roar of it, but when I open my eyes, sunlight is flooding through the gauzy curtains.

Not rain. The shower.

I glance at the clock. 3:11. A Nordstrom dress bag lies draped over the chair, and several smaller bags—Sephora, Saks—sit on the coffee table. Curiosity pulls me out of bed and over to the chair. I don't remember my feet until they touch the floor and pain pulses through them. Gingerly, I stand. It's not that bad. Not that bad. I repeat it a few times before hobbling over to the chair to inspect the dress. I unzip the bag. It's navy-blue silk, the color and sheen of the ocean right at the moment that dusk becomes night. I pull the dress off the hanger and hold it up to inspect. The cut is simple and elegant—a halter with a dangerously low back and a slight flare at the hem.

I'm holding it up to my chin, checking length, when Marcel's voice startles me. "Is it okay?"

I jerk around, like I've been caught stealing, and find him standing there in a towel, dripping wet. "Beautiful," I say. "Thank you."

This shouldn't be awkward. I've seen him in a swimsuit too many times, but something is off between us. He feels it too, or maybe he feels me staring at him. I look away.

"I wasn't sure what kind of shoes you could even wear with your feet all cut up, so I bought two pairs." He gestures to the bags on the table.

"Oh. Thanks." I pull the box from the first bag and slide off the lid. Steel-colored stilettos. They're perfect. The second, navy ballet flats.

I peek into the last bag and discover a rust-colored swirl of hair. I take out the wig. "How did you know I've always wanted to be a redhead?"

"Lucky guess."

I twist my own hair on top of my head and pull on the wig. I make my way over to the mirror and examine my reflection. It's not unnaturally red, but that deep auburn that makes me think of horses and foxes and autumn leaves. I tuck my loose dark strands up beneath the red, then run my fingers through it. "I don't look like myself, do I?"

"No."

"I was worried you'd come back with something blond," I say. The hot tub girl in her gunmetal bikini appears in my mind, and I push her away.

"Blond wouldn't look good on you," he mumbles.

I fiddle with the wig a little more, then lay it out on the coffee table. "So I guess I shouldn't have doubted you."

"Apology accepted. Although I had to ask the lady at Sephora to put all the makeup together." He leans over to get his own clothes from a shopping bag. I've never noticed that tiny mole on his back before, right below the ridge of his shoulder blade. "But I chose the dress myself."

I pull my eyes away from his back to the dress. I rub the fabric between my thumb and my finger. It feels like a petal. "It's gorgeous."

"Aren't you going to try it on?"

I'm dying to. "I think I'll shower first."

I take the dress with me to the bathroom and hang it on the back of the door. The mirrors are still fogged, and the mugginess clings to me, beading on my skin as I remove the T-shirt and shorts. I unwrap my feet and inspect the damage. The bleeding has stopped, but they still look pretty bad—worse than they feel. They probably need air and to be elevated more than anything else, but that can wait till tomorrow. I'll ask Marcel to put more bandages on after my shower.

I take my time washing and conditioning my hair with the hotel's high-end products, scrubbing every inch of skin with green tea exfoliating scrub. Definitely not the Holiday Inn.

Once I'm clean and dry, I take the dress off the hanger and slide it over my head. It falls down around me, cool and slippery.

The fit is perfect. I don't need a mirror to tell. The back feels low but not indecent, and the rest is snug but not tight.

I leave the bathroom, suddenly nervous. There's nothing more awkward than watching someone watch you, so I glance at Marcel and then don't let myself look back. "Is there a full-length mirror?"

"By the door." He's on the couch, flipping channels with his feet propped on the coffee table. I feel his eyes follow me across the room.

And when I see myself full length, wet hair, navy halter, I recognize the dress. But not as a dress. "Oh. It's like Nanette's swimsuit. I didn't realize . . ."

"You like it?" he asks.

"Of course."

I finally look at him. He's wearing jeans and a black T-shirt, bare feet. He turns off the TV and puts down the remote. "If he has to see you in that tonight and know that he can't touch you ever again, he'll want to kill himself. Trust me."

My mouth is too dry to speak. And what would I say, anyway? My hair is dripping water down my back, into the dress. I should go change.

No, I should kiss him.

"Let's leave Miami," he says, and he looks so serious, I almost want to consider it. "You could still call your father and warn him about tonight."

"So he can just keep on doing what he's doing? I don't want that."

"But how are you going to stop him?"

"I'm not. I'm just going to talk to him."

Marcel says nothing, grabs a magazine from the coffee table and flips pages.

"I know," I say. "I sound naive. But I have to tell him that I know who he really is and what he really does and what I think of him. He has to know that I've seen pictures of what he's done. His victims aren't even . . ." I break off. I can't describe the picture of Yolanda to Marcel. "Plus, if we leave, Emilio wins."

Marcel's jaw tightens and the pages flip faster.

"So we stay," I say.

"We stay," he says.

"I'm going to change out of this."

He looks at his watch. "We have a few hours. You shouldn't be walking around. Your feet."

"I'll elevate them after I change." I walk toward the bathroom, then turn around again. "Remember that time when I kneed you?"

"Couldn't forget it if I tried."

"Right. Well, I'm sorry."

He stops flipping pages. "I thought you said you were never going to apologize for that."

"Did I say that?"

"Yeah."

"I guess I didn't mean it."

The rest of the afternoon passes like melting ice—slowly, slowly dripping, then it's gone and I don't know how it happened.

We sit side by side on the couch and go through every detail of the plan: he leaves before me, around nine, in his car with the equipment he bought—kerosene, pliers, metal cutters—and my map to the marina in Coconut Grove where Papi docks the yacht.

"You're sure it'll be there?" he asks.

"That's where he always docks when it's here in Miami. As far as I know."

"And who will be on it?"

"I don't know. Everybody will want to be at Vizcaya, so probably just a few thugs. I only know what Emilio told me—that the shipment came in this morning, and that the FBI isn't seizing it until his guys move in on my father at Vizcaya. They can't have word getting to him before he's in handcuffs."

"So, after midnight."

"After midnight. If Emilio keeps his promise."

I try to picture Papi in handcuffs, but the image is so unlikely, Papi being controlled and subservient to anybody or anything. Emilio knows that. He knows Papi won't go willingly.

Marcel reads my mind. "It's going to be messy, isn't it?"

"Not if I make sure he and my sisters are out of there before it can start."

Marcel takes a deep breath. "If I don't call you to tell you it's done, assume something went wrong and do what you have to do."

I nod. I don't want to think through the list of things that could go wrong for Marcel.

"So when will you leave here?" he asks.

"I'll get a cab at ten."

"Are you sure that gives you enough time?"

"I think so. It'll be easier to slip into Vizcaya once the party is in full swing. And the fire—that gets set at eleven?"

"On the dot. I kind of wish I could go to Vizcaya with you. I'd like to say a few parting words to Emilio. With my fist."

"Which is why it's good you're not coming with me."

"You don't think I could take him?"

I raise an eyebrow and lean back, pretend to inspect his shoulders. I reach out and circle his bicep with my fingers. "You could take him."

"What did you even see in him?"

"Lies." I think of the Emilio I thought I knew. What, if any of that, was real? "But that makes him easier to hate now."

Marcel digests that. The warmth drains from the light around us as the sun sets. Tonight has to happen.

I order room service while he organizes the supplies he gathered, and then we take our final meal out onto the balcony. The night is moonless, but star-heavy. I try not to look up. Instead I watch boats slice in and out of the harbor toward the mouth of the Miami River. The way they carve paths through the water reminds me of being in Venice with Papi last spring, of sitting in a gondola and trailing my fingers in the Mediterranean. I don't want to think about that either.

"Not hungry?" Marcel points to my plate.

I twirl my fork through the pasta—shrimp fettuccini alfredo—and take a bite. I'm too nervous for it to taste good, so

I put the fork down. "I ate too much earlier."

When he's done, we go back inside. I change into my dress and sit on the edge of the bed while he gets ready. I watch him do the little things: unplug his cell phone, slip it into his back pocket, organize his supplies, pack them into a small black bag. His precision is reassuring. He's careful. He'll be fine.

But none of this feels fine. I'm not sure how I've managed to squander so many hours with Marcel, how I wasted it feeling the wrong things. Thinking about Emilio made me blind to everything else.

"I guess it's time," he says, glancing at the clock.

"What if something bad happens?"

"Something bad *is* going to happen. That's the point."

"Right. I know." I nod, trying to keep the worry from creeping up and out of me. I don't want him to see it. "Maybe you should just stay here, though. Forget the yacht and the drugs. I'll go to Vizcaya and warn my father."

"No." His voice is firm. "I'm not doing this just for you."

Lucien. Of course.

He pulls a long-sleeve black shirt over his T-shirt. "Ready," he says, looking around the room. "Don't forget your phone."

"I won't." I follow him to the door, trailing at an awkward distance. "Be careful. And if something doesn't seem right, just leave. Remember, you don't have to do this."

"Yes, I do. And this is the easy job—all I need to do is screw up one little piece of his plan and everything falls apart for him."

"Are you talking about my father or Emilio?"

"Both."

He turns at the door like he wants to say more.

It's my only chance. I'm not sure that I'm going to take it until I'm reaching for him, rolling up on my tiptoes, pulling him down by his arms so my lips can reach his lips. I close my eyes. We're somewhere else.

It's a second or two before his surprise melts and he's kissing me back. The injuries slide away—lies, insults, grief, guilt—those things never happened. He's kissing me earnestly enough that for one desperate second, I forget who I am.

When he breaks away, a chill rolls through me.

"Promise me you'll get out before midnight," he whispers, holding my chin in his hand.

"I promise."

"No matter what. Even if you don't hear from me." He steps away from me.

The chill is stronger now. I want to grab him and make him stay. "No matter what."

He's nods. And he goes to leave, but he hesitates, and in the pause I imagine he's changing his mind. As he's stepping toward me, I think he's decided sabotage isn't worth the risk, and while he's kissing me again, harder and more desperately, I'm almost certain he won't go tonight. He'll wait here for me, and we'll leave Miami together.

But then he lets go of me and he's gone. The door slams so loudly my breastbone rings.

THIRTY-THREE

Six minutes.

I sit. My feet aren't throbbing so much as aching now, and when I prop them up on a pillow, they stop hurting altogether. Or I stop noticing.

I'm waiting again, staring at the clock, but this clock is sleek and silver with black numbers. I don't doubt that it keeps accurate time. I thought I left waiting in Montreal, but this is different because it isn't futile.

I should be thinking about what I'll say to Papi, but it's hard to believe I'm going to be seeing him soon. I've been refusing to think about the conversation in case thoughts lead to feelings and feelings lead to cowardice. I don't want to back out. I can't back out now.

Five minutes.

Vizcaya is a labyrinth, with its dozens of back stairways and corners and closets to hide in. I'll have my pick of them, but I may not need to get lost in the twists and turns, since the balcony rooms that overlook the great hall are hardly ever used during parties. When I was younger, I would spy on the guests from up there. Lola pretended she was old enough to be part of the party and Ana clung to her, but I had a better time watching from above.

Or I could hide safely outdoors. The official Vizcaya Gardens on one side of the mansion stretch for acres, but there's a smaller, torch-lit lawn on the other side between the house and the water. I could wait there, and I'd be sure to see him when he came out to smoke.

Four minutes.

I picture Papi with his lips curled around a Cuban, fat fingers holding it in place, and feel a pang of nostalgia.

But Yolanda Rojas. The image slams me before I can finish the thought. The dainty white earrings and daffodil dress, soaking, dragging, smearing blood. And her toes. The undersides of them were coated, like the soles of a baby's feet dipped in paint to capture a footprint.

I wiggle my toes. It's just my subconscious, but the connection is made, from her to me and me to her. We're not so different. How could Papi do it?

My mind has done something to the image. It's not a photograph anymore. It's a painting, a morbid interpretation. My brain has turned it even more garish, and now this exaggerated version of her death—screaming scarlet, pulsing fuchsia blooms, shrill blue sky—burns behind my eyes. I blink. Still there. My forever nightmare.

Three minutes.

I should let Emilio arrest Papi. I should call Marcel and insist he leave the yacht alone.

Instead I stand, walk over to the table, and stretch the wig over my head. Once I've finger-combed the bangs and tucked all my hair into it, I stare at the girl in the mirror. She's not me. I like her, though. She's guiltless—no sins, no conscience—and she's vengeful. It's amazing how little it takes to become someone else. That I can lose myself behind a little synthetic fringe is miraculous. I'm not the daughter of a monster, or the pawn of a spy, or the model of an egomaniacal artist. I've turned myself into the woman in the mirror. *I* have.

I run my hands over the dress. Is it because Marcel picked it out for me that I feel so beautiful? Our kiss rubs at my thoughts as I pick through the cosmetics. Did it even happen? Will it happen again?

Two minutes.

Then again, they've all lied. I'm not sure why Marcel would be any different.

I shove that thought away and start applying makeup, mentally congratulating the Sephora salesgirl as I go. Marcel bought everything on my list, plus more than a few extra items she must've talked him into. I paint it on thick, thicker than I've worn since the last time I sat for Lucien. When I'm done, my face is as unfamiliar as my hair.

No need to try on both pairs of shoes. This is not a ballet flats dress. I slide my feet into the stilettos, ignoring the burn at the balls of my feet when I stand. Mind over body.

One minute.

It's time. I take a careful look around the hotel room, trying to ignore the strange, sentimental tug pulling at me. I'll be back later tonight. Marcel will be here with me. With that deliberate vow as my last thought, I grab the sequined clutch and leave.

The night is warm and breezy, but the taxi is utterly swampish. "AC's broken," the driver explains before I even ask.

"Vizcaya, please."

He screeches away from the Setai without so much as a nod.

I don't buckle up. I don't want to touch anything in this dark, soggy space, with its sour-breath smell. It feels like I'm inside the mouth of an animal, perched on a moist, panting tongue. Sweat pools under my arms, between my thighs, beneath my breasts as we lurch through traffic. I silently pray it doesn't stain the dress. I don't look out the window. Instead I focus on the ragged gashes in the back of the driver's seat, where it looks like something tried to claw its way out.

Thankfully the ride isn't long. "You can just let me out here," I insist, as we swerve off Bayshore Drive into the entrance. I peer out the window at the brass gates of Vizcaya. The letters of the estate's name gleam with opulence and promise.

"You sure?" the driver asks, gesturing beyond the gate to the skinny driveway. Towering walls of tropical scrub encroach on either side, and only a few lampposts with weak yellow bulbs dot the way. "I can drive you up. It's not so close. And snakes, you know?"

I hand him a few bills from the wad of cash Marcel left me. "I'm sure."

He pulls away and I begin walking. One step at a time, my heels bite pavement, each *click* telling me I'm on the road and not sinking into the sandy shoulder or something worse. Something alive. It feels like I'm climbing uphill, but I know the driveway actually descends, that I'm not so far from the ocean.

The sultry sway of Cuban music hits me first, even before I can see the glow of the mansion itself. Next it's the smell of salt, the breeze lifting the ocean up into the air and throwing it at me. And by the time I emerge from the shelter of the driveway and see Vizcaya's immensity glowering down at me, my heart is flying.

I don't pause. I don't stop to consider which entrance will be easiest to slide into unnoticed. This redhead doesn't hesitate, but powers up the stone steps coolly like her nerves aren't on fire.

I glance up. At the front entrance, a man is taking an invitation from a couple and scouring a list for their names, while the woman readjusts herself, tucking excess flesh into strapless satin. It takes a moment, but I place the man. He bought a silkscreen Warhol print from Papi last year. I look down at my feet, and when I get to the top of the stairs I veer left to where two tuxedoed men are laughing and smoking, one tall and youngish, the other with a wry mouth framed by a right-angled goatee. To my relief, I don't recognize them. I give them my biggest smile, though, and join them as if I'd been looking for them, lacing my hand through the younger one's arm.

"You have one of those for me?" I ask, pointing to the cigar in his mouth. No doubt Papi is dispensing them like candy by now.

He's startled for only a moment before looking me up and down. He grins, canines gleaming. "Don't tell me a pretty little thing like you smokes cigars."

"'Course not." I look up at him through my eyelashes like Lola does when she's on the prowl, then reach out and take the half-smoked cigar from his hand. His mouth drops open in surprise. I smirk, take a slow pull, and hand it back, pretending my head isn't about to explode with memories and fumes.

I'm not a smoker. When I was eleven, Lola swiped three of Papi's cigars for us girls to try, and we smoked them on the stretch of white beach behind our house. Or Lola and I did. Ana refused, but hung around to watch and whine about oral cancer. Ignoring her, we savagely bit off the ends like we'd seen Papi do a million times, lit them, and sucked in like we meant it. We *did* mean it until the smoke hit our throats, and then we were too busy sputtering and gagging to remember what we meant. Ana watched on with a smile. Lola flung hers into the ocean after two pulls, but I kept smoking, braving it out until mine was no longer than my finger. Bitter mouth and burning eyes, I showed them their baby sister wasn't such a baby. Then I threw up.

My sisters. They're probably inside right now.

Both men are watching me, so I will my throat not to seize

up. No coughing, no gasping, I tilt my chin skyward and blow smoke.

"Where do I know you from?" the young one asks with a confused tilt of his head.

I hand him back his cigar and shrug. "Here? Now?"

"Right." He raises his eyebrows at his friend, who is still looking at me but not at my eyes. I resist the urge to snap my fingers in front of his face.

"Are you gentlemen here to buy art?" I ask innocently.

More smiles. "Maybe," the young one says. "Are you?"

I eye the near-empty glass in Goatee's hand. "I'm here to have fun."

Goatee takes the last sip, and I narrow my eyes at him.

"There's more where this came from," he says, tipping the empty glass in the direction of the entrance.

I slip off the arm of the young one and thread my hand through Goatee's arm. I press my body into his side. "Show me," I say.

He doesn't have to be asked twice, and the young one follows close enough behind after I flash him another of Lola's smiles over my shoulder.

As we approach the entrance, the man with the clipboard frowns at me. I pretend not to notice, nuzzling into Goatee's neck like I have a secret to tell him.

"Excuse me," Clipboard says.

My heart lurches. Goatee seems too distracted to respond, but then he pulls a folded wad of bills from his pocket and hands them to Clipboard without even counting it.

Clipboard stares at the money. I can't breathe. He tucks it into his breast pocket. I feel Goatee's hand between my shoulder blades, sliding down the curve of my spine as we glide through the door into the gold light of Vizcaya, into the dizzying swirl of people I'm afraid to look at. I keep my eyes low as we weave around clusters, his hand slinking farther down my back.

I smile through clenched teeth. "I've got to use the ladies' room."

He frowns.

And I twist away, slipping into the crowd before I can hear his response. Laughter and music devour me. And so many people. Ropes of bright colors bind me as I spin, shiny dresses and gemstones screaming and coiling around me. *Breathe.* I stumble on, turning behind the first set of arches, rushing past a couple having an argument and another couple kissing against the wall.

One glance into the ballroom and I spot him. Papi. He's laughing, telling a story with both hands waving like he does, eyes shining, cheeks ruddy. The affection surges fast. It startles me, nearly pushes through my hard and shiny disguise before I can brace for tears. I blink before they spill. I pull myself back together, because this vengeful shell in a red wig doesn't love him; the real Valentina shouldn't love him either.

From this angle it's easy to see that he's the center of attention, as always, but now I finally understand that doesn't mean love. That means fear.

Papi, this party, everything—I've been seeing it all my whole life, but I've never really seen it. I thought I grew up in some kind of garden of cultured beauty and art, but this is excess and rot.

Yolanda Rojas.

I see her face, and I'm on fire. I just have to think it, and he's a monster again, and I'm a monster's daughter. Rage drives me to the top of the stairs and down the balcony corridor, past the chuckling men and the slurring women leaning dangerously close to the railing and waving their jeweled hands and corset-squeezed breasts over the edge.

In the far corner, another hallway leads away from the party below. Those rooms were empty last year. I charge toward them, not caring if anyone sees me. These people are all too pleasure-drunk to notice anything but their own ecstasy.

I turn and start down the hallway. The first door is locked. I rush to the second, which is locked too. The farther I go, the darker the hallway, the shakier my hands are. Locked, locked, locked. I close my eyes, and there's Papi again. If he goes free tonight, it's on me. Did I really think that through? Is it my fault there's not justice for Yolanda Rojas? If Marcel sets fire to the yacht and Papi's business is decimated, does that mean Papi will never hurt anyone again?

The volume of each question inches higher and higher until my mind is screaming so loudly it hurts. When does the daughter of a monster become a monster herself?

I turn back the way I came, but this time I don't look down at Papi. I push through the throng of balcony revelers again, to the far west side of the building. An identical hallway of locked rooms stretches along that side too, but this hall is not as dark as the other, or it starts that way, but lightens at the end. I walk the length of it, trying the locked doors just to be sure. When I get to the end, the hallway turns and ends at a door with a window, starlight streaming through. An emergency exit. Praying it doesn't set off an alarm, I open it and step out onto a small balcony.

Fresh air.

I catch the door with my hip before it slams shut. Getting locked out here would not make this nightmare any better, but there's nothing to prop it with. I take off my right sandal and wedge it between the door and the frame.

There.

Something like a sob shakes my chest, but I don't make a sound. I only let it happen once. I wrap my arms around myself, gripping my ribs, letting the breeze fill my lungs. I didn't know seeing him would be this hard.

I focus on the thin line of the horizon, where inky water meets charcoal sky. It's all black, but it's not all the same. My eyes float along the surface of the water, pulled southward by the palest glow. I can't see around the king palms at the edge of the estate, though. The marina isn't far—two miles maybe, but it's too early. Marcel said he'd start the fire at eleven. I take my phone from my purse. It's only 10:35, and I haven't missed a call. He said he'd call.

But the glow is intensifying before my eyes. It's either a fire or an apocalyptic sunrise, the way that violent orange is seeping over the night and singeing the sky. The faintest tang of smoke hits my nose. I walk to the rail, rise onto the ball of my single stilettoed foot, and lean forward. I can't see from here. The coastline curves inward, hugging Coconut Grove with the marina in the middle. I take a deep breath, and this time the smoke is unmistakable.

The yacht is burning.

He did it. Could it be that simple? I only have to make sure my sisters leave, that Papi leaves, and then it's all over? But maybe Papi shouldn't leave.

I turn away from the ocean, slip my shoe back on, and make my way back to the party. Before I even round the corner, I sense the change. Something is sour. But the music is the same, and the women and men on the upper level are still cackling and chortling just as loudly. They're only five minutes drunker. It's the party below that has changed.

I reach the overlook and stare down into the ballroom. Papi is gone. Renaldo, Jose, Fernando, and the others clumped around him before—they're all gone too, their places absorbed by the throng. It's not so simple, though. I look closer and see that among the oblivious there are some worried faces, furtive movements, people being pulled close and ears being whispered into. People are trickling out.

I need to find my sisters.

Lola and Ana. Ana and Lola. I turn slowly, scanning bodies and faces, and the colors melt, one vibrant gown into the next, into the next, into the next until it's a giant amalgam of satin-glitter-cleavage-curls.

I don't see them.

Does it matter now, though? The skeleton of the party has clearly left, which must mean the raid is off. Pulling away from the nest of the party, I follow the arcade around the perimeter of the room, ducking out onto the balcony at the first set of doors. Burning oil hits my nostrils. The yacht. I wish I could see it. I can imagine orange flames enveloping it, licking it up and pushing it down, all my memories being strangled and drowned with it. It makes me sick. And it makes me happy.

I look down into the ocean, where the breakwater stands waiting to block the next storm. A stoic limestone barge carries the burden of stopping the waves, but it's the ring of statues surrounding it that I've always loved. They rise out of the water with rippling musculature and stalwart faces. Those statues weather hurricane winds.

From thirty feet away I recognize the slope of Ana's shoulders and the curve of her slightly-longer-than-attractive neck. She's at the water's edge, staring out at the row of brave figures with the sky burning behind them. That impossible combination of gawky and poised, that can't be anyone else. The dress—a tight, iridescent tangerine sheath—must be new, but the jeweled clip holding up her hair is familiar. She's got her phone to her ear, and I can hear the soft murmur of her voice.

I've missed her. I knew it, but I didn't really know it until now.

There are only a few men on the patio, and none of them

looks my way as I walk down the steps to the water's edge. She turns around, and I can see in her face that she doesn't recognize me. But then she does. I walk faster.

She puts her phone in her purse and waits for me to come to her. That squint is familiar and that stance—arms straight at her side—is familiar too, and it finally feels like I'm home. When I reach her, I throw myself into a hug. She catches me, but she's stiff arms, hairspray, a crinkly dress. Not much more. I feel tears coming.

"Where have you been?" she murmurs into my hair.

I pull back and wipe my eyes, embarrassed. Ana isn't emotional. "Away," I say.

She steps back, and her dress makes a disapproving *scritch, scratch*. Skin rubbing taffeta. "It's been four months. You owe me more than that."

"I . . . can't I . . ."

She waits. I don't finish. She should know better than to think I'm suddenly going to confide in her. It's been years since that happened. After a few moments of waiting for nothing, she reaches out and smooths my wig like she's petting a doll. It's affectionate, but misleading; her face says I'm not forgiven. "Nice costume."

"I didn't want anyone to recognize me."

"Then why are you here?"

To rescue you. But I never considered she wouldn't want rescuing. Smoke tickles and stings my lungs. I cough.

"Something must be on fire," she says, glancing over her

shoulder and above the grove of palms. Now a black plume is bleeding over the orange sky like octopus ink.

"Where's Papi?" I ask, eyeing the growing spill.

"He got a phone call and left. Or at least that's what Lola said."

"You don't know where he went?"

"Since when do I keep track of Papi?" she says irritably. "It's not like anyone ever tells me what's going on. I don't even know where you've been hiding out, but from the looks of your skin it must've been somewhere lame. Seriously, Valentina, you need to spend a week on the beach in a bikini."

"Good to know you've been worried about me."

She snorts. "Is that why you took off? So everyone would sit around and cry?" The fire-stained sky lights up her hair, making the black flash metallic orange as she twists her head to look back to Vizcaya. "We didn't have to worry—Papi said you were fine."

"You didn't wonder how he knew?"

"Papi knows everything. But you found out all about that, didn't you? Isn't that why you ran away?"

She knows.

"I left because I . . ." I trail off as everything in my mind slides around.

Of course she knows.

The sky, the ocean, Ana—my world is rubber and Technicolor. It's stretching and bending, barely recognizable. Ana and Lola have known for a long time. *I've* been the naive one.

"You left because you found out where the money comes from and decided to throw a tantrum about it," she says.

I sway a little. I train my eyes on a limestone statue, but my center is being pushed and pulled by the waves lapping its base. If she'd seen what I'd seen from Emilio's closet, she wouldn't be so unmoved. She wouldn't be okay. She wouldn't be standing here so calm under such a violent sky. "How long have you known?"

She shrugs and turns her head in the direction of the fire. Hell is seeping over us, but she already knew.

"Why didn't you tell me?" I ask numbly.

"Papi told us we couldn't."

"But that makes no sense."

"You mean because you're the favorite?" she challenges, thrusting her chin out. Ana's face has always been a little less than symmetrical, but this pose—chin cocked, jaw set—offsets it. It's her strongest look.

"That's not what I said."

"It's what you meant."

My pulse rings in the soles of my feet, the waves of blood surging and ebbing. "So what if I am the favorite? How is that my fault?"

"It's not. It is your fault that you responded like such a child, running away like that. So some of the art is stolen. Get over it."

My breath catches.

"Sad, though, finding out the special hobby Papi shared with *just* you was actually smuggling masterpieces."

Smuggling masterpieces. She doesn't know? I'm too confused, and then I'm too relieved to talk, because it's so much better for her to believe the cover. It means she doesn't knowingly live in a bloodstained mansion, spending bloodstained money.

Ana smirks. "He said you were too young, too sweet, but he was really just worried you'd run away like Mama." She ends with a laugh, a disingenuous *ha* that gets swallowed up by the slapping of a wave against the barge.

My crime. Mama's crime. Laid side by side and examined by Ana's discerning eye, they don't look all that different.

"I'm not like her," I say.

Ana's face is hard and shimmery, a clear surface for the light to play on. "You don't know that. You don't even remember her." She shakes her head, like she's bored of this conversation, like it isn't the most substantive one we've ever had. "What did Papi do to get you to come back? What did he buy you?"

"Nothing. He doesn't even know I'm here."

"What do you mean?"

"Nobody knows I'm here."

She reaches into her purse and pulls out her phone. "When he finds out, he—"

Before she can press anything, I step forward and snatch the phone out of her hand. She wobbles and steadies herself, but doesn't try to grab it back. She's too shocked.

"You're not telling him," I say.

"Why not?"

"Because I'm going to do it. I'm going to go talk to him right now."

She narrows her eyes.

"In person," I say. "He has to tell me why. He has to look me in the eye and explain, and know that I know what he does. It's why I came back."

"Did you run out of money or something?" she asks.

"I don't want any of his filthy money."

"Wow. Your conscience is really . . . something."

I shake my head. "I've seen things you haven't seen."

She studies me. "You're different."

My stomach sloshes, with the sound of warm salt water slapping stone. I am different. I'll never again be the old Valentina.

I thought I came here to warn Papi, but now that he's gone, I see it isn't just that. I have to talk to him. He has to know I hate him for Yolanda Rojas.

I'm a monster's daughter, but I'm not a monster myself.

"You're definitely different," she says. "It's a guy, isn't it."

I don't answer.

"Is that the real reason you ran away?"

"No."

"It is."

"It isn't."

"Is he here with you?"

"No," I say, surprised that I'm answering her at all.

"What's he like?"

I stare into the smoldering sky that Marcel made. "I don't

know. He's sad. And brave."

She rolls her eyes. "I meant what does he look like?"

"Kind of like a sculpture."

"This is going nowhere," she says, and holds out her hand. "Give me my phone back."

"Trade you for your keys."

"Seriously?" She folds her arms. "You want to borrow my car? You realize it was bought with *filthy* money."

"Ana, please."

She pulls out her keys but doesn't pass them to me. "And how am I supposed to get home?"

"Lola's in there, right?"

Ana holds out the keys and I take them, passing her phone back.

"It's not as simple as you think it is," she says. "Not so black-and-white, I mean, with Papi being the bad guy."

"I don't think it's simple."

"But you think you're better than me because I'm not running away or confronting him."

I don't. She doesn't really know about Papi. I examine her dress. It's shiny and tight, ruched around the middle, and gaping around her neck like her head is the stamen emerging from some lolling flower. It's couture, but not beautiful. It's not something I would wear, or even something I would've worn. I don't think. Except I'm not sure I remember exactly what my former self preferred or why.

"I don't think I'm better than you," I say. I don't understand her, but that's not the same. "You know where he is, don't you?"

This time she doesn't deny it.

"Tell me."

"Home."

"Are you sure?"

"You insist I tell you, and then you don't believe me?"

Home. I was sure he'd go to the marina to scream at someone as his millions melted and sank. The yacht was insured, but the cocaine, all that money . . . I'd imagined the horror flickering on his face. "It's not that I don't believe you, I just thought—"

"Lola was there when he got a call and started freaking out. He told her he had to go home, but that we should stay here." She stops and sniffs the air. "That smoke is killing me. I wonder what's burning."

There are so many things burning right now, I can't begin to answer. The yacht. My feet. My heart. I turn to leave. "Thank you," I call over my shoulder.

If she responds, I don't hear. Maybe it's swallowed in the break of a wave against the limestone.

I want to slip through the party like a sliver. If I walk fast enough, if I don't make eye contact with anyone, I should be able to glide through it to the valet unsullied. I can envision myself emerging clean and free on the other side of the revelry, leaving this dirty luxury for good. I almost make it, too. The canopy of chandeliers and drunken cackling tricks me into feeling hidden, but Emilio's eyes find me. Or I find them. He glaring down from the balcony over the ballroom. An angry gash carves a ragged line down from his hairline, forking over his left brow. He shakes his head slowly. It's either disbelief or a threat, either *I can't believe you did this* or *I'm going to kill you*.

I smile.

He takes off walking toward the stairs, disappearing from my view. He's coming down.

Common sense says to run, but I don't. I rush to meet him, inexplicably eager to be close enough to see his rage. He thinks I'm still scared of him now? He can't do anything to me anymore!

From the bottom of the stairs, I see him descending. I charge up, reaching halfway before we come chest to chest.

"You did this!" he snarls. "You set that fire. You tipped him off."

My smile grows. He looks so ugly right now with his face pulled tight and that nasty gash. I hope the scar is permanent.

"This is a federal investigation you're screwing with," he goes on. "Do you have any idea how much time you can serve for obstruction of justice at this level?"

"I don't know what you're talking about," I say calmly.

"You think that pretty little smile will keep you out of jail?"

"Obstruction of justice? Gee, those are big words! How have I obstructed justice?"

He ignores me. "I guess I shouldn't be surprised. He *is* your father. I thought you were the one Cruz with a moral compass, though."

"Don't tell me who I am," I spit at him. "And just so you know, I didn't tell Papi about your plans for tonight. I didn't tell him anything. He doesn't even know that I'm here."

"But it doesn't matter anymore, does it? He's gone. Worse, he's gone with everyone he trusts, and I'm here. Do you know what that means?"

"That your little cartel bust is going to be pretty lame," I say.

"Obviously, that's off. Just like you wanted, right? And Victor's somewhere trying to figure out how fifty-five million dollars of coke just went up in flames, probably making a list of people to kill for it right now. I hope you feel good about that, by the way."

"As long as you're on the list, I feel fine." But I don't feel fine. Sinking the yacht was supposed to cripple Papi, make him scramble, make him doubt Emilio. It wasn't supposed to inspire a killing spree.

"I should've told you the whole truth about your family," Emilio says. "I wanted to spare you, but that was clearly a mistake."

"You think you can hurt me? Too late. Ana just told me she and Lola have known about the art for years." I turn and start walking back down the stairs.

"Not that. Your mother—I showed you those other pictures, but I didn't show you the pictures of her."

I stop, but I don't turn around. He can talk to my back.

"Not that you'd recognize her. They had to use dental records to ID the body. We think she tried to leave him."

Horror slices me open from the inside. Am I bleeding here on the steps? I make myself turn now because I have to see him. "Liar," I whisper.

That's the face I remember from starry nights on the yacht. "I'm sorry," he says, and for a second I think he is, because I remember that sad glimmer of wishing things were different.

"Liar," I say again, but it's more of a cry this time, because I think I see in the way he's looking at me that he did love me and he is sorry, which means what he's saying must be true.

"I'm not lying," he says, hardening his features, and the look is gone. "Still think he deserves to get away? Still proud of who you are and what you've done?"

My thoughts aren't fast enough to rein in impulse. I march back up the steps between us, and I spit. It hits his cheek and he recoils in shock. He takes a handkerchief from his pocket and wipes it off while I walk away. Forever.

THIRTY-FOUR

At a certain time of night, at a certain velocity, the Rickenbacker Causeway to Key Biscayne becomes a roller coaster. It's that way now. I'm flying between ocean and sky, strapped into Ana's car, perched on a thin track. I see nothing but the lights of other vehicles dotting the road before me. Am I even steering? Those lights are like blisters, swollen and pulsing, nagging at my eyes as I veer between and around them.

All my dreams of her have been wrong. I imagined her abandoning us. In my most charitable moments, I had her too horrified to know what else to do. And of course, my sisters remember her too well, missed her too much for that kind of charity. They hate her.

How far did she make it? Did she escape in a car, speed across the Rickenbacker at night like this, shaking and crying, too terrified to look in her rearview mirror?

All these years of knowing nothing, I want to know all of it now. How did he do it? Or maybe he didn't. Maybe he sent someone else to kill the mother of his children.

I push my foot to the floor, and the car hums higher, its pitch matching my panic. The causeway crests, and the lights of Key Biscayne open up before me. It's a cluster of diamonds in a black nest—none of Miami's neon glare, just unapologetic opulence. Home. I swing into the exit lane and swerve off the causeway and onto the boulevard that spans the island.

Memory is such a liar. It's been four months since I've seen my home, and I've pictured it every day. But those images were all mopey versions of truth, tearstained and wrinkled like a folded photograph in a back pocket.

Now that I'm here, I feel what I couldn't recall. There's something metaphysical hovering over me as I drive the familiar streets, like a vibration or an invisible crackling. Thrill. Power. Wealth. It's been here all along. It took leaving and coming back to recognize it, though.

I pull into the wide circle of our driveway, under the portico, past the pillars and vine-choked nymph statues. They look more twisted up than usual, strangled by ivy.

I park in front of the cluster of fruit-laden avocado trees and step out of the car. I'm suddenly inexplicably calm. Maybe there's a maximum amount of shock and sadness my mind can hold, and I've reached it. Now I'm holding on to a cold, distant sort of anger, and it's entirely cerebral. I don't feel scared. I feel dangerous.

Should I use the front entrance? The side door? The back?

Indecision binds me. This is my house, but I don't ever want to go inside it again. And I want to confront Papi, but I don't know if I can bear to see his face now that I know.

Without thinking, I reach up to squeeze an avocado. My fingers sink into the flesh, releasing the scent of decay. More than floral. Turned. The avocado slips off the tree without a tug. I begin walking through the flower beds, letting the rotting fruit roll out of my hand and onto the earth as I make my way around the side of the house. At the first set of windows, the blinds are drawn. Papi's office. It's dark.

I keep walking, through bushes and cypress and king palms and jungle growth, past more darkened windows, until I hear the ocean. A few more feet and I reach the gate. Beyond it a staircase goes two ways—up to the deck that wraps around the back of the house, or down to the rocks and the waves.

I edge closer until I hear voices, then shrink back against the house instinctively.

Papi. His voice is the only one that carries over the sound of waves slapping salt and sand against the rocks below. I can't hear the words, only that he's spitting them.

I'm inching toward a disaster, a tragedy, like I can stop it. Why am I here? Loyalty? Love? Revenge?

The image that appears in my mind answers none of it. I see a gun. Papi's gun. I have to be able to protect myself against his goons, don't I? My memory reproduces it as black, thick, shineless. He keeps it in his office, in a locked drawer, but the key isn't hidden, or at least it wasn't. I stumbled upon it years ago.

I slip off the stilettos and abandon them in mulch, turning back the way I came, running, not questioning whether it's still there or what I'm going to do with it. I need that gun. Without it I'm the girl watching from the closet, the girl who finds Lucien's body too late to do anything, the girl too shocked by photographs of her own blood's crimes to do anything more than cry. I need that gun.

The front door is locked. I type in the nine-digit security code, hoping Papi hasn't changed it again. The door clicks, and I slip inside the darkened front entrance. I'm home. But I don't have time to stand still and feel it. I hurry down the hall to Papi's office, head down so I don't see the artwork welcoming me from the walls. Those paintings will not have changed either, and I don't want to see them right now.

Reaching Papi's office, I flip on the lights and go straight for the skinny top drawer. The key is there like I knew it would be, and it slides into the hole in the bottom right drawer. I open it and there the gun is, waiting for me.

I know nothing about guns. But that seems less important than the sureness in my gut that I can't be the coward again. I wrap my fingers around it, surprised by the weight, the solidity. It's cool and smooth like a piano key. Smiles gleam up at me from the picture frames on Papi's desk—my sisters and me.

I leave the way I came, but I'm running faster now. It would be quicker to go through the house, but I don't know who's hanging around keeping watch, or what I'd do if they tried to stop me. The trek back around the statues and the palms and the flowering wisteria feels different now that I'm gripping the gun. I'm solid. I'm steel.

I slow once I can hear Papi's voice again. It's biting the salt-rich wind as I push the gate open, but the rhythm is off. I hear it as I put my foot on that first step up to the deck. I'm three steps up when the unnatural lilt makes sense. Terrible sense.

English.

I freeze. The gun feels slippery, so I try to choke up on it, holding the barrel with my sweaty left hand, sliding my right farther up the grip. All of Papi's employees speak Spanish.

I take another step, and the words become real.

". . . not like you thought, is it? Playing the game?" He laughs. It's the same laugh I've always known, not a villainous cackle, but the resonant boom that echoes in my memories. How many times have I made Papi laugh like that?

"The ankle, you see," he says, "I had no choice. . . ."

Below us a wave crashes, swallowing the rest. I strain, but he's too far away, probably closer to where the deck wraps around the other side of the house.

". . . you even know how much seven and a half tons is worth?"

Mumbling. Too soft to hear. I inch forward, heart pounding. If I turn the corner, I may be visible. But maybe it's too dark, and maybe they won't be looking this way. I look down at the gun and realize suddenly why I'm holding it. I'm going to point it at someone.

Papi laughs, this time bitterly. "One hundred eighty million dollars."

One hundred eighty million. Emilio thought fifty-five. That's more than triple.

"So the ankle was just a start," Papi continues. "We'll get to the other one too, but why not spread them out? Let's do an arm first. Fernando?"

I step around the corner just as a crack and a scream ring out. The crack is crisp and hollow, and the scream . . . It's unearthly. It's split—guttural and high-pitched at the same time, a groan and a shriek woven together in a way that makes my stomach fall and not stop falling.

The visual takes longer to register. It's too dark. The torches on the far side are lit where the figures are clustered, and only faces are lit. Fernando's hawkish profile towers over something slumped, something he's holding up but not entirely because it's just shoulders, a doubled-over mass. Jose is propping the slumped thing from the other side, or I assume it's Jose from the neckless build. Papi's the only one whose whole face is visible. He's sitting, facing the others, florid jowls shining red and flickering under the torchlight. He could see me if he looked a little to the left, but he doesn't. He glares at the slumped figure as it lifts its blond head.

Blond. So blond the torchlight can't paint it with the same bloodred brush. The hair glows white when the head turns from side to side, writhing in pain.

"*Stop!*" I scream.

They all turn. All of them but Marcel, who curls into himself again, his beautiful hair disappearing as he crumples to the ground.

Courage swirls and centers somewhere inside of me, and now it's my arm jutting, my hand clutching the gun, my finger curled around the trigger.

They stare.

I didn't see their guns appear, but they're out now. Fernando's is pointing at me. So is Jose's. So is Papi's.

"*Stop!*" I scream again, stepping forward, and I see their faces change as they realize who I am.

Papi's arm relaxes. "Put your guns down," he says.

Fernando hesitates.

"It's Valentina," Papi barks at him.

Valentina.

Fernando tucks his gun into his pants. Jose drops his arm to his side, but keeps his eyes trained on the barrel of my gun, his fingers wrapped around his weapon.

"Welcome home," Papi calls, placing his gun on the table with a satisfying *clunk*.

"What are you doing to him?" I sob.

He narrows his eyes and looks from Marcel, to me, to my gun, to Marcel, connecting the fractured pieces. "Tell me you didn't have anything to do with this," he says to me.

"Let him go."

He says nothing.

"Let him go."

"Valentina," he says.

I hear it now. Not just the indulgence, but the placation. I thought I was his favorite, that he thought I was the smartest, the most worthy of his attention. He made me think it with that same tone, but now it's clear it was only a way to control me. Flattery. "Put the gun down."

"No."

Jose twitches, and his weapon glimmers at his side.

Fernando bends over and picks up Marcel by the shoulder. Marcel groans, and my heart groans with him. He lifts his face to me for the first time, but only for a second. It's long enough to see the blood pouring from his nose, both eyes swollen nearly shut. I wouldn't know him if it weren't for his hair.

I gasp, and he drops his head again. My finger feels slippery against the trigger. I stretch my hand, tighten my grip.

"Put the gun down," Papi repeats gently. That soothing tone says so much. I'm only a child to be pacified.

I can't think. Marcel's swollen eyes and blood-painted chin are all I can see. I point the gun at Papi.

"You don't even know how to hold it," he says. "Have you ever shot a gun?"

I haven't. He knows it. What am I doing? The answers have been coming to me all night as I stumble along, because I couldn't plan this, or I didn't want to plan this. It's been better to feel like fate was pushing me through, but now I see myself through their eyes. I'm ridiculous. I'm standing before three armed killers who think I'm harmless, pointing a gun at Papi's head like I could pull the trigger.

"It's not a toy," he says.

"And I'm not a child. Let him go."

"Put the gun down." He holds out his hand and takes a few steps toward me. Those steps do something. They stir the whirlwind of courage and fury swirling inside me again. I'm stronger than he thinks I am.

Smarter.

"No." I turn my hand, bend my elbow, and bring the tip of the gun to my temple. The sensation of its tip against my skin makes me shiver. It's so cold.

Papi freezes, mouth open. "Is it loaded? Put it down."

"Let him go."

He shakes his head. "This isn't funny. Put it down."

"*I said let him go!* You don't think I'll pull the trigger?" My voice is shrill. I sound like someone else. "You're going to kill him, and if you kill him, I don't want to live anymore."

He looks at Marcel's bent and bloodied figure. "But you and Emilio—"

"Don't talk to me about Emilio!" I shout.

"But what happens to this fool has nothing to do with you or any—"

"Yes, it does! Setting fire to the yacht was my idea—I made him do it!"

Papi swears, runs both hands through his hair. He's sweating. "What are you saying? No, what were you thinking?"

"I was thinking you deserve to lose everything. And I was thinking about the narc."

"*What?*" he growls.

"The narc. You've got an undercover agent working for you."

He looks from me to Marcel, then back at me again. "Who?"

"Let him go, and I'll tell you," I say, and tighten my grip on the gun. I lift my wrist so it's level with my temple again. Still pressed against my skin, it doesn't feel cool anymore. It's marble smooth.

Papi turns to Fernando and nods. Fernando looks disappointed but shoves Marcel to the ground. Marcel groans, but he doesn't get up. He has to get up.

"Marcel," I call.

"Tell me about the narc," Papi coaxes.

"Not yet. *Marcel*," I say, sternly this time. "Get up." I don't ask him if he can even walk. He has to get up.

Marcel pushes himself up with one arm, then groans as he gets his left leg underneath him and stands. He looks like a marionette, grimace painted on with blood. His left foot hangs at an odd angle, and his left arm cradles his right against his body. And his face. I can't look at his face. "Go," I say. "There's a car in the front. I left the keys on the seat. Go and don't stop."

I try not to watch him as he hobbles and lurches across the deck toward the gate, but I can't look away. He's crooked, gasping and wincing with every step. It's my fault. I should never have told him the truth about Lucien's death, never have let him bring me to Miami at all. And Papi—I pull my focus from Marcel's receding figure back to my father—Papi belongs in jail. No, Papi belongs in hell.

Something's different.

It takes me a moment to realize what's changed while I

watched Marcel go. Fernando's hand is at his belt, gripping his weapon.

"Drop it!" I scream, jerking the gun at my temple. "Papi, make him! I'll do it!"

Papi holds his hand up to Fernando. Fernando scowls and puts his gun on the table next to Papi's. "Jose," Papi says, and Jose does the same.

"Now walk away from them," I order. "All three of you. Over there, by the pool."

They obey. Side by side, unarmed, Papi and his goons stand in a row, defenseless because of me. "So you want to know who your narc is?"

Papi nods.

"First, tell me about my mother."

He blinks. A gust of wind tousles his hair, and for a moment he looks much younger. "What about her? You know everything."

"I know the things that you learn from photo albums and home movies. I don't know the important things. I don't know why she tried to leave you. I don't know how you killed her."

He doesn't flinch. "Stop this, Valentina. Who's the narc?"

"How did you kill her?"

He takes a step toward me.

"You don't think I'll do it now?" I scream. "Now that I know you murdered my mother? Step back and tell me how you did it!"

He moves back but doesn't say a word.

I'm crying. I want to wipe my cheeks, but I can't risk losing my balance or my grip on the gun, so I push on. "He said they identified the body with dental records. Does that mean fire?"

"Who said that?" he asks.

"Does that mean fire?"

"Who told you that! The narc—is Emilio the narc?"

"Does that mean fire?" I scream.

He nods.

I open my mouth, but before I can speak or scream, a strong, hot gust of wind blasts into me and a shudder rolls through me at the same time. Am I dying? The beating is so loud—my heart must be near bursting—but then I realize it's too fast to be my heart.

A white light explodes over me and I gasp, but I don't drop my gun. Its warm, slippery body is still heavy in my hand. The thumping takes on a mechanical rhythm, the angry beat of steel shredding holes in the smoky sky. Red hair whips my face, blinding me. With my free hand I pull the tangle of it back and force myself to turn toward the light.

A megaphoned voice blares down at me, but the words don't come together to make sense. The pulsing is too forceful. But the words repeat and repeat until I do hear. *"This is the United States Coast Guard! Drop your weapons and put your hands in the air!"*

Coast Guard. I do understand. The blinding light above me—that's a helicopter. The fading light behind me, the one without a gun or a prayer—that's Papi.

THIRTY-FIVE

"Let's try this again."

I rub my tongue against the roof of my mouth. It's leathery. Twice scalded, I'm not attempting to drink my coffee anymore. I keep my hands curled around the hot cup, soaking in heat that way instead. "Can you turn down the AC?"

The beefy man across from me—Pearson, I think—snaps his hairy fingers at the younger, skinnier one by the door, who jumps up and leaves, presumably to adjust the temperature.

"Who started the fire?" Pearson asks.

"I did."

He gives me a startled glance and scribbles something on his notepad.

In the several hours I've been at the station, it's the first real thing I've said. It's amazing how long you can stretch out asking for food, faking a few tears, asking for more food, faking a few more tears, and still have them believe you're considering cooperating.

He licks his finger and turns to the next page in his curled-edged notepad. "Are you aware of what was on the yacht at the time you set the fire?"

"No. What was on the yacht?"

He studies me intently. I break his gaze after a few seconds to examine the nail polish that isn't on my nails.

"Drugs. Do you know anything about your father's professional dealings?"

I eye the mirrored wall to my left. It's surprisingly predictable—just like a TV show. I imagine a team of detectives sitting on the other side, analyzing my responses, arguing about my body language. I wonder if Emilio's with them. I look back to Pearson. "He sells art."

Pearson sighs and scratches the back of his thinning hair. His role here is the one of disappointed father figure. The detective before him—Ferreira, I think—he played the intimidating jerk. Maybe if I hold out long enough, they'll send in a good-looking young guy to smile at me and convince me to tell him all my secrets. As if I'd fall for that now.

Pearson gives me sad eyes and shrugs. "You're telling me you know nothing about the drugs."

"Drugs?" I give him another blank stare. He has wrinkles across his forehead. I hold my eyes there.

"You're either a part of helping us piece this together, or you're not. Obstruction of justice in a case of this size—that's not something you want to mess around with."

"You said I'm not being charged with anything."

"I said you aren't being charged with anything *yet*." He leans back, lacing his fingers behind his head, showing off the yellowed armpits of his dress shirt.

"I'm a minor, you know."

"You think that means you can't be charged with obstruction?"

"I think it means I can demand to see my lawyer, right?"

"Is that what you're doing?"

The door swings open and the skinny one walks back in. He nudges his glasses farther up his sunburned nose and sits in the chair closest to the mirror. The AC vent is still blasting cold air at me.

"No," I say.

"So then. The fire. We have a report from an eyewitness saying they saw a young male sneaking onto the yacht."

"Okay, so maybe I didn't set the fire."

"Tell me who did."

"Why would you assume that I know?"

He pauses. "This investigation is pretty big. There's a huge team of people who've been working on it, spanning several different agencies, and apparently one of the FBI agents seems to think you do know who set that fire."

I turn to stare at the mirror. It's large, covering nearly the entire wall, but I let my eyes travel over it slowly, smiling as I go. "I don't think your FBI agent really wants to get my whole story."

Pearson frowns and scratches a flaky patch between his eyebrows. "Let's move on to something else. Do you want to tell me why you were holding a gun to your head when the Coast Guard arrived at your father's house?"

"No. Is pretending to threaten to kill yourself a crime?"

"Pretending? You're claiming you aren't suicidal?"

"I'm definitely not suicidal. I promise."

He looks heavenward, a prayer for patience passing between his eyeballs and the ceiling. He plays the part so well. I bet he has a teenage daughter. Maybe several.

"I was mad at my father," I say.

"Why?"

"I don't know. For taking away my credit card?"

He mutters something under his breath I don't catch, then pushes back his chair. "What was that?" I ask.

"I said damn lucky."

Lucky. Too much. I'm suddenly too tired and the game is too taxing. I want them to leave me alone so I can stop pretending to be an idiot and curl into a ball on my own bed and cry. "I don't feel very lucky," I mumble.

"And why is that?"

"According to you guys, my father is going to spend the rest of his life in prison, and I get to walk around with that shame of who he is for the rest of my life. What's lucky about that?"

Sympathy crosses his face, then he scrubs his stubble with his hand and wipes it away. "Well, for whatever reason"—he glances at the mirror—"the FBI doesn't want to press you on

404

your story. But if you had anything to do with what went down tonight, you're more than lucky. You're smart."

"I don't know what you're talking about."

He takes his notepad and tucks it under his sweat-stained armpit. He stands but doesn't leave, waiting for me to acknowledge what he's said.

I examine my imaginary nail polish again. "Can I go home now?"

"Yeah. But it'd be a good idea for you to stay in Miami for the next week or so in case we need to talk to you. Your cooperation is important if you want to avoid charges. Do you have someone to take you home?"

"I can call my sister."

"Right. And Valentina," he says, "if you did have anything to do with it, you should know you did a good thing. The Cruz organization is responsible for some of the most horrific—"

"*Stop.*"

He looks startled.

I push my chair back and it makes an angry scraping sound, but I don't say another word. I shouldn't have to explain why I don't want to hear what he has to say about my father's legacy. My name. My life.

He nods.

Leaving Miami takes longer than it should. Lola turns into a mother hen, practically forbidding Ana and me to look out the windows for fear of having our pictures end up on TV. That's not even possible—our pictures are already everywhere—but she's too mortified to be reasoned with.

Humiliation. That's the deathblow for Ana and Lola, maybe almost as painful as realizing Papi will never see the light of day. Everybody knows. *Everybody.* How many of them knew before, I wonder? But that seems unimportant to my sisters—like it's so much more shameful having your father incarcerated than having him be a known drug lord.

In quieter moments, though, I wonder if Ana and Lola aren't lost in a darker tragedy. Maybe the public scorn is something benign for them to hate. It's safer to wail about our social demise than to mourn our mother and learn to hate Papi, too. The detective only hinted at what Papi had done to her, but my sisters aren't stupid. Lola was old enough that her loss has a face and a touch and a smell.

She doesn't talk about that, though. She talks about how mortifying it is to be online gossip fodder. She talks about escape.

My humiliation is different. I've already been gone for months, been a different person during my self-imposed exile in Montreal. Maybe that's what makes this embarrassment minor. Not even minor. Nonexistent. Or maybe it's that I'm too busy feeling something else.

While my sisters lick their wounds and wander around our home wondering how much of their lives will be seized by the government, I call Marcel. I call him again and again and again.

Each time I honestly believe he will pick up—I'm not sure why, after the first day of failed attempts—which means each time he doesn't is rich with fresh devastation. I leave a message the first time, and the second, but after that I can't make myself talk to a machine and pretend it's him. It's not him.

The silence drives me crazy in increments. One day becomes two, becomes three, becomes four. First, I'm just a little insane, imagining him driving north through that first night with his ankle broken, arm broken, face bleeding, and who knows what else. I see our trip here in reverse. Does he stop at a hospital right away? Or does he take my advice and not stop at all? How terrified was he, *is* he, that Victor Cruz or one of his enforcers is behind the headlights in his rearview mirror?

By the time I've worked through all the details I can think of, I'm practically senseless with worry. I lie on my bed and stare at my phone, debating whether calling Marcel's parents will result in an immediate international search, or whether they'll pass the phone to him as if nothing has happened.

I'm a complete lunatic by the time I'm considering the worst: Marcel is dead. He was bleeding internally after the beating from Fernando and Jose, and he died in agony on a highway in Georgia. But even if he had no ID on him, Ana's car would have been found. It hasn't been. Ana is still carless and pissed off at me for it. The fact that Lola wouldn't let her go anywhere if she did have a car is irrelevant.

But if he isn't dead, and he somehow made it back to

Montreal, and there's no other physical force preventing him from answering his phone or calling me, then that would make sense. Terrible sense.

If he's alive, he's lucky to have survived his brush with the Cruz regime. He must be thinking that. He must be thinking about Lucien.

I don't think about kissing Marcel. Not consciously. When that memory finds me it's against my will, while I'm asleep or zoning out to Lola's paranoid nattering.

We meet with Detective Pearson again, all three of us together. I'm prepared to play dumb, but I don't have to. The questions are too easy, like he doesn't think we know anything or he doesn't care if we do.

"That's all?" I ask as he stands to leave, ignoring Lola's glare.

"That's all."

I frown, not sure whether to ask the question I've been worrying over since Papi's arrest.

"We don't need you to testify," Pearson says.

He's not the idiot I'd thought he was last time.

"Good," Lola says tersely. "Because we wouldn't. Let's go."

She's wrong. I might.

Ana and Lola stand, so I do too. If they've got enough on Papi without us, then that's probably best. The collection of murders permanently burned into my mind is too much to share, and Marcel's bloody face, his twisted, beaten body as he limped away from me, is just as bad as all the others.

I have to find him.

We go home and eat stale cookies and make plans. Lola and Ana are convinced the only cure for their blistering shame is Aruba, so I sit with them and pretend I'm going to go with them, pretend a tropical island is still the place I want to be, pretend that a month on the beach will be long enough for the reporters to stop calling and the photographers to get bored with milling around the gate and leave.

After I'm done pretending, I go up to my room and pull up a list of hospitals in Montreal. It's a long shot—him making it all the way home in that condition—but where else would I start? According to the internet, in Montreal alone there are at least a dozen places where he could've been treated.

I waste the first call asking if Marcel LeBlanc is a patient.

"We can't tell you that, miss," the receptionist tells me. Her French accent, flattened from what sounds like years of telephone receptioning, makes me oddly sentimental. "Privacy laws, yes?"

"Oh. Right. Yes."

On the phone to the second hospital, I ask for my call to be transferred to Marcel LeBlanc's room.

"Of course," the operator says at first, but then, "I'm sorry, we don't have a current patient by that name."

"No *current* patient? Does that mean he was there?"

He pauses. "I'm sorry, but I can't give out that information."

"When was he discharged?"

"Miss, that information—"

"He *was* a patient, though."

"By *law*, I can't confirm whether he—"

"No, I get it. Sorry."

I exhaust the list. He's nowhere. It's been two days since Ana reported her car stolen (all the chaos and upheaval surrounding Papi's arrest bought me three days of excuses before I made up a story about leaving it on the causeway with a flat tire). But if he made it to Canada, it's less than a long shot. Maybe he made it to an airport and flew . . . anywhere.

I could wait.

I could wait like I waited for Emilio, paralyzed by fear and shame and passivity, starving and cold and useless. But I'm not that girl anymore. I don't hide in closets, and I don't stare at water stains, waiting for my hero. I'm the hero. But I still don't know what to do.

The mandolin appears from nowhere with nothing. It's just there on the porch one day when I'm going out to search for an avocado that isn't yet rotten. Based on the label and the packaging, it came on a UPS truck, but there's no return address to tie it to Emilio's apartment, no letter.

An anonymous apology. I take it in.

My sheets are slippery. I move a little and slide so far, like I'm floating, and it's not good or bad but different. Everything is. Home should feel more like home. The sheet below me feels silkier than water, the one on top smooth like wind. I shouldn't feel trapped by something so loose and light that it might not even be there at all.

I sleep, I think, or I have my eyes closed long enough that when I open them again it takes a while to find the lines of my dark room. It's all curved: the beveled poles of my canopy bed, the oval mirror, the stoic slope of the armoire. Nothing is straight. Sometimes, irrationally, I miss the harsh right angles of my upturned crate and the broken-faced clock.

But my eyes adjust, and the decoratively bowed becomes familiar again.

I can't hear Lola and Ana anymore, so they must've gone to bed. Seven days have passed since Vizcaya, and on every single one of them I've fallen asleep to the sound of my sisters talking across the hall in Lola's room. Tonight, like the other nights, I started out in there with them, but I can only take so much before I start to suffocate. I didn't say much tonight, just lay across the foot of Lola's bed and nodded at the appropriate times. Their woes are justified. I should be more sympathetic. But I've already processed the sting of Emilio's betrayal and mourned the darkest side of Papi's life.

They're worried about money. It's not like I'm *not* worried about money, but I'd already cut myself off from Papi's filthy wealth. There are worse things than poverty.

Papi's bank accounts have been seized, and FBI agents have been traipsing in and out carting off Papi's computers and files and safes. Lola thinks it's only a matter of time before they start taking our belongings—the valuables, at least. I doubt she really knows, but I don't call her on it either. I listen and nod and commiserate.

I think about Marcel. All the time. All the time. All the time.

Once my eyes are fully adjusted, I roll onto my right side and stare at my Degas sketch. Three ballerinas. It's mine, or I've always thought it was, but now that I'm staring at the charcoal figures warmed only by moonlight, I'm unsure. It feels like it's mine, even if all the other art in this house has become tinged with the ugliness of what I know.

Papi bought the sketch because I begged. We were at an auction house in London, one of the first I remember, and despite his detailed explanation of its overvaluation and the unlikelihood of resale at anything close to cost, I wanted it. The economics meant nothing to my seven-year-old mind.

"But can we buy it anyway?" I asked him.

"Tell me what you like about it," he said.

I frowned. I was sure there was one right answer, but I didn't know it. I liked that it made me feel sad—nostalgic, if I'd known the word. It made me want to close my eyes and dream those dancers real, but I couldn't close my eyes and risk losing them. It made me feel like I knew a secret, but that reason made the least sense of all.

Papi watched me as I frowned at the sketch. I remember his face-crinkling smile when I turned to him and shrugged.

There's something in that smile for me now. It's the one I'm going to remember, the one I'm going to intentionally recall when the facts of his life make me doubt he was ever sincere about art or about me.

We left the auction house that day with the Degas wrapped in a tube, my hand tucked under Papi's arm.

It's mine. Legally, who knows, but I feel no moral qualms as I slip out of bed, reach up, and lift the sketch from the wall. I know enough to at least estimate what it would go for. Two hundred thousand dollars. Maybe even three. That's more than enough to go somewhere new, start over again, be anyone I want to be. Not Jane and not Valentina, or at least not the Valentina I've been. I'll know exactly who it is once I get where I'm going.

There. Even before I've thought about it, I know where *there* is.

"Here you are," Señora Medina says, handing me the cardboard tube.

I give her the check. "Señor Lopez will love these. The last ones sold quickly, and these ones are so beautiful."

"I'm glad. You have an eye for beauty, don't you?"

I smile. I do.

I slide the tube into my satchel. Four small watercolors of Girona: a Mediterranean beach, a Catalonian meadow, a young girl playing with a dog, and my favorite, a boy in front of an easel. Unframed. Originals. I handpicked them all.

I couldn't go without real art again. That had been a mistake in Montreal, my barren walls, my refusal to go into the museums

I passed. Lucien's amateurish attempts were the closest I came to seeing art, and the result was emptiness and loneliness.

Here in Girona, my walls are covered with my postcard prints—a poor girl's gallery, as Rosa calls it. Rosa, my only roommate, has her own poor girl's gallery, except hers alternates between French and Spanish *Vogue* pages, and the torn-out pages of a firemen's calendar. She's studying fashion at the university. Her study of firemen is somewhat less official.

"Where are you from?" Señora Medina asks.

I hesitate. I've come up the hill to buy her watercolors several times now, and we've always conversed in Spanish. But she must hear that mine is slanted with South American tones. There's no need to lie, but it takes an effort to tell the truth these days. "America," I say.

She frowns, eyeing my short cotton shirtdress and brown sandals. I bought them here.

"You don't look American," she says bluntly, "but you don't sound Spanish."

It wasn't a question, so I don't try to explain. I intentionally bought my clothes here so I would at least blend in when I wasn't speaking. Spanish clothes were a carefully weighed expense, and worth every penny.

Señora Medina stares harder at me. Smooth-faced and beautiful. "I'll see you next week, then?"

"Next week," I say, and slip out the door into the sunlight.

I pull the strap over my head. Like the clothes, the sturdy leather bag was a bit of a splurge. The Degas sketch brought in more than I expected, but every purchase I make now has the feel of finality. There's plenty of money, but once it's gone, the only thing replenishing it will be my own earnings at the art shop, which are . . . not huge. Last I heard from Lola and Ana, the trial was underway, but all of Papi's assets have been seized now. If I'd wanted his money—which I didn't—I couldn't have it.

I start the walk down the hill and through the park, bag swinging on my hip. Señor Lopez's operation is small, but beauty doesn't have to be big. I sell prints and postcards (the tourists love their Dalí), as well as the work of local artists. Most of them stop by the store to replenish the stock themselves, but Señor Lopez sends me out to pick up also, and sometimes, like today, to buy. My shifts there earn enough money to pay my rent at the apartment building across the plaza and for food, but not much else.

Not that I need much else right now. I'm drunk off freedom and anonymity. I had that in Montreal, but fear washed it with gray. Fear chilled me more than ice or wind, left me lonelier than I'd imagined possible. But I'm not afraid anymore.

The walk from Señora Medina's is fifteen minutes, but it's oddly warm for January and the sun slows my feet. We're closed for siesta for another hour anyway, so I take my time, wandering Girona's now familiar cobbled streets.

Girona was unplanned. I'd been sure I wanted to be in Madrid. But then I got there and realized it was too much, or I was too little. I was too frazzled for bustle, too overwrought to be inspired by the buzz of a thriving city, no matter how beautiful. After one day of anxious wandering, I knew that I needed to be closer to the ocean. I needed a place to think. So I took the train to Barcelona and then kept riding farther east and farther north, vaguely aware that I was getting closer and closer to France, but not ready to decide exactly where I was going. The coast. That seemed good enough. Minutes before we arrived in Girona's station, I realized it was my last stop before Spanish become French, so I disembarked.

Crinkled and exhausted and suddenly brimming with self-pity, not to mention the broken heart I'd been running from, I probably should've hated it. But Girona wouldn't let me come and keep my fingers entwined in my grief. It made me let go. Something about the depth to its romance, the stoicism to its prettiness. Right away, it felt like a painting.

I stayed the first few nights at a hostel, exploring the spider-web of Girona's cobblestones by day. By the time I found Señor Lopez's shop, I'd already decided I would stay. The bright abstract prints propped in the display window, the mustard-yellow awning like a gold frame itself, the SE NECESITA EMPLEADO card taped to the door—they were all confirmations of what I already knew. This could work. Maybe this was even meant to be.

I wasn't looking for home. I'm not so naive or optimistic to think that home is a place, but in Girona I recognized something scrubbed clean and quaint and earnest that make it perfect for starting anew. Alone.

Finding Rosa and the apartment across the plaza made me certain. She's silly and honest and warm, but nosy and messy too, which makes her an average roommate and a better-than-average friend. Rosa actually likes it when I play the mandolin. She isn't sweeter than Nanette, but I'm better than Jane, so it works.

After my first paycheck, I mailed a stack of my favorite postcard prints to Nanette. It's surprising, the relief of saying thank you, even if the thank you is anonymous.

I called Lola from a pay phone to let her know where I was and tried not to listen as she informed me of the latest pretrial injustices they had been subjected to. The credit cards, the cars, the jewelry, all gone.

The art too. Seized. All of it.

It's taken weeks here in Girona, but now I can think about it without tears. I can do this—walk down the hill, satchel of art bouncing on my hip, and acknowledge without crying that the paintings and sketches and silk screens and sculptures that decorated my childhood aren't mine. They never were. Somebody else is looking at them now, and me, I'm finding my own.

I don't go straight to the shop. Instead, I head across the plaza in the direction of my apartment to grab some lunch, pausing at the window of the café on the corner. I've got crusty bread and mozzarella at home, but those pastries behind the glass look divine.

"Valentina," a voice calls from behind me. "Or are you going by something else now?"

Even out of context, Marcel's voice doesn't surprise me. I've been hearing it in my head for weeks. Every day I have at least one imaginary conversation with him, and even now, as I turn around, I half expect to see nobody. But it's him, sitting at a café table no more than ten feet away, that smirk on his face. Exactly the same.

"I wasn't sure," he says. "I thought you might be Jane again."

"Not Jane." I walk toward him, suddenly off balance, like the cobblestones are sinking in places. When I go to pull out the chair across from him, I can't. It's weighted by a large gray boot. A cast. Crutches lie at angles beneath the table.

He leans to the side and swings a chair from a neighboring table with his left arm. His right is in a sling and looks to be casted too, wrist to shoulder. He pushes the chair toward me. "Here."

I sit. "You're okay. I mean"—I glance at the mammoth medical boot—"you're not okay, but you're alive."

"More or less. You thought I was dead?"

"You didn't return my calls."

He laughs, and he looks good. Happy. Strong. "A guy doesn't return your calls, and you automatically assume he's dead? That's confidence."

"I just . . . the last time I saw you, you weren't exactly in good shape. I didn't know how badly you were hurt. I didn't know anything. Did you drive all the way back to Montreal?"

"I made it to Atlanta, then called my dad."

"What did you tell him?"

"Some story about partying with friends and getting jumped outside a club. He flew me home from there."

I swallow, wanting to ask him why he didn't call back, but not wanting to bare my desperation. "You should have called to let me know you were okay."

"I hardly remember those first couple of weeks. Two surgeries on that one." He points to his left leg. "A cracked rib and collapsed lung. Dislocated shoulder. Fractured ulna." He lifts the cast on his right arm. "I didn't know Victor had been arrested until after I was out of the hospital, and by the time I was with it enough to get your messages, you weren't picking up. By the way, your sister says to hurry up and get a cell phone here."

"Lola told you how to find me."

"Yeah," he says.

"If I get a cell phone here, she'll be able to call me whenever she wants."

"So will I."

I smile and it feels right, in the same way that Girona and the shop and Rosa all feel right. But dreaming and imagining someone is here puts a strange shadow on reality. Did I wish it true? His real face is clearer and brighter than in my imagination.

"Miss me?" he asks.

"Yes."

"Good. I'd feel like an idiot if I came all this way and you didn't want me here."

"I want you here."

He smiles. That feels right to me too.

"Your parents—I can't believe they let you come," I say.

"That's only because you don't know them. I have to be back in two weeks to get a walking cast. That'll be on for eight weeks, at least, then physical therapy for a year or something ridiculous like that."

"A year." I stare at the row of toes peeking out of the end. He has nice toes. I've never really looked at them before, but now I'd kind of like to examine them.

"It wasn't your garden-variety fracture," he says.

"But do they expect you to make a full recovery?"

"Mostly. They think. The bones in my ankle were totally shattered, so I've got steel rods and stuff in there now. Don't look so horrified—it's not like I had a career as a professional runner ahead of me or anything. You should've seen me setting off alarms at airport security. They practically strip-searched me right there. Apparently, wearing two casts is the same as asking to have every body cavity thoroughly examined."

I laugh.

"You're too far away." Before I can inch forward, he reaches out and pulls my chair toward him so our knees touch.

Being so close to him, so suddenly, it feels like the breath has been sucked out of me. I stare down at the cast on his leg. "Does it hurt?"

"Not anymore."

"I'm sorry."

"You didn't do this," he says gently. His hand drops to my leg, where cotton meets skin.

I shake my head. "I made you bring me to Miami, and I made you set fire to the yacht, and then my father—"

"Both of those were my idea, and you aren't your father. Besides, being temporarily crippled has its perks."

"Such as . . ."

"Hot nurses."

I roll my eyes.

"Actually, my nurses were mostly old and hairy. Seriously, though, my injuries are the only reason my parents didn't ship me off to military school."

"You would not do well in military school."

He snorts. "You're telling me."

"So instead of getting sent to military school, they let you come to Spain?"

"I told them you'd reform me."

"In two weeks? Not possible."

"I know."

"But you can start by going to my apartment"—I pause to point at the tall, red building across the plaza—"and making me dinner while I work my shift at this shop right there." I point to the yellow awning.

"I've already been to your apartment. Rosa is probably rifling through my suitcase right now."

I narrow my eyes. "What makes you so sure I'll let you stay with us?"

"Rosa already said I could," he says. "And because you're glad I'm here."

He's got me there. I am. I put my hand over his hand, and he turns it palm up, circling my wrist with his fingers.

The clock tower rings. I stand, pull my key out of my satchel, and give it to him. "I have to go to work."

"You aren't going to make me stand up to kiss you, are you?"

I blush. There's no reason for the sudden shyness. It certainly isn't the people wandering past in the plaza. This is Spain. Kissing is breathing.

I sit back down, close my eyes, and lean into Marcel's lips. I'm right. Kissing Marcel is breathing. His hands move up my arms, pulling me close, and I'm suddenly sure of what's happened to me. I'm free. I belong to myself. I'm Valentina.

ACKNOWLEDGMENTS

I'm torn. I could make these acknowledgments a love letter to Anica Rissi, or I could sprinkle my affection all over the place, but truthfully I owe her the biggest thank-you. Having an editor who believes in your manuscript is one thing (an awesome thing), but when that editor is willing to pour her buckets of love and wisdom into it, that's another miracle altogether. Thank you also to Alex Arnold, Amy Ryan, Katherine Tegen, and the whole team at Katherine Tegen Books who worked on this book.

Hemingway said write drunk, edit sober. I didn't do this. I wrote pregnant and edited not-pregnant, which might not be all that different. And while I'm thrilled with the results, I can't say I recommend it. It was tough. So, thank you to my heroic husband who listened to my rants and told me it was going to be okay, even when the only thing I could do was lie on the couch and watch *The Bachelor*. He deserves a second thank-you for allowing himself to be tricked into a research trip to Montreal. He really is wonderful.

The Best Writer-Friends of the Year Award goes to Jenny Sanchez and Lauren Gibaldi. Ladies, I'll let you know when the award show will be. Start writing acceptance speeches and shopping for your red carpet dresses immediately.

And finally, a constant and sincere thank-you to Mandy Hubbard, agent extraordinaire. Smart, encouraging, and intuitive. I'm not sure how I'd do any of this without her.